Praise for

The Last Storyteller

"*The Last Storyteller* spans three gencrations, two continents, and one family's desperate attempt to mend the tears in the fabric of their hearts. All three women—grandmother Victoria, mother Isabel, and daughter Taite—ring true to me as genuine, complex, yet sympathetic characters. A rich thread of Welsh history is woven throughout this poignant modern tale, even as it explores the very contemporary issue of medical ethics. The real storyteller here is Diane Noble, whose novels never fail to touch the heart with tenderness and truth."

—LIZ CURTIS HIGGS, best-selling author
of *Thorn in My Heart*

"I waited years for Diane to write this book, and it was worth the wait! Within these pages you'll find heartfelt longing, holy desire, trials, and triumphs. Diane has seamlessly drawn together an ancient and contemporary story line, making it a delicious choice for any taste in fiction."

—LISA TAWN BERGREN, best-selling author
of *The Captain's Bride*

"Like all of Diane Noble's wonderful novels, *The Last Storyteller* overflows with warm sensitivity and pure entertainment. The love story of Taite and Sam will long be remembered and cherished. I enjoyed it very much!"

—LINDA LEE CHAIKIN, author of *Yesterday's Promise*
and *Today's Embrace*

"True-to-life characters in heartbreaking situations with hope as their only buoy—these are the elements of Diane Noble's *The Last Story-teller*. A story of redemption and forgiveness as only Diane Noble can tell it. I look forward to every novel crafted by this master storyteller."

—TRACI DEPREE, author of *A Can of Peas*
and *Dandelions in a Jelly Jar*

the LAST
STORYTELLER

Other Books by Diane Noble

Heart of Glass
The Veil
Tangled Vines
Distant Bells

The California Chronicles Series
When the Far Hills Bloom
The Blossom and the Nettle
At Play in the Promised Land

Novellas
Phoebe
Come, My Little Angel
"A Place to Call Home" in *Christmas Homecoming*
"Birds of a Feather" in *Unlikely Angels*

Written under the pen name Amanda MacLean:
Westward
Stonehaven
Everlasting
Promise Me the Dawn
Kingdom Come

Nonfiction for Women
It's Time! When Your Children Have Grown, Explore Your Dreams and Discover Your Gifts

the LAST STORYTELLER

A NOVEL BY

DIANE NOBLE

WATERBROOK
PRESS

THE LAST STORYTELLER
PUBLISHED BY WATERBROOK PRESS
2375 Telstar Drive, Suite 160
Colorado Springs, Colorado 80920
A division of Random House, Inc.

The characters and events in this book are fictional, and any resemblance to actual persons or events
is coincidental.

ISBN 1-57856-399-2

Library of Congress Cataloging-in-Publication Data
Noble, Diane, 1945-
   The last storyteller : a novel / Diane Noble.—1st ed.
      p. cm.
   ISBN 1-57856-399-2
   1. Grandparent and adult child—Fiction. 2. Women storytellers—Fiction. 3. Welsh Americans—
Fiction. 4. Terminally ill—Fiction. 5. Pregnant women—Fiction. 6. Single women—Fiction. 7. Grand-
mothers—Fiction. 8. Storytelling—Fiction. 9. Wales—Fiction. I. Title.
   PS3563.A3179765L37 2004
   813'.54—dc22

                                                    2004010014

Printed in the United States of America
2004—First Edition

10 9 8 7 6 5 4 3 2 1

To the one who's tasted motherhood's tears,
Both of sorrow and joy,
And the one who's held her daughter's small hand,
With a heart so filled with wonder she could hardly breathe,
To the one now grown who, if she'd been asked long ago,
"Where's home?"
Would have answered, "Where my mommy is."

To mothers and daughters

Youth fades; love droops; the leaves of friendship fall;
A mother's secret hope outlives them all.

—OLIVER WENDELL HOLMES

I

Taite Abbott hoped she had the courage to utter the words that had kept her in a cold sweat at night, heart thudding, for over a week. She stood barefoot in the wet sand at the ocean's edge, her toes tickled by the lacy foam of retreating waves. She glanced at Sam, who was sitting a few feet away and staring out to sea, and her heart ached. Their lives were about to be changed forever.

The air was full of winged song. Gulls banked and soared, their shadows crossing the sun. Long-legged shorebirds dipped and waddled and chattered across the wet sand. In the distance, harbor seals yipped in staccato counterpoint to the rhythm of the breaking waves.

The place awakened something tender and beautiful inside her as she stood on the damp sand, toes curled into its gritty warmth. When she felt especially unacceptable, undesirable, and less than all she needed to be, the ocean drew her. It always had. Maybe because it was here that her heart found strength to float above her failures, take wing with the seabirds, and soar heavenward toward castle-shaped piles of clouds.

With a sigh, she sat down again on the warm sand, then lay back on her side, elbow bent, her cheek resting in her palm. She faced Sam, whose brow was furrowed in thought. On the horizon beyond him, a gaggle of shrimp boats chugged slowly through the gray green swells. He was likely figuring out something about work-hours versus profits, how much more money they could make if they stayed out an hour longer.

She smiled to herself. Not that Sam knew any more than she did about shrimping. But too often his analytical mind kept him from enjoying the beauty of a day like today. He'd sometimes said that trait in her was one of the things he loved most. She reminded him to stop and breathe, to celebrate such moments before they disappeared. It always surprised her that he found something of such joy in her. She seldom saw such things in herself.

Sam's jaw was backlit by the late afternoon sun. His familiar silhouette, in repose, showed both strength and good humor. When he turned, she would see love in his expression, just as always. Until she confessed her secret.

Watching him, she tried to predict what his reaction would be once she uttered the awful words *I'm pregnant*. Would it be the same as hers: disbelief followed by dismay, then anger?

Somehow she thought not. Sam came from a big, noisy, loving family. Children were treasured, each baby a gift from God to be celebrated through every milestone of his life. No small feat considering Sam's parents had borne four sons and raised them all to be good men.

Sam would do the right thing, but that right thing wasn't what Taite wanted.

Not that she didn't ache with longing for them to be together for the rest of their days. She lived and breathed dreams of their wedding. She didn't have a ring on her finger, but they had often talked about how they would someday marry. Well, maybe she had talked about it more than he had, but he had never stopped her from daydreaming. Sometimes he told her to slow down, to remember that they couldn't make plans until he had completed his medical internship and residency. And that was years away. But mostly he listened with a silly, crazy-in-love smile on his face.

The only thing her daydream hadn't included was children. She had never mentioned this part of her daydream to Sam: no children. Not now. Not ever.

Family meant pain. And she was more or less certain her genetic makeup was predisposed to reject those she loved and to have them reject her. Much as she loved Sam, a fear gnawed deep inside that he, too, might abandon her someday. She had never told him how she felt. He wouldn't understand. Rejection by someone he loved was as alien to him as finding polliwogs in a bottle of designer water.

She was having difficulty drawing the line between honesty and self-preservation. It was one thing to keep something hypothetical from him, such as her desire to have no children. It was quite another to keep the actual pregnancy to herself, especially after the test strip turned bright blue. Twice.

Sam turned to her, raised a quizzical brow, then stood and moved closer.

"Come back to me," he said, surprising her, as he sat down. He took her bare foot between both his hands and brushed off the sand. His touch was gentle.

"Come back?"

He smiled. "From that place in your mind where I'm not invited." He was too close to the truth. In her nervousness, she had created a safe, emotional distance between them. When she didn't comment, he traced the newest tattoo just above her ankle. "Whatever made you decide on Snoopy?"

She let out a pent-up breath, glad for the distraction. "It was Snoopy typing on top of his doghouse as if nothing could stop him."

Sam grinned and, placing her foot back on the sand, flopped down on his back beside her and stared up into the sky. "Why didn't you just get a typewriter? A real one, I mean." Though she could see only his profile, he looked amused. "I would have gotten it for you. Or a computer."

"As long as I just talk about writing, I can't fail." She laughed, but it sounded thin. "Once I try on my dream and it doesn't fit, the dream melts away. Dies. It's happened too many times in my life." Maybe it was the same thing that caused the dark stirring in her heart about motherhood. She studied him and silently practiced the words: *Sam, I've got something to tell you… It's about the death of hopes and dreams (yours) and about fears so dark they bring nightmares and choking tears (mine).* Yes, those words would work. He would see the futility of their plight. She would make him understand.

Sam rolled over and looked at her, his elbow bent, cheek resting on his palm. "You've got talent, Taite. You should use it."

"Someday," she said quietly, biting back the words she'd almost uttered. She let a few seconds float by with the sounds of gulls and harbor seals. She didn't look at him but sat up, cross-legged, elbows on her knees, her gaze on the horizon where the heavens met the waters, where she supposed eternity might begin. Absently, she touched the tiny jeweled stud above her lip. It was a nervous habit she acquired soon after the piercing, which she'd had done at the same time she'd had seven rings and studs set into her right ear. She closed her eyes in concentration, ready at last to tell him.

Sam didn't seem to notice. "I've been waiting to tell you my news," he said quietly.

His news? Taite turned to look at him, his serious tone catching her attention and making her heart skip a beat. Was he about to tell her it was over, that he didn't love her anymore? She was afraid to breathe.

"You know that fellowship I've been hoping for?"

She swallowed hard, relief creeping in beside her dread. "The one in Boston? The INR, didn't you call it?"

"That's the one. The Institute of Neurological Research." He said the words reverently, grinning as if he'd just won the biggest lottery in California history. "There's an unexpected opening. They've offered me the spot. I received the call yesterday."

"How soon?"

"I leave in a week."

"Oh, Sam," she breathed, sudden tears stinging. For his happiness—how he had longed for this opportunity!—and for the muddle she was in, especially now that he would be gone.

He stood and took her hand, helping her to her feet. A breeze had kicked up off the ocean, ruffling his sandy hair and the hem of her long sundress. He raked back the hair blowing across his face and pulled her closer. "It's my dream, babe. Our dream. It's for our future."

"Can I go with you?" If he said yes, she might be able to set aside her fears. For now.

He stepped back. "We couldn't be together. Nights on call. Day after day of nonstop study. Plus I don't have enough money to take care of us both. With the scholarship and my parents' help..." His voice trailed off, but he'd said it before, and she knew his thoughts: His parents had sacrificed everything to see him through med school. He couldn't ask them for anything more.

He pulled her closer. "You know how much I love you. I'll be home for holiday breaks." He touched her cheek, giving her a gentle smile. "This is a twelve-month program. And think of it, Taite. The time will pass quickly...especially when you consider that we've got a whole lifetime stretching out ahead of us." His affection was clear.

"I'm all wrong for you," she blurted, suddenly wanting to hurt him.

For a moment he didn't speak; then he said, "You always go there—to that place where I can't reach you." His shoulders drooped. "I love you, Taite. I have since the first day I laid eyes on you. But you can't seem to accept it."

She wished she could be happy for him, but she felt empty inside. "Honestly, Sam, can you see me as a doctor's wife?" She laughed lightly, as if it didn't matter. She looked down at her foot, turning her ankle toward him. "A tattoo, for goodness' sakes...another on my shoulder." She glanced at her bare shoulder beneath the strap of her camisole. "I can just see the expressions on the other wives' faces."

"There're always high-neck sweaters." His attempt at humor dropped like a stone between them.

Her voice rose an octave. "I'm me, Sam. Don't you see?" Dread of what she must do made her heart pound even harder. When she touched the jeweled stud, her finger trembled. "Don't expect me to change."

"You're spoiling this for me," Sam said. "This fellowship will make all the difference in the position I may be offered later—the research I want to do. Not to mention the contacts I'll make. Who knows where this will lead?" He paused. "I thought you would want to celebrate our good fortune."

She glared at him. "*Your* good fortune." She had to make this good to drive him away. Now they stood apart, but she didn't know who had moved first. He didn't answer, and she could feel his sadness. It was palpable. "Oh, why don't we just face the truth." Her voice was little more than a whisper. She tried to console herself with the thought that if she ended it first, she wouldn't have to worry about him leaving her.

"What truth?" His tone said that he suspected something and that he was angry.

Tears were streaming now. Unplanned, and not the image she

wanted, but she couldn't help it. "That it's...that *we're* all wrong. We have been for a very long time."

Several moments passed before Sam spoke, and when he did, his voice was low and hoarse. "Is this what you want, Taite? To end it?"

She pressed her lips together to keep from screaming, "No!" But if she told him about the baby, he would drop his dreams of the fellowship, of med school, and insist they marry. He would hate her for it. Then would come the day when he'd leave her. "Yes," she whispered, looking out to sea, to that hazy line at the horizon. "Yes." She longed for him to pull her into his arms, to declare his love, to tell her he would do anything to keep her by his side. But when she turned back, he only stared into her eyes with anger and dismay.

"I'm tired of trying to convince you otherwise, babe," Sam said. "Maybe you're right this time." The words left his lips before his heart realized what he'd said. Taking a deep breath, he turned away from her to pick up the picnic plates and cans of drinks. He tossed them into the basket with a dull clatter.

Sam loved Taite. She was everything he was not, everything he wanted to be but had never discovered how to pull from the creative side of his imagination. Taite had. She was a free spirit where he was an uptight planner; she was poetic where he was analytical. He was all about goals. She was all about singing the music of her soul.

He looked down at her upturned face. Her expression held an unfathomable sadness, and he longed to hug her close, assure her of his love. He longed to tell her that the image of her floating into an elegant soiree, dressed in hiking boots and a handkerchief skirt topped with a lacy camisole top, was enough to lighten his heart for a week. She had no idea how others saw her, how they warmed to her quirky, sometimes outrageous ways. She was a poet, a wordsmith who understood the music of language, with an innate intelligence and creativity that no college degree could provide.

They'd met seven years before at Stanford when he was a senior and she was a sophomore. His brothers had insisted his right brain needed stimulating, so on a lark he had enrolled in a creative writing class taught by a short-story author, a young woman a friend had told him was an intelligent beauty. He'd expected the elective to be amusing at best and at worst a way to add three extra credits before graduating. Instead, his well-ordered world was turned on its ear, and not by the beautiful, talented professor.

It happened the first day of class. While sitting in the back row, teetering his chair against the wall, he saw the waiflike coed enter the room. Her thicket of dreadlocks caught his attention first, then her heart-shaped face. She hesitated at the doorway, her luminous dark eyes seeming to take in the lay of the land, assessing its safety before she took another step. Then she moved through the forest of chatting students and up the aisle toward him, her grace reminding him of a doe crossing a clearing.

As she approached, he was captivated by every detail that made up this odd though beautiful girl, from the freckles scattered across her nose to the boots beneath her ankle-length gypsy skirt. She flashed him a smile, and he was surprised at his disappointment when she chose to sit just ahead of him instead of in the empty seat at his side, even after he pointedly moved his books.

After she was settled, he bent near her ear, taking in the faint fragrance of something that reminded him of wildflowers in the sun, and whispered, "My name's Sam Wellington. What's yours?"

She turned, the corners of her mouth curving upward. Her gaze fell on him like sunlight, and he couldn't stop smiling. "Taite," she said, humor sparkling in her dark eyes. "Taite Abbott."

He was captivated from the beginning, but two weeks later when the professor read Taite's short story to the class, an allegory about love and loss amid a village of gnomes in a primeval forest, Sam's heart was stolen straight out of his chest.

The gulls cried as the big round wafer of a crimson sun sank lower into the horizon and brought Sam back to the present. He watched her standing a short distance away, the sea breeze ruffling the wisps that had come loose from her dreads, the sunset turning her face golden.

Unexpected tears filled his eyes. He wanted to draw her into his arms and whisper, "Oh, Taite, if you only knew how much I love you! You tempt me…oh, sweetheart, how you tempt me to throw away everything I've worked so hard for! But we have this goal, and I intend to see it through."

He remained silent, unable to speak the words in his heart, as they rode back to her rental cottage. No matter how he tried to lighten her mood, she wouldn't respond. She simply stared out her side window without speaking. She wasn't the type to use silence as a weapon; his going away was troubling her more than he'd expected.

He reached for her hand, but she pulled away. He couldn't imagine she meant what she'd said about breaking up. Their arguments never lasted longer than a day or two. He had no doubt that they would patch things up before he left for Boston.

When he called the next morning, she wasn't home. Or didn't answer. He left a message, but she didn't return his call. By the time he boarded the plane, he'd left at least a half-dozen more. Still nothing from Taite. A strange uncertainty troubled him as the attendants readied the cabin for takeoff. He pulled out his phone to try calling Taite just once more.

He dialed, then stared at the number he'd pressed, hesitating before hitting the Send button. What if she said she needed him? Would he be willing to get off the plane, give up everything, and go to her? His new fellowship would begin at dawn the next day. He couldn't show up late.

But Taite was all that mattered. If she needed him, he would stay. He pressed the button. It rang three times on Taite's end, but as her answering machine clicked on, the announcement came that all electronic devices must be turned off immediately. With a sigh he flipped the phone closed and placed it in his jacket pocket.

The flight attendant finished her instructions, and the plane rolled back from the gate. Ten minutes later it roared down the runway and angled into a steep climb. The glint of sunlight on the ocean blinded him briefly before the airliner banked into a turn.

He leaned back and closed his eyes. All he could see was Taite: her lips turned up at the corners, the pale freckles across her nose, the pleasing curve of her cheek, the grace of her movement. He could almost smell her wildflower scent. And the music of her voice... He sighed, smiling as he remembered the sound of it.

The plane hit an air pocket, jolting him from his reverie. He turned to stare through the window. They were now well above the clouds, and the sky, so blue it looked purple, made his eyes ache.

As soon as he settled in, he would call. Surely she would answer this time. Surely she missed him as much as he missed her.

2

I t's inhumane." Taite fought to control the anger in her voice. "Besides that, the way you ignore the needs of those in your care is just...just..." She stammered with rage, then stopped to count to ten silently. With an annoyed sigh, she began again. "Mrs. Field says she's been ringing for help since midnight. No one came. She fell trying to get out of bed."

She glared at Josiah Bond, the facility owner and manager who was lolling against the doorjamb across the room. "I intend to report you and your so-called golden-age home to the proper authorities." She held Mrs. Field's arm and applied ointment to the abrasion on her wrist. The elderly woman gave her soft smile.

"You're fired," Bond said without expression.

"You can't fire me—there's no one to take my place." She continued ministering to Mrs. Field, keeping her gaze down so Bond wouldn't see her cry. He'd threatened her before when she pointed out areas that in her opinion fell below standards of decency. She hoped he'd back down again. She couldn't lose her job now, not when she needed the money for the abortion. Not when she needed as much distraction as possible to keep her from thinking about Sam.

"Your kind is a dime a dozen. You're outta here." When she didn't move, Bond crossed the room toward her, and the squeak of his rubber soles on the cheap linoleum made her hair stand on end. He stood next to her in icy silence. She knew what it meant. She'd been fired before, too many times to count. Always for insubordination.

"I'm not finished," she whispered, upset that he would stop her in the middle of treating Mrs. Field. She gave the woman a loving pat before cutting another length of gauze and covering it with a ribbon of ointment.

Slowly she wrapped the wrist, taking her time as Bond stood beside her, breathing audibly in short, angry puffs. "Oh, but you're wrong, Abbott," he growled. "You are most definitely finished." As soon as she completed the wrap, he propelled her through the doorway and down the long, poorly lit hall. Several patients in wheelchairs raised their hands in greeting when they saw her, then looked puzzled as Bond whisked her along toward the entrance, still holding her elbow.

She looked to her narrow cubicle as they swept past the front desk. The receptionist sniffed as if she was expecting Taite's termination and was glad for it. Taite had reported her the week before for smoking cigarettes in the patients' rooms.

"But what about my things?" she protested.

"I'll put them in the mail," Bond said without missing a step.

Good thing she didn't believe in the use of a handbag, or she would have had to leave it, too. She kept her ID and money—what little she had—in her pocket. "My coat…"

"It's a warm day," he said. "You won't need it." He reached in his jacket pocket and pulled out an envelope. "Here's your final check." So he'd known ahead of time that he would fire her. He reached for the door and swung it open.

Taking the envelope, she stepped through. "I'm serious about contacting the authorities," she muttered.

"Abbott, take it from me. They roll their eyes when they hear from you. Just like they have over all your other letters through the years."

She stopped short and frowned. "How did you know about those?"

He sneered. "I've got a friend on the state board. I happened to mention the trouble I'm having with you, and he knew right away who I was talking about. Says you write good letters, but the board laughs every time. Says you've got more of a flair for fiction than for reality." He gave her a small snort of a laugh. "And the word's getting around, Abbott. You'll be hard pressed to get another job in this field if your would-be employer does any checking."

Tears filled her eyes. She pressed her lips together to keep from crying. "Take care of Mrs. Field, will you?" she finally managed.

Bond shut the door in her face.

Taite walked to her cottage, unable to stop her tears. She'd failed again. Mrs. Blythe, her landlady, met her at the gate. "You're in arrears, dear. When can I expect payment?"

"How much is it?"

The woman told her. Taite pulled out the check and glanced at the figure. It was a dollar over, but she handed it to Mrs. Blythe anyway. "I'll be leaving this afternoon."

"Dear, I hope you don't think that I—"

Taite waved away her concern. "It's time for me to go," she said softly. "That's all."

Mrs. Blythe pushed up her eyeglasses and peered at the check. "You'll need to endorse this," she said. She thrust it back into Taite's hand, quickly following it with a pen. "Say, do you have any friends who might want to rent the cottage?"

Taite sat heavily on the bed, holding her head. Her life was a mess. What would she do now? Where would she go? If it were a matter of simply finding another job, she could deal with it. But the abortion weighed on her mind. And Sam. Always Sam.

She needed to start her life over. Maybe it would turn out better this time. But she had no idea how to start. She had a knack for muddling things up, which was why she was in this pickle.

She stood, went to the room's single window, and stared out toward the ocean. It was a tiptoe view, little more than a silver glint between trees and houses. But it was there: a constant made up of ebb and flow, the rhythm of waves on the sand, the music of life.

A place of healing.

Years ago her grandfather had bequeathed her an old fishing cottage on Pelican Island. It sat on acres of land on the seaward coast, a deserted lighthouse the only structure visible within any distance. Her mother and father had vacationed there when she was four and Anna, her sweet, pretty sister, was six. Those were the happy days before Anna died and her mother's heart turned bitter and her father went away. Her memories were vivid, like old Technicolor movies: fishing with her grandfather in his dark green canoe, sitting in front of the flickering orange fire while her grandmother spun stories, watching her father pop yellow corn in an old-fashioned cast-iron pot, cuddling in her mother's arms as she read to Taite and Anna from picture books of bright reds and blues and purples and golds. It seemed the whole world had been colored with laughter and love in those days.

"The fisherman's cabin." Something beckoned her as she turned the idea over in her mind. A small village where she might find work lay within walking distance. Anything would do, from bartending to hotel-room cleaning. Her needs were simple: food and clothing and enough money to pay for the procedure, which needed to be done by the end of her first trimester. Or at least that's what she'd heard was the least expensive and safest timing for abortions.

She turned to her closet, grabbed a few clothes and toiletries, stuffed them into her backpack, unplugged her phone, and headed down the driveway to the street leading out of town.

Just like that, she put her plan in motion. She would hitch a ride down Highway 1 to her grandmother's house in Crescent Bay, spend the night, then continue on to the island the next morning. Her heart was light as she headed into the late-morning sunshine. She had a plan at last.

It was twilight when she let herself out of the beat-up van's backseat. She leaned back in through the window and thanked the five college girls inside for taking pity as she tramped along the highway, thumbing a ride. Then, swinging her backpack to the sidewalk, she stopped to look up at the imposing three-story house at 99 Sea Horse Lane in Crescent Bay. Its curved roof was barnlike in shape, and a turret spiraled toward the sky near a tall brick chimney on the north side of the house. Stone pillars stood squat and solid on either end of the wide porch; two more rose like sentinels, flanking the leaded-glass-and-oak front door. For as long as Taite could remember, the house had been white with black shutters, its slate roof a faded green gray.

This house had provided the only solid foundation she remembered in her life. No matter how much turmoil Taite went through with Isabel, her mother, it seemed the elegant house and Naini remained unchanged. When her mother's career rocketed and she chose it over Taite, Naini had welcomed her granddaughter with open arms.

Victoria wasn't a cookie-baking kind of grandmother, clad in a cheery apron and smelling of cinnamon. Neither did she quilt or knit. Instead, when Taite lived with her, she drove her into the city to museums, plays, and rock concerts. Sometimes to fine restaurants where the chefs knew Victoria liked her tiramisu served in a crystal goblet and where the black-tied servers knew her name.

Taite remembered the nights, just before bedtime, when they would sit together at the bay window in Taite's bedroom, both of them lonely for those who had left them. Victoria would wrap her arms around Taite, and with that beautiful, resonant voice she'd spin the ancestral stories. Taite didn't know how Naini knew them; she just did. Some were of medieval Wales, others of the first ancestors to sail the Atlantic to the Virginia coast, still others of the migration west by wagon train, the rush for gold, the settling south of San Francisco. Victoria was the consummate storyteller, sometimes digging so deep into the story that she seemed to become the people she described, taking on their voices and mannerisms. Some of Taite's happiest childhood moments were spent lost in her grandmother's stories.

She smiled, thinking of the unstoppable, unflappable Victoria Kingswell. Even now, in her eighties, Victoria was on the board of directors of the local community theater, a greeter at church, a driver for Meals-On-Wheels, and head of the literary guild readers' circle, which she had founded. She couldn't imagine her grandmother ever slowing down.

Taite hoisted her backpack, slung it over one shoulder, and approached the door. The house was dark, which worried her. By this time of early evening, the parlor window should have been glowing with light while Naini read her latest book-club pick. Taite lifted the brass knocker and rapped sharply against the ornate metal plate. She waited, then tapped again, this time harder. A moment later she pushed the button to ring the bell. Still no response.

Puzzled, she headed to the wooden gate at the side of the house, lifted the latch, and let herself in. The back door was unlocked, just as she knew it would be. She opened it and stepped through. The only sound was the squeak of loose boards as she moved up the back inside stairs to the sunroom. She tossed her backpack on the sofa. "Naini?" she called "Naini, I'm home. Are you here?"

"Dear one, is that truly you?" a voice called from upstairs.

"Naini, you've nearly scared the socks off me!" She raced down the center hall to the stairs beside the entry. "Are you up there?"

The sound of her grandmother's chuckle relieved her fears. "And scaring your socks off would be quite a feat," Victoria called down. "No pun intended." She descended the staircase, tapping a jeweled cane with each step. Taite marveled yet again at her grandmother's classic beauty. She was slim, wore her gray-streaked brown hair swept up, and dressed impeccably, reminding Taite of Katharine Hepburn in her later years.

She waited until Victoria had stepped onto the polished oak floor of the entry, then gave her a hug. "I've missed you."

Her grandmother held her a moment, then pulled back and frowned. "What brings you here, honey? It's not even the weekend…" She peered at Taite, studying her face. "It's your job, isn't it?"

"Me first," she said, grinning as she reverted to a childish mannerism. "I was worried. Are you okay? The house is so dark—not like you at all."

Victoria laughed lightly. "Of course I'm all right, honey. I was busy upstairs. Did you knock at the front door?"

"And rang the bell."

Her grandmother smiled, looking a little embarrassed. "Sometimes I get lost in thought. And I hate to admit that this was one of those times. I was thinking about the family stories…" She nodded toward the sunroom. "Let's go in and sit for a while. Would you like tea?" They headed down the hall. "Now, tell me again about your job… It *is* the job, isn't it? What happened?"

"Seems I'm too picky for my bosses. And there's this little thing called not being able to take criticism."

"You?" Victoria glanced back and raised an incredulous brow.

Taite laughed. "Not me, them. Seems no one likes to be told they're inhumane in their treatment of others. Even when it's true."

"You love working with the elderly. I'd hoped this job might last."

"Me, too, Naini. But—well, here I am on your doorstep once more."

They reached the sunroom and sat down in the two overstuffed floral-chintz chairs by an old-fashioned Franklin stove. "You're welcome here anytime, you know that. This will always be your home. But you look pale, tired. Is there something else?"

Taite's fingers seemed to fly to her stomach. She swallowed hard, wanting to get the words out before she gave away her despair about the pregnancy. "Sam and I have…ended it. This time for good."

"I'm so sorry. I know how much you care for each other." She nodded to a small stack of cut wood. "Why don't you light a fire for us, honey?" She settled back, her gaze following Taite as she stood. "Now, tell me what happened."

Taite didn't answer until flames were licking from the kindling and she'd laid some larger pieces of orangewood on top. "There's not much to tell. When Sam told me he'd received a fellowship to the Institute of Neurological Research—the INR—in Boston, I knew this was his first step away from me." She shrugged as she plopped down in the floral chintz again, swinging one leg over the chair arm. "He's outgrown me, just as I'd always suspected he would."

"Did he say that?"

"Not in so many words. But it's still true."

"Is the INR affiliated with Boston University Medical School?" There was a curious, intent gleam in Victoria's narrowed eyes.

"Yes, it is. Do you know of it?"

"I've heard of it. I have a dear old friend who was once affiliated with the medical school, taught there for years." She smiled and gave Taite a wink. "I knew him before your grandfather came along—in case you're wondering."

Taite raised a brow, surprised. "You mean you loved someone before Grandpa?"

Victoria laughed, sounding decades younger. "Oh my, I can't say that I loved Luke—or that he loved me. But we were an 'item,' as we called it one summer. Met in the High Sierra where our families had taken us for summer church camp. I was fifteen and he was sixteen. We walked hand in hand together under the stars and promised that every summer we'd meet under a certain tree where Luke had carved our initials. And we pledged a letter each week during the rest of our lives."

"That sounds serious. What happened?"

"The next summer his family didn't come because of his father's financial difficulties—the Great Depression had finally taken its toll. We continued to write for a time, at first weekly, then monthly. A few years later he met a lovely woman he soon made his wife, and I met your grandfather. We exchange Christmas letters, even after all these years." She paused, staring through the tall windows into the deepening dusk. "He and Martha live in Boston. Retired by now, of course, but in his last letter, Luke told me he still lectures at the medical school from time to time. In the area of ethics, if I recall correctly."

"Sam wants to go into research...stem cell transplant. Ethics is a subject of great interest."

Victoria gave her a sharp look. "How do you feel about it—the ethics of such research?"

That was the least of her problems. "Embryos are embryos. If they're going to be killed anyway, why not use them for research?" She shrugged. "I don't see the harm. In fact, I see that they could be used for the good of mankind.

"By *killed,* you mean abortion?"

"Of course."

Victoria pursed her lips, a signal of her disagreement. Taite had seen that look countless times.

"It's just a cluster of cells, Naini. Nothing more. No form. This is all done in the early stages before organs form...or anything." She tried not to think of the cells in her womb forming into anything recognizable. She had no emotional attachment to them. Why should she? They represented her worst fears. They were something to be rid of as quickly as possible. "If a woman chooses to have an abortion, what's the harm in donating the cells for a good cause?"

"Harvesting," Victoria said. "It's called harvesting." Taite wasn't surprised her grandmother knew the term. She kept up with current issues. "Besides the fact that it's illegal in our country, it's immoral. Unethical." She seemed to study Taite with a scrutiny that saw into her soul. Or maybe her womb. "And that cluster of cells is a child. A being touched by the hand of God, unique in every way, its soul already breathed into being—the essence of life itself."

Taite held up a hand. "That's just a theory, Naini." Out of respect she didn't call the theory old-fashioned. "And if you're talking about life within a cell, how can these be any different than bacteria or protozoa? Those are living cells, aren't they? Yet we don't try to protect bacteria. Save them." She sniffed.

"What's happened to the values you were taught, Taite?"

"They disappeared when I lost the one who taught them to me."

"Your mother." Her voice was sad.

Taite snorted. "So much for the values I learned at her knee."

"You can't throw out the truths you learned from her just because she took a different turn—"

"What good are the truths I learned from a loving mother who wound up turning her back on me as if I didn't matter? Her 'truths,' as you call them, her moral values, mean nothing to me."

"You can't go on carrying such a load of bitterness."

Tears stung Taite's eyes. "I don't know how to erase it."

"Write to her. Answer her letters. Seek reconciliation."

Taite didn't try to disguise her annoyance. "She doesn't deserve it."

"But you do."

Taite's annoyance threatened to turn into full-blown defiance. For Naini's sake she tried to keep her voice under control. "What good could it possibly do? I'll only get hurt again. And this time, perhaps even worse."

"It's been years since she left you," Victoria said softly. "And there was Anna. She's gone through a lot of heartbreak. Don't you think it's time for understanding? for forgiveness?"

"She hasn't asked."

"How do you know? You haven't read her letters."

She willed herself to release the anger that had so quickly filled her heart. After a moment, she said, "I was more comfortable when we were talking about stem cell research."

"Which brings us back to the sanctity of life—yours, Isabel's, mine, the embryos' in the wombs of mothers around the world."

This was worse. Again her hand covered her abdomen and lightly rested there. What would her grandmother think if she knew about the cells within her womb? She felt ill. "You do have a way of making your point."

"And I'm not finished." Her grandmother always did love a stimulating discussion about anything from science to ancient history. This was no exception.

"Go on. I'm listening." Taite tried to smile through clenched teeth. "Though don't think you'll change my mind." It would be an impossible subject if she didn't love her grandmother so much.

Victoria cleared her throat. "Back to the harvesting you brought up. If embryos are such a fine commodity, who's to stop harvesting for profit? What if young women who need the money purposely become pregnant to sell their embryos?" She shook her head. "That would be quite a business enterprise." She paused, and when she continued, her voice was low with conviction. "And what's to stop us all from becoming coarse in our attitude about life? Where will the line be drawn between a human being's precious, intrinsic value and the same group of cells' value as 'medicine' to heal others?"

Taite's stomach lurched. For the first time since she discovered she was pregnant, nausea threatened. She moistened her lips, unwilling to let go of the topic. "What if someone you loved suffered from some debilitating disease, perhaps Alzheimer's? Would you feel the same way about this 'medicine'?"

Victoria met her granddaughter's gaze, her expression solemn. A fleeting uneasiness seemed to darken her eyes. Almost before Taite could wonder at its cause, the look disappeared. Of all the emotions Taite expected to see in her grandmother's beloved face, fear wasn't one of them.

3

T aite waited for her grandmother to speak, but Victoria remained silent. It was as if the question about curing debilitating disease with help from aborted embryos was too difficult to face.

"We can't know such answers," she said at last, "not until the questions score a direct hit to our hearts."

Taite felt suddenly that she might suffocate. She had to talk of something else, anything else but embryos and wombs and mothers and daughters. "I'm going to the island." The words came out in a rush. "I need time to think, to get my life together. It came to me this morning that I must go there. I've lost so much. Sam. My job." *My direction.* "I've got to put the pieces of my life back together." Integration, a shrink had once called it. She pictured her life flying off in little bits, floating into the atmosphere, never to be retrieved.

Victoria smiled. "The island does have the capacity to draw one. I don't know if it's the love I remember in the cabin…or the beauty of the lighthouse. What a delight it would be to see it again." Her expression softened. "Sometimes I dream about it. Though the lighthouse has long been deserted, in my dreams its light is brilliant; its beam turns slowly, almost conquering the darkness like a fiercely radiant sword." She laughed lightly. "Oh, the stuff of dreams—so silly and imaginative."

"Your imagination is just one of the reasons I love you, Naini."

"My stories...," Victoria mused, letting her gaze drift away from Taite's face. "You always enjoyed them so."

"Tell me more about your dreams of the island."

"There's a fisherman who rows to the point where the lighthouse stands. I've never seen his face, but somehow I know if I did, his kindness would shine as brightly as the reflecting glass in the lighthouse." She paused. "I always wake before I see his face."

Taite sat forward, intrigued by her grandmother's dream. "Let's go there...together."

Victoria gave her a sharp look, then stood to tend the fire. She reached for another piece of wood, tossed it in the stove, and closed the door before turning to sit down. "I have my volunteer work here in town. I'm needed, and truly, I couldn't just walk away from it all. There's no one else to drive on Tuesdays for meal delivery." She reached for Taite's hand. "Perhaps I'll visit you later."

Taite grinned. "After the cabin's cleaned up and you're sure the plumbing's working."

"You know me well." Victoria seemed pleased that Taite wasn't pressing her to come to the island. She'd always been quite vocal in her admiration of young people who were self-sufficient, and Taite hoped she understood that the invitation didn't reflect a clingy kind of neediness. But the subject quickly passed when Naini said, "Now, how about that tea? I made lemon cookies yesterday, your favorite."

"I'm starving."

"Oh my, I hadn't thought to ask—have you had supper?"

Taite shook her head, realizing she was famished.

"I ate early." She laughed. "Just like all old people do. Would you like a few slices of marinated ahi and sticky rice?" Taite wondered how many grandmothers would fix such a delicacy for dinner. "I found a new recipe, and it's delicious, if I do say so myself."

Taite sat at the kitchen table while her grandmother warmed the rice and steamed a few spears of baby asparagus.

Soon Victoria carried the plate to the table. "Chopsticks?"

Taite smiled up at her. "Asian food isn't nearly as tasty without them."

"I raised you properly." Victoria looked pleased as she sat down.

"You taught me to use chopsticks almost before I could hold a fork." Taite dug in with relish. "I remember practicing with popcorn during story time. One puffed kernel at a time. I must have been six or seven."

"Ah yes, story time." Her grandmother glanced toward the window facing the backyard as if recalling some important memory. Taite understood. The stories were part of an unbreakable bond between them.

"I would love to hear them again."

"There are many you haven't heard, child," she said softly. "Some that have come back to me only recently. I don't know where I heard them before; I just know they're as vivid as anything I've experienced firsthand. Sometimes I dream them at night." She shrugged and laughed. "Perhaps it's part of the aging process. They say long-term memory gets sharper at the same time the short term is fading."

There was something wistful in her grandmother's face, and for a shadow of a moment, Taite was afraid for her. "Speaking of popcorn and stories, how about tonight?" She stood to clear the table. "I'll pop the corn."

Victoria brightened and stood to load the dishwasher while Taite pulled the popper from the cupboard. They chatted while dishes and

silverware clinked and popcorn danced and exploded. It reminded
Taite of evenings from childhood she'd spent with her grandmother,
feeling cherished and protected while performing the everyday tasks
that somehow had kept her fears of the unknown at bay.

Night had fallen by the time Taite and her grandmother returned to
the sunroom. They sat down, and Taite placed the large bowl of but-
tered popcorn on the table between them. Outside the window shadows danced as a breeze rattled the trees, and a glow from the rising
moon in the eastern sky competed with the silver spangle of stars.
When Victoria smiled and pointed to the corner of the yard, Taite followed her gaze.

"There, do you see them?" Her grandmother sat forward, her face
alight with pleasure. "Over there, just beyond the walnut tree."

Taite frowned, squinting through the window into the darkness.

"The young couple."

"Neighbors?" Taite stood and went to the window, puzzled. Why
would neighbors trespass so blatantly? But she saw no one. Only the
trees, shadowy in the moonlight, waved their branches.

"It's Taran and Gwynedd," Victoria said. "They come here often
at twilight or on moonlit nights. You remember who they are, don't
you, dear? The young couple from Wales? The earliest members of the
family tree."

Taite turned to her grandmother, expecting to see a twinkle in her
eye, a wink, followed by a soft laugh to signal that she was teasing. But
Taite's heart sank when she saw Victoria's face. Naini was serious. Dead
serious.

"There they are again," Victoria said. She stood and moved to
stand beside Taite. "They look so happy. Perhaps their troubles haven't
yet begun."

"Naini? Are you feeling all right?"

"Of course, honey. I'm fine." Her voice dropped. "Are you sure you can't see them?"

"There's no one there. No one at all."

Victoria laughed then, sounding embarrassed. "It's just those family stories, I suppose. I've lived with them so long I feel they're part of my life."

Taite took her hand. Perhaps it was the strain of living alone. She hoped it wasn't anything more serious.

"They always come in the evenings, these visions." Victoria was looking into the moonlit yard again. "First it was the dreams at night—so real I would wake up in a sweat, my bedclothes in a heap, after dreaming of those who came to steal our heritage, the sacred heritage of our people."

Taite felt as though the breath had been sucked right out of her lungs. "How long has this been going on, Naini?"

"The dreams? Maybe for five years or so." She shrugged. "I didn't worry at first. Just thought they were products of my vivid imagination. Then the visions started. They're always at twilight. Always the same young couple. Sometimes there are animals with them. Goats, lambs, maybe a sheepdog." She turned to the window, peering into the darkness. "They're still there. But only the young lovers. They didn't bring their animals tonight."

"There's no one there," Taite said again, though she couldn't help looking. Her grandmother sounded so certain.

For several minutes Victoria didn't speak, and then she said, her voice soft, "Sometimes I fear I'm going crazy."

"I've never known a saner—"

Victoria held up a hand. "Ninety-nine percent of the time I'm fit as a fiddle. I deliver food to shut-ins; I volunteer at the hospital; I'm a docent at the Museum of Modern Art. In fact, I *know* there's not a thing wrong with me. Then I'll have another of my nightmares and wake up on the floor with my bed looking like I fought off a regiment of Vikings barehanded." Her uncertainty seemed to return. "And now the visions—hallucinations, if you like. And they're always the same. I wasn't going to tell you, didn't want you to worry, honey. But here they are again.

"I'd hoped you might be able to see them too, these sweet young lovers from the ancient days." The tense lines on her face deepened. "I swear they're so real that when I see them I almost believe I walked beside them in twelfth-century Wales. Even their clothing is perfect in every detail."

Taite studied her grandmother, her anxiety growing with each additional description of the twilight visitors. "Have you talked to your doctor?"

Victoria nodded. "He thinks it's simply the stress of growing older, dealing with things on my own since your grandfather died, the worry over…" Her voice dropped, and she let her gaze drift away from Taite.

"Family?" Taite filled in softly. "Estrangement from Isabel, worry over my wild ways and what in the world will become of me."

Her grandmother smiled, her earlier uncertainty fading. "Well, he didn't exactly use those words. But yes, that was the gist of it."

Guilt overwhelmed her. "Would it help if I stayed here?"

"Oh goodness no, child! I wouldn't hear of it. You know how I feel about independence—for us both. You have your life to live, your plans to make. You are right to be off to the island to 'get your head on straight,' as you young people used to say." She glanced out the window. "They're gone now." A small smile played at her lips. "I just wish you could see them." She sighed and seemed to compose herself. Her expression reflected the control that Taite knew her grandmother was surely fighting to regain.

But Taite was still trying to get her emotional bearings and, feeling faint, reached for the windowsill in case her quivering knees gave way. Her grandmother had always been a rock. She studied Naini's face, searching for signs of emotional instability. She looked as sane as ever.

Victoria's voice was lighter when she spoke again. "Here, child. Sit down and let's get to the story you requested."

But a story of ancient Wales was the last thing Taite wanted to hear. She reached for a handful of popcorn and plopped again into the chair near Victoria, planning to suggest they watch a movie on television instead. Then it came to her that her grandmother's stories might be like anything else that people buried deep in their hearts—grief, emotional pain, anger—only to find that those emotions resurrected themselves of their own accord. Could Naini's stories have taken on their own life in much the same way? Perhaps if she spun her tales, the visions and dreams would go away.

She shored up her courage. "Tell me about Taran and Gwynedd." Perhaps the words would give her insight into what was causing the troubling dreams and visions.

But Victoria, always sensitive to Taite's own psyche, merely smiled and patted her granddaughter's hand. "Some other time, dear. Right now, let's talk of your plans, the island, and what lies ahead."

Taite's sleep was restless that night. She woke before dawn, still worried about leaving Naini. Her grandmother seemed in high spirits, as right as rain, as she bustled around the house, searching for her car keys. Then Taite's heart stood still as a laughing Victoria produced them from the meat drawer in the refrigerator.

She bit back her tears as she followed Victoria to the car, tossed her backpack in the rear seat, and slid into the passenger side. An hour later, as the train pulled from the station, she peered through her window, through the heavy mist that hugged the ground, to see the figure standing tall and proud in her dark raincoat, a red umbrella in one hand, jeweled cane in the other. And without knowing exactly why, Taite wept.

Victoria sat down before the small oak secretary in the parlor and pulled out a sheet of ivory stationery and her favorite fountain pen. Her dear friend Luke was a neurologist, and often in the past few years, she'd wanted to ask his opinion about her dreams and visions, her lapses in memory. But as always, she hesitated, not wanting to admit her mental instability. So, burying her worries in her heart, she wrote about another concern, one even closer to her heart.

> *Dear Martha and Luke,*
>
> *No, it's not Christmas! I thought I would break tradition—mercy me, what a wonder—and write six months early!*
>
> *I trust this missive finds you healthy. I so enjoy hearing about your life now that you're retired, your trips to warmer climes, your involvement in your church, and of course your activities there at the University . . . which brings me to the reason for this letter.*
>
> *My granddaughter Taite, as you may remember, is very close to a young medical student. He has recently been accepted into a fellowship program at Boston University. Stem cell research, I believe, is his field of study within the neurology institute.*
>
> *Could you keep an eye out for him? (You do not need to*

tell him I asked you to—and neither am I telling Taite.) He is an exceptional young man and clearly brilliant. Yet he is also generous of heart. Though they've had their ups and downs, he and my granddaughter love each other and will no doubt marry someday. (They've had a tiff and say not, but Grandma knows better.)

I don't understand very much about this field of research and medicine, but I know your good hearts (both of you) and also your expertise in these matters (also both of you). I pray for God's guidance if you come across dear Sam Wellington. He has promise. God's hand is on him, though he doesn't know it. I have prayed for him (though I didn't know his name) even when Taite was a baby.

I send my love and prayers across the miles.

Sincerely,
Victoria Hamner Kingswell

Her pen hovering above the paper, she considered adding a postscript about her health concerns, perhaps suggesting they speak by telephone. She stared at what she'd written, her still-elegant penmanship in sepia ink, and drew in a deep breath. She didn't want her suspicions confirmed just yet.

She folded the page and pulled a matching envelope from a drawer. Quickly she penned the address on the front, added a stamp, and sealed it before she could change her mind.

4

By early afternoon Taite stood in front of the long-deserted fisherman's cabin at Point Solana. It was in worse shape than she remembered. She stared at the weather-beaten shack and wondered if she was crazy to think she could start her life over here. Slowly she moved up the rocky path. A wave of nausea caught her by surprise, and she halted in midstep, her hand on her stomach, before continuing on to the crooked door. As she rummaged inside her backpack for the key Naini had given her, her desperate circumstances brought on an involuntary shudder.

She had come here to think things through, have the abortion, and seek renewal in the peaceful atmosphere of the rocky wilderness, amid the unceasing music and motion of the ocean. Already she feared her inner turmoil roiled more powerfully than the sights and sounds she'd hoped would bring her peace.

She found the key and breathed easier, resting her head for a few seconds against the weathered planks that served as a front door. "Oh, Sam," she breathed, "if only you were here to shoulder some of this. I'm scared. What if I'm not doing the right thing by not telling you?" How she wanted to tell him her fears about Naini. He would have the expertise—or find it—to know whether the symptoms were stress related. Or something worse.

It seemed her whole world had rocked off its axis. She remembered a theory about a massive meteor hitting the earth sixty-five million years ago with such force that the axis indeed shifted. The poles changed positions, and massive tidal waves swept over the continents, tossing boulders as if they were pebbles. The landscape changed forever.

Just like the landscape of her heart was changing.

Sam was in Boston. She was here on the deserted side of a small island. Alone. She missed him desperately and tried not to think about him. An impossible task. His face was in her dreams, his memory always with her: the sound of his voice; his rare, full-bellied laughter; the way he had of brushing back the hair that fell across his forehead; the way his eyes studied her with curious intensity.

Determined to banish thoughts of Sam from her mind, she straightened her shoulders and turned the key in the lock. The door creaked open on its rusty hinges, and she stepped inside. There was no electricity in the cabin. Years ago when her grandfather lit the oil lamps, Taite and Anna had thought it the grandest thing ever to see the flickering, dancing lights. She had followed Anna everywhere that summer, worshiping her golden sister just as everyone else did.

Anna had been learning to ride a two-wheeler, and though the training wheels were still on, she had hollered in delight for everyone to come to the porch and watch as she wobbled up and down the dirt road. And they had. Though Mama and Papa had said not to, Anna had also helped Taite up onto the bicycle seat, holding her upright as they seemed to fly down the road. Anna always did like to take chances.

In those years they were a family, just like a Norman Rockwell painting—Mama, Papa, Anna, and Taite. The air smelled of ocean and salt and pine forest, the breakers crashed, the seagulls sang, and even the lighthouse worked then, shining its rhythmic light on them all. Taite had thought her world would always be secure, filled with light and love.

Who would ever have thought it would come to this? A rickety shack once resonating with the rollicking sounds of family was now occupied by a lone pierced and tattooed rebel who couldn't hold a job. The one who planned to kill the first of the next generation. She almost laughed at the irony.

The warmth she remembered between her parents was long ago. Times had changed. Anna and her father were dead. Isabel lived in England, though the last Taite had heard, her mother was basking in the sun somewhere in Portugal "for some brightening of the spirit after the incessant gloom of the U.K.," she'd written Naini. Taite couldn't remember the last time she'd heard from her mother. But it didn't matter; she'd tossed out Isabel's last several postcards without reading the first line.

Brushing a cobweb from her face, she looked around, taking in the room and its musty, spare furnishings. The faint shadow of an oil lamp on a small table in the corner caught her attention, and she headed gingerly toward it. When she jiggled the metal base, the answering slosh meant oil was inside. The lamp wasn't heavy enough to be full, but even a thimbleful would bring welcome light.

She found a box of kitchen matches, struck one, and coughed as the odor of sulfur filled her nostrils. The match was damp and went out before she could remove the glass chimney to light the wick. She tried three more times, her fingers now shaking from the damp that chilled her to the bone. Finally, on the fourth try, the wick sizzled, then ignited.

The room seemed smaller than she remembered. Cobwebs filled

the corners, and tattered curtains sagged from the room's three windows, two of them flanking the dark cave of a fireplace. Rickety stairs opposite the sectioned-off kitchen area led to a loft above, divided into two rooms. A small bathroom adjoined the downstairs bedroom, but just as she had figured, the plumbing was broken. She shivered at the thought of trips to the outhouse in the middle of the night.

The kitchen consisted of a rusty, chipped sink with a hand pump and a hundred-year-old wood stove, something that her grandfather had brought by dory from the mainland just after he had finished building the cottage as a first home for her grandmother when they were still newlyweds. Once they moved to the mainland, it remained where he'd built it, standing strong against Pacific storms, serving as a fisherman's getaway. She'd been surprised when he left it to her in his will.

A handwritten note accompanied the deed.

> *You are loved beyond measure. God even says this about you, dearest Taite: "You are precious in My sight, you have been honored, and I have loved you." Don't ever forget this love— God's, your grandmother's, and mine.*
>
> *Love, Poppy*

He'd meant well. But then, and now, the last thing Taite could believe about herself was that she was precious to and beloved by a God who'd obviously turned his back on her. And factoring in her failures clinched it. God's love was lavished on those who deserved it. Not her. Not now.

Taite swallowed the sting at the back of her throat as she thought of her grandmother and grandfather. After her grandfather died, Taite thought she'd never get over missing him. It wasn't long until she suffered another loss: Isabel left for Europe. Taite cried herself to sleep for weeks, then woke one morning, shook her fist at God, and swore she'd never shed another tear because of her mother again. Taite and her grandmother were the only ones left, and they became inseparable.

Naini didn't blink when Taite got her first tattoo, a small Winnie the Pooh on her right shoulder. Naini only wondered how it would look when Taite was eighty and moved into a retirement home. Taite explained that she would move there only if her friends went with her, and her friends accepted her just as she was, tattooed or not. So in short, it really wouldn't matter. Naini smiled elegantly, as was her way, and asked Taite to go with her to get one of her own to test her own friends' loyalty. It had taken Taite nearly all day to talk Naini out of getting a tattoo. Taite had worried that the samples in the tattoo parlor window, more than the tattoo itself, might upset Naini's weak heart.

Coming to the cabin had brought an unexpected flood of memories. Too many. And too much sorrow behind them. It was time to press them down someplace deep inside where she didn't have to deal with them, just as she always had. She went back to the stack of wood in the corner, set the kindling in the old kitchen stove, and then arranged some larger sticks in the shape of a tepee. This time the first match started the fire nicely, and soon the fire glowed as the heavier wood ignited. Taite held her hands to the warmth and breathed deeply for the first time since letting herself into the cabin. She got the fireplace going as well, then swept the hearth with the same broom she'd used as a child.

One by one, she checked the necessities: the water at the sink, which was too rusty to drink; the well out back, which proved to be filled with pure, sweet water. The outhouse was next, and it, too, was adequate. Then she tackled the cobwebs, first inside the house and, shivering with worry, in the corners of the necessary, keeping a sharp lookout for eight-legged critters. She beat the furniture, sneezing as clouds of dust rose, then shook out the curtains and swept the floor.

Finally she put a kettle of water on to boil and rummaged through her backpack for herbal tea bags and a granola bar. When her tea was ready, she pulled a chair close to the fire, removed her boots, and settled back to toast her bare feet near the fire. She yawned and let out a long sigh, content for the moment. Maybe in time she could learn to breathe again and go on with her life without Sam. Maybe she could find the courage to do something she loved without fear of failure. Absently, she traced the tattoo on her ankle with her fingertips: Snoopy bending low, paws pounding the keyboard of the typewriter. Taite grinned and whispered, "It was a dark and stormy night..."

Maybe it wouldn't be a Snoopy kind of night on the island, but as dusk drew closer, the sun played hide-and-seek with wisps of fog. She stretched and headed to the door, thinking fresh air might calm her spirits and queasy stomach. She stepped to the small porch and leaned against the rail, gazing up into the thick branches of the cedars and pines that sheltered the cabin, then to the distant rocky promontory that gave this part of the island its name: Point Solana. Point of Sunlight.

As if on cue, the sinking sun struck the lens of the abandoned lighthouse, giving it a brief but brilliant glow before disappearing. The bright, solid look of it gave her comfort.

Sam headed across campus to the adjoining hospital, his white coat flapping. It was nightfall, and a full moon rose in the eastern sky. But his day was far from over. He'd been up most of the past twenty-four hours, last night studying for his lecture classes between calls to the emergency room, today sitting through intensive classes on neurological anomalies, acute stroke treatment, and the latest advances in stem cell research, especially cloning human eggs for stem cell extraction.

His first two weeks had gone well, though he worried about keeping up with the pace. Already he was too weary to go on much longer without sleep.

He stopped by the hospital cafeteria for a cup of coffee, then, checking his watch, saw that he had fourteen minutes until he was due to observe in ER, just enough time to wolf down a quick supper. He picked up a salad, a bowl of macaroni and cheese, and two slices of paste-colored bread. On his way to the checkout counter, he grabbed a couple cartons of milk and dropped them on his tray.

He had applied for this fellowship because of his interest in stem cells. He had no doubt about the morality of such research. In his first year of medical school, he'd settled on Webster's definition of life: "an organismic state characterized by capacity for metabolism, growth, reaction to stimuli, and reproduction." Viruses, bacteria, mosquitoes, and flies fit the criteria for life, he'd told himself, and people thought nothing of killing them.

They destroyed living creatures for their own use daily. What was so troubling about harvesting one hundred fifty or so fetal cells for study? They were no more or no less alive than any other cell.

Besides, the idea of using stem cells for research ignited a wonderful sense of destiny, of purpose, deep inside him. If lives could be saved, what was the harm? If fetuses were going to be aborted anyway, why not use the stem cells for the good of humankind? Since he'd begun his intensive studies, he'd had little use for those who questioned the morality of the research.

With a sigh, he set his tray on a Formica table in the corner and settled into the orange-plastic-and-metal chair in front of it. The tables around him were empty. Just as well, since he was too tired for light-hearted banter and had no time for meaningful talk with other students or physicians. He'd just popped open a carton of milk and poured it into a plastic cup when an older doctor came through the cafeteria line, spotted him, waved, and headed toward him, tray in hand.

Sam stifled a groan and managed a smile of greeting. The doctor, Luke Stephens, had retired from active practice but still guest-lectured in the ethics sections. Sam had enjoyed his presentation in class just last week. But afterward he had heard the other students talking about him. They saw Dr. Stephens as behind the times in his approach, simplistic in his views of contemporary scientific advances, and utterly backward when it came to the moral issues involving abortion, stem cell research, cloning, and the rights of the unborn.

And now, as Dr. Stephens headed toward his table, Sam hoped the conversation would keep to the lighter side.

"Dr. Stephens," he said with a polite nod. He scooted his chair back to stand.

"Please, don't get up," the older man said with a friendly grin. "And call me Luke." He was slender and tall and held himself with dignity. He looked to be in his late seventies, perhaps even eighty, but spoke in a strong, genteel voice with undertones of a Southern upbringing.

"We met my first week here," Sam reminded him. "Name's Samuel Wellington."

"Good name for a doctor," Dr. Stephens said as he opened his own carton of milk. "You observing in ER tonight?"

Sam couldn't help grinning. "Wellington. Hadn't thought of it quite that way." He stabbed a forkful of macaroni. "And, yes, I'm due in ER in a few minutes."

"These first days in the program are tough. Intense, to put it mildly."

"I enjoyed your lecture last week."

"Ah yes—the psychology of patient trust."

Dr. Stephens's blue eyes bored into Sam's, as if searching for something inside him. Perhaps a kinship, though Sam at once dismissed the thought as ludicrous. Why would this experienced physician care about Sam, a medical student still wet behind the ears?

Dr. Stephens swabbed a pat of butter across his bread. "Yes, I noticed you—first row, third from center."

Sam laughed, remembering his lack of sleep the night before that early morning lecture. "I hope I looked as interested as I felt."

"You yawned once or twice."

The heat of embarrassment crept above Sam's collar. "I'm sorry…"

The older physician laughed again. "Actually, halfway through the lecture you leaned forward, suddenly and quite obviously alert. Your expression said you might disagree with me. It was right after I mentioned how doctors have slipped several notches in public opinion. How we must act decisively to turn the tide."

Sam finished his first carton of milk in two long swallows, then wiped his mouth with a paper napkin. "I was wondering why it matters. So long as doctors do the best they can for their patients, shouldn't that be enough?" He checked his watch, then dug into his salad. "Does it matter what the public thinks?"

Dr. Stephens took another bite of bread and nodded. "General public is one thing. Individual patients are quite another. And en masse?" He shrugged. "They're one and the same. We've got insurance companies on our backs, paperwork that takes us away from important time with our patients, and frivolous litigation to deal with…which makes all of us nervous about our practice. We're tempted to overcompensate by ordering too many tests, just to cover ourselves.

"The result is distrust. Patients hear about malpractice—sometimes truly legitimate cases—or they faint dead away when they see their bills for the expensive tests we've ordered. They see less of their doctor, and when they do get an appointment, sometimes weeks after their call, they find themselves sitting in front of a grumpy, over-worked, overstressed physician."

Sam chuckled. "I hope that's the extreme."

Dr. Stephens didn't laugh with him. "Trust me, it isn't. It's no won-der we need to learn ways to connect with our patients for those few minutes we're with them."

Sam didn't say so, but from what he'd observed watching residents on rounds, there simply wasn't time. Again, he thought about Luke Stephens's reputation for being old-fashioned. "Maybe the days of one-on-one practice are over. Just as the days of house calls bit the dust in the fifties."

"And the alternative is..." Dr. Stephens's startling blue eyes were fixed on Sam.

Sam had finished eating and, checking his watch, saw that he had six minutes to get to ER. But in deference to the older doctor, he stayed seated a little longer. "New technology," he said. "Maybe that's the alternative. With the incredible scientific advances already in place— and still more miraculous advances around the corner—perhaps the practice of medicine will be vastly different. More intervention to pre-vent disease, which in turn makes people more content with the doctor-patient relationship." He grinned sheepishly, suddenly aware that this knowledgeable doctor was listening intently to his opinion. "You know better than I do about all this, but one might think it follows that physicians can rest easier too."

"You're talking about the miraculous cures. Perhaps those such as stem cells could provide?"

Sam met the older doctor's unblinking gaze and nodded slowly. He leaned forward, elbows on the table. "We've been barred from stem cell research on humans here, but in other countries the advances have been astounding. The possibilities of curing diseases, enormous."

"That's the field that beckons you?"

"I'm considering it, yes."

"Rather than practicing medicine."

"Isn't it the same thing?"

"Research versus hands-on healing?" Dr. Stephens studied him, arms folded. "Don't get me wrong, Sam. I'm not putting down research. It's a vital and necessary part of medicine. Some are called to it; others are called to bringing about healing through treatment on the other end. You're at a turning point. You've indicated your field is neurology, but my question has to do with your calling and what you'll do with it."

Sam leaned back thoughtfully. "Calling. Interesting choice of words. Sounds like something my grandmother might say about a preacher being called to preach."

He meant it as a joke, but Dr. Stephens's expression remained as serious as before. "Perhaps it isn't much different," he said.

"As to my calling"—Sam shrugged as he stood—"it's a question I think about a lot." He smiled and extended his hand as Dr. Stephens got to his feet. "I've enjoyed talking with you. Thank you for joining me."

Dr. Stephens stood and nodded. "We'll continue this discussion some other time. I'm interested in your views."

"I'd like that." Sam turned toward the swinging doors, still pondering the older man's words.

Luke watched Sam hurry from the dining room. The letter from Victoria Kingswell had arrived the day before his first lecture to the incoming class, and he'd recognized Sam's name on the class roster. By now it was apparent that Victoria was right, the young man showed exceptional promise. It seemed the strong convictions behind his passion and intensity were the same Luke had observed in class.

He'd spotted it again while they talked. Sam cared, oh yes, obviously cared deeply about his calling, whether or not he acknowledged that he cared. Too many students arrived at the university hospital with their exemplary GPAs and letters of recommendation but fell to the back of the pack when they discovered the grueling schedules, the hours or days without sleep, the unending study.

Already Samuel Wellington had caught the attention of the dean, the faculty, and several resident physicians. They had noticed that he was among the first to arrive and last to leave the lecture hall, the first to step forward with probing questions during lab, the last man out the door— reluctantly, it seemed—when rounds were finished.

Luke saw past the fatigue, past the assumptions about modern advances, into the deeper questions in the young student's heart. The moral issues facing medicine today, perhaps? Taking one life to save another? Choosing the sanctity of one life and dismissing another? Difficult questions that demanded deep thought.

Sam's choice among the paths before him held consequences far beyond what he could imagine. Life—and death—depended on his choice.

5

On Pelican Island, one foggy summer day after another slipped by. As each afternoon faded slowly into night, Taite worried about the abortion—where to get it and how to pay for it. She had marked her calendar with the remaining days of her first trimester. Nearly every morning she trudged the two miles to town, past the small general store, past the one-room church with its graceful steeple, past the scattering of Cape Cod houses, past a pale yellow Victorian with peeling paint and a faded sign that read Happy Acres Retirement Villas to the health clinic next door.

For several days she could only stop and stare at the building. Finally, on one cold, overcast morning, she found the courage to walk to the entrance. Heart pounding, she slipped through the door and made her way across the waiting room to the receptionist. But before the round-faced woman could ask what Taite needed, she lost her courage and fled. She fell to her knees in a clump of mustard weeds between Happy Acres and the clinic and lost her breakfast.

"Honey," a voice said behind her, "are you all right?"

Taite, without looking up, just shook her head.

A gentle hand touched her shoulder. "Please, come inside until you feel better."

Taite allowed herself to be helped to her feet. The receptionist supported her with one arm and opened the door with the other so she could step back inside the clinic.

"I'm Grace," the woman said as she led her to an overstuffed chair.

"I-I'm Taite. Taite Abbott."

Grace smiled. "How about some tea?"

Taite nodded and swallowed hard.

"And maybe some soda crackers?" Grace looked sympathetic.

She must have guessed Taite's condition. Soda crackers were the age-old remedy for morning sickness. She nodded. Grace bustled through the doorway and, after a brief hum from a microwave, returned with a teacup and a saucer stacked with crackers.

Taite's stomach settled after the first bite. "Thank you," she murmured, gratefully taking a sip of honey-sweetened tea.

"You need to see Doc Firestone?" Grace looked concerned.

"Yes, but I haven't any money."

"For prenatal care?" Her voice was gentle even as she probed.

Taite couldn't bring herself to say the word *abortion*, so she just nodded. She could always tell the doctor later if she could get in to see him.

"Doc takes certain patients without charge," Grace said. "If there's a need, then he willingly gives his time." She stood to go back to her desk. "He's in meetings on the mainland today, but he'll be in tomorrow. Can you come back in the afternoon? Say four o'clock?"

Taite finished another bite of cracker and nodded. "Yes, that will be fine."

"About how far along are you, Taite?"

"Two months."

"And you're staying out at the old Point Solana cabin all alone?"

When Taite looked surprised, Grace laughed. "This island's so small everyone knows everyone else's business. Your grandmother is Victoria Kingswell?"

"Did you know her?"

"Oh goodness no, your grandparents left here long before my husband and I arrived. But we've heard how your grandfather helped build our community church, Chapel by the Sea, just across the street. Same year he brought Victoria here as a new bride."

"He did?"

"You weren't aware?"

She shook her head, still nibbling a cracker.

"You'll have to stop by and take a look. His name is on the bronze plaque in the narthex. Your grandmother's, too. They bought the bell for the tower as a love gift to the congregation on their first anniversary."

Taite took a sip of tea, feeling somehow gladdened to learn this. "I haven't heard it ring since I've been here."

"You won't, either. It's rusted up something terrible. I guess we've gotten used to not hearing it, so no one's bothered to take it down and send it for repairs."

Taite left the clinic feeling better than she had in weeks. She'd taken the first step toward getting rid of her problem. Soon she could press it into that place inside with the rest of her better-forgotten memories. She lifted her chin and headed for the church across the street.

A woman in a large straw hat was kneeling in front of a flower bed beside a stone walkway. Wildflowers grew in organized chaos. The brilliance of the display pleased Taite. If she could have a garden, she'd want it exactly like that.

"Hello there," Taite said, trying not to startle the gardener.

"Well, my goodness, hello," the woman said, standing and dusting off her denim overalls. As soon as she turned, Taite realized she wasn't plump, as she'd first thought. Not in the ordinary sense. She was preg-nant. Very pregnant. "Welcome to our chapel—and to town. You're new, aren't you?"

Taite nodded, staring at her round stomach.

The young woman laughed, noticing. "Don't worry. The clinic's right across the street—in case I go into labor." She laughed again mer-rily. "But I've got six weeks to go, according to Doc Firestone." She paused to slap the dirt from her gloves and pull them off. "My name's Susan. What's yours?" She extended her hand, and Taite returned her firm clasp.

Susan was a curious mix of delicate beauty and robust health, per-haps from her gardening, and there was something in her luminous eyes that reflected both peace and merriment.

But it was Susan's swollen stomach, looking ready to burst with life, that caught and held Taite's attention. She was surprised by how it repelled her. Another wave of nausea threatened. Swallowing hard, she struggled to keep her feet still instead of fleeing to the safety of her cabin. Breathing slowly to regain her equilibrium, she finally managed, "My name's Taite, and I am new here. I've moved into a cabin on the other side of the island."

"Oh, of course. The Kingswell cabin."

She laughed. "Word does get around. It was my grandparents'."

Susan beckoned. "You must see this—we've been waiting for you to come by."

Taite trotted after her to the small covered porch and the entrance to the church. "We?"

Susan looked over her shoulder as she headed to the door on the right. "My husband, Tom, and me. He's the pastor here." She held it open while Taite stepped through.

"And you're the gardener?"

Susan laughed heartily. "It would appear so. Actually, I putter around the place because I love to garden." She flipped on a light switch in the narthex. "I have a real passion for it. The growing season on the island is shorter than I'd like, but I've done wonders with wild-flowers and my herb garden at home. I grow rosemary, oregano, thyme. You name it; I grow it. Or try to." She paused at the entrance to the sanctuary and looked up at a bronze plaque. "Here it is."

Taite looked up. The metal had darkened with age, but she could easily make out the words:

CHAPEL BY THE SEA
DEDICATED TO THE GLORY OF GOD
IN THE YEAR OF OUR LORD, NINETEEN HUNDRED AND FORTY-FIVE.
MAY ALL WHO ENTER THESE DOORS FIND SOLACE OF SPIRIT
AND UNENDING JOY IN CHRIST.
WITH DEEPEST GRATITUDE TO THOSE WHO PROVIDED
THE FOUNDATION OF LOVE
FOR THIS CHURCH THROUGH FAITH IN ACTION,
ESPECIALLY DANIEL AND VICTORIA KINGSWELL,
WITHOUT WHOM THIS CHURCH WOULD NOT HAVE BEEN BUILT.

An empty ache seemed to gnaw at her soul, and without warning, her eyes filled. Embarrassed, she brushed them away.

"How proud you must be of your family," Susan said, squeezing her hand. "What a heritage."

At her words, Taite turned and almost ran from the church. She didn't want Susan to see her anguish.

The next afternoon she arrived at the clinic at four o'clock for her appointment with Doc Firestone. Grace smiled and led her into the doctor's office. "He'll want to take a medical history first," she explained. "I'll be back afterward to show you to the examination room."

A few minutes later a middle-aged, balding man stepped through the door. Doc Firestone's expression was kind but businesslike as he studied her face. "And what can I do for you today, young lady?"

"I-I'm, ah, well…" She felt her face flush, and her gaze slid from his.

"Pregnant," he finished gently. "And I take it you're not married."

She took a deep breath and started again. "Yes, I'm pregnant. And I'm not married."

He was writing something on her chart and didn't look up when he asked, "Do you know who the father is?"

"Of course."

"Does he know about the child?"

Child? She hadn't thought of her condition as anything but a condition, period. There was no child. There would be no child. "He doesn't know about my condition, if that's what you mean."

Though her voice had risen, the doctor's voice remained calm, even gentle, as he continued his questions. "Do you think he should know?"

She thought of Sam, his kind ways, his loving heart, the hurt this would bring if he did find out about her deception, about the child. She shook her head. "No, he shouldn't." Her heart seemed to shrivel with the words.

"What was the date of your last menses?"

"Around the end of April…or maybe it was May." She sniffed and offered an indifferent shrug. "I wasn't paying attention, so I don't know for sure. Sometimes I miss one here and there. That's what I thought this time…well, until I took the home pregnancy test. The second one, actually. I took two just to be sure."

He met her eyes. "How are you feeling?"

"Physically?"

"We'll start there."

"Tired. No, make that *exhausted.*"

"That's normal in your first trimester," he said. "We can give you vitamins. You especially need iron."

She wanted to blurt out that it wasn't vitamins she wanted or needed. But he interrupted her thoughts when he went on.

"And emotionally," he said. "How are you feeling in here?" He thumped the place over his heart and gave her a kind look that reminded her of Sam.

Her throat constricted. "Not so well," she whispered.

"That's to be expected too."

She stirred uneasily in her chair, looked to the window, then back to his face. "The reason I'm here," she said finally, wanting to get it over with, "is to discuss an abortion."

He put down his pen and studied her thoughtfully for a moment. "Tell me why you think it's necessary."

Taite tried to adopt a tough-as-nails expression, but when she couldn't get her chin to stop trembling, she dropped her head into her hands and started to cry.

6

Behind his desk, Doc Firestone scribbled some words on Taite's chart. She tried to read them upside down, but either his handwriting was illegible or his notes were in Latin.

He finally looked up, cleared his throat, and nodded slowly. "You carry a life inside," Doc said quietly. "A human being, not just a cluster of random cells to dispose of. It's not a growth."

Swallowing hard, she lifted her chin and boldly met his gaze. "You're saying you won't do it." She was surprised to see the compassion in his face. Embarrassed, she looked away. "What if my life was in danger?"

"I'm bound to protect life, yours and your child's, not destroy it."

"You can't stop me from aborting this fetus myself." She gathered her courage to glare at him again, hoping to mask her uncertainty, her fear. "There are ways, you know," she added defiantly.

Somehow he seemed to see through her bluster. "Ways that will only bring harm, perhaps death, to you both…" He went on to describe in grisly detail what she might expect if she tried such a thing or went to a cut-rate practitioner for the procedure. "Even at a professional clinic, you might be unharmed physically, but let me tell you what will happen to the child you carry."

She stared at him, feeling sicker at every word as he continued. "If you abort the child in the first twelve weeks, your cervix will be dilated to an opening the diameter of a ballpoint pen. A slender suction or vacuum device is inserted, and your baby is broken apart and sucked through the opening. The whole procedure takes about fifteen or twenty minutes." He let out a bitter laugh. "And do you know what they'll call it?"

Mutely, she shook her head.

"Removing the pregnancy." He shook his head. "They never call it a child. A baby."

"You have no right to talk to me this way—"

He interrupted her. "What about your child? Does she have any rights in this?" He didn't wait for an answer. "Let me tell you about the procedure in the second trimester. The cervix requires dilation by a substance called laminaria, made of various materials that absorb water from the cervix, then slowly expand, causing dilation. Once this is complete, the suction tools are put into action, and the child is cleaned out of the womb, usually in small pieces." He spoke with grave deliberation, his obvious disgust for the euphemism growing with each word. "It's called cleaning out the products of conception."

Annoyed, Taite stood. "You're using scare tactics just like the picketers I see on television. The same ones who kill abortion doctors. Terrorists, that's what they are—what *you* are!" She felt faint, and swayed enough to cause Doc Firestone to stand and reach across the desk toward her. But she shook her head fiercely and backed away from him. "You've helped me enough today." She turned toward the door.

"There's just one more thing," he said, and she hesitated, bracing herself for more gore. "By now your child has a brain and spinal cord—even a heart, a liver, kidneys, and intestines. In just a few weeks, if you play music, she'll hear it. Also your voice, and she'll feel your heartbeat." He came around the desk and met her gaze. There was no condemnation in his look, only caring.

"Eleven years ago a Dr. Paul Rockwell was giving an anesthetic for a ruptured ectopic pregnancy when he was handed the embryonic sac—which was intact, transparent. It was still attached to the wall by the umbilical cord.

"He said this tiny human was perfectly developed, with long, tapered fingers, feet, and toes. It was a boy who moved vigorously in the amniotic fluid with a natural swimmer's stroke. When the sac was opened, the tiny human immediately lost his life and took on the expected appearance of an embryo at this stage of life—what you'd normally see in photos."

"I don't believe it," Taite said quickly. "Likely one of the Internet stories that gets started and told and retold as gospel truth."

"I knew him," he said quietly. "We were once colleagues. He doesn't lie."

She shrugged. "A pro-lifer, no doubt, who'd do or say anything, true or not, to sway the undecided." She almost smirked at the obvious, pathetic attempt by this country doctor to change her mind. Women had abortions every day. She was no different. The thing wasn't even a baby yet—no matter what Doc said. Heart and liver? She almost laughed. "Give me the name of a free clinic."

"Most advertise free consultations but not free procedures. Depending on how advanced the pregnancy is, they range from three hundred to four thousand dollars."

She gasped, then figured this was probably a lie as well. She feigned another indifferent shrug and again turned for the door.

"Take some time to think it over," Doc Firestone said, following her to the hallway. "You're so young. The emotional and psychological consequences will haunt you all your life."

She met his gaze without blinking. "Just who do you think will take care of my baby once it comes? I've made a terrible mistake, but I don't want this…this…I don't want *it* to suffer for my own sins. It's better that it not be born at all."

"Not *it*," he said kindly. "He. Or she."

She clamped her lips in a tight line and started for the door. The man wasn't going to give up.

That night she sat in the cold cabin, trembling, afraid to move from where she was curled in the worn, overstuffed chair by the fireplace. Six cans of chicken noodle soup, two boxes of crackers, a bottle of lemon-lime soda, and a box of ginger tea sat untouched in two paper sacks on the kitchen table, where she'd dropped them after her trek from town. She now had less than twenty dollars left. She needed to find a job at once. She thought about stopping by Happy Acres Retirement Villas, but she remembered Josiah Bond's threats and decided to look elsewhere. There had to be other employment on the island. Maybe Susan would help her.

Making a plan helped ease her panic: first the job, then the procedure.

She leaned back and closed her eyes. She was exhausted from her day, but instead of a welcome haze of sleep, her mind swirled with images of the bloody procedures that Doc had described.

Her eyes flew open. She ran for the door, threw it open, and hung over the rickety railing to be sick once again.

"Susan?" she called from the street in front of the church.

The young pastor's wife didn't hear her, intent as she was with trimming the ivy around the sign announcing the week's sermon topic: Rejoice in the Lord! Again, I Say Rejoice!

Rejoice? Over what? she almost asked aloud.

Susan turned and grinned, laying her pruning sheers aside. "Taite!" She crossed the grassy distance between them. "I was just thinking about you."

"You were?"

"There aren't many people our age on the island. I need a friend." She gave her another engaging smile.

Well, I don't, Taite was tempted to say. The less Susan knew about her, the better. She wouldn't want to be friends if she knew about the abortion.

"I thought maybe we could go to tea sometime. There's a great tea shop just next to mine."

"You have a shop?"

"I sell homemade candles and soaps. Scented, of course. Make them myself from the herbs and wildflowers in my garden." She laughed. "My shop's called Wild Thymes."

Taite couldn't help smiling. "As in wild t-h-y-m-e-s?"

"One and the same. I can introduce you to my friends, shop-keepers just down the street from me. There's a great stationer's, also a bookshop run by a published mystery writer. You'll love the gals— Marihelen Westrick owns the Ink 'n Quill, and Linda Sue Udell, our very own famous mystery writer, owns the Cloak 'n Dagger."

"I'm looking for a job. Do you think either of them needs help? I've never worked in retail sales, but I'm a fast learner."

"We can ask. Trouble is, we're seasonal. Whatever you get around here lasts only through mid-September at best. After that, we don't get any tourists."

Taite's heart sank. She couldn't earn what she needed in what was left of summer. "I'd like to meet them anyway," she said.

She must have looked as downhearted as she felt, because Susan laid her arm around Taite's shoulders. "Is everything all right? Do you need help? Financially, I mean. We have a small fund for that through the church."

Taite considered it. They would never have to know how she spent the money. She was instantly ashamed and shook her head. "No, I'll be okay if I can just find something to help me get by."

Susan took her hand. "You let me know if things get rough. Promise?"

Again she considered taking the money. She didn't want to close the door entirely. "Thank you. That's very generous. I promise I'll come to you if I need anything."

Susan motioned her into the church. "I'll wash up, then take you into town and introduce you around. Then some tea…" She smiled. "I've come to love honey-lemon-ginger with an almond *biscotto* on the side."

"So do I—love the tea, I mean."

Eyes shining, Susan gave her a knowing smile. "Same thing happened to me in my first trimester."

It had been three weeks since Sam arrived at the university, and though every morning he woke intending to write to Taite, the hours sped by, a rush of classes, study, papers, and ER observation rounds. Yet always when he fell into bed exhausted at the end of the day, thoughts of Taite filled his heart. Finally, one late afternoon, he found a free hour and headed to the library. He chose a table behind double stacks near a floor-to-ceiling window and sat down. For a moment he just breathed deeply, thinking of Taite, the joy of her presence, the ache of missing her. Her image filled his senses. He lifted his pen and began to write.

My dearest sweetheart,

I hope you've forgiven me by now for not reassuring you of my love that last time we were together. How I wish I could take back those things I said. Taite, I should never have let you think for a moment that I would ever let you go. No matter what you said about your role as a doctor's wife—I should have taken you in my arms right then and assured you that I will never leave you, that I'm proud of you just the way you are.

I love you and want to marry you. But I hope you understand the reasons why we must wait. My work here makes me all the more sure of our grand plan: finish this year in Boston, complete my course work and internship—then, dear one, we will marry! That will be perfect timing, because I'll be equipped to support the two of us while you complete your English lit degree.

I have so much to tell you about my work here. I've tried to call, but your phone is disconnected! Please write and tell me where I can reach you. I know how close you are to your grandmother—and luckily I have her address, so I'll send this letter through her.

Taite, your smile is always with me. I hold you in my arms each night and dream of the day we'll be together again.

> *With all my love,*
> *Sam*

He folded the letter and placed it in an envelope. Then he pulled out another sheet of paper and began to write again.

Dear Mrs. Kingswell,

I hope this letter finds you well. I don't know if Taite told you, but we had a bit of a spat before I left for Boston. I can't reach her, and her phone has been disconnected. I know of her love for you and figure that she'll probably contact you before she goes anywhere else. She seemed troubled that last day I saw her, and I'm eager to know that she's healthy and well.

Would you please give her the enclosed letter if you see her—or perhaps forward it to her if you know of her whereabouts?

I remember you with such affection. Our visits with you were some of the most enjoyable of our times together. I look forward to seeing you when I return.

Sincerely,
Samuel Wellington

Victoria woke with a start. Her bedclothes were knotted and damp with perspiration. Shivering, she drew in a deep breath, trying to calm herself. Then she opened her eyes and looked around the dimly lit room. The blankets were twisted around her legs and torso, and she was lying on the floor.

She lay still, remembering. She had gone back in time once more to the village of Hanmer, walked along the abbey wall with Brother Cadwallen. They had spoken of the sacred Scriptures he was copying.

Then the landscape grew dark as the clouds gathered. He warned her to leave, told her about the gathering danger, but when the thunder of horses' hoofs began, she stayed beside him.

Then Taran and Gwynedd had strolled into the garden below the walls. In the distance the daffodils colored the hillsides bright gold, the blue green mere sparkled nearby, swans gliding along its mirror-like surface.

And there was music, the beautiful song of Taran's voice as he sang to his lady love.

She struggled to be free of her bedding, wondering about the fearful images of the gathering storm, the thunder she'd heard before waking. It had been like a thousand mounts racing toward the village. She needed to warn Taran and Gwynedd tonight when they came.

Grabbing hold of the side of her bed, she stood shakily and then crossed the room to her dressing table. She sat wearily on the dainty chair and leaned forward, squinting into the mirror. She gasped. Her forehead was bruised, and dark blood had congealed above a small cut on her cheek. Her left eye was blackened at the lid.

Dropping her head into her hand, she prayed for her heart to stop its erratic beating. A moment later she returned to sit down on the edge of her bed. She picked up the phone from its cradle on the nightstand, asked the operator for the number in Boston, and within sixty seconds she was connected.

Luke Stevens answered the phone.

"Luke, it's Victoria Kingswell."

After a moment of stunned silence, he cleared his throat. "Victoria…"

"I need help."

It was just past sundown a week and a half later when a loud rapping woke Taite, who had drifted off in front of the warm hearth. Though she had enjoyed meeting Susan's shopkeeper friends, neither of them could offer her work, so she'd taken a job cleaning vacation rentals for minimum wage. Now she couldn't seem to get enough sleep.

The knocking sounded again. She rubbed her eyes and stumbled across the room. Lifting the sagging curtain, she peered through the dusty window to the right of the door. Nearly hidden in the shroud of falling dusk, a figure stood with a letter in his hand.

Curious, she opened the door.

A young man of about fifteen gave her a quick nod. His bicycle leaned against a tree behind him. "You Taite Abbott?"

"Yes."

"This came for you on the afternoon ferry. Postmaster thought you might not stop in for a time, so he sent me out with it."

"Nice of him," she said absently as she took the letter from his hands. Even before she glanced at the familiar handwriting, she knew the letter was from Naini. No one else knew her whereabouts.

The boy shifted his weight from one foot to the other, seeming in no hurry. A jay cackled from a nearby pine, and in the distance a gull called.

When the boy still didn't leave, she remembered her manners. She reached in the pocket of her wrinkled broomstick skirt and handed him a dollar, trying not to calculate how much soup it might have bought.

He grinned, showing a mouthful of teeth that seemed too big for his face. The smile was contagious, and Taite grinned back. "Thanks for coming all this way," she said.

He gave her a mock salute and trotted to his bike.

Wanting to draw out as long as possible the gift of Naini's communication, Taite put the envelope down while she lit the lamp, stoked the fire, and fixed herself a cup of tea. Finally she pulled the chair close to the fireplace and slipped her finger beneath the seal. She was surprised first at the one hundred dollars in cash that fell to her lap, then at the brevity of the letter itself. Her grandmother was usually as wordy as Taite, sometimes more so. Her trembling fingers shook the paper as she read the words:

Dear Taite,

Can you come quickly? I need you. I'll explain when you get here.

Love,
Naini

Stunned, Taite sat for several minutes, weighing the words in her mind. Then she reread the note. There was only one explanation. Someone had told Naini about the pregnancy. With a huff, Taite stood, crumpled the letter in her hand, and tossed it into the fire. It could be no one other than Doc Firestone. Or possibly Grace.

Both were do-gooders, goody two shoes, judgmental, self-righteous. Her face flamed with anger. Yes, self-righteous and judgmental. Doc and Grace didn't know what it was like to be alone and penniless. Pregnant. Abandoned. And scared.

She paced the room, wringing her hands. To think they had taken it upon themselves to write to Naini and burden her with this.

Taite's anger grew. If it weren't so dark, she would head to town this minute and bang on the front door of every house until she found either Doc or Grace. And she would give them a piece of her mind. Oh yes, and she certainly knew how to do that. She'd picked up words in some of her jobs that would shock a Marine recruit.

She might be petite, but she had a mouth on her when the occasion arose. Yessiree bobcat, and she planned to spit out every one of those words. A virtual tirade. She stopped, frowned, and thought about those words. Well, yessiree, she would do exactly that.

Then she thought of Naini and how disappointed she must be. Taite quit pacing and focused her anger on what Doc and Grace had done to her grandmother. Quick tears stung her eyes. How could they dare?

Especially now, when she seemed troubled and stressed about those dreams and visions. It wasn't right for her to be burdened with this any more than it was right for the cluster of cells growing inside Taite's womb to be burdened with a life it didn't ask for.

Taite's hand went to her stomach and hesitated there for just a heartbeat. *I'm getting sentimental, and I can't let that happen,* she told herself, but without conviction. *I cannot. I will not.*

The next morning as soon as the sun crept above the blanket of fog, Taite started for town. Her backpack was slung over her shoulder, and she had donned a fresh broomstick skirt that hung just above the tops of her hiking boots. First stop, the clinic, and after she'd said her piece, she would catch the afternoon ferry to the mainland.

She walked briskly, her eyes stinging in the brisk sea air. A single gull circled overhead, calling on the wind, and near the crumbling lighthouse a couple of sea lions barked back and forth like trombones. A formation of pelicans emerged from the fog, and one dropped suddenly toward the sea to dive for a fish.

She drew in a deep breath in wonder at how quickly her spirits lifted. If she'd thought to bring her journal, she'd be tempted to sit down at the base of the lighthouse and write her feelings. She almost laughed. How many times had she thought about doing such a thing, only to put it off for some other time? But that time never came. She'd told Sam she didn't write because she was scared of failure. And she was afraid. Afraid to find that her thoughts, so eloquent in her head, were just yammering emptiness—or worse, purple prose—on paper.

How could she face another failure? Only this time, instead of stumbling out of a job because she was hotheaded, judgmental, picky, and unafraid of authority, she would fail because she wasn't good enough.

She stopped in the shade of a cypress tree, watching another gull soar high, then land on the weathered brass fixture at the highest point of the lighthouse. For the briefest moment, the image of Naini's light-house dream came to her, along with the notion that she wasn't alone. She glanced over her shoulder to make sure a hiker wasn't coming along the path behind her. But no one appeared. She shook off the notion and continued on the dirt road into town.

"Why did you contact my grandmother?" Taite, hands on hips, glared at Grace. "What happened to patient confidentiality?"

Grace frowned. "I didn't, and I can't imagine that Doc Firestone did either." She shook her head, then pulled a file from a long drawer. "We don't even have your grandmother's address or phone number listed on your chart." She looked up at Taite. "What makes you think we did?"

"I had a letter from her yesterday." Taite swung her backpack to the floor. "She said I needed to come to her at once."

From the hallway behind Taite, Doc Firestone spoke. "What is it you're concerned about?"

Grace met his gaze with a frown as if looking for something written on his face. Guilt maybe? "She's had a letter from Victoria Kingswell, her grandmother."

Taite moved her glare from Grace to Doc. "I wonder what lengths you'll go to in order to stop my abortion. I also wonder what the Department of Health and Human Services would think about this breach of confidentiality."

Doc walked slowly toward her, put some files on Grace's desk, then turned again to Taite. "I wouldn't break patient confidentiality even if I could—no matter what you decide about your baby."

There was that word again. *Baby.*

"You didn't call my grandmother then?" Her voice sounded small even to her.

"No. I don't know your grandmother. I wouldn't know where to begin to find her"—he smiled gently—"even if I'd thought of contacting her. Which I didn't."

As a mother holding a crying baby came through the door and approached the desk, Grace bent toward Taite and lowered her voice. "I didn't either, Taite. Believe me."

They were telling her the truth; she could see it in their faces. "It's worse than I thought," she said quietly.

Doc looked worried. "What is it?"

"Naini needs me." She picked up her backpack and almost ran to the ferry dock.

7

Taite trotted up the walkway to the front door where Victoria stood with open arms. Her grandmother hugged her fiercely, then pulled back, looking relieved. "I'm glad you're here."

"You said you needed me."

"I did." She took Taite's hand, led her into the parlor, just off the entry hall, and nodded toward the twin high-back chairs in front of the gas fireplace.

Taite sat down, legs crossed at the knee, her foot wiggling, while her grandmother turned the key to ignite the flames beneath a stack of three imitation logs.

"Two reasons prompted my note," she finally said, then settled into her chair and leaned back, regarding Taite. "One has to do with you, the other with me. I have a letter for you. But I was afraid that if I forwarded it to the island, you'd take one look and toss it out—"

"Why would I do that?"

Victoria laughed. "I know you."

Taite uncrossed her legs and leaned forward. "It's a letter from Mama." Her heart lifted as she spoke the words, which surprised her. "She's coming home."

It took Victoria a moment to answer, and when she did, her voice was soft. "No, honey. I'm sorry. Nothing from your mother."

Something seemed amiss with her grandmother. It wasn't in her voice, which was as soothing and resonant as ever. No, it was something else, an unreadable light in her eyes. Had Doc Firestone contacted her after all? She wouldn't put it past the man to lie through his teeth.

"So you know, then?" she blurted. "Well, don't believe a word of it. He lied. Everything he told you was a lie."

Victoria looked up sharply. "Who lied? Sam? He said in his letter he'd been unable to find you."

For a moment there wasn't a sound in the room. "Sam?" Taite finally managed to squeeze out. "Sam wrote to you?"

Her grandmother tilted her head as if trying to follow Taite's reasoning. "You said he lied."

Taite let her hand flutter to her lap and thought about what she'd just said, how she'd almost given away her secret. "Yes, a lie," she said letting her eyes drift away from Naini's. "Of the worst sort. Flat-out rejection. It was a, ah, a lie about our relationship, about marriage, the things we'd, ah, promised each other." She tapped the tiny jewel above her lip.

Naini knew her too well, knew that tap meant nervousness. And worse, knew that she was the one doing the lying. Taite swallowed hard before turning back to her grandmother.

"What else is it, Taite?" Victoria leaned back in her chair, a troubled expression shadowing her face. She lifted her hand to secure a strand of hair into the twist at the back of her head. Taite noticed a yellowish discoloring of the skin, like an old bruise, on her forehead. But her grandmother spoke before she could comment. "You've lost weight, honey, haven't you? Is everything all right?"

Taite laughed and shook her head. "I'm still upset over Sam." She sighed, twisting her lips into a lopsided smile. "And of course, I'm worried about you. Your note frightened me."

Victoria tilted her chin in that elegant, in-charge, Katharine Hepburn way she had. Taite breathed easier. She hadn't seemed to notice the nervous jewel tapping. Victoria stood and headed to the tall roll-top secretary across the room. After a moment she returned with an envelope and handed it to Taite. "I'll fix us some tea while you read Sam's letter, honey. Then we can talk, if you like."

She left the room and Taite opened the envelope, folded back the flap, and pulled out the letter.

Victoria filled the kettle, lit the burner, and whispered a prayer for guidance. Taite looked thin and drawn, even more than when she had visited a few weeks earlier. And those dark circles under her eyes stirred an even greater worry. She'd read articles about eating disorders and briefly considered that Taite might be suffering from some such thing. Lack of control in a young woman's life was a likely cause. Her granddaughter had been like a little boat with no rudder, adrift on an ocean of emotions, since her father died and her mother left her all those years ago. Now, with Sam's leaving for Boston, it was no wonder that Taite might grab control wherever it could be found.

Again she whispered a prayer for Taite. After reading Sam's letter, she had felt compelled to send for her granddaughter. Of course she'd missed her. In the end it was a growing concern about her own diagnosis that prompted the note. But her worries over Taite now superseded even that.

She set two cups beside the sugar bowl on the tea tray.

"Naini?" Taite called from down the hall. A moment later she rounded the doorway into the kitchen.

When Victoria looked up, she saw that Taite had been crying. "Taite… What did he say?" She gently led her to the table. "Is it something you can talk about?"

The teakettle whistled, and Victoria returned to the stove to turn off the burner. Taite was more important than pouring tea, so she quickly slid into the chair beside her. "Tell me what's wrong, honey."

"He loves me; he said so in the letter."

"That's good news, yes, child?"

"Sort of." Taite's voice was weak, and her gaze drifted away. Then she swallowed hard and leaned over the table, her face buried in the crook of her arm.

With a sigh, Victoria rested her palm lightly on her shoulder. How many times God had led her through life's darkest moments by giving her someone else to help. By turning her focus outward instead of inward. This was one of those times. "You can tell me anything, Taite. Just like always. I'll not judge or condemn… I'm here to love and to help."

Taite looked up at her with red-rimmed eyes. Victoria handed her a tissue.

"This…this is too hard," Taite said. "You don't understand…"

"Try me."

She swallowed hard, and her hand seemed to flutter to her stomach without conscious thought. All at once Victoria knew. She patted her hand. "This is it, then, honey? A baby?"

Taite started to cry again, and her head bobbed down to rest on her arm. "Y-e-ss," she cried miserably.

"Oh my," Victoria breathed as Taite continued to sob. This did call for a cup of tea—the stronger the better—for Victoria's sustenance, even if her granddaughter didn't want one. She moved to the counter and poured two cups, dropped in tea bags, and with a heavy sigh brought the tray to the table and sat down again. "All right." She added a bit of starch to her voice while running through the implications in her head. "You're pregnant, Sam doesn't know, and you're afraid to tell him." Taite sniffled and nodded. Bingo. If only the rest would be so easy. "Why don't you want him to know?"

Taite looked up finally, but her eyes would not hold Victoria's gaze. "This research fellowship means everything to him. If I told him, he would insist on marriage—immediately."

"And you're worried that would ruin his career plans."

Taite nodded again. "There's something else." Her eyes filled again. "I don't ever want children. I can't, after what happened—"

"With your mother," Victoria finished. "Go on." She was walking a fine line between loving acceptance of Taite and dismay over her circumstances.

"I-I wasn't going to tell you…and especially, I wasn't going to tell Sam…because, well, I plan to, well…"

Victoria understood the end of the unspoken sentence. Her reaction was swift—as if a fist had taken hold of her heart and squeezed it. She forced her voice to remain calm. "You're planning to have an abortion."

Eyes now defiant, Taite leaned forward as if steeling herself for the argument to come. "I don't have a choice, Naini. This, this"—she patted her stomach—"this didn't ask to come into the world unwanted."

"Shouldn't Sam have a say in this? Your child is his, too." This wasn't the time for a lecture about the self-indulgence of youth, living together without the sanctity of marriage, or the emotional fallout of an intimate relationship before their wedding night. The deep guilt and confusion in Taite's eyes told Victoria that such a discussion needed to wait. And when it did happen, Taite's heart would need a liberal dose of God's grace and forgiveness to find true healing. Victoria breathed an inward prayer that she would be attuned to God's nudging—of her heart *and* Taite's—when the time was right. She only hoped there would be enough time. She reached for Taite's hand. "You've been bearing this all alone, haven't you…even when you were here before?"

Taite pulled back her hand, swiped at her eyes, and blew her nose. "I talked to the doctor on the island, also his assistant, Grace."

"About an abortion?"

"Yes." Her voice was a tight-lipped hiss.

"And…"

"He wouldn't talk about it."

Good. Victoria breathed easier. God's protective hand was already on this little one. She looked down at Taite's abdomen, thinking about the miracle that grew there. "How far along are you?"

"I've known for a few weeks. I need to have the abortion before the end of the first trimester. It's much cheaper that way. If I have it later, I'll have to spend time in the hospital. I'm still trying to earn enough money." She looked up at Naini hopefully.

Victoria gave her granddaughter a *c'est tout dire* smile, accompanied by a gesture that said, *Don't even ask.* "Tell me about your letter," she said, taking a different direction. "What did Sam say?"

"He loves me." She sniffled then blew her nose. "He misses me and wants to talk with me."

"Why don't you call him?" She glanced at the phone on the little desk in the corner of the kitchen.

"It's too late."

Victoria assumed she meant the time difference. "He's a med student and probably still up studying."

"It's too late for us, I mean." Her eyes filled again. "Look at me, Naini. I don't have a job. I'm pregnant. I'm a mess." She paused, then added in a whisper, "And I'm scared to death." She stood and started to pace the kitchen. "Sam's brilliant. He knows everything about… well, everything. Things I can't begin to comprehend. The human genome, stem cells, genetic disposition, cloning." She shrugged. "Can you imagine being saddled with a woman who can't get her life together? What can he possibly see in me?"

"I've seen the two of you together, Taite. He adores you." There was no doubt about their love. Sam's expression nearly glowed with love and laughter at Taite's quick and quirky way with words, her insights into the world and people around her. The girl's IQ was likely off the charts, but her self-esteem hovered somewhere around zero.

"I-I'm all wrong for him." Taite leaned back against the counter and crossed her arms. "That's all there is to it. I can't call, because I don't want to be tempted back into a relationship that won't work. I don't want to be tempted to keep the baby and regret it for the rest of my life."

Victoria took a sip of tea, watching Taite over the rim of her cup. God had brought her back into Victoria's life for such a time as this. Now that she knew what they both faced, she only hoped there was time to do what needed to be done, to speak of the long-buried family secrets. Time was a precious gift, one that slipped by too quickly. She breathed a prayer that God would extend the days she had left. That he would grant her the time to help Taite.

"I think it's time to pull out the family stories and dust them off." She smiled at her granddaughter. "We didn't quite get to them last time."

Taite stood up straight, looking every bit the in-charge young woman she could sometimes be. "You said you sent for me for two reasons. One having to do with me—and we've covered that. The other having to do with you. What's up?"

Taite had borne too much recently, and adding the burden of her diagnosis would be unfair. "It will keep," Victoria said. "We'll talk about it later." She patted the chair next to her. "For now, back to the stories..."

Taite smiled, seeming to understand that Victoria didn't want to talk about herself. She blew her nose again, then slid into a chair beside Victoria. "What do they have to do with my circumstances? I mean, why do you mention them now?"

Victoria patted her hand. "I mightn't always be here. I need you to hear them, write them down for future generations before they're forgotten forever." A shadow crossed Taite's face. Victoria quickly squeezed her hand. "But enough of that. Let's retire to the sunroom. It's more comfortable there."

Taite tended to the tea tray. She had just poured steaming water in the teapot when the phone rang. Victoria headed across the kitchen to the corner desk, gave her greeting, listened for a moment, and smiled when she recognized the decidedly masculine voice.

With her hand over the receiver, she whispered, "It's Sam!"

Taite turned, her face pale. "I-I can't, Naini. Please, I can't." She covered her mouth and ran from the room.

When the sickness had passed, Taite joined her grandmother in the sunroom and settled into the chintz chair. Victoria had brought in the tea tray and set it on the coffee table, and gratefully Taite sipped the warm liquid and bit into a cracker from a stack of several on a nearby saucer.

Darkness had fallen, and mist floated among the ancient live oaks outside the long row of windows. In the corner, a fire flickered and glowed from behind a square of clear mica in the parlor stove.

They sat in silence for a short time, and Taite leaned back and closed her eyes to soak up the warmth of the room. Naini covered her with a crocheted throw, tucking it in around her shoulders. The gesture brought back memories of childhood: the sound of her grandmother's voice, the touch of her hand, the comfort of her presence. She breathed in the peace of the moment. Naini was her anchor. She hoped there would be no more mention of the young lovers outside the window.

"We're from a long line of storytellers," her grandmother was saying. "The tradition must continue." She settled back into her chair and took a sip of tea. "The tales have been kept alive by their telling. My mother told me, and her mother before her did the same, my grandmother, great-grandmother, and so on…back so long ago we don't even know the names of the storytellers…only their stories of the ancient ones." She paused, staring out the window, but not speaking of what she saw there. "They're graven so deeply on my heart that sometimes they turn up in other ways."

"Visions and dreams?" Taite didn't want to believe that illness was involved.

"Stories in every form."

"How do you know if they are true?" Her eyes were wide open now, and she sat up and leaned forward. "You've heard the stories told, you've dreamed them, envisioned them. What if they're products of a vivid imagination—yours and others'?"

Victoria laughed. "Someday I'll tell you how I know, but it's always been up to the listener to determine fact from fiction." She winked at Taite. "That's the fun of storytelling." She paused. "In the old days, there was more time for such entertainment. Nowadays people don't have time to sit and listen. I tried with your mother. She didn't have the patience." She chuckled again. "Neither did you when you were younger."

Taite started to interrupt, but her grandmother gestured with one hand to stop her. "Oh yes, you listened when you were small enough to sit on my lap. Once you were grown, turned into a teenager who knew more about everything than anyone else, who thought life began the day she was born…"

"Oh dear, was I that insufferable?"

Her grandmother raised a brow, but there was a twinkle in her eye. "Insufferable. Hard headed. Spunky. Delightful. All these things."

"I remember your story about the Welsh brothers who came west to look for a lost tribe of Gaelic-speaking people."

"You could never get enough of that one."

"What were their names again?"

"My goodness, this takes me back… Bleidd was the older brother, fierce as the day is long. His name means wolf. And the other…" She looked toward the greenhouse window into the lush foliage beyond. "Adwr. That was it. Adwr. It means coward."

"What a name to be stuck with." Taite laughed. "Can you imagine trying to overcome a label like that? I'd take Bleidd over Adwr any day."

"It was my own grandmother who loved to tell that tale. Seems these two were first cousins of Nicolas, the first Hanmer to arrive in the new country. That was the original family name, you know. Hanmer in Wales, Hamner in America."

Taite nodded. "Then carried on through the generations from father to son"—she raised a brow—"until the Civil War."

Victoria seemed pleased she remembered.

"I sat on your lap, listening as you told the story of my great-great-grandfather. How he was a hero at Gettysburg, saved his best friend's life, then died from his wounds."

"It was heartbreaking," Victoria said. "He left a young widow and a baby daughter."

"And that baby was your great-grandmother." Taite had heard the story at least a dozen times when she was a child.

"Gwen Hamner, who married…" Victoria frowned. As the silence stretched, she moved her gaze to the window. "I'm sorry. I'm having trouble remembering," she finally murmured.

"You once told me her married name was Johnson," Taite reminded her gently, her heart skipping a beat in mild alarm. "She was Gwen Johnson." Her grandmother nodded, but her expression held a shadow of worry. "Naini? Are you all right?"

"*Naini*…now that's something I'm glad you never outgrew. Did I ever tell you that we've always called our grannies Naini? It's left over from the old days. A small part of our heritage that's been passed down through the generations."

"The Welsh word for *grandmother*," Taite said softly. And for *love*. "Yes, you told me." She reached for Naini's hand and squeezed her fingers.

Victoria smiled again. "Sometimes I wonder if there will be time to tell the important stories, the earliest ones."

"I'm here now. I'll listen."

"It's late. Are you certain you want me to start one now?" When Taite nodded, Victoria closed her eyes as if to recall something she had seen firsthand. "Nearly nine hundred years ago there was a monk named Cadwallen, Brother Cadwallen. He was an artist, a musician, and he loved God with all his heart. He was on a mission from the abbey at a place called Caer, several weeks by foot away, when he found a fertile meadow beside a mere—that's what the Welsh call a small lake—a mere. It was holy ground; he knew it the moment he saw it. He planted his staff upon a small rise and declared that this would be the home of a new abbey, a place where the sacred Scriptures would be copied for missionary work throughout the known world."

"Is this the story of Taran and Gwynedd?" Taite couldn't help glancing toward the window.

"It is. And it's probably more important than the other stories. It's about a family blessing that continues through nine centuries. It's about a planting of the Lord," she said thoughtfully, and again Taite wondered about the soft worry in Victoria's face. "It's about the trees of righteousness that no force on earth can supplant—then or now." She seemed to search for understanding in Taite's face. "God tells us he'll give 'beauty for ashes, the oil of joy for mourning.'" Then she chuckled. "But I'm getting ahead of myself, aren't I?"

Taite leaned back in her chair and tucked the throw beneath her chin. "All that's missing is popcorn."

"Now, I like that idea," Naini said. "While you get the popper out, we'll speak of Sam."

Taite sat up straight and bit back a groan. "I was an idiot, running away from the phone like that." She had wanted to talk to Sam. Desperately. She wanted to tell him everything but couldn't bring herself to utter a simple hello. "Thank you for explaining why I couldn't talk." Victoria raised a brow, and Taite hurried to add. "Well, you didn't tell him why *exactly.*"

"I simply said you were indisposed. A good word that covers a multitude of conditions." She fell silent for a moment, then added, "But the longer you wait, child, the harder it will be. Time's passage has a way of robbing us in the cruelest way imaginable and creating a chasm that can't be crossed." Her voice quieted. "At least in human terms. Those sweet good-bye kisses missed, those words of love unspoken, those moments of forgiveness and grace withheld—all lost to time. Before a person knows it, opportunities have passed and the mind becomes dead to the need to make amends. Walls are built around the heart."

Taite stood up and stoked the fire. "Sometimes walls are needed. The thicker the better."

"They may protect you from pain, but they also keep out the joy."

Taite's eyes filled. The image of the wall was familiar, but it wasn't just Sam on the other side. Her mother was there too. Perhaps even the child in her womb—but she couldn't bear to think in those terms. Not a child, only a cluster of cells. That's all. Her back was to Victoria, and she drew in a long breath to steady her emotions.

She closed the heavy door and turned again to her grandmother. "About that story," she said, forcing a lighter tone into her voice. "I'd rather hear about the monk than talk about Sam. And I don't think I feel like popcorn after all." She settled back in the big, overstuffed chair again, legs folded beneath her, a throw pulled under her chin.

Her grandmother zeroed right in on her heart as if the rest of her was transparent. There was no condemnation in her expression, only understanding mixed with that same soft worry she'd seen earlier.

Taite's cheeks warmed. She was the cause of Naini's worry and didn't deserve such consideration. "Taran and Gwynedd?" she prompted, to turn her grandmother's thoughts elsewhere.

"Yes, the earliest ones we know," Victoria said. She inclined her head toward the foliage in the yard beyond the sunroom windows, as if to the unseen visitors, and began to tell the ancient story.

8

Brother Cadwallen planted his crook in the spongy soil beside the boggy mere. The hammered crosier at its top caught the light of the sun just before the orb slipped behind a blanket of mist. For a moment he studied the crosier, its chased scrolls and fruit-laden vines, then he dipped his head slightly, something he was prone to do when agreeing with the Voice in his heart.

"Ah, my Lord," he breathed, "may your blessings rest upon this place. May your Word go forth with diligence, and may we, your faithful servants, be worthy of the work you have given us. Protect the works of our hands, O Father. Protect these sacred writings."

He raised his head and studied the sun glowing like an ember through the mist. *Protect.* It seemed the word appeared in his prayers all too often in recent days. Long ago monks worried about raids from the fiery-haired giants of the north, but it had been centuries since the last invasion. Why did the worry of such things nag him now?

Several yards below Cadwallen, Brother Rheged and Brother Vaddon stood near the blue gray waters of the mere. Rheged leaned his head wearily against the crook of his staff and sighed audibly. He was the eldest of the three Benedictine monks by at least a score of summers, and the long journey from Caer Abbey had sapped his strength.

As if reading Cadwallen's mind, Rheged turned slowly to meet his gaze. "Do not be troubled." A fringe of white hair circled the older monk's head like a halo, accentuating his long face and aquiline nose, and his habit hung soiled and worn from bone-thin shoulders. "God has brought us thus far," he wheezed. "He will see us home."

Vaddon chuckled, and then he walked toward Cadwallen and planted his own staff in the soil near Cadwallen's. "Perhaps we have found our home in this place, Rheged. Perhaps we will not return to Caer." The squint lines at the corners of Vaddon's eyes deepened as he studied the fertile lands beyond the mere.

Cadwallen followed his gaze, assured that it was indeed God who had spoken earlier in the deep center of his being. "Aye," he said quietly. "This is the holy place that we have sought, a suitable home for the new abbey."

His thoughts turned to birth, growth, and fertility as he pictured the abbey a few years hence. Bustling with life in the inner sanctum where the brothers would toil. The church and its cloister, where he and the other scribes would put nib to vellum, the chapter house, the infirmary, the dormitory, the refectory. Perhaps later a bakehouse, a mill, and a malthouse. He smiled. All within the abbey's walls.

And outside the abbey's walls families would move near, their village cropping up like wild Welsh daffodils in spring. And farther out, in the lush grasses beyond the mere, sheep would graze, their lambs skipping joyously nearby. There would be flocks of them, for it took an entire herd to make the vellum for the pages of a single copy of the Bible.

Now the air was quiet except for the chirruping of a few sparrows and the low voices of the swans that glided effortlessly across the mere. But someday, once the abbey's stone walls were built and the brothers' work on the Holy Scriptures had begun, the voices of the village children at play, the hum of workers in their fields, the bleating of lambs as they followed their shepherds, and the lullabies of young mothers inside their thatched cottages would all ride on the wind, playing a music of life that would proclaim itself a gift from the Father.

"Dreaming about where you will plant your herbarium, Cadwallen?" Vaddon leaned against his staff. "Or musing on the meaning of life?" The youngest of the three monks was outspoken, an attribute that frequently caused disquiet among the cloistered brothers. His flame-hued fringe of hair moved in rhythm with his laughter, and too often the monastery halls echoed with a voice that was too loud, a footfall too hurried. Though the abbot counseled against such behavior, Cadwallen found the young man as agreeable as he was exasperating.

Cadwallen chuckled. "I was imagining the life to come—not ours, but those who will someday tread this ground."

Brother Rheged walked laboriously toward the two younger men. "We have been called to preserve the sacred texts for those who follow. Perhaps for those who will follow in worlds we cannot know." He paused for a moment and then continued, breathing with difficulty. "We have been called to this task at risk of death. No less than our Lord has called."

Cadwallen looked at the old man with affection. Rheged seldom spoke these days, and when he did it was often with gentle reprimand. Or with wisdom that Cadwallen would muse upon for weeks or months afterward. "Yes indeed," he said, meeting Rheged's bright gaze. "For those who will follow."

It came to pass just as Cadwallen had prayed, though years later his heart still held uncertainty about the abbey's safety. Daily he prayed for the Han-mere villagers who had built their homes near the abbey to care for their flocks and gardens. And he lifted the precious texts before his Lord, asking that they be preserved from harm, that their words of forgiveness and mercy and life might never be lost.

On the day of the twelfth anniversary of the abbey's founding, Brother Cadwallen knelt in the herbarium, thinning a row of cabbage seedlings, as he awaited the bell calling him to morning lauds. Shading his eyes, he glanced up at the sun, newly risen above the mist-enshrouded mere. It would be a fine, sunny afternoon for the newly planted garden. It would also provide a few minutes of warmth on that place between his shoulders that ached from huddling over the book of Saint Mark as he scratched his nib on vellum, painstakingly copying the sacred Word.

He smiled to himself, thinking of the illumination he had begun after saying his prayers during prime. Inspired it was, and he chuckled as he thanked his Lord for the ideas that seemed to flow these days. His did not have the bright-hued grace and liveliness of Brother Vaddon's work, but it pleased him nonetheless.

Cadwallen stretched his shoulders, then reached down to pluck out another seedling from the row he was thinning. But instead of the tolling he awaited, the sound of two villagers' voices—a deep voice of a young man followed by a maiden's musical lilt—carried toward him on the brisk spring wind.

Villagers understood that the gardens of the abbey were forbidden by order of the abbot, but Cadwallen saw no harm in an occasional stroll by a courting couple or the lively play of children, so long as they kept to the paths and didn't trample his seedlings.

Stretching to relieve the crick in his back, Cadwallen peered through the rosemary hedge. Between the thatch of leaves and twigs, he spotted the brown homespun of the girl's skirt and the sheepskin leggings of the boy. He lifted his eyes to their faces and smiled. A youth of little more than sixteen summers, dressed in a hooded tunic, bent near a maiden so comely, Cadwallen's heart caught at the look of her standing amid the gold carpet of wild daffodils.

"Gwynedd, my own," the shepherd said, his voice low, "your beauty brings song to my heart. Even in the fields, I think of you and my very soul breaks into song."

Gwynedd's laughter seemed but a whisper on the breeze, so loving and light it was. " 'Tis I who should hear your music, m'love, not your sheep. Sing to me now!"

Ah, the Welsh! Cadwallen grinned and nodded heavenward as the young man began to sing. No matter how lovelorn or joyful the hearts of the Welsh, they gave voice to their feelings with song. He rocked back on his heels and listened, adding his own silent blessing to the young man's music.

When at last the bell tolled for mass, Cadwallen rose reluctantly. A twig snapped beneath his foot, and the startled couple turned to him with expressions of surprise and worry. The young man swallowed hard, tongue-tied in the presence of a monk, not a usual occurrence.

"Your name, good sir?" Cadwallen said pleasantly, approaching them on the path.

"Taran," the shepherd said, twisting his hat in his hands. "And this, m' pretty lady, is Gwynedd."

"Both of Han-mere," Cadwallen said.

"Aye." The shepherd bowed, and when he stood upright once more he swallowed so hard his Adam's apple bobbled. "Yonder lies my flock." He nodded to the sheep outside the abbey's gates.

"And I, sir, am a shepherdess," the fair girl said, blushing prettily. "My family's flock lies beyond the mere. 'Tis a healthy one." She lifted her chin with pride. "Already good vellum has been made from the hides of last year's ewes."

"Likely some that I used this day," he said. Then he added, "You are welcome to visit this place. It is sacred ground, but that I do not need to relate. I see from your expressions you know it is so." The bell's final tone was fading, and Cadwallen smiled at the two. "I must take my leave," he said, "or I shall be late for prayers."

"Pray for us, good brother," Taran said as Cadwallen hurried away from the herbarium, his habit snapping in the brisk wind.

Cadwallen glanced back and waved a hand. "I have done so even before your words were thought to be spoken," he said, "and I will from this day onward."

Sometimes weeks would pass before he saw the young lovers again. He was true to his word and prayed for them whether he saw them or not as he worked the soil, planting, weeding, and fertilizing.

He took joy in their laughter, their song, and their looks of love. In early summer, Taran wove necklaces of daffodils for Gwynedd, and in the chill of fall, they walked with hands lightly touching, as Taran sang of his love.

In early spring, when the sun was still winter-thin, banns were posted for their marriage. The church bells tolled joyously, and Brother Cadwallen offered his public blessing over the two during midday mass.

Two days later a horse thundered toward the abbey, its rider wild eyed and frantic to warn that a hairy and flame-skinned warrior who called himself Gunnolf, the fighting wolf, had descended upon the abbey at Neath, reducing its church and grounds to rubble and ash. Dozens of sacred texts were burned. Holy treasures of immeasurable worth were looted and relics of the saints desecrated. Beloved abbots and monks were slain and their heads set on rows of spears that flanked the road to Neath as a warning.

Brother Cadwallen was among the monks who met the rider at the abbey gate. The frightened man cried out his warning as his horse shook the foam from its mouth and rolled its blood-hued eyes.

"Gunnolf roared of his family's retribution as he slaughtered the innocents," the rider said. "He shouted in blood-curdling cries that he has come to reestablish the honor of his forebear, Eryk, and to stamp out memories of battles Gunnolf imagined were stolen generations ago.

"'Tis more than a rogue Viking band, displaced by time. He is insane with retribution. Insane with hatred toward the Welsh because we refused to be conquered centuries ago.

"And he comes when we are weakest. Even our own prince and his warriors cannot protect us. Alas, they are busy with campaigns in the south against the English."

He turned his horse back to the path leading from the peaceful abbey. "Be warned and take cover!" he shouted over his shoulder. "Caer is the crown jewel he seeks because of her wealth. But this peaceful village lies in his bloody path. May God have mercy on your souls."

For two days the monks secreted their relics and treasures, especially the Holy Scriptures, in caves beneath the abbey. Cadwallen carried his beloved book of Saint Mark near his heart as he descended the circular stone stairwell leading into a maze of tunnels and the largest of the caves. Gently he placed it with those brought by Vaddon and the other scribes, then knelt to kiss it reverently.

It was just after midday mass on the third day when Cadwallen, standing atop the gatehouse wall, leaned against his staff and searched the horizon for signs of Gunnolf and his marauders. All looked deceptively peaceful, but soon he heard the low, rumbling thunder of pounding hoofs from the far side of the mere, beyond the carpet of wild daffodils. A light snow was falling, pure and chill. Soon its purity would be stained crimson.

The end was near.

He hurried down the steps to the rock-lined path, intending to run back to the cloister. But when he rounded the corner of the gatehouse, Gwynedd and Taran stood before him, unaware of the approaching danger. She turned to Cadwallen with a smile, her long plaited hair adorned with a single daffodil blossom. A dusting of snow had fallen on its petals.

"Quickly," he shouted, "follow me!"

Gwynedd's eyes widened and her smile disappeared. "Surely they are not yet approaching."

Taran's face paled to the shades of the winter-gray mere. "We must help gather our flocks, help our families…"

"There is no time!" Cadwallen shouted over his shoulder. "Follow me." When still they hesitated, he added a firm, *"Now!"*

The next sound was of their footsteps and labored breathing as they ran behind him. When the three reached the rectory, he snatched up a torch and led them beyond, to the hidden passage, pushed against a stone that allowed the heavy door to open, and waited to pull it closed when they were safely inside.

Gravely he passed his staff to Taran. Then holding the torch high, he hurried down the circular stairs until they reached the underground tunnel. "Do not be frightened," he said, though his own knees were knocking together like dry bones in the wind.

The dank air smelled of fresh earth. In the distance, water dripped from a natural spring. They reached the cavernous room carved from granite. Heavy leather chests had been filled with the abbey's sacred treasures. The volumes of Matthew, Mark, and Luke, all partially completed, were carefully stacked nearby.

"I cannot stay with you," Brother Cadwallen said, placing the torch in an iron holder beside the door.

Gwynedd's eyes were dark and round in the torchlight. "Will you return?"

He did not answer. There mightn't be enough time, but he did not want to speak of it.

Taran stepped closer to Gwynedd, and after giving her a loving glance, looked back to Cadwallen. "I will go with you."

"We are a peaceful order," Cadwallen said, understanding his intent. "There will not be a fight." He put a hand on the young man's shoulder. "You need to stay here—with your Gwynedd." He looked with sorrow at the sacred books. "Protect these. Above all else. Protect these, the works of our hands."

Taran swallowed hard and nodded. "Aye, good brother. You have my solemn word."

"And promise me," Cadwallen continued, "that birth, growth, and fertility will go on no matter the destruction of this day. That when you wed"—he smiled gently—"and wed you will, promise me you will remember this moment. That no matter the strength of the adversary, our sovereign Lord's intent for mankind, for his world, will prevail in the end. His power knows no bounds; his strength knows no limit. The abbey may be destroyed on this day, but God's love will never die.

"Brutes such as the one who calls himself 'fighting wolf'—with arrogant, fierce resolve to destroy all that is good—are but chaff on the very breath of God. 'Tis they who will be destroyed in the end." Cadwallen moved to the tunnel entrance, but halted when he heard footsteps following.

It was Gwynedd. "Please, dear Cadwallen," she entreated, touching the sleeve of his habit, "please, offer us your marriage blessing…to keep us till the day it is sealed in our nuptial mass." Her expression said she knew that day would not come.

Without awaiting his response, she knelt on the stone floor before him. Taran dropped to his knees beside her, still holding Cadwallen's crosier. Cadwallen placed a hand on each of their heads. "Almighty

God, our heavenly Father, fill these your beloved children with faith, virtue, knowledge, temperance, patience, and godliness. Knit together in constant affection your son Taran of Han-mere and your daughter Gwynedd of Han-mere from this day forward. For their children, their children's children, and for all who will follow through the ages: turn the hearts of parents to children, and the hearts of children to parents. So enkindle fervent charity among them all, that they may evermore be filled with love one to another as members of your family through your Son, Jesus Christ our Lord.

"This will serve as your wedding rite, my children," he said. "Please repeat your vows after me."

Solemnly, sweetly, they vowed before heaven and earth their undying love to each other and their Lord. He touched their foreheads with the sign of the cross and blessed them.

When he had finished, the only sounds in the granite cavern were the drip of an underground rivulet and the crackling flames of the burning torch.

Taran stood and, taking her hand, helped Gwynedd to her feet. Then he turned to Cadwallen and held out the crosier.

Before the monk grasped it, he removed a gold ring from his finger. The torchlight illumined its intricate, knotted design.

"'Tis yours, dear ones," he said, "the ring of my consecration." Then answering the question in her eyes, he added, "'Tis of a design matching a cross in Caer Abbey. Some say it is the Tree of Life. Others say the knots are made of lilies, symbolic of the risen Christ."

"'Twas given you by the bishop, I am certain." Gwynedd's alarm caused her eyes to widen.

Cadwallen smiled at her acute observation. "Indeed." But he would rather make it a treasured gift to Gwynedd and Taran than allow the marauding evil ones to slice off his finger and rob him of it in death.

"I give it now to you to keep in remembrance of God's love for you, yours for each other, and for your children and your children's children." He reached for Gwynedd's hand and slipped the ring onto the third finger of her right hand. "Consider it my gift, a marriage ring and token of God's abiding love for you and the generations to follow."

She raised her eyes to her beloved and smiled. "Aye," she said quietly.

Smiling once more to give them courage, Cadwallen lightly touched the golden trumpet-blossom still tucked above Gwynedd's ear, and then took the staff. Without another word, he turned and made his way into the tunnel.

9

The torch had long since sputtered to sparks and died, and the catacomb was now darker than the blackest night. In the distance an underground brook seemed to weep like a woman in mourning. For hours it seemed—but there was no way to measure time—Gwynedd paced the stone floor, now listening for voices at the tunnel's entrance, now clinging to Taran for comfort.

"Prithee, do you think it is time, dear Taran?"

"Not yet," was the whispered answer.

"I quake in terror for what we will find." She imagined the attack, her family's fear, and she shuddered. *O God,* she whispered in her heart, *the strength of all who put their trust in you, have mercy on us, help us in our weakness, give us the help of your grace.* She pictured her mother and grandmother, her father, and wept. He would defend to his death his home, humble though it be, and all entrusted to his care. She imagined the worst and wept. *Lord, have mercy; Christ, have mercy.*

Taran didn't speak, but she heard his deep intake of breath. She knew him well. This gentle shepherd was also a man of fearless strength. She had seen him fight wolves barehanded to snatch his sheep from danger. His father had died three years before, and his mother and sisters depended on him. He must be wondering about their fate and berating himself for not being there to defend them.

If not for Brother Cadwallen placing the weight of his request on their shoulders, they would be with their households now. As if understanding her fears, Taran reached for her hand, and his fingers brushed Cadwallen's ring. "I promise it will not be long until we discover for ourselves what lies beyond the tunnels."

She trembled, then absently touched the ring with her thumb and felt the warmth of Taran's hand above hers. She remembered the kindness in Cadwallen's face, the peace that seemed to shine from his spirit, the joy in his voice. Then her thoughts turned to the rubble, the destruction of what was once so beautiful, and cold dread took root in her heart. When she spoke, her voice was but a hoarse whisper. "I fear what lies beyond, the horror that might greet us. Truly, I mayn't find strength in my quaking knees to stand once we leave the tunnel."

"I will help you, m'love." Taran's voice sounded a furlong away.

"We must make a promise," she said, squeezing his hand tight. "Should we become separated, we must know where to meet again. I am surprised we have not considered it before."

Since Cadwallen had left them, fear had filled the cavernous room as surely as a chill mist over the mere. But at Gwynedd's words, Taran laughed quite suddenly. The sound bounced off the granite walls, startling Gwynedd. "I have seen you determine the path of your flock," he said, still chuckling. "Whereas I let mine rather wander as we look for a suitable place for the day, you reckon rainfall and sunlight to find the greenest grasses." He paused. "Perhaps that is why your ewes and rams grow plumper than mine." He laughed again, and her heart slowed its frightful rhythm at the sound. "But never did I imagine that in a circumstance such as we face, you would make preparation aforehand."

She smiled into the darkness. "My heart may be melting in fear, but my stout determination remains."

He brought her hand to his lips before releasing it. "I daresay your spirit will never change."

"And our plan?" she prompted. "What shall we do?"

"Your greatest fear is that we will be separated in the confusion that awaits us beyond these walls?"

"Aye," she said quietly, "that and still other worries abound." She remembered her family again.

"We shall meet here, then, m'love. In this very place. No matter who asks or how they entreat, we'll tell no other of these caves or what Cadwallen has entrusted to us."

"Aye," she whispered, glad for his wisdom.

"And m'love…" Taran's voice deepened as if in sadness. "There is something else I fear." Gwynedd's heart caught as Taran continued. "'Tis about the ring Brother Cadwallen gave you."

She touched it again, thinking she knew before Taran spoke what he would say. "Should we—should you, m'love—be caught wearing it, I fear the consequences."

"It will be considered stolen?"

"It wouldn't matter, stolen or not. It's made of purest Welsh gold. There are those who would as soon kill for it as not. Even those with no evil intent would rob you of it to exchange for a loaf of bread, if their family was starving."

"I already considered such things, dear Taran," she said. "We will conceal the ring here in this cave—somewhere near the sacred texts."

He chuckled, again surprising her. "You have done it once more, m'love. You are always a league ahead of me in thought." He fell silent, and when he spoke his voice was solemn. "If separated, we will return each summer equinox at dawn…"

"Until the day we die," she said.

He took her hand as she stood. "I will love you forever, dear Gwynedd." He kissed her, at first tenderly, then with greater passion, holding her as if he never wanted to let go.

Her heart leapt at the nearness of him, and with a sigh, she nestled in his arms, feeling the thud of his heart against her cheek. "Sing me one more song before we go," she said.

Resting his jaw on the top of her head, he began to sing,

> O, m'lady fair, my only love…
> O ffanni, blodau'r ffair,
> Ble mae mor hardd ei phryd?
> Mae'n cyrraedd cymaint gair,
> Mae'n ben ar ddeuparth byd!
> Brydyddion mwynion maith,
> Hyd eitha'n hiaith a'i mod,
> Nid cu nacáu, ond llon neshau
> I ganu'n glau ei chlod!

She wept when his voice fell silent again, and she remembered their days in Brother Cadwallen's garden, the lighthearted moments spent together in song, laughing as the mists rolled across the mere, walking the fields with their flocks. "How I love you, my Taran," she whispered, "but never will I give up searching should we be lost from each other."

"Nor will I for you," he said hoarsely into her hair, and then, taking her face between his hands, he kissed her again. After a moment they groped their way across the dark cavern and, testing the wall, found a slatelike sliver of loose stone near the sacred books. Taran chipped away at the slate as Gwynedd took the ring from her finger.

" 'Tis a good hiding place," he said. "Hidden from any who might pry."

Gwynedd held the ring for a moment, kissed it lightly, and then she placed it in the hollow he made. A small thud echoed through the cavern when Taran set the stone back into place.

"Are you ready?" he asked.

"Aye," she said softly, and placing her hand in his, started for the opening into the tunnel.

"May God be with us," Taran said, his voice strong and brave. He stepped in front of her and took the lead.

"Lord, have mercy," she whispered as she followed. "Christ, have mercy."

Minutes later they came to the end of the damp, winding passage and halted before the great stone at the opening. "Once we step outside," Taran said, "we must close the door behind us with haste so it cannot be found by those—"

She touched his arm. "M'love, I know full well. Once we leave this place we cannot reveal where we have been. We cannot let anyone see us return, no matter the danger. 'Tis not for the ring, but for keeping hidden and safe the sacred books."

Taran sighed. "Would that I might do this alone," he said. "That you remain here, safe, until I return for you."

"We will go together." She laughed softly to lighten his spirits. "God is with us. There are those who may await our hands of healing and words of succor." *If anyone survived Gunnolf's attack,* she added silently. "Now open the door before I do it myself."

With a grunt, Taran rolled the large stone just far enough to provide a space for them to slip through. "I'll go first," he whispered as a chilling breeze swept in, "then I'll signal you to follow."

"Aye," she said, creeping closer. A faint light appeared beyond the opening, making it seem either dawn or dusk. The air smelled of damp earth and crushed wet leaves. Then another haunting stench assaulted her nostrils. A smell that came from burning wood and flesh. Closing her eyes, she whispered a prayer of hope that it was animal flesh, not human.

"My love," Taran whispered, "come now. Follow me. Quickly."

She stepped outside and, letting her eyes adjust to the light, waited for Taran to roll the stone into place.

A heavy mist hid the abbey—if any of its walls remained—from sight. It also hid Taran and Gwynedd from suspicious eyes. Voices rose in the distance, speaking the guttural sounds of a language she had never before heard. She could make out the glow of fires, and she hoped they were cooking fires. Then she raised her eyes and saw a dull orange haze above the village.

Taran took her hand again, urging her to move quickly. He headed away from the abbey grounds, and she knew he would head first toward the village to see whether families remained, which thatched houses hadn't burned. Darkness seemed to be falling faster now, and a brisk wind off the mere burned her cheeks.

They had traveled only a long cast of a stone from the tunnel entrance when they reached a rise. At the same time, the emerging moon brightened the mist and brought the landscape into view.

"Oh Taran," she moaned, bringing her hand to her mouth. Bile stung her throat, and she bit back her tears. "Oh no…" The village, or where it had once stood, was rubble. Every dwelling, every stable, every pen, had been burned or trampled or both. Even in the moonlight, she saw strewn bodies of the young and old. With a sob, she buried her face against Taran's chest. His arms closed around her, but he said not a word.

When she looked up into his face a moment later, a terrible anger blazed in his eyes. "They will pay," he said between clenched teeth. "They will be made to pay."

She clung to his hand. "Taran, do not fight them. Promise me this. We must remain together."

"I will see you to safety," he said. "But I will not rest until vengeance is done." He let go of her hand and ran down the rocky hillside, almost falling as he went. She heard his sobs of anguish as he went from house to house. Some still smoldered, others were black shells. She couldn't bear to see the bodies, any of them, and stayed back.

When he reached the pen that had sheltered his sheep, just beyond the edge of the village, he fell to his knees. In the pale light of the moon, Gwynedd saw his shoulders shaking with grief as he gathered a slain lamb into his arms.

It was then she followed, stumbling over stones and brambles in her haste to reach him. When she was a few footsteps away, she halted as raw grief overtook her. His robe and his face were smeared with the lamb's black blood; his anguished cries filled the night air.

Dropping to the ground, Gwynedd gathered him to her bosom and rocked him like a baby, crooning as she, too, wept. "Sh, m'love. We are here. We are alive. We must flee."

Then she heard heavy footfalls tramping down the hillside whence they had come. Voices followed not long after, deep and guttural, interspersed with laughter, coarse, raw. Terrifying.

"Come, Taran," she whispered. "Quickly. Come!"

The moonlight caught the glint of hatred in his eye, the smear of dark blood on his jaw, just before he stood and turned to face those who marched toward them.

"Taran, no!" she cried.

10

Long after the house was quiet, Taite sat in the window seat of her upstairs bedroom. Her thoughts turned to Gwynedd and Taran. Her grandmother told the story as if the young people existed today. Not surprising, since she walked and talked with the young lovers in her dreams, fantasized that she could see them at twilight in her garden.

Taite wasn't one to be impressed by genealogical research and had often dismissed her friends' claims to ethnic or national origin as incredibly boring, especially when their stories claimed a connection to royalty or bigger-than-life historical figures. But her grandmother's stories caused a stirring as she came into a new sense of family continuity. If what Naini told her was true—and she had her doubts—Taite was part of a direct lineage that stretched back through the generations, blessed by an ancient monk's prayer.

In recent years she had dismissed God—and nearly everything of a spiritual nature she'd once believed to be true—but her thoughts returned to him now. And to the blessing in Naini's story: *Turn the hearts of parents to children, and the hearts of children to parents...*

She drew her knees to her chest, wrapped her long skirt around her legs, and stared out into the deep night. *That God would turn the hearts of parents to children…* Bitterness rose inside her as she thought about her mother. Though she'd been only five when Anna died, she remembered the attention her mother lavished upon her sister. She had felt left out, like a traveler walking behind her sister and mother, but the journey had nothing to do with her. They were walking in some sort of light that she couldn't penetrate. She merely walked in the afterglow, worshiping Anna, her bright and beautiful big sister, and wondering why her mother didn't turn the same eyes of love on her.

So much for that part of the family blessing. God must have overlooked it at Taite's birth—and Anna's death.

She touched the place on her abdomen where the seed lay hidden in the dark womb and felt unsettled, unsure. *Turn the hearts of parents to children?*

She stood abruptly and crossed the room to begin getting ready for bed, but she couldn't shake the image of a child growing inside her, one with the unique mix of genes from her family and Sam's. A child began to dance into her thoughts…a little girl with hair as dark as hers, with eyes like Sam's, a nose like Naini's, a child with a combination of traits that came from generations past, perhaps even those of Taran and Gwynedd.

Almost angrily she pulled Sam's worn flannel shirt from her backpack, jammed her arms through the sleeves, and buttoned it up the front. She was getting sentimental again. She couldn't afford the luxury of such feelings. She headed into the bathroom and grabbed her toothbrush. With each rough stroke she promised herself she would see about the abortion first thing in the morning—before Naini rose, before any further thoughts about babies or children changed her mind. She would find a way to pay for it; she had no choice. Surely they would perform the procedure on credit.

She rose at dawn after a restless night. The house was cold, and she shivered as she set kindling and three small oak logs in the sunroom stove. After she tossed a lighted match inside, she stood back, pleased, as the kindling caught and sparked to life. Next she headed into the kitchen to find the phone book and, she hoped, the address of a clinic. After rummaging through the drawers in Naini's kitchen desk, she found the book, sat down as she flipped it open to the yellow pages, and discovered several listings under physicians. Four seemed promising, each ad declaring confidentiality. She pulled out the middle drawer, a narrow space that held pens and stationery, and reached for a scrap of paper to write down the addresses.

At the top of a notepad, a few words in Victoria's elegant script caught her attention. She picked it up and held it to the light. Written there was the name of a neurologist with an address and phone number at Stanford Medical Center. Beneath the doctor's name was a date and time. The appointment had been last week, just a few days before the letter that Naini sent to the island asking Taite to come.

Taite sat back, stunned. Naini had sent for her because she needed her. Yet Taite had blown in like a small tornado awhirl with her own troubles. Naini had said there were two reasons she'd sent for her. After Taite had dropped her bombshell, they'd never gotten around to reason number two, the one having to do with Victoria. Guilt settled into her heart, and she bowed her head, struggling with waves of nausea.

She swallowed hard and headed to the pantry for crackers. She asked herself why else her grandmother might have jotted down the name of a neurologist. Perhaps she had driven a friend to the doctor, someone from church or one of her clubs. Maybe it was a coincidence that the appointment was close to the date of Naini's note. Taite bit into a saltine and sat down again at the desk.

Apprehension washed over her as her grandmother's vivid dreams and hallucinations came back to mind. She remembered Sam once mentioning that nightmares sometimes preceded the onset of Alzheimer's. She clutched the edge of the desk, feeling dizzy. It couldn't be. Not Naini.

"Child?" She looked up to see her grandmother in the doorway. "My goodness, what gets you up so early this morning?"

Taite turned as her grandmother moved across the room. She wore an ivory sweater and camel-hued wool slacks, and her hair was arranged in a soft swirl around her head. She was as elegantly dressed as always, but her lined face showed weariness and something deeper. Taite remembered the shadow of fear she'd noticed on her last visit and recognized it again.

Her world seemed to tilt the wrong direction. "Naini, I should be asking you that question." She gestured toward the note. "I was looking for a piece of scratch paper"—too late she remembered she'd left the phone book open to the page listing women's health clinics—"when I came across this."

Her grandmother's gaze went to the phone book before meeting Taite's eyes. "It seems we both have our health issues," she said calmly. "And yes, we do have something to discuss."

Taite dropped her head, feeling sick again. At once Naini was beside her. "Fresh air is the best antidote for what ails us both. Let's walk to the harbor. I know a little coffee shop that serves dynamite cinnamon rolls."

"I-I don't think I can eat..." She swallowed hard.

"Nonsense. You're not eating enough. That's why you're feeling sick. You need carbohydrates." She smiled as she laid a hand on Taite's shoulder. "I think a roll swimming in melted butter—real butter, mind you—might be just what the doctor ordered. And a cup of herbal tea."

Taite forced herself to think of a walk in the fresh air, nothing more. Not what Naini was about to tell her. Not what she planned to do.

"And I see you're ready to go out—boots laced and jacket on." Victoria's lips were in a tight line; the headings on the yellow pages had clearly given away Taite's plan. But she said no more. Instead, she headed to the sunroom stove, closed the damper, and then moved down the hallway. Taite followed without speaking.

Minutes later they were on the road, walking toward the harbor. The fog had moved out to sea, and the day was promising sunshine and warmth. The promise didn't match the darkness in Taite's heart.

After they had walked a half mile or so, Victoria pointed to a weathered building at the end of the wharf. "New owners just took over, a husband and wife team. And oh my, can that woman bake."

The sting of the brisk air on her face, the sounds of seagulls flapping and calling overhead, the sight of pelicans diving for breakfast in the rippling gray water, and the bark of harbor seals all came together as if orchestrated by Naini herself to lift Taite's spirits. She caught her grandmother's hand to help her over a spit of sand and onto the worn, uneven planks of the wharf. "You were right," she said as the sun crept into view over the rolling hills. "This is just what I needed."

Victoria turned her face to the sun. Her smile said, I told you so.

About halfway to the coffee shop, they stopped near a deserted fisherman's bench and sat down in a pool of sunlight. "My favorite time of day," Naini said. "Many mornings I walk here to have my prayer time. I claim this bench as mine. God seems closer somehow, here by the ocean with its rhythm of waves and salty sea air."

Taite tilted back her head and drew in a deep breath. If she believed in a caring God, she might agree. "What is it you have to tell me?" She glanced at her grandmother.

Victoria faced the ribbon of beach where long-legged sandpipers skittered across the wet sand. "You found the name of a doctor I saw at Stanford Medical Center last week. Normally, appointments must be scheduled months in advance, but a friend cut through the red tape."

"Was it because of the dreams, the…visions?"

Gulls called overhead, and almost as if in answer, a sea lion barked from beneath the wharf. A short distance away, two fishermen talked about the morning's catch. Taite waited, her stomach clenched tight.

"He ordered tests," her grandmother said. "I received the results the morning I sent for you."

"So it wasn't Sam's letter after all." And it certainly wasn't because of Doc Firestone spilling the baby beans.

Victoria watched her carefully, her brow furrowed, as if measuring how much to say, perhaps what to say. So many times through the years, she had looked upon Taite with a curious mix of caring, exasperation, and humor. Now, caring seemed to have taken precedence. Finally she spoke. "I've become concerned about the nightmares and hallucinations. I tried to put them out of my mind, hoping they were just signs of my eccentricities." She smiled. "Signs of my storyteller's heart."

"But they're not."

Victoria shook her head. "Partially, perhaps. But the bigger answer is no."

"What is it then?" Taite suddenly wanted to cover her ears.

"I've never been one to do things the simple way. And as I head through my golden years, it appears, they won't be simple. The tests aren't entirely conclusive, but the neurologist is fairly certain of his preliminary diagnosis. It's got a name longer than Methuselah's age. And part of it sounds more like a person than a disease." Her smile faded. "Are you ready for this?"

"Of course."

" 'REM sleep behavior disorder with diffuse Lewy bodies' is one name for it."

That didn't sound so bad. She'd never heard of it, which was a good sign. And it certainly didn't sound fatal. She took Naini's hand. "That's a relief."

The creases on Victoria's face deepened. "I'd never heard of it either."

Taite chuckled. "Lewy bodies? Hey, that would be a great name for a private investigator. Lewy Body." She laughed again.

"During the first phase the nightmares begin," Victoria said, as if Taite hadn't spoken, "vivid dreams in which the dreamer loses the normal sense of paralysis accompanying most REM sleep."

"REM is rapid eye movement?"

"The person often wakes up bruised and cut on the floor beside the bed."

"That's happened to you?"

"Many times over the past few years. Then the hallucinations began. My family doctor misdiagnosed the cause and sent me to a psychiatrist. He said I was suffering from schizophrenia." Her gaze drifted out to sea.

"You said it was misdiagnosed."

Victoria nodded. "The medication I was given made me feel worse than before. I was in so much pain I couldn't walk. After two days I flushed the pills down the toilet and didn't return to the doctor."

"Until now," Taite said. "Explain this new diagnosis. It doesn't sound too serious."

Something in her grandmother's voice, her expression, told Taite she was wrong even before Victoria went on to explain.

"If my doctor is right, I'm in the early stages of dementia. Another name for this disease, the one it's usually known by, is dementia with Lewy bodies. Or DLB."

Suddenly Taite found no humor in the name. "Your doctor's wrong," she said, struggling to keep the catch from her voice. "The tests will show that you're fine." Besides, something with a silly name like Lewy bodies couldn't be serious. "I refuse to believe it."

"The second phase is the one that causes visions. Just like mine, they are so vivid, the patient—though understanding intellectually—refuses to accept that the people and animals she sees aren't there."

"No! I still don't believe it." In her dismay she again had the sudden childish urge to cover her ears.

"In the third stage," Naini began, and Taite stood, hands clenched, looking out at the thundering surf, her back to her grandmother. Victoria stood and moved close to Taite, putting one arm around her shoulders. "In the third stage, Parkinson's-type symptoms begin. Rigid limbs, shuffling walk, extreme fatigue to the point of falling asleep in midsentence, and in the end—"

"Don't say it!" Tears rolled down Taite's cheeks. "It's not true. It can't be true." A new anguish seared her heart.

For a moment they stood without speaking, Taite crying quietly. Above them, gulls circled and cried. Now and then a pelican swooped, flapping its broad wings awkwardly to keep airborne. Taite sniffled into a tissue and glanced at her grandmother.

"The doctor told me what to expect from this point on…if indeed his diagnosis is correct."

"I'm listening."

"I need your help, Taite."

The words brought a willing response, but Taite knew her limitations. She'd never had what it took. Not that innate ability some people had to do the loving and right thing at the right time. Sam had it. Naini had it. Such strength and capability that she didn't ever seem to need help from anyone. Till now. "What do you need from me?" Her heart didn't match the words.

"Until now I've been at peace with old age, assuming all I needed was right here where my heart is. But I've been doing a lot of thinking since the diagnosis—" Taite opened her mouth to protest, but Victoria held up a hand. "Please, this time let me finish."

Taite nodded and tried to ignore her unsettled emotions.

"As I was saying, I always assumed I would go on living here, just like always, until the day I die. Now everything has changed." Victoria paused. "So I've decided to sell the house. I'll need your help to ready it for the market." She studied Taite with a hopeful expression.

From the far side of the harbor a foghorn blew, and another pelican swooped down, its wings extended, and landed on the railing, wobbling as it sought balance. Their perplexed expressions had always amused her, but now as the creature stared at her with an unblinking, hopeful look, she waved it away with an annoyed gesture. It swooped again toward the sea.

"You can't sell," she said finally. "I think you should get a second opinion about this Lewy body business, maybe a third, before you make any drastic life changes. Having a home is too important; you can't sell it." Her voice dropped to a bitter whisper. "Besides, it's the only place where I've known love. If it's not there…" Her voice trailed off, and she was immediately ashamed.

"Stanford is the best," Victoria said quietly. "And I know my symptoms. I'd guessed what was ahead long before I saw the neurologist. As for the other, I don't have a choice. Your grandfather left me enough to get by, but nothing close to what it will take for extended care in a facility."

This was her cue to assure Naini that she would step in, take care of her, see her through whatever might lie ahead. She didn't need more than a half second to assess her qualifications: pregnant, unwed, about to seek an abortion, no career, no savings. Who was kidding who? She couldn't take care of herself, let alone an elderly grandmother suffering from dementia. Tears of self-pity filled her eyes. How much worse could it get?

Seeming to sense her thoughts, Victoria leaned forward and searched her eyes with a penetrating gaze. "Lest you think that life is unfair right now, God has given you a precious gift—"

"If you're about to lecture me about not having the abortion, don't bother." She knew she sounded petulant. She didn't mind. Life *wasn't* fair right now. "I feel more alone than ever. Talk about another reason not to have a child..." She looked away from her grandmother, hating herself for the words that had just pierced Naini's heart.

"I was about to say that your life, Taite—yours—is a precious gift. Maybe you don't see it now, but let me tell you, it passes too quickly. When you're my age, looking back over the blessings of family and friends—those times when your heart swells so with love and laughter that you think you'll never forget the moment..." Her voice, soft with emotion, trailed off. "Then you do forget," she said finally. "Maybe not right away. But it happens."

Taite felt like weeping. "Is that how it is with you, Naini? The forgetting, I mean. Already?"

Victoria's gaze was on the horizon, following the flutter of birds above a fishing boat. "There are those moments," she said. "But I'm blessed; they aren't many. They aren't often." She caught Taite's hand and squeezed it.

That night after her grandmother was asleep, Taite walked through the house, letting her fingers trail along high-back chairs, chests, and occasional tables as she passed. All spoke to her in the silent language of her grandmother's heart.

As she wandered from room to room, her emotions roiled like the surf off Point Solana. "This is too much," she whispered into the darkness. "Too much!" She wanted to shake her fist at God. How could he do this to a woman who had loved and served him nearly all her life? How could he take her fiery spirit, good sense, and creative energies?

Eventually she stood in her grandfather's library. The room was bathed in a filtered glow from the gas streetlight in front of the house. She walked to the window and pulled back the filmy curtain. Fog ebbed and flowed with the breeze, creating an otherworldly look in the night. She shivered, suddenly afraid of the darkness.

She settled into the worn office chair that had been her grandfather's and rested her head in her hands, elbows on the big oak desk in front of her. The troubles of the day, the fear of her tomorrows, brought a new wave of nausea. She swallowed hard and tried to gulp deep breaths, but her emotions had her breathing so rapidly that she felt lightheaded.

"Sam," she whispered, picturing him on that last day, "I need to talk with you. I need your wisdom about all this. Your thoughts about the baby…our baby. Your thoughts about Naini. And mostly, just to hear your voice and know I'm not alone."

Oh, how she missed him. But Sam was in Boston, going on with his life, likely not giving her a second thought. He was her best friend, the one with whom she could always share every heartache, every joy, every failure, every triumph. Until now.

She traced circles on her abdomen with her fingertips over the place where the baby grew. Again it occurred to her that this child carried the genes of ancestors past, of her grandmother, of those who lived in her grandmother's family tales.

The irony didn't escape her. Just when she was beginning to wonder about the relevance of the family blessing by the old monk in twelfth-century Wales, she found out that her grandmother's stories were the result of dementia. She almost relished her moment of cynicism.

She stared through the window, setting her lips in a defiant line. It wasn't her fault that Sam had left her in this condition. It wasn't her fault that she didn't have the means—or the will—to save the child growing beneath her heart.

No, it wasn't her fault. Any of it. She might have believed in God's goodness when she was a child. But now? She let out a bitter laugh. If there was a God, he certainly showed no compassion.

She bowed her head and wept great tears of self-pity.

Later that night, sitting in the window seat of her bedroom, she opened a spiral notepad and smoothed the first page. Then she lifted a pen and began to write.

Dear Sam,

I have something to tell you that can't wait.
I sent you away that last day so you would never
know what I planned for the child, our child. You've
dreamed openly of the family we would someday have.
You've talked about a house full of love and laughter—

babies and boisterous toddlers with their noisy ways and
sticky hugs and kisses, the soccer games and piano recitals,
the commencements, weddings, grandchildren, all the
family milestones we'd enjoy through the years.

And now I carry the child who might be part of that
life of laughter and love.

If you knew what I plan, you would be appalled.

I deceived you, Sam. I never told you that I don't want
children. You know about my issues with my mother and
my dead father. What I've never told you is how deeply I
am wounded. Rejection, indifference, is worse than open
hostility. I can't imagine bringing a child into a world so
cruel as the one I experienced.

Some might think my experience minor compared to
what other children have endured. But for me, the rejection
cut to the bone. My fears are too great to love completely. . . to
accept love completely.

My guilt—for the times we gave in to personal intimacy,
for deceiving you, for what I must do to end this "problem"
—sometimes brings me to my knees in pain. I want to pray,
but I don't think God would want to hear from me. So
I just weep. That's all. I just weep until my soul is empty.

I am the one who must bear the consequences. I get an
ache in my heart every time I think of what I must do.

You've long urged me to write—the stories that spin in
my head, the poetry that sings in my soul. Perhaps someday
I will. But for now—just as the iron bands of emotion have
squeezed the breath from my lungs, all creative thoughts and
words seem to have been squeezed from my mind.

I won't mail this. But it helps to pretend, at least for a short time, you are there in Boston, thinking of me just as I am thinking of you. That you might read this if I were brave enough to mail it.

For all my childish, self-centered ways, there is one part of me that is solid and true. And it is this, Sam: I love you.

But I'm afraid that in this new, terrifying world I've been called into, even that may disappear. It frightens me to death to think of it.

Love,
Taite

11

Victoria watched her granddaughter with a heavy heart. They had caught a train into the city early this morning, tended to real estate business, and now sat outdoors at a small café overlooking the gray waters of San Francisco Bay.

"I made an appointment for you with an ob-gyn recommended by my doctor," she said to Taite, knowing good and well the frown that would surely follow the announcement. "It's at two o'clock."

"Today?"

"Of course."

Taite twisted her hands in her lap. "You're making this harder for me, Naini."

"Good."

"I can't go."

"You don't have a choice."

"Yes, I do." Her lips were set in a straight line.

"I told you I need your help."

Taite's look was one of rigid challenge. She was as stubborn as her mother had once been. "You said you needed me to help with selling the house."

"You must be healthy for what's ahead. You need a checkup, vitamins, that sort of thing."

Taite had declared more than once that at her first chance she would visit a clinic to have the procedure done. Victoria had spent the last several days making sure she didn't have that chance. She had kept Taite busy readying the house to sell—scrubbing floors, vacuuming, cleaning out closets, transporting clothes and blankets to a homeless shelter. Besides, in Victoria's opinion, nothing beat back the blues like hard work. Cleaning closets and weeding gardens were better than any emotion-soothing drug. Of course there were those severe cases that needed true medical help. But for her granddaughter, so like herself and Isabel in temperament, cleaning and weeding would work just fine.

"Don't start in feeling sorry for yourself again. You're strong. You're talented. You've got a bright mind. You belong to a God who says in his Word that you're the apple of his eye." Victoria leaned across the table as a waiter brought two glasses of milk. "You've got youth. You've got a man who loves you with enough passion to last several lifetimes, and he has said—in my hearing—that he wants to spend his life with you. The whole world is yours for the taking."

"You're my grandmother. You have to say those things."

Victoria sighed and stirred two teaspoons of honey into her milk. There was no getting through to the child. Unless she played the guilt card. She smiled behind her linen napkin. "I'm an old lady. I don't have to say anything I don't want to. And I may be losing my mind soon, so humor me."

Taite smiled for the first time all morning. It was like a sunrise after a foggy dawn. "The last thing in the world anyone would call you is an old lady."

"And what would they call me then?" She shot her granddaughter a demure smile.

Taite laughed. "Incorrigible."

She laughed with her. "Of all the words I've heard when people try to describe me, I rather fancy that one right now."

Taite played with her milk, but grimaced when she tried to take a sip.

"Bottoms up," Victoria said pleasantly. It had been her idea to order it—just after she cancelled Taite's coffee request. "As I was saying, it won't hurt to at least see to your vitamins and minerals. Iron is important too. Do all this while you're waiting to decide about…the other."

"I've decided."

"Humor me," she said again.

Taite shook her head. "You're impossible," she muttered and lifted the glass of milk to her lips.

"Actually, I liked incorrigible better."

Taite laughed. "All right, I'll take vitamins. But that's all." She signaled the waiter and asked for chocolate flavoring.

Victoria settled back, satisfied. She hadn't won the war. But chocolate milk and vitamins said she'd won a small battle. Maybe Taite hearing her baby's heartbeat through a stethoscope would help win the next one. She closed her eyes and whispered a prayer as the server brought their sandwiches.

Taite was still dealing with the emotional aftermath of the doctor's visit when they stepped down from the train in Crescent Bay. She tried not to think about the sound of the baby's heartbeat, but the lively rhythm of it wouldn't leave her.

With an impatient sigh, she hailed a taxi. Soon they were on their way through the small seaside town to the outskirts where her grandmother's big Victorian loomed against the gray landscape. They climbed the front steps. Victoria took her key chain from her handbag and unlocked the door.

"Beginning now," Victoria continued as they passed over the threshold, "we must decide about the rest of my things." She paused. "And lest you get sentimental on me, keep in mind they're just *things*."

Again Taite thought about the house and all it meant to her. She wanted to weep. She turned away and walked to the sunroom window. A few ticks of the kitchen clock passed before she felt the touch of her grandmother's hand on her shoulder.

"Child," Naini said, "I wish I could tell you everything will be all right—just as I did when you were young. But the truth is, it won't be. Not for a long, long time." She paused, gazing through the kitchen window at something in the distance. "As terrifying as that prospect is," she said, her voice dropping, "as scared as I am sometimes, I only know I trust God…even in this."

When Taite didn't answer, she went on, "Knowing what's ahead makes me even more aware that I need to cherish every day that my legs still carry me, every word I'm still able to write, every moment my memory is clear. Each is a gift."

Her words made Taite angry with God all over again. How could he strike her mind, her body, with this worst of all diseases? And yet Naini still trusted him. She fought down nausea at the thought. "How can you say that? How can you think of anything besides what's ahead? The darkness…" She bit her lip and looked away.

There was a smile in Victoria's voice when she continued. "Fear can't exist in the light of God's love. It's the knowledge of that light I cling to." She paused. "And I don't have to see the light to know it's there. That knowledge gets me through my darkest fears."

Taite remembered the lighthouse dream her grandmother had

described and had a fleeting thought of taking her to Point Solana, caring for her there, while she could still understand the light's meaning. Just as quickly she pushed the notion away. Becoming a caretaker for a patient with a debilitating illness called for someone heroic, and she was no hero.

"Promise me, child, that when I can no longer remember, you'll tell me. You'll say these words to me."

Taite nodded stiffly, unable to bear thinking about such a time. "I still say you need to get a second opinion."

Her grandmother went on as if she hadn't heard Taite. "In Ecclesiastes there's a verse that reads, 'Truly the light is sweet.'" She smiled. "And it is, Taite. Oh, there is never a sweeter light than that which shines after the darkness."

Sam trotted across campus, shoulders hunched, coat clutched against the wind as he hurried though a summer cloudburst to an evening seminar on ethics and the law. As he passed the library entrance, his friend Blake Frey came out through the glass-and-steel doors and took the broad steps two at a time. Knowing they were headed to the same class, Sam waited for him.

He grinned and winked. "Wet enough for you?" Hailing from Portland, Maine, he never missed a chance to rib Sam about his California roots. He wasn't Sam's only friend who thought all Californians hung out on beaches that looked like Malibu, teeming with tanned and blond surfers, and ate nothing but bean sprouts and tofu and drank green tea and carrot juice. Their politics were laughable as well, though Sam would never admit it to this group.

Sam grinned back. "Reminds me of summers in San Francisco. Though not quite as cold."

"Yeah, right," Blake said as they both picked up their pace. "Say, you interested in going after a grant to work in Stockholm? I just heard that the Stein-Rutherford Foundation is sponsoring a six-week study-abroad program for a half-dozen outstanding med students." He chuckled. "Key word here is *outstanding*, which disqualifies you."

Sam raised a brow and laughed. "I'd come closer to it than you."

"Yeah, I almost forgot. You beat me in the last ethics exam by a half point."

"That's because it's my favorite subject."

"And that's because you're the teacher's pet," Blake said. "The old man seems to home in on you with his questions."

"I disagree with him almost all the time. Maybe he likes the challenge. Or else he's trying to convince me of the flaws in my thinking." It did seem that Dr. Stephens picked on him—especially when Sam was bleary-eyed and sleep deprived, barely able to mutter his disagreement. Not that it was the most stimulating class in the program. Many students complained that Stephens was long past his prime and impossibly old-fashioned in his thinking and that he should be given the academic boot. Blake had laughed more than once that the old man must know where bodies were buried to be kept on so far past retirement age. "But back to the grant. What's it all about?"

They'd almost reached the lecture hall, and Blake moved aside to let Sam through the double doorway. "Age before beauty…"

He gave Sam a mock bow, and Sam stepped through the doorway, shaking his head. "The grant?"

"Stockholm's pretty liberal, right?" They headed up the stairs, Blake in the lead.

Sam frowned at the obvious. "True."

"It's hands-on research, my friend. Working in a lab. Stem cells, baby. Stem cells." He raised a brow. "Something we'd never get a chance to do here."

"Fetuses?"

"That's right. The real thing. Not computer mockups."

They reached the lecture hall and found their seats. The vast room slowly fell silent as the stately Dr. Stephens entered. "I'll fill you in later," Blake whispered as they pulled out their notepads.

"Just tell me when."

"I said later."

Sam chuckled. "I mean, when Stockholm?"

"Winter break—mid-December through the end of January."

Sam leaned back, arms folded, thinking about the opportunity. He couldn't wait to get back to California to see Taite. For the past few weeks he'd thought of little besides the moment he would take her in his arms, feel her melt against his chest, breathe in the fragrance of her hair. He'd thought his days would be too busy to think about her. How wrong he'd been. No matter the rush to and from the hospital and classes, the sleepless nights observing in ER when acute stroke victims were admitted, the endless time in the books—no matter what he was doing, her image came to him. Standing by the ocean, tossing her sun-drenched mop of dreads, turning to grin at him with that sparkle of a beauty mark above her lip…she was always with him.

As he weighed the Stockholm fellowship, he couldn't help realizing that Taite hadn't exactly been open to working on their relationship. She wouldn't speak to him on the phone, hadn't answered his letter. Maybe she really had given up on him. Or maybe she didn't love him after all. What if he flew home for Christmas to be with her but she wouldn't see him?

He forced his attention back to Dr. Stephens. The old man's introduction was less than stimulating until he hit upon the core issues of ethics and law.

Sam sat up straight, almost annoyed that the subject was so fascinating. It seemed that in every area of the field that drew him, there were more questions than answers. Especially this one.

Dr. Stephens moved from behind the lecture table and studied the faces of the students before him. The pause was dramatic. When he spoke again, his voice was solemn. "As physicians we are committed to pursuing every means possible to heal the sick, to alleviate disease, to study the hard questions, to seek answers that might restore health to the handicapped and those suffering acute or chronic pain, to bring aid to the dying.

"What if you had the means to heal the suffering but the laws of the country forbade you to use that means?"

Sam frowned. So what else was new? Of course there were laws forbidding the use of hundreds of untested drugs and experimental methods of fighting disease. And for good reason. The jury was still out on many of the drugs and procedures. He was content to wait for judgment. But Sam knew the doctor must be leading up to the question of embryonic stem cell research, and he leaned forward expectantly.

"What if, my friends, someone close to you was suffering from a debilitating disease, one that created chronic pain so intense that it was almost unbearable? What if you had the means to alleviate that pain? Not only that, but through these means, to restore this loved one to health, to a life free from pain?" He paused, looked away from the students, took a page from a stack of papers, and then raised his eyes once more.

"And I propose another question for debate: what if, when you are practicing medicine, say forty years from now, you and your colleagues find there's no longer room to care for the human beings who are living longer because of miracle medicines but are succumbing to dementia? Their suffering is past because they don't know where they are, who they are. They have no future, no past, no present. Their caretaker's suffering is great—if they are fortunate enough to have a caretaker.

"As a side note, did you know that sixty percent of caretakers of such patients die before their ill loved ones? But I digress. Let's return to your practice a few decades into the future. Dare we whisper the word *euthanasia?*"

Sam saw that the professor's face conveyed a measure of sorrow. It was so still in the classroom he could hear the breathing of his colleagues around him.

"What about the economics of keeping these patients on life support or just keeping them alive?

"Gentlemen and ladies, I bring this question before you as an example of what your generation will face in the coming years. Some of you are heading into research, and though—as you know—I preach hands-on medicine, healing one patient at a time, I commend you who are going into research. Because it will take all of us working together to discover the answers to the deeper questions.

"We can't just talk in this class about healing and research as esoteric subjects. This shouldn't be a course to attend and shoot for a grade that looks good on your record." He leaned on the podium. "We've got to look to our future, as a country, as a world.

"Of course, you know where I'm going with this. Ethics versus the law. Which is the higher calling? To obey the law? Or to obey the Hippocratic oath? Lest you've not had the opportunity to review...or to sign...this oath, let me read it to you." He adjusted his eyeglasses and smiled. "From the original."

He lifted the sheet he had retrieved earlier. After clearing his throat, he began to read aloud:

I swear by Apollo the physician…that, according to my
ability and judgment, I will keep this Oath and this stipulation—to reckon him who taught me this Art equally dear
to me as my parents, to share my substance with him, and
relieve his necessities if required; to look upon his offspring
in the same footing as my own brothers, and to teach them
this Art, if they shall wish to learn it, without fee or stipulation; and that by precept, lecture, and every other mode
of instruction, I will impart a knowledge of this Art…to
disciples bound by a stipulation and oath according to the
law of medicine, but to none others.

I will follow that system or regimen which, according
to my ability and judgment, I consider for the benefit of
my patients, and abstain from whatever is deleterious and
mischievous.

I will give no deadly medicine to any one if asked, nor
suggest any such counsel; and in like manner I will not give
to a woman a pessary to produce abortion.

With purity and with holiness I will pass my life and practice my Art.… Whatever, in connection with my professional
service, or not in connection with it, I see or hear, in the life
of men, which ought not to be spoken of abroad, I will not
divulge, as reckoning that all such should be kept secret.

While I continue to keep this Oath unviolated, may it
be granted to me to enjoy life and the practice of the Art,
respected by all men, in all times. But should I trespass and
violate this Oath, may the reverse be my lot.

Dr. Stephens's gaze seemed, as usual, to home in on Sam as he
opened the lecture to questions and comments on the oath. Sam didn't

take the bait. He couldn't get past the words "I will follow that system or regimen which, according to my ability and judgment, I consider for the benefit of my patients." Ability and judgment. His own ability, his own judgment, after training, after he took the oath.

"You see," Dr. Stephens concluded, after several of the students had given their comments, "in the section having to do with euthanasia and abortion, the Hippocratic oath is quite clear. For the sake of discussion, allow me to read it to you again: 'I will give no deadly medicine to any one if asked, nor suggest any such counsel; and in like manner I will not give to a woman a pessary to produce abortion.'" He removed his glasses and rubbed his eyes. "Tell me," he said, looking up again, "can you take this oath seriously? Can you take a life, no matter the help you might bring another human being?" He paused, again seeming to stare at Sam.

"Tell me," he repeated, "can you use the aborted tissue of a human being for research to save others' lives? And what if taking the aborted tissue of one human being saves another from becoming the shell of a human being I mentioned earlier? In simplest terms, an infant saves an octogenarian from euthanasia."

The room was silent.

Sam raised his hand. When Dr. Stephens nodded to him, Sam spoke. "Could it also be that certain parts of the Hippocratic oath are hopelessly out of date in today's world? Could it be that science and medicine have advanced far beyond what was once ethical to a new level of..." He faltered, searching for the right words. "...of understanding of our profession?"

Watching him intently, Dr. Stephens gestured for him to go on.

Sam cleared his throat and stood as the other students craned to watch him speak. "Could it be that a higher 'calling,'" he said, "if I may refer to it as that, in the oath is to...and I quote...'follow that system or regimen which, according to my ability and judgment, I consider for the benefit of my patients'?" He paused, gathering his thoughts.

"I have to question," he continued after a moment, "whether this section contradicts, perhaps even negates, the section that follows on euthanasia and abortion." He held up a hand. "Not that I'm ready to determine that I'm for or against either one. But I believe we can't discount the advances that could be made if scientists were allowed to do research on human embryonic tissue."

He sat down as several of the students around him applauded. Dr. Stephens held up one hand to restore order. "A thoughtful response," he said. "Let's return to my earlier question but take it a step further. If someone you loved was dying, or suffering terribly, and you had the ability to alleviate that suffering through means unlawful, or even unethical, would you do it?" He again stared at Sam, his blue eyes unblinking behind his thick lenses.

"Me?" Sam had to ask.

"You."

The class tittered.

He grinned and stood again. He couldn't help enjoying the interchange with the old doctor. He had to hand it to him: Dr. Stephens always gave him something to think about. "Until class today," he said pointedly, "I didn't have knowledge of the section in the Hippocratic oath to back up my thinking. But by using those words I just quoted, I can't help but think I would go above the law, above what might be considered 'ethical' by standards that aren't my own, to do whatever was necessary to save the life, or alleviate the suffering, of another human being." It was solid reasoning. He bit back a smile of triumph as he met Dr. Stephens's gaze.

Dr. Stephens was now leaning back against the lecture table, legs crossed at the ankles. "Where is the line drawn then?" His voice rose with passion. "Do we each make up our own rules based on our own code of ethics? We ignore society? The laws of our nation?"

"But do we let our patients suffer because we might break the law?" Blake argued, from Sam's right. "Just let them die?"

A lively discussion ensued, and Sam again sat down.

"We're nearly out of time," Dr. Stephens finally said. "This is a discussion that will continue throughout your career, believe me. We certainly can't come to a conclusion during one lecture—isn't that true, Mr. Wellington?" He laid aside the page containing the Hippocratic oath. "But I want you to think about medical practices in Nazi Germany, the practice of eugenics and euthanasia that began in the 1930s, some say, because of economic reasons and developed into the horror of the Holocaust. And I want you to consider the slippery slope of subjective thinking."

"Nazi Germany?" Blake muttered as he gathered his lecture notes. "How can he possibly equate it with America today? The good doctor's gone over the edge with this one."

Sam looked past his friend to Dr. Stephens. The tall doctor stood near the door and met his gaze as if waiting to continue the discussion. Sam stifled a groan. It wasn't the first time. It probably wouldn't be the last.

12

Luke Stephens watched Sam Wellington stride confidently down the concrete steps of the lecture hall aisle. Sam was a hodgepodge of opposites. He had the stocky build of a college football player, but the artistic hands and tapered fingers of a surgeon. He had the blond and fit look of a California surfer, but an expression of studious intensity. He wondered if the young man knew how to laugh.

"Thought-provoking lecture," Sam said when he reached Luke.

Luke shot him an amiable smile. "Ah yes, I could see that you were engaged throughout."

"These are difficult questions. Just when I think I've got all the answers, you throw another ball into the game."

"It's not a game, Sam. That's the tragedy." They headed down the hallway, following the other students toward the exit. "I'm on my way to OR. Dr. Edwin Liu is meeting with his surgical team to discuss a new procedure he'll be performing tomorrow morning."

"You're part of the team?" Sam didn't hide his surprise.

"At my age?" Luke chuckled. "I find the advances in this particular surgery extraordinary. Dr. Liu is a friend and invited me to observe tomorrow but also to get up to speed tonight." At the door he stopped to put on his raincoat. Outside, he opened his umbrella.

"What's the procedure?" Sam hunched his shoulders and zipped up his jacket. The umbrella was big enough for two, and Luke gestured for Sam to step underneath.

"Dr. Liu studied with Mahlon DeLong at Emory. They've made tremendous advances with deep brain stimulation for treatment of Parkinson's disease."

Sam nodded. "I've done some reading on it."

"Want to come along? I think I can get you a front-row seat."

The answering grin was clear. Something about Sam Wellington grabbed Luke and wouldn't let go. Maybe Sam reminded him of his own son at that age. Or himself.

He was about to mention his lecture and further probe Sam's thinking, when the young man brought it up himself.

"As I said earlier," Sam said, "sometimes I think I have everything laid out neatly in my mind...about the ethical issues...when you throw out something, a new idea that I hadn't considered before. Then I find myself back to probing the issues again."

Luke chuckled. "That's what this is all about, Sam. That's why I brought up Nazi Germany." He sobered as they rounded the women's studies wing of the hospital. "What do you think was the purpose of the experiments done in the camps?"

"I suppose it was for the goal of refining the so-called Aryan people. Hitler wanted a healthy, pure race."

He could see Sam's uncertain frown in the glow of the gaslights along the brick sidewalk. The rain fell steadier now, and the smells of wet leaves and damp earth filled the air. The scent of wood smoke wafted from somewhere in the distance, making Luke suddenly miss

Martha. She was home, likely sitting by the fire reading and listening to Mozart.

And here he was, just as on so many nights of their fifty-four years of marriage, tending to his other passion—medicine and teaching those called into its service. Martha was his primary passion, and always had been; he hoped she knew it.

The bright entrance to the hospital loomed before them. "You're partially right, of course," he said as they began to ascend the stairs. "But we have to wonder about the doctors who performed the experiments. Did they rationalize that they were doing it for the good of mankind? To make advances in the field of alleviating disease? To someday relieve the suffering of those they loved?"

The automatic doors swung open. Luke folded his umbrella, tucked it under one arm, and headed across the lobby to the elevator. Sam followed.

"The point you're making," Sam said when the elevator doors closed, "is that to those doctors the end justified the means."

"Exactly." He locked on to the younger man's gaze. "And isn't that what you're telling me about stem cell research using aborted embryos?"

"It's not a black-and-white issue," Sam said thoughtfully. "Roll back the argument to the meaning of life and potential for life, productive life. What is it that's so troubling about using a hundred and fifty or so embryonic cells for study?" He shook his head slowly as if thinking though his argument. "What is the difference between a human stem cell and an amoeba, for instance?"

"Potential?" Luke said, to encourage him to continue.

"It has to be. The capacity to become an independently functioning, reasoning human being. But they are a long way from that in their first days of existence." He frowned. "From what I understand, this potential begins when neurons have formed primitive connections and some pathways have been programmed."

"During what appears to be REM sleep in utero," Luke said. He'd read the same research papers. The elevator doors opened, and they stepped into the hallway. "You're saying life isn't life until these connections have been made?"

"It's later, of course, through experience and environment that they become fully human." He stopped, again frowning in thought. "So my point is that it's the potential that makes these cells special. But they haven't reached that potential, so what is the problem with harvesting?"

Luke nodded. "Go on." They stepped aside while three doctors in white coats, stethoscopes looped around their necks, strode to the end of the corridor. A nurse raised her hand in greeting as she hurried along the opposite direction.

Luke and Sam walked slowly to the OR. "Certainly there is nothing supernatural about them in these early stages," Sam said. "No life force beyond biology. They are just cells no different than amoebas or paramecia."

"They have potential."

"Exactly."

Before Luke could respond, a group of doctors joined them. Luke introduced Sam to a colleague who fell into step with them, and a few others nodded politely but seemed surprised to see a student among them. Luke knew what they were thinking, but he'd never been one to be intimidated by what others thought. One of the benefits of being professor emeritus.

They sat in the front row, just as he'd promised, and soon after Dr. Liu began speaking, Luke glanced sideways at Sam, who was completely engrossed. He remained as immobile as a statue during the ninety-minute discussion.

Afterward they walked down the back stairs to a side exit near the parking lot where Luke had left his car. The rain had stopped, and a stiff wind had kicked up in its place. Sam shook Luke's hand, looking genuinely grateful for the experience.

"You want to observe the procedure?"

Sam grinned. "I thought you'd never ask." Looking thoughtful, he paused, and then he spoke again. "This is an opportunity few students get. I want you to know how grateful I am."

Luke opened his car door and turned to Sam before sliding into the driver's seat. "Four o'clock sharp, then. We'll meet here at the back entrance."

"I'll be here." He nodded and waved as he turned.

Luke slid behind the wheel, but looking into the mist-filled night, he thought about the miracle of medicine they had just observed. If only Sam and others like him realized that there was more than one way to go with research for diseases like Parkinson's. Of course these doctors in training had a passion to save lives, but in the rush of youth, they didn't always reflect on all the alternatives. He hoped, he prayed, that Sam would consider deeply, thoroughly, the morality and ethics involved.

His mind went back to the Christmas Eve when he and Martha lost their firstborn son. Four months earlier when they discovered she was pregnant, they had barely been able to contain their joy; that tragic night, when the hemorrhaging began, it seemed their despair had no limit. He'd held the baby in his hands and wept over the child who would never grow up. The tiny fingers were perfect, the toes like a string of miniature pearls. Even now, he felt the same rush of love, of pain, that he had felt when he saw his son.

Didn't the researchers know what they were working with? Didn't they care? He started the ignition and backed out of the parking space. He was still thinking about Sam Wellington, about all the young med students, when he turned into his driveway and looked up at the sturdy brick house that had been their home for a half century. A light glowed from the library window, and smoke rose from the chimney. He smiled. Martha was waiting up, just as she always had.

His heart suddenly glad, Luke hurried from the car and up the walkway.

Sam sat at the desk in his room. His thoughts were full of what he had observed tonight. He wondered if he would be able to sleep at all, though he needed to be awake by three thirty in the morning. He pulled out a notepad, and as always when his heart was stirred to the core, he wanted to write Taite.

She would understand. She always did. Whereas he saw the miracle of science, she saw poetry in the same information. He looked at problems and how to solve them. She looked beyond the problem solving to the outcome, the glorious outcome. She saw the hidden hand of...well, not God so much as nature. She saw nature's poetry, its design. He lifted his pen and began to write.

Dearest, dearest Taite,

Tonight I had the privilege of listening in on a discussion—led by a team of doctors preparing to perform deep brain stimulation tomorrow morning on a patient suffering from acute Parkinson's disease.

He went on to explain the details of the procedure, then, his pen poised, he thought about Taite, her smile, her look of curiosity and interest whenever he talked about medicine. He began to write again.

Taite, I'm telling you this because I love sharing my life with you. My hopes, my dreams, my excitement over the profession I've chosen. How I would love to tell you about those other areas that intrigue me—stem cell research, embryonic tissue transplant, and so much more. Oh, the miracles of medicine—and of Mother Nature, as you would say.

There's something else that I absolutely must discuss with you. After you receive this letter, I plan to telephone to see what you think of the idea. Here's the big news: I am planning to apply for a six-week research program in Stockholm. All expenses are paid—airfare, room, and board. As you probably know, scientists in Europe are forward-thinking in their approach to medical research. Research can be conducted there that can't be conducted anywhere in our country. It would be the opportunity of a lifetime—if I'm accepted.

What would you think, Taite, about coming with me? It would be just the two of us, exploring a new country, a new society. Think about how that would broaden your thinking. Think about how it would open your heart to new and exciting ideas. The research on embryonic tissue—how I would love to talk more with you about the miracles such study might bring to the future of medicine. Can you tell I want to share my life with you, today and always?

We must find the money for you to come with me. Taite, my darling, I love you and can't bear the thought of not being together as we had planned during winter break. Please say yes. We'll find a way to finance your trip. I promise.

I love you. I will call soon.

Sam

The morning fog had rolled in off the ocean when Taite returned from her walk along the sand. She opened the mailbox at the end of the walkway and headed for the front door, thumbing through the stack and glancing at the bills and real estate and mortgage ads. Her heart caught when she spotted Sam's familiar scrawl on a legal-size envelope. With trembling fingers, she tucked the rest of the mail under one arm and headed into the house, down the long hall, almost afraid to open Sam's letter.

Naini looked up with a smile. "Anything interesting?"

"From Sam." She handed the rest to her grandmother, then sat down on the big ottoman and tore open the envelope. The sunroom was quiet except for the sound of the pendulum clock and the rustling of paper as Naini opened her mail.

Taite smiled when she read that he wanted to share his discoveries with her—that he wanted her to go to Stockholm with him. Then she bit her lip as the impossibility of his request hit her. She couldn't leave Naini, not now.

Her fingertips rested on her abdomen as she read his words about stem cell research. Images of a needle, an embryo, test tubes, blood, and death caught in her mind and lodged there. First nausea hit, followed quickly by a sense of panic, bringing with them a dry mouth and heart beating so fast she thought she might die.

In that fraction of a second, she realized that somewhere, deep in her heart, a seed of hope had been born. She hadn't recognized it until now, but that hope had a name: Sam. She didn't care about a trip to Europe with him or even seeing him right now. No, that hope had been that Sam might welcome a child. Their child.

For days her grandmother had talked of little else—the coming baby, her desire that Taite and Sam and the baby might become a family. That's where it had started, and now, Taite realized, that seed of hope had caused her to put off the abortion.

"Child, is something wrong? Is Sam all right?"

Taite closed her eyes for a moment, forcing herself to breathe deep, slow, in, out, again. And again. Her heart rate slowed, the nausea lessened, and she looked up at her grandmother. "Sam is fine."

Victoria tilted her head, her sharp eyes telling Taite she wasn't fooled. "What did he say to upset you?"

Taite wadded up the letter and crossed the room to toss it in the flickering flames of the parlor stove. The movement gave her time to think about the answer. She didn't want to lie, but neither did she want Naini to know the whole truth. She closed the stove door with a soft thump. "He's going to Sweden—Stockholm—over winter break."

"You're disappointed that he's not coming back here…to see you?"

"He made a choice. It's a wonderful opportunity for his research." She sat down again, facing her grandmother. "He hasn't applied, but he's thinking about it." She let out a small, bitter laugh. "But no doubt he'll go. I don't think he's been denied a single fellowship or grant he's applied for."

"He's a very bright young man." Naini settled back in her chair and took a sip of tea. "Tell me about the research."

"Has to do with stem cells transplanted from embryos into patients with debilitating diseases."

"Oh yes, of course. But it's illegal here, isn't it?"

"Lab studies can be performed, but not on humans. That's why Sam wants to go to Sweden. It's legal there, apparently." She paused. "This has long been a passion of his. Research, that is."

"So he would be working on human embryos?"

"Yes."

"Where do they come from?"

Taite sidestepped, letting her gaze drift away from her grand-mother's face. "We've talked about harvesting before."

"I'm assuming they use aborted embryos in this Stockholm lab."

"Some naturally aborted, others…" Taite couldn't finish. She swallowed hard and bent over, dropping her face into her hands. In an instant, she felt Naini's hand on her shoulder.

"Child…what is it?" She dropped to the ottoman and put her arm around Taite.

"I can't bear the thought of it, that's all." She sniffled and rubbed her wet eyes. This had gone on too long. She would wait no longer to have the procedure. Then there would be nothing to worry about. No worries about Sam. He could go off and do what he needed to do. No strings attached. If he really loved her, they could go back to the way they were before the nightmare of the pregnancy. Everything fixed.

There was Naini, of course, and her disapproval of abortion in general and Taite's specifically. But her grandmother loved her without condition. She would forgive, and everything would return to normal there as well.

Everything except Naini's health. Taite's conscience stabbed her when she considered her grandmother's disappointment about not having a great-grandchild in her life. She made such a big issue about the family stories, the genetic links to the past.

"The longer I wait, the harder it is," she mumbled. "That's all. There's so much confusion in my life right now about Sam, about my future." She sighed. "That's why I've got to take this first step. Today."

Victoria frowned but kept silent.

"I've got to have the abortion, Naini." She reached for her grand-mother's hand, imploring her to understand. "I can't go on without taking charge. I've only waited because of you, thinking you might be right. But this letter… Sam's words about the research made me realize what I carry inside me is no more than a bunch of cells."

Her grandmother held up her hand. "You're wrong, Taite. You must realize that I've followed this research for the obvious reasons. Even before the diagnosis, I wondered if stem cell transplants might help me.

"I've told you how frightened I am of the future…of being alone with this disease as it takes over my limbs, my movement, and my mind. Yet would I consider such a transplant from another human being if it meant a return to good health?" She stood and moved to the stove, opened the door, and stoked the fire.

Taite went to stand beside her grandmother. "Please don't say anything more, Naini. You have your opinion; I have mine. I must do what I must do before it's too late."

"How do you mean, too late?"

"I'm losing myself in a maze of uncertainty. I've got to take charge of my life again. I can't wait." She thought of all the things she would do once she recovered from the procedure. Get a job, go to school, reconnect with Sam. Take care of Naini. Get on with life. This was just the first step.

Naini interrupted her thoughts. "You're going today?" The clock struck eleven.

Taite nodded wordlessly.

"Do you need me to be with you?"

Taite was touched that she asked, but she was also certain the offer wasn't to be there to hold her granddaughter's hand. It was to talk her out of the procedure before they reached the front door of the clinic. "No," she whispered, unable to look at Naini for fear of the sorrow she would see there. "No. I can…do this…alone." Without another word, she ran from the room, headed up the stairs to grab her backpack.

Minutes later the front door slammed behind her, and with tears blinding her vision, she rushed into the street.

Victoria sat without moving in the front parlor, awaiting Taite's return. She wondered if she should have gone after her. Just after Taite ran out, she went to the door, ready to step outside. But something stopped her, and she turned back.

That had been an hour ago, and she hadn't for a single moment stopped praying for Taite. She'd had plenty of experience. Years past, her daughter Isabel had also chosen to go her own stubborn way, had defied her, caused anger and sorrow. It was hard enough to endure the pain brought on by Isabel's self-centered attitudes, but when that pain spilled over into the life of Isabel's troubled teenage daughter, Victoria had taken matters into her own hands.

She pulled back the lace curtain and peered out into foggy midday gloom. No sign of Taite.

She had relived the moment dozens of times through the years, wondering now as she always did if she had done the right thing. Said the right thing. Spoken when she should have remained silent. Kept quiet when she should have imparted words of wisdom. But she knew Isabel wouldn't have listened anyway. And Taite was just like her mother.

"Mama," Isabel had said that day in this very room, "it's the chance of a lifetime. I've worked hard for this opportunity, and now it's here."

Isabel, pretty Isabel, had twirled in delight, her dark hair flying around her porcelain face. "I've been accepted for special studies in Madrid," she'd said breathlessly. "It's a special program offered through the Prado."

"How long?"

"A year."

"You can't go," Victoria said with a frown. The Prado was prestigious, but it wouldn't matter even if El Greco himself was the private instructor. "How can you even think of it?"

Isabel narrowed her eyes. "I should have figured you'd disapprove."

"What about Taite?" She had asked the same question too often through the years: When Anna was diagnosed with acute leukemia and died and Isabel said she might not live through the grief. When Isabel was distracted by her marriage difficulties with Brady. And when he died. *What about Taite?*

True to form, Isabel had gone tight lipped the day she announced her plans for Spain. "Taite is adaptable. She'll get along fine."

"You're planning to take her with you then?"

"Of course. It will be a wonderful opportunity. We'll travel, see Spain, Portugal, maybe France and Italy while we're there."

Brady's accident came just a year after Anna died, leaving Isabel deeply in debt with a six-year-old child to raise. She worked her way through the university with two jobs, supplementing her income with scholarships and her sporadic artwork sales. The trip to Spain was her first big break out of the ordinary. Victoria understood the glitter of excitement in her eyes. Her years of single-mom drudgery were about to end.

"Taite is at a tender place in her life, Isabel. I hope you're not planning to backpack around Europe with her in tow." Isabel had been known to hitchhike during her college years. "She needs proper schooling. She's barely into her teens. You need to be here to give her the stable environment she needs."

"You don't believe in my mothering skills. You never have." Isabel's tone was heavy with resentment. "For your information, we'll be going first class."

Warning bells went off somewhere in Victoria's head. "How can you afford first class?"

Her daughter had the decency to look embarrassed. High color spotted her cheeks. "Not first class, exactly. But far better than staying in youth hostels and hitchhiking." She leaned back in her chair, keeping her gaze on Victoria. "I've met someone, Mother. His name is Adam Gilchrist. He's from San Francisco, a newspaperman. He plans to cover the first week of the Prado experience, do a feature article on me for his newspaper. He used to live in Spain, and he knows the ins and outs of travel there. We plan to leave before the program begins to do some touring—by train. He wants to introduce me to some of the ancient wonders, art museums, cathedrals, monasteries, Roman ruins, palaces…"

Her voice dropped, hinting at a sense of wonder. "Mama, I've discovered something wondrous in my work. Something unique. It's got a meaning that's—well, almost spiritual." She paused. "Adam thinks it's—"

Victoria held up a hand to interrupt. She didn't want to hear about Adam or Isabel's work. "So Taite would be carted around Europe—"

"Spain. Mostly around Spain."

"Carted around Spain then, with you and your new boyfriend."

"He's not my boyfriend. He's a friend, a dear, dear friend." She denied it, but Victoria saw something in her eyes.

"How long have you known him?"

Isabel blushed. "Just a few weeks, but—"

"You're thinking only of yourself, Isabel. You've got to think of Taite. She's at a vulnerable age. She's having trouble fitting in."

Isabel frowned. "She's always had trouble fitting in. She's artistic. Not to mention brighter than ninety percent of her classmates."

"You can't just run off to Spain with a man you barely know," Victoria said, hammering in her point, "and drag your daughter along."

Isabel narrowed her eyes, her earlier good spirits gone. "The trouble with you, Mother, is that you always think the worst of me. I'm almost forty years old. I was left alone when Taite was six. I worked to support us both, went back to school to follow my dream, and all the while raised a beautiful, artistic daughter. Now I want to expand her world, take her on the adventure of a lifetime."

"Put off your trip, Isabel. The Prado can wait."

Isabel seemed to consider her mother's words. "This is my time. An opportunity that may not come my way again. I want to do this for me. I want to do it now. And before you lay another guilt-inducing, scathing remark on me, I'll say this: I'm not choosing pursuit of art over raising my daughter. I'm choosing both."

Victoria stood and went to the window. She didn't look at Isabel when she asked the obvious question. "Why don't you ask Taite what she would like to do?"

Isabel's quick intake of breath spoke louder than words. There had always been rivalry between them for Taite's affection. Taite spent more time at her grandmother's than with her mom, especially in the early years when Isabel worked two jobs and sometimes three to make ends meet and pay off Brady's debts.

"Ask me what?" twelve-year-old Taite asked from the doorway. She looked frightened, and Victoria wondered how long she'd been standing there, listening to their raised voices.

Victoria remembered how Isabel had told Taite about the trip. Taite had looked confused, glancing from her grandmother to her mother and back again.

Victoria had known even then what she needed to say: *Go with your mother, honey. You'll love every minute and be back before you know it.* But she remained silent. Now, with the wisdom of time, she knew her words could have changed everything.

All these years later Victoria sat in the same room and remembered the look on Isabel's face when Taite chose to stay with her grandmother. Victoria had manipulated the outcome, but she had never found the strength to ask Isabel to forgive her. Instead she'd tried to make it up to Taite by taking her mother's role, advising her as she thought Isabel would if she had been a part of Taite's life.

She didn't know Isabel—her values, her ethics, or really anything about her. But there was something in her heart that clung to Isabel, unable to ever forget the little girl who once thought the sun rose and set on her mama, who had followed her around the house with shining eyes. Now the same little girl was a grown woman, alienated from both her mother and her daughter.

Victoria dropped her head into her hands, wondering if she should have spoken up before Taite left for the clinic. Victoria squeezed back the sob in her throat. Though she'd had good intentions, her actions, her words, had been wrong. Unforgivably wrong.

She thought of Taite at the clinic, alone and scared. If Isabel had been with her, perhaps things would be different. She pulled back the curtain and, staring into the fog, whispered a prayer for Taite…for Taite's baby…for Isabel…and another for herself, for forgiveness.

Taite lay on the gurney, covered with white sheets. The clinic took only what a woman could afford. Taite had paid with what was left from her grandmother's one-hundred-dollar bill: sixty-three dollars and fifty cents.

The prep was finished, and she was waiting to be wheeled into the room where the procedure would be performed. She had taken a white pill that brought drowsiness within minutes. The nurse-practitioner had explained that the IV drip wouldn't start until she was in the operating room. After that, she wouldn't know anything until she woke up in recovery.

In her drug-induced drowsiness, a parade of images seemed to come alive in her mind: Sam reached out to her, his eyes bright with affection and pride. And Naini, sweet Naini, offered words of love and encouragement. Next a beautiful woman with dark hair danced into Taite's imagination. She was small like Taite, long hair gleaming as it fell across her shoulders. She whirled in a cloud of bright-hued gauzy clothes, laughing and reaching out to Taite with both hands.

Their faces warped and changed. All three images lifted their hands, abnormally large in proportion to their bodies, and pointed to Taite with expressions of agonizing grief.

She screamed as they marched closer, crying out now as if in excruciating pain.

"What have I done?" she whimpered to all three. "What have I done?"

They pointed to her stomach. Taite looked down, and she saw that she was covered with blood. Her baby's blood.

"Mama!" she sobbed, reaching for the dark-haired woman. "Mama, help me!"

13

Isabel woke with a start. She reached for the travel alarm clock on the bedside table, rubbed her eyes, and squinted at the dial: 3:24 in the morning. With a groan, she flopped back against her pillow and stared into the darkness.

She had just heard a baby cry. She was sure of it…or had it been a dream? She held her breath, straining to hear it again. But the only sound coming from outside the rental cottage windows was the moaning wind off the ocean and the brush of eucalyptus on the tile roof.

Impatient that a dream would disturb her so, she sat up and flipped on the light. She grabbed a novel from the table and paged through to where she'd stopped reading the night before. The words blurred, and she let the book drop to her lap, her heart still listening for the cry.

She tried to recall the dream, if indeed it had been a dream, but both images and sounds lingered at the edges of her mind, disappeared, and then drifted into her consciousness once more.

It had been Taite's voice, she knew now, caught in an echo from infancy. Taite had cried out to her, had needed her. Isabel closed her eyes, pressing the image to her heart: Taite as a baby, standing in her crib, reaching out her little arms to be picked up.

The cry had been so real. A chill skittered up her spine, and she leaned back against the pillow and closed her eyes. What if Taite needed her? What if the cry had been sent from her daughter's heart straight to her own?

Taite need her? She almost laughed at the ridiculous thought. Her daughter hadn't needed her for years. She'd made it abundantly clear that she didn't need her mother for anything at any time. Her refusal to answer Isabel's letters and return her telephone calls was positive proof.

The only way Isabel knew anything at all about her daughter was through Victoria. She was thankful her mother cared so deeply for Taite. Feeling a lump form in her throat, she glanced around the room to get her emotional bearings. Her gaze touched on the white plastered walls crowned with dark oak beams, the dancing, lighthearted Miró prints in primary colors, the vase of fragrant cream roses on the table by the window.

The straight-backed rocker sitting next to it drew her attention, and a rush of anguish seared her heart. Her sins were great and forgiveness too long coming. Perhaps she had too much pride to utter the necessary words of healing to her mother and daughter. She didn't know if it would ever be different.

Her life was different now, but the guilt from the past sometimes was too much to bear.

Mothers and daughters—a relationship steeped in pain and sorrow and joy and complexity. It seemed, even in her own childhood, to be either a dance of grace and love or else of regret and despair over failed expectations. She'd been determined not to make the same mistakes her mother made. Instead, she'd far exceeded them. She wondered again if redemption would ever come, if forgiveness and reconciliation would ever be theirs.

Perhaps the last chapter in the relationship wasn't yet written. The notion gave her hope until she remembered Taite's stubborn, angry ways. She sighed, flipped off the lamp, and pulled the goose-down comforter over her shoulders. She tossed fitfully until daybreak.

When she finally rose, she put on a pot of strong Portuguese coffee. While it brewed, she donned a sundress, sandals, and wide-brimmed straw hat. Then, mug in hand, she went outside, through the front gate to the winding cliffside path above the ocean. The sun was about to rise when she sat down on a low rock wall at the edge of the cliff. Waves lapped against the white beach below, and the rhythm of the surf blended with the cries of the seagulls circling in the violet sky of dawn.

She drew in a deep breath, savoring the salt air, the sounds of the waking earth. Taite again came to mind, and she wondered if she still found delight in the sights and sounds of the ocean. She remembered the elfin toddler on a similar day, digging in the sand, pirouetting as the lacy waves tickled her bare feet, pointing to the sky, then looking back at Isabel and declaring, "Mommy, don't you just love today?" She had run into Isabel's arms then, fitting herself completely into her mother's embrace and covering her cheeks with kisses.

Bookish little Anna hadn't liked the beach at all. She found it messy and didn't like to get sand on her feet. She much preferred sitting on a blanket under an umbrella, reading a book. Taite was always much more like Isabel in temperament, from her quirky artistic bent to her love of the wild wind and crashing waves. Funny she would think of such things now.

Her thoughts were interrupted by a gaggle of ducks noisily marching across the trail, their tail feathers waggling, into a forest of tall sea grass. Suddenly quiet, they launched themselves into a pond, ripples spreading behind them.

Isabel removed her hat and lifted her face to the rising sun as the first fingers of light appeared over the ocean from the east. The earth seemed to hush, just as it always did at the very moment of sunrise, before it burst to life again with renewed vitality at the start of the new day. Isabel put aside musings of the dark night, the longing for years she couldn't recapture, for the child she'd let go.

No matter her sorrows, fears, or heartaches, these fleeting moments when earth seemed reborn lifted her spirits. Perhaps they reminded her that when night shadows fell across her heart, they would be followed by a rebirth of joy at dawn. *Weeping may endure for a night, but joy cometh in the morning.*

It was true even this day.

She clutched the thought close to her heart and set off along the path to the white-walled villa. Its warmth beckoned, just as it did every morning.

She drew closer, shading her eyes against the early-morning slant of the sun. A crimson bougainvillea cascaded across the roof of the cottage, nearly covering the Spanish tiles, before spilling to the ground on the opposite side. Another, of a soft salmon color, spilled across the squat rock wall on the right side of the house, just beyond the eucalyptus tree. Rows of sunflowers, heavy heads just now tilting toward the morning sun, stood like sentinels in a patch by the gate.

She had rented the villa on the Algarve coast two months earlier, and already it seemed like home. She loved London, where she lived the rest of the year, but having a place to paint where the light seemed almost magical more than made up for the dearth of plays, museums, and five-star restaurants. Her first exhibit in London was to open in only seven weeks. She had two paintings to finish, and last night a third concept had ignited the flame in her artist's heart. She now planned to leave the other two unfinished for now and turn her attention to the newest portrait, Saint Francis of Assisi. She had promised the curator an exhibit of twenty-five paintings, and she would be hard pressed to complete the last three.

She painted contemporary renderings inspired by medieval portraits of biblical figures and the early saints of the church. She had developed the idea years ago, just as she was becoming established as a portrait artist. One afternoon, after an unexpected confrontation with Taite that had nearly twisted her heart in two, she had visited a museum and had come across a Byzantine painting of Mary, Christ's mother, done in the twelfth century.

It had reminded her of the recent research showing that a broken heart actually causes the same sensation as physical pain. Isabel had known it firsthand, and looking up into Mary's face, she'd thought about the intensity of physical pain she must have experienced watching her Son's agony on the cross.

That day she had stopped and stared, moved to tears. She slipped to the bench in front of the portrait, unaware of time passing. The artist had captured Mary's heartache, fears, and love so beautifully that Isabel felt she was looking straight into the heart of a mother who knew great pain. And deep peace. Isabel was just beginning to understand how a mother's love, forgiving love, grace-filled love, was sometimes not enough.

Soon her spirit was drawn to researching the ancient art dating back to the sixth century. And, almost as if her fingers were connected to her soul, she began to paint her own versions, her own contemporary portraits, of this ancient, spiritual art form.

She named her style Sacred Doorways, and orders poured in, some from churches, many more from individuals who wanted to hang them in home chapels or simple retreats set aside for contemplative prayer. Her portraits of Mary—sometimes alone, other times holding her infant Son—were requested by mothers who often shared their heartaches with Isabel when they placed their orders.

And now the idea had come to her in the night to paint Saint Francis. At the thought, she breathed in the familiar words of his prayer, something that had become an integral part of her daily prayers through the years. "Lord, make me an instrument of thy peace."

She had nearly reached her gate when she looked up to see a welcome figure standing beneath a pepper tree by the porch.

"Adam!" The sun was higher now, and she pulled down the brim of her hat. "I wasn't expecting you until later."

The smile lines around Adam Gilchrist's eyes deepened as he strode down the front path to meet her. "I caught an earlier train. I've got meetings in Lisbon this evening, so I'll have to leave earlier than planned." Before she could comment he stopped in front of her, his expression softening. "I must say, just seeing you makes this glorious day even brighter."

She smiled up at him. "And you, my dearest friend, never fail to cheer me." She tucked her hand in the crook of his arm as they turned toward the villa. "Would you like a cup of tea…or some thick, sweet Portuguese coffee? I made some earlier."

Adam held open the front door. "I had coffee on the train from Faro, but I'm ready for more." He paused. "I'll get it. You sit down and read this…then we'll talk." He placed a folded newspaper in her hands. When she gave him a questioning look, he added, "It's good news, Isabel. Your exhibit is going to be bigger than we thought. It was even mentioned in the *Economist,* if you can imagine. Not their usual fare, but I suppose after your profile in the *London Times,* they wanted to get in on the action." He laughed.

Isabel crossed the room, sat on the window seat near the stone fireplace, and unfolded the newspaper. "Oh my, this is good news." She looked up and smiled. "I can't imagine you didn't have something to do with this."

"I've got my connections." He nodded to the paper. "You read it, and I'll be right back." He left the room, and a moment later she heard him pouring coffee.

The article, taken from the Sunday *Round About the City* section of the *Times,* reported that the Queen herself was interested in Isabel's art. She grinned and called to Adam with a laugh, "Can this possibly be true? The Queen?"

He came through the doorway, cups and saucers in hand, his face alight with pride. Adam had been her champion from the first time they met. He was the first to believe in her abilities, her gift. When she was married to Brady, the most mention he gave to her paintings was to mention her "hobby" to his friends and business associates. And her mother always seemed more interested in recounting Isabel's failings than in taking pride in her accomplishments. As for Taite, she had probably never seen the Sacred Doorways. Or cared to.

Adam's tender expression as he stood near the window, bathed in sunlight, made her glad this dear man was in her life. He placed the mugs on the bay window shelf, then sat facing her, at the opposite end.

He leaned back, looking relaxed and rested in spite of his grueling trip from San Francisco—usually across the pole to London, another flight from London to Lisbon, followed by a puddle-jumper to Faro and a train to the town of Albufeira from there. A wave of affection washed over her when she considered all he'd been through and his eagerness to see her. She reached for his hand. "Thank you for coming, Adam."

"I sensed from our last conversation that you might need to talk. In person, not on the phone."

She nodded and took a sip of coffee, American style, not Portuguese. "Amen to that, my friend. You have a way of sensing my moods."

He watched her over the brim of his cup. "I know you well. What troubles you isn't just a mood."

"It's Taite…my mother…family." She sighed and leaned back against the cool plaster of the window seat alcove. "Maybe this season of life causes one to remember, to regret, to agonize over losses that might have been avoided. It seems that no matter how successful I am in other areas, it doesn't make up for my longing for Taite. I just want to see her… No, more than that, I want to hug her, to tell her how much I love her." She paused. "Tell her I have so many regrets…ask her forgiveness."

"I know you've tried to write."

"Many times, but I don't know if she's ever read one of my letters. I've sent Christmas and birthday gifts that were never acknowledged. I finally gave up. The last two letters I sent were returned with an Addressee Unknown stamp on the envelope. I've kept up with Taite through Mother, but it's not the same. There is such a root of bitterness in her—toward me. Deeper than that, I think she's afraid to love, to be loved. And I feel helpless to do anything about it."

Adam looked thoughtful. She could always count on him for good counsel. He would cut through the extraneous and get to core issues. It was his gift. It was the same thing that made him a good newspaperman.

"You know how I feel about how you raised Taite," he said. "You've told me how you struggled to make ends meet—and fill the roles of both mother and father."

"Even when I could have relaxed my schedule, spent time at home with her, I chose my career. I should have tried to work it out so I could have been home more. I shouldn't have left her to come here, or I should have insisted that she come with me, no matter what she or my mother said."

He looked thoughtful. "And then there was Anna."

"Yes, Anna." She looked away. "I was so broken by her illness, her death, I feared loving that much again. I didn't mean to, but I was never the same with Taite."

"You loved Anna more than you did Taite?"

"She was the firstborn, excelled in everything, talked early, became my little shadow. I doted on her. I realize that now. But my favorite?" She had asked herself the same question a hundred times, attempting to analyze what went wrong between Taite and her. "I hope not. I didn't intend it."

"Did you ever tell her about Brady?"

"No. It was painful enough for me; I didn't want to burden a child with it." The pain was still as acute as it had been twenty years ago. "As it was, she felt abandoned when he died. If I told her why..." She shook her head. "I'm afraid it would have convinced her she was right."

His voice held a reasoned resonance, his tone comforting. "Now that Taite is grown, she needs to know. Maybe it would help her understand why you made the choices you did." He gazed down at her, his compassion clear. "She needs to know why he left you both that day. And I think you need to talk to her about Anna. Was she ever allowed to grieve?"

"She was too young to know what happened."

"I think she knew, and remembers. She lost two significant people in her life, and she lost you as well, emotionally if not physically. Maybe her bitterness is just a cover-up for grief she can't express." He paused. "Maybe getting it out in the open, no matter the pain, will finally allow her to heal. Allow you both to heal."

She swallowed hard. "Oh, the regrets," she breathed, shaking her head slowly. But he reached for her hand, and they walked to the front window. As they stood there, looking out, he wrapped his arms around her and pulled her close. She sighed deeply as he rested his cheek atop her head.

"You want to go to her, don't you?"

She pulled back and looked up at him. "I had a dream last night…" How could she explain? "She needs me," she finally said. "In spite of time and distance, I sense it in my heart. My daughter needs me."

"You realize, of course, there's no postponing London." He paused to regard her.

"That part doesn't matter. What does matter is that Taite doesn't want me in her life. She's made that obvious. As for my mother…" She let her gaze drift to the window again, to a place above blue green waters where a formation of ducks was taking wing. "I think she's quite content to keep me on the opposite side of the world." *So she can have Taite to herself,* she added silently.

"Healing is paramount," Adam said softly, "in everyone's heart— not just yours. And you can't do it long distance."

She attempted a light laugh. "As usual, you've bored right into the heart of things. My burden is heavy. And if mine is, my mother and my daughter must feel this too." She contemplated living out her days without making peace with the two women she loved more than any others in this world. "Someday," she whispered.

Suddenly the room felt too small, life too short, the pressures too great. The floor seemed to tilt, and she touched the windowsill to steady herself. As if sensing her distress, Adam wrapped his arm around her shoulders and gently led her to the door. They strolled down the path leading to the cliffs, climbed down to the beach, and walked along the water's edge. Adam took her hand as they continued to a point of rocks about a half mile away.

"Come back to San Francisco," he said after a time, "even if it's for just a few weeks. Contact Victoria. See if she can arrange a meeting between you and Taite." He reached in his pocket for his satellite phone. "Do you want to call her? Find out how Taite is doing? It might relieve your mind."

She shook her head. "I can't."

His eyes said he understood her fear of rejection, and he put the phone away.

Adam loved her. Many times through the years he had asked her to marry him. She couldn't imagine life without Adam, but neither could she imagine their relationship encompassing anything but friendship.

For as long as she'd known him, Adam had been in the newspaper business, first as a reporter, and now as chief international correspondent with the *San Francisco Register*. Just as he concerned himself with her well-being, she in turn worried about his health. He traveled to London, Paris, Madrid, or Lisbon as often as every other month, giving him too many air miles to cover, odd foods, and long hours. In his fifties, though he was silver-haired and distinguished, his shoulders were beginning to droop, his gait slow.

A wave of tenderness overcame her, and she reached up to rub the ache from his shoulders. He stopped and grinned down at her. "Does it show that much?"

"Your jet lag always does."

He let his head loll back and sighed deeply. "I'll give you all day to stop that."

She smiled as they sat down on a flat stone, and she rested her cheek against his shoulder. "How are the meetings going?"

"The situation in Nigeria is dangerous. Worse than the Middle East right now. These guys were lucky to get out. And now they're insisting on better, safe, working conditions."

"They should." As they talked, they both removed their shoes.

"But some are making unreasonable demands. I think they expect to stay in five-star hotels with satin sheets instead of in the roach-infested dives they usually get." He laughed. "When I was with AP overseas full-time, I wasn't surprised to find questionable sheets, cockroaches the size of my fist, and tarantulas hiding out under the bed. Figured it was part of the adventure. Kids today are too soft."

"When are you flying back?"

"I have a dinner meeting this evening. More meetings all day tomorrow. If all goes well, I fly to London Wednesday morning and hope to catch a connecting flight in the afternoon."

Adam took her hand again and drew her to her feet. They walked barefoot slowly along the water's edge. The waves crept across the wet sand, and overhead the gulls swooped and cried. She could breathe again, and she lifted her eyes heavenward.

"Thanksgiving is just a few weeks after your show," Adam said. "Shall we meet in London?"

She stopped walking as an idea began to form. "There is an inn on the English-Welsh border, not far from Shrewsbury. How about doing something wild and crazy and going there for Thanksgiving?"

He grinned. "I doubt that they serve turkey, dressing, and all the fixings."

"I have an idea that they'll do something completely Welsh and Old World in our honor."

A wave rolled against a spit of jagged rocks, and the spray shot into the azure sky. He grabbed her hand and pulled her close to the water again as foamy wavelets tickled her feet.

"Can you promise that?"

Her heart swelled. "It's the place of my ancestral home. My mother used to tell some tall tales. I have no idea if they're true, but they're entertaining, to say the least. She didn't think I was listening, but I loved them. I've been to the little village twice…and strangely, it does feel like home. The family that runs the small inn knows me, and they'll be delighted we've returned."

"I like the idea," Adam said. Then he stopped and turned to her again. "But are you certain you don't want to come to California?"

"I'm sure, Adam. I can't. I don't know if I'll ever be able to take that step."

"I understand."

They lunched in Albufeira at a small café across from the train station while Adam regaled her with the latest happenings in the San Francisco art scene and in the ever-wacky California political arena. She told him about the painting of Saint Francis she'd just conceived and her growing desire to research illuminations from medieval manuscripts.

"Have you ever seen the *Book of Kells*?" Adam asked as they walked across the dusty street to the train station. "It's on display at Trinity College in Dublin."

"About a year ago. I'll never forget my reaction. My, those beautiful illuminations in the margins. As colorful as if they'd been set down yesterday, not in the ninth century. I felt, well"—she shook her head, grasping for words—"as if it, or something, was beckoning me." She paused, thinking about the spiritual significance of the thousand-year-old Gospel manuscripts. "Though what, I don't know. Or why. But I have to say, the experience took hold of my heart and hasn't let go to this day."

"Maybe God is drawing you to something he'll reveal later."

"That's been my conclusion. But I still feel impatient to know." She shrugged the thought away. "Meanwhile I'm studying old illuminations and manuscripts and painting my medieval knockoffs." She laughed. "Sometimes I think it's in my blood."

Adam left on the three o'clock train for Faro to catch his return flight to Lisbon.

Isabel returned to the cottage and, while the late afternoon sun bathed her studio in light, began to work on Saint Francis.

But it wasn't the saint whose image filled her mind. Her thoughts returned to Taite, and after a few minutes, she put down her brush and moved to the window. A breeze floated in, and beyond the dancing branches of the pepper tree, the ocean sparkled in the distance.

"Father," she breathed, "wherever my daughter is, whatever she is doing, be with her this minute. Surround her with your love. Draw her into your loving arms. I can't be with her, but I know that you are there. Hold her, Father, and please don't ever let her go."

14

T aite tried to open her eyes, but the pain was too severe. She was covered with a light blanket, and though she hadn't seen it, she was certain it was white. It had to be. Somewhere in the fuzzy shadowlands of a fading nightmare she remembered being on a gurney, covered in white. And in her dream—or had it been real?—crimson blood had stained the white swaddling wrapped around her.

She lay perfectly still, assessing where she was. A hospital, judging by the sounds, the soft-soled footsteps of nurses, the beeping of monitors, the smells of disinfectant. She wondered if she had been in a traffic accident. The thought brought fleeting images of her father: a big, dark-haired man tossing her in the air, then hugging her to his chest, pushing her high in a swing, up high…as high as the clouds, tying an apron around her waist so she could help him stir the batter for blueberry pancakes, the laughter, the songs, the smiles. It seemed he loved her more than anybody else did, even Naini. Later, much later, she heard the confusing and hateful words that her daddy would never come home again. It wasn't until a little boy in her kindergarten class said her daddy died in a car crash that his death became real.

She could smell disinfectant again. She swallowed against the sudden urge to gag. Her head still throbbed with pain, and after another brief struggle, she gave up trying to open her eyes.

She was immediately soothed by the sound of her grandmother's voice, gentle, soft, comforting. It meant she wasn't alone, and somehow the fear roused by the smells and sounds lessened. Naini's words, her phrases, floated in her addled mind like a mist, obscuring the familiar, the known. Whatever the familiar or the known was, she wasn't ready to face it.

Neither was she ready to talk, so she lay perfectly still as her grandmother began to speak of the ancient ones; she let the words envelop her like a blanket, fill her with music that only her soul could hear, pull her into their velvet depths. Naini had probably been telling the story for hours, hoping to reach Taite's heart. Though she didn't remember where the story began, she listened now. "…the rising sun," Naini was saying in a hushed voice, "cast a shimmering glow on the crumbling abbey walls as Gwynedd and Taran emerged from the cave. You remember, dearest, the night Gwynedd saved brave Taran from certain destruction by pulling him into the brush before Gunnolf's patrol had seen him. Well, soon after, they slipped into the boggy forest near the mere. There they remained hidden from the marauders, drinking water from a nearby brook, sleeping near each other for warmth…"

Twice Taran slipped into camp in the predawn dark for food. He found roasted carcasses of sheep, thrown into a pit beyond the main camp, enough flesh on the bones to feed them for a day. The smell of the meat turned Gwynedd's stomach, and her first meal didn't stay down long. Next time she ate more slowly, trying to think of anything but the lambs she had helped birth and later carried so tenderly.

On the morning of the fourth day, they huddled together as a light snow fell. "We cannot stay here much longer," Taran said, looking toward Gunnolf's encampment.

Gwynedd agreed. Few words had passed between them since he had fixed his mind on vengeance. It was almost as if he blamed her for saving his life that first night, as if he felt he deserved to die for deserting his family in their need, and her interference had prevented him from making an honorable sacrifice. His face seemed frozen in a solemn, bitter expression that caused her heart to twist almost in two.

"My husband," she said, meeting his eyes, "I cannot stop thinking that some in our village may have escaped." Taran turned from her, just as he had each time she mentioned it before, and gazed through the tangle of winter branches toward the place where their thatched village once stood. He shook his head slightly, his demeanor reflecting a sorrow too deep for words. This time she would not allow the turning of his heart away from her. She stood, crossed the small clearing, and then knelt in front of him.

She folded her hands in her lap, resting them on her soiled woolen tunic. "Taran, my own, your grieving is a good and honorable thing, and my heart weeps with yours for our families, our friends, for Brother Cadwallen and the others and their work. Cadwallen once said to us that weeping may endure for the a night, but joy cometh in the morning.

"Gunnolf has brought darkness to our land, but how will others know that joy will dawn in the morning if the sacred texts are lost forever? Do you realize that we, beloved, are the only ones who know where the texts are hidden? That our Lord has placed a mission here under our noses? Yet we weep like lost lambs, afraid to do the bidding of our shepherd."

He looked down, as if puzzled to see her kneeling before him. It seemed that he was living in a different world, a different time, so far away was he. Perhaps his mind simply could not contain the horror of what had come to pass. She understood because hers was much the same, especially deep in the night when she imagined the brutes crashing through the woods and discovering their hiding place.

"You want to make a plan," he said with a hint of a smile, his first in days. "I can hear it in your voice, just like always."

"Aye, m'lord," she said softly. " 'Tis time."

He reached for her hand and, lifting it to his face, closed his eyes and held it there as if it were the dearest possession of his heart. After a moment he met her gaze, his pain evident, but also his love. The fixed set of his jaw, the light in his eyes, brought her peace; she could survive anything so long as she was certain of Taran's love.

"We must go to Caer Abbey," he said, "to tell the bishop what has happened here and let him know where the Gospels are hidden."

She nodded. "And we must leave soon, before this encampment breaks."

"Some may already be gone. I heard horses in the night…galloping out as if to journey…hoofs pounding the earth as they moved north. They have not returned."

"Mayhap they plan to continue their encampment here, those who remained behind?"

"We have no way of knowing."

She stood and walked across the clearing, clutching her hands so tightly her knuckles turned white. "Could it be they hold captive some of our people, our families?" She could not bear to think of those she loved suffering at the hands of the army.

"Legend tells of the Norsemen who made slaves of our people many years ago," he said. "Some of our grandmothers and grandfathers were carried off to the lands of the north, never to be seen again. But many of the invaders settled here, claiming properties as their own, blending in with the rest of us." He frowned in thought. "From what we know of Gunnolf and his legions, they are from the same lands—renegades, methinks, reliving old glories of their own legends." He paused. "And vengeance, according to Brother Cadwallen, passed through the generations from one called Eryk the Great. One who had no luck conquering the mighty Welsh."

"Both good and bad can be passed from parent to child. Think what heartache this has wrought, the loss of the sacred, both people and God's holy writings."

"Things of God are never lost." Taran fell quiet. He was a deep thinker, her husband. A storyteller and songster, he spun tales and sang ballads of long ago, told by his father to him and by his father's father before that, from the time of the ancient ones who sat around their fires, how they crossed from a place called Gaul where the apostle Paul himself was said to have visited. Stories were among the good things passed from parent to child. How much better than grudges that might only fester and lead to bloodshed.

The story they were living might someday be told by this dear one, put into song or poem, so that it would be told again and again. That was simply the way of their kin, Taran of Han-mere had often told her. The ancient songs and poetry flowed in his veins, just as in the people of ancient days. She gave him a gentle smile, her heart swelling with love. She might be the planner in their family, but Taran was the poet. Oh, to hear him sing again! She hoped it would not be long.

"We should go out tonight and see if our people are here. If horsemen have left for the north and their stockades are not guarded well"—she smiled—"it follows that we would have a better chance of success."

He drew himself up in a way that showed a stubborn desire to protect her. " 'Twould be dangerous, m'love. If anyone goes, it will be me. Alone."

She started to protest, but Taran held up a hand. "I am your husband, do you remember?"

Her cheeks warmed. "Aye, m'love," she said, looking down at her hands. "How could I forget?"

"I will go just after midnight." He leaned back, watching her. It seemed that a glimmer of hope shone in his eyes, mixed still with his sorrow and now fear. "But promise me this, m'love…"

"Anything."

"If I do not return, promise you will steal away to Caer, to the refuge of the abbey." He stood and gathered her into his arms. "That is the only reason I fear to leave—'tis for your sake. I would rather stay and be with you. I shudder to think of you making the journey alone."

"Would it be wiser to go to the bishops at Sarisberie?" she asked. "Or perhaps Amwythig?"

Wise Taran shook his head. "An easier journey, yes, but I heard before the raid that Bishop Roger of Oxford has broken King Stephen's peace. His nephews Bishop Ely and Bishop Lincoln were brought before him, weak as he is rumored to be, with a demand to surrender the keys to their castles. One is in prison, and the other escaped—though the teller of the tale knew not which—and war is about to break out in Sarisberie."

She sighed. Would there ever be peace anywhere? "Tell me how to go to Caer then, if I must."

He pointed through the thicket of barren branches to high ground away from the valley. "Walk for an hour until the river's bend is at your feet, then follow the river until you reach a low range of mountains. 'Tis a journey of many days." His face sagged with worry. " 'Twill be cold this time of year. Snow might fall."

She pulled back and touched his face. "First, m'love, we will not think that this will be a certain fate. I pray you return tonight with good news about our friends." Her heart lifted at the thought. "Mayhap our loved ones are living still, and we will set them free."

He did not comment, and in the silence that followed, she realized her hope was futile. "Continue telling me the way to Caer," she said quietly. "Every detail."

And he did. He gave her landmarks, should she need them. "If you lose your way and if the night is clear," he said, " 'tis the North Star you should follow without fail." He smiled then and hugged her close, whispering into her hair, "And whither you go, no matter where, when you see its bright glow, remember the one who loves you. Should I not be there to tell you myself, love, remember I will be looking upon the same star, praying for Godspeed on your journey."

That night after they had eaten the cold lamb meat scavenged the day before, Taran made ready for his furtive journey into the encampment. The campfires glowed against the ruins of the abbey, and raucous laughter and shouts pierced the night air. If Gunnolf's brutes followed their pattern of sleeping after bellies were full of mead and beer, it would not be long before Taran could easily slip among them and make no disturbance.

Taran and Gwynedd sat perfectly still, Taran with his arm tightly around her shoulders. She shivered with cold, and he held her even closer. "Tell me, husband," she said when the sounds of the encampment had died, "would you think of attempting to kill Gunnolf with his own sword if you happened upon him?"

"I cannot promise," he said quietly. In the dark she could not see his face, but she heard the bitterness creep back into his voice.

She took his callous hand in hers, clasped it between both of hers, and held it close to her heart. "Brash acts are akin to being human, Taran of Han-mere. With the devastation of all we love and know of our village, how could you not want to exact revenge?" She turned to him. "But m'love, I prithee, mind your temper this time. I will not be there to hold you back." She paused, unwilling to say more, but praying for his safety.

Taran left their hiding place after the only sounds drifting from the encampment were the invaders' snores and the nickering of horses somewhere behind the abbey ruins. He kissed her lips, then stepped into the moonless night.

She could not sleep. She lay down on a bed of leaves and stared at the sky. A smattering of stars shone brightly, and under their crystal light, she prayed for Taran's safekeeping. She rose finally after a few hours and walked in a circle around the sleep bower. She shivered with both cold and worry and wondered about Taran. Finally toward morning she curled among the leaves in her bower and fell into a deep and troubled sleep, only to be awakened shortly by the sounds of horses and men's voices.

She pulled aside a slender branch and peered through the evergreen tangle. A morning mist had risen from the mere, obscuring her view and muffling the sounds of the encampment. She strained to peer through the gray fog. It took her a moment to comprehend what lay before her.

With a gasp she stepped back. Not a furlong away, a shadowy knot of horses and men were readying to take their leave. At their rear, barely visible to her, another group was rounding up a cluster of old men, women, and children, driving them from behind the ruins of the abbey's outbuildings. Even in the heavy gray mist, she knew: these were her people.

Now it made sense that Taran had not come back to her because he'd had to hide away during the night to avoid being caught as the marauders broke camp.

A big man with hair like fire sat astride a dark horse at the head of what was quickly becoming a procession. The arrogant carriage of his head, the set of his powerful shoulders, told her it was Gunnolf. The Norse could not have brought their own steeds across the waters, so all these must have been taken from farms and villages as they pillaged along the way. Yet here they were, an army on stolen mounts, well-guarded prisoners taking up the rear, riding two to a horse, or three if small children.

Gwynedd felt the sorrow and fury Taran had carried ever since they'd emerged from the caves. She fought the impulse to run out at Gunnolf and knock him to the ground. But what good would that do? She would only be forced to join the prisoners at the rear. Or worse.

Gunnolf raised his arm, and the company moved forward, slowly at first, then with gathering speed. The left flank came dangerously near her hiding place, and she stepped back, but not before taking a closer look at the prisoners as they rode by.

Joseph, the village baker, stared straight ahead, and Thomas, the blacksmith, sagged atop his mount, looking tired and broken and older than his years. There was Bess, her mother's dearest friend, with her daughter Philberta, who helped at the abbey laundry, and Mary, the eldest of five orphaned sisters, who raised sheep for vellum to support her family. Sometimes she and Gwynedd had whiled away their days, giggling and running through the grasses, their limbs feeling as young and graceful as a lamb's. Tears quickened in her eyes as she watched Mary ride by. The dark-haired young woman held her head high as if undaunted by what lay ahead.

Gwynedd watched two dozen more Han-mere villagers cross before her, and then she saw Taran. Covering her mouth to keep from crying out, she stepped back to remain hidden. His hands were tied in front of him, and as he rode so near, he did not so much as incline his head toward her. Such a nod would give her away, she knew, and she forgave him.

She watched the procession round the mere and ride to the north until they faded into the heavy mist. Then she sat down, cupped her face in her hands, and wept for Taran, for her family, for Mary and the others, until no tears were left.

All that morning she remained hidden, listening carefully for the sounds of those who might have been left behind. When the sun was high and the mists had burned away, she finally ventured forth. Tentatively at first, she slipped from her hiding place, then when the only sounds were the calls of geese and the blowing winds across the plain, she took bolder steps into the open.

The devastation was even worse than she imagined. The magnificent stone walls had been reduced to rubble, the abbey's furnishings burned to ashes, Cadwallen's lovely garden trampled flat.

Walking slowly to where the cloister once rose in graceful splendor, she stared up into the heavens. "Where are your blessings, heavenly Father?" She wanted to shake her fist but dared not. "Where are they?" she cried out again and fell to her knees, tears welling up where none had been. "Brother Cadwallen prayed for Taran and me, blessing our family through the generations. And now Taran has gone from me... There will surely be no generations to follow."

She stood and turned a full circle, her arms outstretched in supplication. "Look at this rubble. How could you allow this? It was a place built for your glory, a place where your work could advance, where your people labored"—the tears were streaming down her cheeks— "where those you love labored for you."

She ran to the place where the altar once stood, where Brother

Cadwallen and the other monks had worshiped seven times each day. Stinking smoke still rose from the wreckage. Off to one side, the bell had fallen and lay in two pieces. She touched its smooth metal, remembering the mellow sounds that had floated through the fields where she grazed her sheep, and again she cried.

She knelt and bowed her head before the missing altar. "I am so alone," she wept. "Have mercy on me, my Lord. I am afraid, and I need your strength. Help me, for I know not which way to go. Guide me, Father, for I will stumble if I do not have you to lean on. Christ, have mercy…"

She paused, sensing she was not alone. There was no one with her in the ruins, but when she looked toward the hillside just beyond the outer wall of the abbey, she saw a shepherd. Silhouetted against the bright noonday sky, he stood holding a crook to one side. He did not speak, but there was no need. Just knowing that someone else had survived the marauders' attack gave her comfort.

Her eyes never left his face as she stood. She intended to go to him and ask how his family and village fared. But before she could move, he raised his crook as if in greeting and set off down the far side of the hill.

She left the rubble soon after and, after picking up a torch left in the encampment, lit it with dying embers from their night fire and headed up the hillside to the caves. With stubborn resolve as her guide, she found the entrance and, after three attempts, moved the stone doorway far enough aside to squeeze through. She held up her torch to dispel the darkness. Beyond its glow, the air seemed as thick as black pudding.

Shivering, she took hesitant steps, praying her memory would serve her well as she picked her way through the maze of tunnels. With relief, she heard the underground stream and knew she was drawing close to the cavern. The musty scent of vellum, ink, and lambskin greeted her as she stepped into the cavernous room. Soon she was alone in this deep-earth place where the only sounds were the dripping of water, the sputtering of her torch, and the hammering of her heart.

She set the torch in the holder by the doorway, then quickly crossed to the stone where she and Taran had hidden the ring. A moment later she clutched it in her hand, whispering a prayer of thanksgiving. It was a small first step in the journey that lay ahead. She tore a strip from her tunic hem and threaded it through the ring. Then she tied it around her neck, tucking it beneath the bodice of her garment. Before taking up the torch again, she turned to look at the place where she and Taran had knelt before Brother Cadwallen and spoken their holy vows. And now her beloved Taran was a prisoner of the Norse brutes, and their friend Cadwallen, so generous of heart and spirit, was doubtless dead.

Though Cadwallen could not have known, he had given her a purpose for today, a reason to go on, no matter her sorrow and pain. She would see to it that the mission he had bequeathed her was accomplished. She would go immediately to Caer to tell the bishop about the sacred hiding place.

At last she went back into the tunnel. When the stone door was replaced and her torch extinguished, she scavenged through the ruined abbey for food, finding dried crusts of bread, morsels of meat, and a pouch filled with nutmeats. She bundled her provisions into a square of cloth, knotted at the top for carrying.

She walked to a knoll overlooking the mere and stood for a moment, facing north. Caer Abbey might not even be standing a fortnight hence. If she reflected on all that lay ahead, or even what she'd already endured, she would be overcome with despair.

So she resolved not to worry over food and water or the dangers on her path. She simply looked north, thinking about Taran. "Knit together in constant affection your son Taran of Han-mere and your daughter Gwynedd of Han-mere from this day forward," Cadwallen had said in his prayer of blessing. Whether they were together or apart, their love would not diminish. She would watch for the North Star to guide her and to speak of Taran's love.

Looking toward a bank of gathering storm clouds and the trampled barren grasses of the valley, she shivered with apprehension. Then she gathered her courage and took her first step. Strangely, the image of the shepherd she'd seen beyond the abbey ruins returned to her, and she didn't feel so alone.

"Naini…," Taite whispered.

"Are you awake, honey?" She heard her grandmother cross the room to stand beside the bed.

After a struggle, Taite managed to open her eyes. She breathed easier, realizing the pain had dulled to a throb. The light streaming through the room's single window said it was morning. "Where am I?"

"You're at Eisenhower Community Hospital."

"What happened?"

Her grandmother moved closer and took her hand. "You've had quite a time of it."

"Water…," she whispered. Her grandmother lifted a plastic tumbler and brought it to where Taite could take the straw between her dry lips. Taite swallowed with difficulty, then took the glass in her free hand and sipped again. "Was I in an accident?"

"You don't remember?"

Taite shook her head, gave the tumbler back to her grandmother, and leaned back against the pillow. She felt as if she had been run over by a herd of runaway goats, but at least the pounding pain in her head was gone.

"You left the house to go to a clinic, honey." She seemed to be waiting for Taite to respond.

"Clinic?" As the word formed on her lips, she remembered. "Oh... yes. The clinic." She drew a shaky breath. "They told me it was a simple procedure. You said this is a hospital... What am I doing here? Did something go wrong?"

"We almost lost you, honey. You had a reaction to the anesthetic at the clinic. You stopped breathing for nearly four minutes. They brought you here by ambulance. Luckily, you'd given them my name and telephone number on the contact sheet when you checked in. I got here as fast as I could."

"I'm sorry, Naini. You shouldn't have had to deal with this." Watching her grandmother's face, she moved one hand to her stomach. Naini looked unbearably sad. "The baby... Did they take my baby?" Her voice was a hoarse whisper.

"Maybe you should rest, honey. We'll talk about what happened when you're feeling better." It wasn't like Victoria to put off bad news, or any news for that matter. Taite was like her that way.

But did she want to know? For weeks she had thought about little else besides getting rid of her problem. A sob caught in her throat. "My baby," she choked, remembering the nightmare of blood on her white blanket. "The abortion... Did they perform it after all?"

Naini shook her head. "No, honey, they didn't. There wasn't time."

Taite took a relieved breath. "I don't know what happened in my heart, or when..." She gulped hard, hot tears slipping down her cheeks. "But I want this baby."

For several moments her grandmother didn't speak. "There's something else you need to know, Taite." Again that look of unbearable sadness came over her face.

"What is it?" She stared at the ceiling, focusing on the little holes in the acoustic tile, focusing on anything but Naini's face.

"You stopped breathing. The baby was deprived of oxygen…"

She drew in a shuddering breath. "Oh…" was all she could squeeze out. But the pain inside was just beginning. She had caused it. The baby hadn't asked for life, hadn't asked for it to end, yet Taite had caused both. And now this. "Brain damage…," she whispered and turned away from her grandmother's compassionate gaze.

"There is a possibility." Naini rounded the bed to stand beside the IV drip. She took Taite's hand. "The doctor will be coming in to talk with you about your options."

"Options?" Though even as the word formed, Taite knew it would be up to her to choose life or death.

"Tests, then decisions about what to do should the results be…" Moisture gathered in Naini's eyes; she blinked rapidly and cleared her throat. "The doctors feel that your baby's father should be in on the decisions."

Taite sat up, plumped her pillow with her fist and settled back. She remembered the dream about the blood, her aching arms, and her sense of devastating loss. "That's impossible. I don't want Sam to know." She shook her head vigorously. "I simply won't tell them who the father is."

Victoria met her gaze. "I already did."

"You told them?" Taite settled deeper into her pillows, one hand still resting protectively over her abdomen. The hospital might have called him already. She imagined Sam's reaction. What would he say? Maybe he was on his way here already. She closed her eyes and pictured his face. But it told her nothing. Would he blame her? She was already heading down that road all by herself. She already carried enough guilt in her heart to last a lifetime, and the thought of more blame being heaped on her head was a heavier load than she could bear.

Taite turned toward her grandmother and saw her worried expression. "I was asked at Admissions," she was saying, "to help with the forms. The admitting nurse asked me specifically about the baby's father." She sat down with a heavy sigh. "I gave them Sam's name, but I asked them not to call him. They said they would wait." She reached for an already damp tissue. "If it weren't for the critical decision you need to make, I don't think contacting Sam would be an issue."

The conversation returned to the choices that Naini had mentioned earlier. If the worry was that the child might be handicapped, there was no decision to be made. She didn't care what Sam, the doctors, or anyone said. She would not abort the baby. Not now. "What if Sam and I can't come to an agreement?" She didn't care that her whisper was hoarse with fear. "What then?"

"You'll face that when the time comes."

They were interrupted by a white-jacketed doctor hurrying through the door. With a brisk nod, he moved to the foot of the bed, picked up her chart, and scanned the page. "I'm Dr. Browne," he murmured, still reading. After a moment he glanced at Taite, then came around to the side of the bed, lifted her hand, and looked at his watch while he took her pulse. "You've had a close call, young lady," he said when he was finished. He gestured for her to sit up, placed the diaphragm of the stethoscope on her back, and asked her to breathe through her mouth.

She nodded, trying to read his expression. "Tell me what happened."

"The fetus was starved of oxygen long enough for us to assume brain and nerve damage. The predicted outcome is premature delivery with the strong possibility of severe mental and neurological disorders in the infant."

"My baby will be handicapped."

"*Handicapped* is a mild way of putting it—in the worst case scenario," the doctor said. His tone was matter-of-fact, but kind. "I understand that you were about to abort the fetus when you had the reaction to the anesthetic. I will schedule you to complete the procedure tomorrow morning. You'll be sore for a few days, but your recovery has come along so nicely here that I predict you'll be up and around and back to your normal self in a week."

"I don't want to have the procedure," Taite said, meeting his surprised gaze. "I've decided to have the baby."

He shot Taite's grandmother a puzzled look, then focused again on Taite. "Maybe you didn't understand. There is a strong possibility of your baby being severely handicapped. I would strongly advise—for your child's sake, if for no other reason—that you terminate the pregnancy. The sooner the better."

"I'm going to have this child."

Dr. Browne worked his jaw as he hooked the chart at the end of the bed. "Have you contacted the baby's father?"

"No."

"You need to get his input and make the decision together."

The doctor left the room, and Taite settled back into bed. "Am I wrong?" she said, watching Naini intently.

Her grandmother lifted the pitcher, poured a glass of water, and handed it to Taite. "You must search your heart…and decide this on your own." Taite didn't think she'd ever seen her grandmother look so sad.

Guilt washed over her for the chaos she had brought to everyone from Naini to Sam to their unborn child. She didn't know how to express her anguish, so she turned her head away from Naini and closed her eyes. "I need to sleep now," she murmured.

After a few minutes her grandmother's footsteps faded down the hallway. Taite wept.

15

It was just past noon when Taite padded to the closet where she found the clothes she'd worn to the clinic. She had just finished dressing when an orderly came in, saw what she was doing, and rang for a nurse.

Taite waved them off. "I'm checking myself out."

They almost blocked the door as they tried to convince her to wait for the doctor's release. But she merely smiled and brushed past them. She took the elevator to the lobby, stopped at the gift shop, and asked an elderly volunteer to call a taxi. She climbed into the first one that appeared.

For the first time in years, perhaps for the first time in her adult life, Taite knew what she had to do next. She had a focus, right or wrong. Lifting her chin, she reached for that steely gumption she'd always suspected was inside and stared out at the bleak gray sky. Despite all she had been through, despite her concerns about the baby she carried and her worries about Sam and what he would say, despite her fears of failure, she wanted to do this one thing right.

She had to because of the baby. Her baby.

She walked into the house and kissed her grandmother's cheek.

Then before she changed her mind, she headed upstairs to her bedroom. Exhausted, she lay down and reached for the phone. Sam's cell phone number was etched in her heart. She punched it in with a trembling finger.

He answered on the third ring.

"Sam?"

A heartbeat of silence followed. "Taite?"

"I have something I have to tell you. Don't say anything. Just listen."

"I'm listening."

A faded and worn quilt lay folded at the foot of the bed. Feeling her courage ebb, she reached for the closest edge and pulled it over her. "This is hard, terribly hard. The hardest thing I've ever had to do in my life."

On the other end of the connection, a wave of apprehension swept through Sam. For Taite to call after all these weeks, her voice shaking, meant only one thing: she must be about to break it off with him completely. He leaned back in his desk chair, teetering on the scarred back legs. He tapped his pen on the desk and waited.

"That day at the beach," she began, almost breathless in her hurry, "I had something important I needed to tell you, but after you told me your news, I couldn't get the words out. And now… Oh, honey, it can't wait any longer." She started to weep.

"Taite," he said hoarsely, "if it's what I think it is, that's okay. I've tried hard to let you know how much you mean to me, but obviously—"

She interrupted him before he could continue. "Please, if we change the subject, I'll never get this out."

"Another subject?"

"Please, Sam."

"Go ahead."

He heard her quick intake of breath, and then she said, "It's about a…child. Our baby."

Baby? He was too stunned to speak. But he didn't need to, because Taite hurried on. "I had just found out I was pregnant that last day I saw you. I wanted to tell you, Sam. But I couldn't. I-I couldn't tell you that I didn't want to have children, ever—whether or not we were married. So I decided to take care of it myself. Get rid of it…"

"You've had an abortion?" He could hear her sobs, but her distress didn't soften his heart. There was too much going on inside him. Fear for one, anger for another. How could she keep something like this to herself? How could Taite do this to them? She had deceived him. "Did you?"

She didn't answer, and his anger grew. He slapped his pen on the table. "Did you, Taite?"

All he could hear was her weeping. He let out a heavy sigh and let the chair fall forward again with a bang. "Go on," he said between clenched teeth. "Tell me everything."

"I didn't think I could—we could—have children because of how I think of family…" Her voice dropped to a hoarse whisper. "Family and love equal rejection and pain…" He could hear her sobs through the phone line. "The pregnancy was a burden to get rid of, something I hated because of my deception, my guilt. I thought I could have the abortion and you would never know."

Something inside him constricted. "You've done it, but you can't live with your conscience? Is that what this is all about?"

She was crying harder now. "I went to the clinic, signed all the papers, and got as far as the room where they do the procedure."

He listened with growing dismay to the rest of her story. When she had finished, he found himself blinking back unexplained tears. Hadn't he argued that these same cells were not much more than amoebas, protozoa…that it was their potential that made them different? Why did he feel he'd just been kicked in the gut?

"Sam… Are you there?"

He let out a deep breath. "Yeah."

"There's something else."

"Oxygen depletion," he said without emotion. "I already know what you're going to say next. Now there's no choice. The abortion is necessary."

She fell silent again, but when she spoke, her voice sounded different. Resolute. "No, there is a choice," she said. "I don't want to abort the baby. While I was out, I had this dream about the abortion…" She paused, sniffling. "About the child, what its death would mean. Something has happened that I can't explain. Everything was different when I awoke. It goes against everything the doctor told me, every bit of wisdom that anyone in the field of medicine might say. It goes against my own fears, Sam. But in my heart, I know I'm taking the right path this time."

"Isn't this a decision for both of us to make?"

At first she didn't answer, and then she said, "I was hoping you'd agree with me."

They were just cells, and damaged at that. "You're letting your heart overrule your head, Taite." He picked up his pen again and tapped it on the scarred wood of the desktop. His tone was cold; he didn't care. "If the attending doctors agreed that the fetus was without oxygen long enough to cause damage, they're right. You can't argue with the facts. It's not fair to our…the child who might have been"—his voice dropped— "to bring him into the world as less than a whole person."

"Are any of us whole?" she said softly.

"We're not talking about broken emotions or physical challenges. This might be something else entirely."

"What if it isn't?"

His medical training was in direct conflict with Taite's wishes, and perhaps his own if he let go of his anger. "You might as well face the facts now, Taite. It's easier to take care of the problem now rather than later."

"It that what you want, Sam?"

He pictured Taite, her face wet with tears, and he imagined the anguish she must be feeling. His voice was gentler when he spoke again. "I don't know what I want. I've just now found out about this. It's a lot to be hit with."

"I should have told you sooner."

She obviously wanted him to forgive her, but he couldn't bring himself to say the words. His heart was numb. "Taite?"

"I'm here."

"I've got to think this through."

"I knew you would."

"I'll call you tonight after class. It will be late, but with the time difference…"

"It's all right, Sam. Call whenever you can."

"Okay, then. I need to go."

She waited a few seconds, and then she said, "I love you, Sam. I always have."

He couldn't bring himself to answer; instead, he mumbled a good-bye and flipped the phone closed.

Overcome with grief, he sat with his head in his hands, fingers thrust through his hair. The news was unexpected. He tried to blame Taite, but deep inside, he knew that his guilt was equal to hers. His greatest sorrow came from the knowledge that the deepest conse-quences of their careless lovemaking would not fall on Taite or himself but on their son. Or daughter.

He couldn't remember the exact words, but phrases from a Bible verse read to him in Sunday school long ago came back: *whoever harms a little one such as this, better a millstone be hung around his neck and he drown in the depths of the sea.*

He considered himself an agnostic. He had no use for a God who couldn't prove his own existence, who allowed suffering and war and terrorism seemingly without punishment. But his unbelief didn't relieve his guilt. He sat utterly still, trying to comprehend all that Taite had told him, trying to rid his mind of his responsibility. But he couldn't get beyond those old-fashioned words of condemnation from the long-ago Bible verse.

He grabbed his pen and began to make notes, trying to get past his emotions to the analytical side of his brain. Pushing the thought of getting rid of a human life from his consciousness, he concentrated on what was best for all involved. He made a list.

1. *Cruel to bring a child into the world less than whole.*
2. *We aren't ready to marry.*
   a. *Not a convenient time.*
   b. *My opportunity for study in Stockholm cancelled.*
   c. *Might have to drop out of med school, yet it's vital for our future.*
3. *Taite doesn't want to be a mother, is scared of the responsibility.*
   a. *If the child is handicapped, how will Taite handle that kind of pressure? How will the child?*

He glanced at the list, and he drew a line through reasons 2 and 3. The only one that really mattered was the first. What was best for the child.

And that single thought was too much to dwell on. With a shudder he rose, slammed his textbooks into a stack, grabbed his notepad, and headed for his class. He grimaced when he thought of sitting through an ethics class today of all days.

Luke Stephens watched Sam head up the stairs to his place in the middle section of the hall. Sam was pale, his eyes red. The students were nearing midterm with its exam schedule and paper deadlines, but the slope of Sam's shoulders made Luke guess that he might be ill.

He opened the class as usual with a description of an ethics case from his own studies. The discussion at the end of the lecture was lively, but Sam didn't participate. Usually, he led the discussion, nine times out of ten defending the opposite—and usually very liberal—side of the argument. Puzzled, Luke didn't goad him as he usually did. Ten minutes before the class ended Sam raised his hand.

"You've got a question, Sam?"

The young man stood, and for a moment he didn't speak. Again, Luke noticed his somber demeanor. "I have a question I've been mulling over. I thought it might be interesting to throw it out for general discussion."

"A bit irregular," Luke said, noting the time. "But we've wound down the earlier topic, so go ahead."

"We've talked about abortion, and you know my feelings about the need to harvest embryonic tissue for the sake of science." There were murmurs of agreement around him, plus a few groans from the back of the room. Sam held up one hand. "Please, hear me out," he said.

"Go on," Luke said, glancing at the clock. "We don't have much time."

"A woman discovers she's pregnant, goes to a clinic to have an abortion, and has a dangerous reaction to the anesthetic. She stops breathing for a significant time, is resuscitated and hospitalized. Because of the trauma to her body, the doctors decide not to go forward with the abortion, though they highly recommended it once she is conscious."

Sam looked uncomfortable when he met Luke's gaze; at once Luke knew that this was intensely personal.

"In the haze of her trauma, perhaps hallucinating, the woman dreams of the child she carries and suffers from guilt and despair when she awakens." Sam paused. "Now she wants to keep the child."

Sam's friend Blake, sitting beside him, spoke up. "The fetus was deprived of oxygen for how long?"

"Four minutes," Sam said.

"She should abort," Blake said to the class. "The doctors surely advised her of the danger to the fetal brain and nervous system to be oxygen-deprived for that length of time."

"They did indeed." Again, Sam met Luke's eyes. "But it has become a moral and ethical issue with the woman. She feels responsible. Instead of accepting the fetus as only a mass of cells, she's looking at it as if it is a child."

"It is a child," Luke said. All eyes were on him. He could almost hear their thoughts: *The old man isn't up-to-date in his thinking. He doesn't realize the importance of modern science, the great advancements made because of progressive thinking. He's hopelessly old-fashioned. Laughable.* Oh, they were polite to him on the surface, but he knew the jabs tossed his direction when they thought he couldn't hear. "It is a baby," he repeated. He glanced at his watch. Students had another class within a few minutes, so he needed to wrap this up. "May I recap the woman's dilemma?"

"Please," Sam said, sitting down.

"It comes down to this: Which is the greater moral travesty? Is it killing a child who has a slim chance of being born healthy? Or is the great mercy one of taking the life of a child who may be born a vegetable?"

The room was silent. "That is the heart of the dilemma, isn't it?" he prodded.

"I would opt for the mercy killing," muttered Blake quietly, though he didn't sound all that sure of himself.

"How about the rest of you?"

Sam was leaning back in his chair, his expression unreadable.

When answers weren't forthcoming, Luke glanced at his watch again. "I'm sorry, people, that's all we have time for today. But the subject calls for contemplation. I'll see you Monday, and we'll spend a few minutes talking about Sam's questions. I'd like to hear your thoughts."

When Sam reached the bottom of the lecture hall stairs, he glanced toward Luke and then continued on through the open door with a group of the other students. Luke gathered his lecture notes and reference texts and headed for the door behind them. He wasn't surprised to see Sam waiting in the hall.

"You've figured it out, haven't you? That it's my child?" Sam was blunt. And accurate.

Luke nodded. "I have to admit, it crossed my mind that you might be involved with the woman in question."

"I just found out this afternoon." His look was grim as they headed down the hall toward the stairs to street level. "I'm still in shock."

"That's a lot to take in." Luke breathed a quick prayer for wisdom, especially if Sam asked for his advice. "Did you know about the pregnancy—or her plans for the abortion?"

Sam shook his head. "No."

"Tell me about it…perhaps starting with the young woman."

"Her name is Taite," Sam said, smiling for the first time. "And she's a wonder. Beautiful. Talented. I've loved her forever, it seems, and we plan to marry when I'm closer to finishing med school. She found out about the pregnancy around the time I told her that I was accepted into this program, so she didn't tell me for a lot of reasons." He shrugged. "She figured that she would just get rid of the 'problem,' and I would be none the wiser."

Luke knew the rest of the story from what Sam had said in class, so he didn't probe. They exited the building and walked toward Luke's car, but before they reached it, he glanced at Sam. "Would you like to stop by for supper?"

Sam looked surprised.

"You don't have another class, do you?"

"I'm finished for the night. But are you sure it's okay? I mean, your wife isn't expecting me."

Luke laughed. "There was a time when we always set an extra place at our table. When my son was in med school, he often brought home starving students for a bit of relief from cafeteria fare." He opened the car door. "Here we are. Climb in, son. I'll drop you back by your room later."

Sam looked grateful and slid into the leather seat on the passenger side. "Your son's a doctor?"

Luke backed out of his parking spot and turned into the street. "Luke was killed the week before he was to graduate from med school. This school, as a matter of fact." He paused. "Motorcycle accident. He was hit by a drunken driver."

Luke heard Sam catch his breath. "I'm so sorry," he finally said. "That must have been terrible."

"It's been thirty-two years, but not a day goes by when I don't remember him. Same with Martha. Losing a child is something you never get over."

"I'm sorry," Sam said again.

Luke smiled. "I didn't mean to drop something this heavy on you when you're going through struggles of your own." He shot Sam a glance. "Please forgive me."

Sam said, "Nothing to forgive." He fell silent as outside the car the fall-barren trees and gray evening passed by. A light and chilly drizzle slicked the streets. They had just pulled into Luke's driveway when Sam said, "Your thoughts on the sanctity of life, on the ethics of abortion, are they colored by your loss?"

"I'm sure they are. I learned a great lesson about the fragility of life, the gift of it, when Luke Jr. died. As a physician, I had already sworn to be an instrument of healing and comfort, but when the death of a loved one entered the equation, that sense of dedication—at least for me—suddenly became a hundredfold deeper. A thousandfold." He smiled. "Let's just say immeasurably deeper." He parked, and they got out of the car.

"Interesting word, *instrument*," Sam said. "That indicates there is a high power wielding the instrument, as if you think someone else— God, I suppose, in your opinion—is guiding your actions." His tone had a cynical edge. "Isn't it enough to take responsibility for your work yourself? To be called to this deeper sense of dedication just because that's who you are?"

Martha had left the porch light on, and the scent of wood smoke filled the night air as they walked to the front door. At the top of the steps, Luke paused and turned to his young companion. "God is the One who called me to this work. I take very seriously the prayer of Saint Francis of Assisi. Do you know it?"

"I've heard of it."

Luke smiled. "Martha insisted it be sung at our wedding. It's of course a map for living in peace. But as a physician, I read into the words the concept of allowing God to use me as his instrument of healing—whether of body, soul, or spirit." He patted Sam on the shoulder and opened the door to let him pass through. "I've got it around here someplace. I'll give you a copy before you go home."

Luke stepped inside and drew in a deep breath. "Smells like Martha has a pot roast in the oven. You hungry?"

Sam's face lit up. "Talk about healing for the soul," he said, grinning. "I think this is just what the doctor ordered." They both laughed and headed into the kitchen.

Sam hadn't spent such an enjoyable evening since arriving in Boston. Martha Stephens captured his heart with her laughter and lively conversation. Luke obviously adored her. She ruled the household like a queen, speeding around the big kitchen in her wheelchair. When Luke went to his office to return a phone call, Sam offered to set the table, and she accepted. By the time he was finished, she had made him feel like family.

The talk at dinner covered everything from national politics to new administration policies at the hospital. After a dessert of hot apple dumplings swimming in vanilla ice cream, Luke seemed to sense that Sam might want to continue their discussion about Taite. Sam and Luke cleared the table and offered to help with the dishes, but Martha wouldn't hear of it.

"You two look like you've got something you need to take up alone," she said in her soft Southern drawl. "You go on now, take your coffee with you, and let me do the rest." She shooed them through the doorway.

The men retired to Luke's study, a richly paneled room with floor-to-ceiling bookcases on two walls. Two worn, overstuffed leather chairs with a small round table between them sat beside a brick fireplace that glowed with embers from a dying fire. The men set their mugs on the table, and Sam settled into a chair while Luke added two logs to the bed of coals.

"I know you must be at war within yourself," Luke said when he'd finished and sat down. "I don't know if I can help with your decision, but I'm willing to listen."

Sam studied the licking flames for a moment. "War is a good analogy," he said. "The choices are overwhelming."

Luke leaned back, steepling his fingers, his expression thoughtful. "And my questions at the end of the lecture? What did you think?"

Sam nodded and paraphrased, "Is the greater moral travesty killing a child who has a slim chance of being born healthy or mercifully taking his life because he might be born a vegetable?"

"And I might add," Luke said, "another question into the mix: if a child is born less than perfect, does that make the child less human, less valuable?"

Sam's heart caught, and he looked away from Luke's intent gaze. "Sanctity of life. It seems your argument always comes back to that— whether we're talking about harvesting embryos for research for the greater good of mankind or we're talking about what life is worth, what risks are worth taking to protect that defenseless life."

Luke stood and turned one of the logs with the poker, then replaced the fire screen and sat down again. "It's not what I believe that will help with your decision. It's what you believe that matters."

Sam thought about the damaged fetus in Taite's womb. He shook his head slowly. "Taite wants this child no matter what. Right now, I just can't agree. The risks are too great," he said. "And I'm angry and disappointed over what she did. I love her; I just don't know if I can marry her." There, he'd said it.

"You're angry over the pregnancy itself or the botched abortion? Or the fact that she didn't tell you?"

Sam grimaced, looking toward the fire. "All of the above." He turned again to meet the older man's gaze. "Is that any way to start a marriage?"

Luke didn't answer. Instead, he said, "I heard that you plan to apply for the Stockholm fellowship."

Sam found the intensity of Luke's gaze uncomfortable. He couldn't read either approval or disapproval in his expression, but what did it matter anyway? It was his life, his career. True, he'd come to Luke for advice, perhaps to get him to agree with him on terminating the pregnancy, which Luke obviously wasn't going to do. Now the Stockholm question? The last topic he wanted to discuss was anything else having to do with ethics. "Yes," he said with a sigh. "But I don't know if I have what they're looking for."

"If we're talking about grades, skill, and an early showing of competence in your field, I would say you do."

It was a compliment, and Sam inclined his head to accept it. "I'd planned to take Taite with me. But now..." He shrugged. "I suppose it depends on...on our decision." He stared into the fire. "I don't even know if I want to see her again after this."

"So you plan to make this decision over the phone?"

It struck Sam that Luke Stephens could read his mind and probably didn't like what he saw. If he flew home to be with Taite and missed several days of classes, his professors might be less inclined to write letters of recommendation for Sweden.

"I've thought about it," he said, "but now isn't a good time to leave school. Midterms, papers...you know the drill."

Luke leaned forward. "I would encourage you to go, no matter the cost. Even if it's just for a few days, I think you need to make this decision together. In person." He paused, and in the silence a log fell with a shower of sparks. "Stockholm can wait," he said quietly. "Taite needs you, Sam. Your decision has the magnitude of life itself." He stood and crossed the room to his desk, rummaged around, then retrieved what he was looking for.

Holding the paper in his hand, he stood by the fireplace, facing Sam. "You've got an analytical mind. You're struggling with a question that has stumped scientists for years: when does life begin? You've given me your own scientific analysis of cells and their life potential. I suspect you're applying this hard analytical data to the fetus Taite carries, causing even greater confusion."

Sam nodded.

"How far along is she?"

Sam hadn't thought to ask but did a quick calculation. "Ten weeks, maybe eleven or twelve."

"At twelve weeks your child is already squinting, swallowing, moving his tongue. He's already got fingernails." He smiled. "He can make a fist, even suck his thumb."

Sam could feel his throat closing up; he looked away from Luke to study the fire.

"After only three and a half weeks, he had brain waves; his skeleton was complete." He walked back to his chair and sat down. "Sam, your child's heart has been beating since he was eighteen days old." His tone reflected his awe. "We're not talking about amoebas or protozoa here. We're talking about a real human being, a child."

Sam stared at the licking flames, trying to find an analytical comeback. He couldn't bear to think of destroying a child. It was easier to think of it as a fetus, with potential, yes. But fully alive? No matter how Luke described in utero development, he didn't think so. Not yet. Wasn't it experience and environment that created life?

Luke broke into his thoughts. "This is the prayer I mentioned." He handed a wrinkled and worn piece of paper to Sam. "Take it home, read it, and see if it might help you with what lies ahead."

Later that night, in his room, Sam pulled out the folded paper. He sat down on his bed, shoulders hunched forward, exhaustion settling in. And he began to read:

> *Lord, make me an instrument of your peace.*
> *Where there is hatred, let me sow love;*
> *where there is injury, pardon;*
> *where there is doubt, faith;*
> *where there is despair, hope;*
> *where there is darkness, light;*
> *and where there is sadness, joy.*
>
> *O Divine Master, grant that I may not so much seek*
> *to be consoled as to console;*
> *to be understood as to understand;*
> *to be loved as to love.*
> *For it is in giving that we receive;*
> *it is in pardoning that we are pardoned;*
> *and it is in dying that we are born to eternal life. Amen*

He fought the urge to crumple the paper into a ball and toss it in the wastebasket. It was only out of respect for Luke and Martha Stephens that he didn't. He took out his cell phone to call Taite, because he'd promised he would. He didn't know what he would say. He only knew that forgiveness wasn't in his heart. He couldn't imagine that it ever would be.

16

W hen the phone rang, Taite was sitting on the window seat in her room, sipping the ginger tea Naini had brought earlier. She picked up the phone, but at the tone of Sam's voice, her palms dampened, and a sudden dizziness made the room spin. "It hasn't gotten any easier for you, has it?" she said as soon as she had regained her emotional equilibrium. She knew the answer before he spoke.

"It's only been a few hours, Taite." His words were clipped, cold, and somewhere inside her, a flicker of hope died.

"I'm so sorry, Sam. I wish I could go back in time…" She let the words fall.

"I wish we both could," he said. Dead silence fell between them.

"Are you there?"

"Yeah, I'm here."

"Have you come to any conclusions?"

"It sounds like you don't want my input. Your mind is already made up. At least that's what you told me."

"I thought, well, I just thought maybe…" Her tears choked her, and she drew in a deep breath before going on. "I want this baby, but Sam…I thought maybe there was a way, perhaps research you could do on the statistics…of survival…the probability of brain or nerve damage…" Her voice fell off, but Sam didn't rush to fill in the blanks.

"I'm still thinking things through, Taite. I'll try to find out what I can, but I'm afraid the answers won't be the ones you want to hear."

She sat up straighter and cleared her throat, trying to bolster her confidence. It would be easier if she didn't love him so much. "I'm sorry I fell to pieces there for a minute. What I really wanted to say was that I intend to take the risk—no matter what."

"Don't you think I should have some say-so?"

"I would love for you to, Sam. But right now I'm alone, dealing with this alone, making decisions alone."

"Alone?" he sputtered. "You called me just hours ago to tell me that we're having a baby I didn't know about, that it may be handicapped or worse, and that you've already made up your mind about what's best to do. You haven't given me much of a chance to be part of this." His tone was darker than before, which frightened her.

"Then come home. Just for a day or two. Let's talk it out, discuss it together with the doctors."

"I can't get away. Not now. All this is requiring more sacrifice than I'm able to give. It couldn't have happened at a worse time."

Her eyes stung. "I know." Even if he wanted to marry after all this, she didn't think she wanted to marry him. How could she, knowing what he would give up? How could she, knowing the resentment he might hold against her in the future? "Believe me, I know."

Silence fell between them again.

Finally she said, "Now I wonder if I did the right thing by telling you at all. I didn't want to, but the doctors said I ought to." She played with the rim of her teacup, carefully thinking through what she had to say next. "I've done what I needed to do, and that's that. I tried to end our relationship, if you remember, knowing that no good could come of what I'd done. And now I'm relieving you of your responsibility in this pregnancy. I'll put it in writing, if you'd like, so you won't need to worry that I'll come to you, trying to get payment for doctors' bills or hospital expenses."

She hoped he would argue with her, but when he didn't, she added, "Good-bye, Sam." Without giving him time to speak, she placed the receiver back in the cradle. *Good-bye, Sam.* Though it was still evening, she went to the bed and lay down, weary from the emotion, from all she had been through. Her hand on her abdomen, she thought of the cluster of cells with new wonder, how they had already formed into a tiny child. She blinked and stared up at the ceiling, a slow smile forming.

With her hand resting above the child, she whispered, "Don't you worry, my wee one. I'm going to take care of you. If it's the last thing I do, I promise, I'll protect you."

A smile playing at the corner of her mouth, she drifted into that netherworld between waking and dreaming. Images of Taran and Gwynedd danced into her mind, as if on an ancient mist from across the mere. She thought she heard Taran singing, then almost laughed, realizing it was only a dream. Then just as vividly snatches of Brother Cadwallen's family blessing drifted into her mind. "Our heavenly Father…knit together in constant affection your son and your daughter from this day forward. For their children, their children's children, and for all who will follow through the ages…that they may evermore be filled with love one to another as members of your family through your Son, Jesus Christ our Lord."

"This blessing was for you, little one," she whispered, "as much as it was for Gwynedd and Taran and their children."

The thought struck her so profoundly that she sat up to make sure she was awake. Her grandmother had always said that God was the same yesterday, today, and forever. When this blessing was bestowed on Gwynedd and Taran, could it be that the child she carried had been included?

Just as quickly, doubts rushed in. What if the blessing wasn't true, that it was only the product of her grandmother's illness? Gwynedd, Taran, the old monk, all of it fit too closely into the pathology of this strange form of dementia.

Then other words, phrases, and verses from some place, some time long ago, filled her heart. She didn't know how she knew where to find their source; she just did. She hurried downstairs to the room off the entry hall that once was her grandfather's office. A large family Bible, well worn, lay on the bottom shelf of the bookcase behind his desk.

A snatch of an idea about God's knowing everything about a human being while still in the womb came to her. She flipped to the concordance and ran her finger down the W column until she came to the word *womb*. Psalms. Of course. When she was just a little girl, her mother read a psalm to her each night at bedtime. They brought her comfort as she fell asleep.

She thumbed through the heavy, leather-covered tome until she came to Psalm 139. She glanced down the verses, growing more excited as she read. "There it is," she whispered, when she reached verse 13.

> For You formed my inward parts;
> You covered me in my mother's womb.
> I will praise You, for I am fearfully and wonderfully made....
> My frame was not hidden from You,
> When I was made in secret....
> Your eyes saw my substance, being yet unformed.
> And in Your book they all were written,

The days fashioned for me,

When as yet there were none of them.

If the old monk's family blessing had really been uttered, then it was true that it was meant for her child. God knew all about this baby before his days were fashioned.

She touched the leaf of her grandfather's Bible with her fingertips as she read the words again, then she bowed her head.

"O Lord, I am unworthy to ask your help. I've done so many things wrong. I've brought such terrible consequences to bear in the life of this innocent little one. Don't punish him for my prideful acts, my mistakes.

"O heavenly Father," she cried silently, "touch his frame, cover him even now in my womb… I don't know the outcome. I only know that he is yours. Help us both."

"Taite…," her grandmother called softly from the doorway. "Are you all right?"

"I am," Taite said, wiping her eyes with her fingers. "Finally." She smiled at her grandmother. "I've just realized it's about time we got on with life."

Victoria looked at the still-open Bible, then lifted her eyes to meet Taite's.

"My child is known and has been since…" Taite followed her gaze, "Well, forever, I think."

Naini looked pleased and nodded. "The family blessing," she mused, tilting her head almost as if she didn't remember.

Concern filled Taite, but she went on, hoping it was her imagination. "I want to think about the future instead of all the mistakes I made in the past."

Her grandmother laughed lightly. "I've had some things I've needed to talk to you about. I was waiting until you felt better." She sounded and looked perfectly normal, and Taite let out a sigh of relief.

"You mean until I got my mind off myself?"

Victoria smiled softly. "Under normal circumstances, pregnancy is a time of self-examination. That isn't a bad thing. And with all you've had to think about..." She came into the small office and sat down in the easy chair across the desk from Taite. "With all you've had to think about, honey, you've needed this time of decision making, weighing your choices."

Taite's worries returned. She leaned forward. "Naini, is there something else you need to tell me?"

Victoria smiled. "We've certainly had our share of family revelations in recent days, haven't we?" She paused. "I only need to discuss where I will move once the house sells. I've looked at some graduated-care facilities that are quite nice. They begin with independent-living quarters, a small apartment or single occupant room."

Taite felt her mouth go dry. All she could think of was Josiah Bond and his treatment of the elderly people at his facility, his anger with anyone who tried to interfere. "Oh, Naini, no—"

Naini held up a hand. "Let me finish. Please. I have enough money—providing the house sells close to the asking price—to set myself up nicely. It won't be the Ritz-Carlton, but I've heard about places nearby that are clean and functional. When I need extended care, I'll be moved to a nursing facility."

Taite came around from behind the desk and sat beside her grandmother. "You said there wasn't as much equity in the house as you'd thought."

Victoria nodded. "There's enough."

"When that 'enough' runs out, what then?" She'd worked in nursing homes long enough to know. Once their resources were depleted, elderly patients were moved to government facilities, sometimes clean and well run. Too often, not. And those without the mental acuity to know the difference, without caregivers to oversee the system, were too often put in those facilities where the conditions were the worst. "Oh, Naini...," she said softly and reached for her hand. "I won't allow it. How can I help?"

Victoria leaned her head back, closed her eyes, and for a moment didn't speak. Taite pressed her hand. Her grandmother looked up, confused. "I'm so tired these days, honey. Did I doze off? I'm sorry...what were you saying?"

"You were about to tell me how I can help."

Victoria bit her lip, obviously trying to recall the conversation.

"About the care facility? Did you need my help...maybe to go with you to check them out?"

Victoria paused again, the blank look still on her face. "We'll talk about it later, honey. Whatever it was must not have been important." She stood and walked from the room. Taite could hear the light tap of her cane on the oak floor as she crossed the foyer and headed down the hallway to the sunroom.

For several minutes Taite leaned back in her chair and stared out the window. It was nearly dark, and the fog was again creeping in from the ocean, casting a gray pall over the landscape. She fought the emotions that roiled inside.

Again it came to her what she needed to do. But could she take on the burden of caring for her elderly, failing grandmother? And what about the coming baby? All her old insecurities drifted into her heart.

Could she carry such a load of responsibility? Her head told her no; her heart said yes.

What if she botched it the way she had so many other things in her life? She set her jaw in a stubborn line, and her hand dropped to her stomach. She'd read that a new mother is as fierce as a lioness when it comes to protecting her young. Perhaps something wild and fierce had happened within her heart when she decided to keep her baby. She gazed out at the approaching bank of fog in wonder, knowing what she had to do.

She stood in the doorway between the kitchen and the sunroom. Naini was dozing in her chintz easy chair, a copy of *Atlantic Monthly* open on her lap. Affection washed over her…and no small measure of fear.

"Naini…" Her grandmother didn't move, so Taite moved closer and touched her hand.

Victoria started, blinked, then sat up.

"I have the solution."

Victoria yawned, covering her mouth daintily. "Solution to what, honey?"

"We'll go to the cottage." Victoria started to protest, but Taite pressed on. "You've talked of the lighthouse, your dream, its importance to you."

Her grandmother nodded slowly. "I have."

"My plan is this. We go to the island to live in the cottage. I will care for you as long as I possibly can. I will get a job—maybe at Happy Acres—and we'll care for the baby, raise her right there at Point Solana."

"Happy Acres?"

Taite laughed. "It looks like it's straight off the coast of Maine—or Cape Cod. More like a home than a facility."

For a moment her grandmother seemed at a loss for words. "It might not be long until I need extended care." She frowned. "And the island is no place for a young woman with a baby. It's isolated, honey." She shook her head. "I think my plan is best for all concerned."

"I want you in my life. I want my baby to know you, Naini. I want her to hear your stories."

"There may not be time for that," Victoria said.

"Promise me you'll think about it."

"I don't think you realize what's ahead, what to expect from my illness, the strength it will take to lift me, to see to my…other needs." She shook her head as if dismissing Taite's plan.

In truth, Taite did have some inkling of the care required from her work with the elderly in San Francisco. But it didn't matter. Now was the time to help others for a change, especially this woman who had given her so much. "We'll take it one day at a time." She gave her grandmother a wide smile, feeling better than she had in weeks.

Victoria reached across the small space between them and hugged Taite. Her embrace was fragile, as fragile as her life seemed to be right now. "I'll think about it," she said. "But only if you'll take me to Happy Acres when the time comes for greater care."

The next day Taite plunged once more into preparing the house for sale, dusting and vacuuming, and packing her grandmother's belongings.

While Victoria napped in the afternoon, Taite climbed the pull-down stairs to the attic, feather duster in her hip pocket, her hair covered with a bandanna. When she reached the attic, she sneezed twice, then crossed to the room's single window and pulled up the sash. Late afternoon sun slanted through the window, illuminating the dust particles that danced in the bar of light. She turned slowly, surveying the piles of boxes and old trunks. To one side two standing rods held large, zippered, plastic garment bags, and opposite them rose at least a half-dozen tall stacks of shoeboxes.

Almost lost in the midst of the shoebox stacks was her grandfather's old Underwood typewriter sitting on a rusted metal table. She tapped the typewriter's keys and felt their sturdy movement beneath her fingers, pulled the return lever, and grinned when the little bell dinged somewhere inside the boxy case.

After a moment she turned again, rubbed her back, and stretched. She felt her energy ebb and dropped to her knees in front of one of the larger trunks beneath the window.

For a few minutes she didn't move. She was bone tired, still recovering from her ordeal with the anesthetic. She hadn't whispered a single complaint to Naini but instead tried to be as upbeat and cheerful as possible.

Taite lifted the lid of the old steamer trunk and peered inside. Another cloud of dust rose, and she sneezed again. One by one, she lifted the objects first to her lap, then to the wood-planked floor around her: a leather-bound diary, some old scrapbooks, crocheted baby clothes, two pairs of booties, one pair of high-top toddler's shoes, and a beat-up, dented letter box, about half the size of a child's shoebox.

Briefly she turned the rather homely box from side to side. It looked vaguely familiar; perhaps she had seen it—or heard her grandmother talk about it—when she was a child. Taking up the rest of the deep space in the trunk were three worn and faded quilts, folded carefully inside out, and beneath them, wrapped in muslin, her mother's wedding gown.

Taite rocked back on her heels. She hadn't seen it since she was a little girl playing dress-up, not long before her father died. She held the fabric close and closed her eyes, drawing in the musty scent, remembering how her mother and father had looked at each other that day when she tottered into the room in Isabel's high heels. Her father had picked Taite up and danced her around the room in his arms, and in the background her mother was laughing.

Dropping the wedding gown into her lap, she folded back the muslin and touched the yellowed satin and lace trim with her fingertips. A row of seed pearls and faded silk roses graced the stand-up collar; the design was matched on the cap sleeves. Taite stood and held the dress by the bodice, letting the folds in the long skirt cascade to the floor.

She carefully refolded the gown, wrapped it again with muslin, and laid it back in the trunk. Her mother had always said she dreamed that Taite would wear the same gown on her wedding day. Taite thought of Sam and her broken dreams and felt sick.

Taite's hands trembled as she next picked up a tiny sweater. It was pale pink, hand crocheted by Naini for Taite when she was an infant. She knew it from photographs, rather than from real memories. She lifted it to her cheek, thinking that one day her little one would wear a garment this small. She imagined the baby's scent, the warm snug feel of him in her arms.

Then her attention went to another small sweater, also hand crocheted. It was yellowed with age, its daisy design tattered with use. A small tissue-wrapped square lay nearby. Gently she unwrapped the thin paper, and a rectangular picture frame fell to her lap.

Anna. Her sister must have been under a year old. Sitting in a puddle of sunshine, she was smiling at the person behind the camera. Taite touched the glass above her sweet little face, and a sting pricked her eyes. What would it be like to lose a child? For the first time in her life, she thought about the grief her mother…and her father…must have endured. "Oh, Mama, I never knew…," she whispered.

The sun was hanging low in the afternoon sky, and wisps of fog brought fleeting shadows into the room. Taite examined some of the other treasures her grandmother kept in the trunk.

After a few more minutes the room dimmed, and Taite stood and stepped across the items on the floor to the window once more. The fog was thicker now and darkened the sun. It was too dim to see clearly from the single light bulb hanging in the center of the room.

She dusted herself off, deciding to wait until tomorrow to tackle more of the boxes and trunks. There was room at the cottage only for what was functional, though she would keep some favorite toys for her baby, maybe a small rocker and some tea-party dishes. When thoughts about her baby's mental and physical ability came to mind, she quickly pushed them away, though a sense of fear lingered in the corner of her heart, as dark and foreboding as the fog outside.

Taite walked to the door. Resting her hand on the crystal knob, she turned to glance at the trunk, almost reluctant to leave it. There on the floor near the still-folded quilts was the homely, dented letter box. As if drawn by some unseen force, she crossed the room again, the floorboards creaking beneath her feet, and picked it up to take downstairs.

A few minutes later she flipped on the overhead light in the kitchen and headed for the table. She frowned as she bent over the strange box. On its worn sides was a wide ribbon of embossed metal, dull and tarnished. She could barely make out a design of Celtic knots interwoven with daffodil trumpets and crosses. The trumpets seemed to be made of a pink-hued gold.

"So you found the family treasure," Naini said from the doorway. "I was going to look for it tomorrow."

Taite turned and smiled at her grandmother's look of wonderment as she approached. Victoria took the box in her hands and gazed at it, turning it this way and that. "It's been a long time," she mused. Then she looked at Taite. "It's perhaps two hundred years old, passed along through the family. It's said the design is Welsh and was probably brought over by some ancestor. The narcissus, you know, is the national flower of Wales."

Taite was disappointed. The thought was ridiculous, she knew, but she had hoped the box was something passed down from Gwynedd and Taran. "What's inside?"

"It hasn't been opened, at least not by anyone in recent generations. Legend is that it's a letter box, and judging by the weight of it, we think it contains letters, maybe an old journal. I had it appraised about twenty-five years ago. The appraiser said that the design is a copy of original Celtic art. But the gold, the pink-gold inlay, is certainly from a gold mine in Wales. The color is very distinctive."

She handed the box back to Taite. "The appraiser pegged the period as eighteenth century." She peered at the lock. "He also said that the value of the box would lessen if it was opened without the key. Because of its age, the lock is worn and thin. There's a chance it might break the minute someone—even an expert—tries to open it. So through the years, it's been part of the family tradition to keep it locked."

Taite slid into the chair and peered at the box. "It's beautiful," she said, touching the intricate design. "You speak as if there is a key someplace."

Her grandmother gave her a surprised look, smiled, and sat down beside her. "Perhaps there is," she said.

Sam couldn't get Taite out of his thoughts. Within a week his studies had slipped to second place, and he found his mind wandering during his lecture classes. For days he avoided Luke Stephens, knowing the questions the doctor would have, spoken or unspoken. He also kept uncharacteristically silent during ethics class. Luke seemed willing to let him keep his thoughts to himself.

He spotted Blake Frey in the library a week after his conversation with Taite.

"You get your application in yet?" Blake dropped his books onto the table, spun the chair next to Sam, and straddled it. "I picked up my letters of recommendation yesterday, got the whole kit and caboodle off to the institute this morning. Now begins the waiting game."

Sam shook his head. "I can't go."

His friend looked shocked. "I thought you were ready to fly to Stockholm as soon as they gave you the word."

"Personal reasons, that's all. I've got to go back to California for break."

"Does the pregnant girl have something to do with it?" His tone was full of concern.

"Yeah. Everything to do with it."

Blake tapped his pencil eraser on the tabletop. "From what you said, she oughta have that abortion. She being stubborn?"

"She's always been stubborn. I think she might agree to it if I fly in and convince her it's the best thing for us all. So looks like instead of heading to Stockholm I'll be heading to California."

His friend looked worried. "You're not doing yourself any favor by staying here right now."

Sam laughed and pulled at the bags underneath his eyes. "I look that bad, eh?"

"I've seen worse. But not much." Blake grinned. "What I'm saying is that you could fly home over the weekend, be back for school Monday. Arrange for the abortion, be free to go to Stockholm with me." He waggled his brows. "It'll be a good time in the old town tonight." He chuckled. "I hear it's a pretty freewheeling society."

"If you're talking about the club scene, I'm not interested."

"Because of the girl?"

Sam let out a sigh. "Yeah. Taite. I can't let her go through this alone. We've got a lot of decisions to make. It's all I can think about.

Research opportunities will come up again, but making a decision like this with Taite—well, there's too much on the line. I've done research, and the trauma to Taite was no small thing. I should have flown home the minute she called. I was mad, and I took it out on her."

"Hey friend, don't flagellate yourself with cactus like those dudes in New Mexico."

"Dudes?" He grinned. "I believe they're called *penitentes*." He gathered his textbooks, stacked his notepad on top, and stood. "You always have a way of putting things in perspective for me. I'll drop off the cactus on the way out."

He punched her speed-dial number on his cell phone the minute he was out of the building. "Taite?"

"I'm here." She sounded distant. Tired.

He was alarmed. "Is everything okay?"

Silence fell between them. "Okay?"

"Wrong word. I'm sorry. How could things possibly be okay with what you're going through?"

"Actually, I'm doing very well."

"Taite, I'm coming home. I'll be there this weekend."

"You don't need to, Sam."

"No, I want to."

"Maybe you didn't understand what I said. I mean, I don't want you to. I don't need you."

"I need to see you, Taite. Please let me come." He waited for her answer, but the phone went dead. For a moment he thought she'd hung up on him, then he glanced at the power icon on the screen. The signal had disappeared. Probably not strong enough. He stepped into a clearing and dialed again.

It rang several times before he gave up and flipped the phone closed. Taite obviously didn't want to talk with him.

17

Sam walked along the winding path through campus. Thunder rumbled across the sky, and a blast of wind stung his face. He shivered, but not from the coming storm. The weather meant nothing; it was Taite who filled his mind. He wanted to see her. He intended to see her.

At the sound of footsteps on the brick path, he looked back to see a figure in a black raincoat walking toward him. It was Luke Stephens, carrying his umbrella and looking as distinguished as ever. He gave Sam a big smile and, when he was close enough, extended his hand in greeting.

"Martha was just asking about you this morning," he said, holding the large umbrella over them both. "I told her I'd see if I could find you, invite you to dinner. She's planning Southern fried chicken and gravy tonight."

"I'm planning to catch the midnight flight to California if there's a seat available."

Luke's expression was at once understanding and approving. "You need a ride to the airport? I'll be happy to oblige."

Sam appreciated the offer and was immediately sorry he'd been avoiding the good-hearted man. "Thank you. I'd appreciate it."

"Tell you what," Luke said. "Why don't you check on your flight, then give me a call?" He reached into his pocket for a notepad, scribbled his number on a piece of paper, and handed it to Sam. "If there's time, plan on fried chicken at our house." He grinned. "And if there isn't, I bet my Martha will be happy to fix you a care package to take with you."

"I'll be the envy of every passenger on the plane." Sam again kicked himself for staying away from them. Luke and Martha were offering friendship and with it a sense of comfort—something he desperately needed—but his feelings of guilt kept him at a distance. Guilt he couldn't rise above. These two had probably lived in an exemplary way, rising above life's complications. His life, in comparison, seemed a tangle of errors, wrong turns, bad choices, and painful consequences. Day by day the painful awareness was growing on him that he had caused those consequences.

"Tell Martha I'm looking forward to it. Thank you for the invitation."

Luke lifted his hand in a mock salute. "Until later, then." He stepped past Sam, umbrella jutting in front of him like a shield. With a quick wave, he disappeared around a curve in the walkway.

The rain suddenly hit the ground in sheets, and Sam ducked into the shelter of a nearby building. He made his call to the airline, flipped the phone closed, and pulled his collar up. He'd just stepped back onto the walkway when the faint sound of voices lifted in song caught his attention. He turned in surprise.

The covered doorway he'd ducked into was that of the campus chapel. He'd passed the New England–style brick building dozens of times in his hurry to get to class, but never once had he so much as peered inside.

The music rose again, more beautiful than before. He tried the door and found it unlocked. He slipped inside and sat down in the back row just as the music died.

In the chancel a choral group was just breaking up after a rehearsal. The director was giving instructions for the next practice, and in the orchestra, musicians were chatting in clusters among themselves as they put away their instruments and drifted toward the side door.

Within minutes Sam was alone. He stared up at the cross, suddenly afraid. His guilt returned. "Better a millstone be tied around my neck…" He bowed his head, but his soul was so parched that he couldn't even cry.

"I've really blown it this time," he groaned. "Botched everything, from throwing away the sacrifice my parents made to send me to med school to causing the death of a child. I've not stood beside Taite, and I may have lost her forever."

He raised his head again, reason setting in. The wisest thing to do was obvious. He would convince Taite that it was reasonable—no, necessary—to see the abortion through. He would stay with her through the procedure, support her afterward. He would bring her back to Boston. Things would go on just as before. They would marry after he graduated. She could go back to school, work on her writing. They would start a family. Someday.

It was a plan. A wise plan. The most logical plan. He stared at the cross behind the nave. Why then did he feel something was dying inside him?

Across the rain-soaked green, Luke Stephens watched the double doors of the chapel. He'd seen Luke duck in, and something told him the young man's struggle was continuing. He wondered if he should follow, but an unseen hand seemed to hold him back.

"Father," he prayed instead, "do a mighty work in Sam's heart.

Turn his troubled thoughts to you so he will find solace...forgiveness...mercy...grace. Grant that Taite and Sam will grow to understand that these gifts are freely given, they are undeserved, they cannot be earned.

"And this unborn child...this innocent one...who dwells in the secret place of your heart, shelter him in the refuge of your wings. Father, may he be borne up in the hands of angels..."

The doors of the chapel banged open, and Sam headed out, scowling and looking anything but refreshed from being in God's presence. Luke watched as the young man, collar turned against the rain, bent low against the wind. Though Sam's back was to him now, the despair he'd spotted, just before Sam turned, frightened him on behalf of the young man. Despair meant the death of hope. And that death might equal the death of the child.

He thought of Victoria Kingswell and all she had meant to him through the years. He was in awe of how God's providence caused paths to cross, God's people to connect. He wondered if, without her letter, he would have noticed Sam Wellington other than as an outstanding student.

Yet, here he was, watching the young man from a distance, praying for him and Victoria's granddaughter. He knew that Victoria was praying for them as well from her side of the continent.

Victoria herself needed his prayers. After her phone call, he'd known immediately the severity of her symptoms and the probable outcome of her diagnosis. He and Martha talked with her again after her doctor's appointment, assuring her of their love and prayers. And when they hung up, they wept.

Sam continued down the path and out of sight. Luke's heart was heavy as he thought of Victoria's family. Though he'd never met them in person, Victoria's letters had made him feel close to each one: Isabel,

Brady, Anna, Taite, and now Sam. *If things had been different all those years ago...* He smiled to himself, refusing to dwell on the sentimental thought. As another clap of thunder bumped its way across the sky, he headed to his car.

By six o'clock Sam had packed his duffel and trotted down the stairs and out to the front of the dorm where Luke would pick him up. During the evening, Martha's laughter and animated conversation helped him not to dwell on his misery. He tried his best to enter into the conversation, grateful for the quick repartee between Martha and Luke. Just as he had before, he found himself envying their relationship. He wondered if he and Taite might enjoy such a lively, loving, comfortable bond forty years from now. Forty years? He almost laughed aloud. He'd be lucky to get her to keep the door open forty seconds once he arrived on Victoria Kingswell's porch.

"Are you worried about seeing Taite?" Luke asked once they were on their way to Logan. He glanced toward Sam in the dark. "I don't mean to pry, so if you don't want to talk about it..."

Sam shook his head. "I don't have anything new to report. I'm just as confused as ever."

"I'll be praying for you, son."

Sam frowned and glanced at the man quizzically. He figured he was religious, judging from his mention of Saint Francis. And there was that painting of a kneeling Christ that hung over the fireplace in his office. But this personal talk of prayer brought to mind the word on campus about Dr. Stephens's old-fashioned thinking. And right now, anything remotely religious reminded him of his guilt. "It should be decided by the end of the weekend."

"Decided?"

He knew the doctor's thinking, knew he might be offended, but he figured he might as well tell the truth. He would have to sooner or later anyway. "I plan to encourage Taite to have the abortion," he said. "I've done research. It's for the best."

"I did some study on the issue myself this week," Luke said. "Since you brought it up in class, I thought further study might give us a broader picture." He flipped on his directional signal and changed lanes. "You might be surprised to learn that in the earlier stages of pregnancy, the trauma to the fetus is less significant. Surprisingly, even in the later stages of pregnancy, oxygen depletion can actually strengthen the baby's lungs, causing the chest muscles to expand and contract as if trying to breathe."

Sam sat back, stunned. "I didn't find that in my search."

Luke raised a brow as if saying, *Who's the expert here?*

Sam felt his ears heat. "I'm sorry; I didn't mean that—"

Luke chuckled. It had started to rain again, and he flipped on the windshield wipers. "Do you think you've wanted to believe the attending physician? Make his hypothesis yours because it is easier?"

The wipers continued their dull rhythm. The traffic slowed to a crawl, and Sam checked his watch. "I assumed that he knew what he was talking about."

"He was speaking in generalities," Luke said, "and of course in that regard he is completely correct. But in recent studies on development in utero, amazingly, the mother's blood oxygen levels remain high enough, even in a state of asphyxiation, to maintain the exchange of oxygen between the mother and child. From what I read—and I can show you the sources, if you like—even though your child has a significant chance of being born less than perfect, he's got better than a fifty-fifty chance of being born whole, physically and mentally." He gave Sam a quick glance before looking back to the highway. "I would recommend seeing a specialist in the field. I've written down the names of some people in the Bay Area. Remind me to give you the note."

Sam sat back in his seat, taking in this latest news, which only added to his confusion. The cars ahead of them surged forward again, and Luke accelerated. The reflection of taillights gleamed crimson on the wet pavement. "Just a week ago I thought I had my life mapped out, the future was certain, my path into it secure. Now..."

Luke steered the car to the right-hand lane and the airport approach.

"In the wisdom that comes with years, I can only say that life is never certain." At the entrance to Sam's carrier, Luke pulled to the curb. "But there is a plumb line, Sam. One that can keep you steady no matter the upheaval. Someday I'll tell you about mine."

Sam opened his door, grabbed his duffel bag, and leaned back in. He thought of the tragedy of Luke Jr., how Luke and Martha's hopes and dreams were pinned on their son, how their hearts were filled with love for him, how they had to learn to live with their loss, their grief. Luke was talking about God; Sam knew it from all he had observed. Yeah, it would be good to believe in a God who would help you through the tragedies, the confusion. But if you didn't believe in a Supreme Being unless he could prove himself, what then? And even if this One did prove his existence, what if your life was so polluted with wrongdoing that this Being didn't want anything to do with you? What then?

These weren't questions he could ask Luke. He cared what Luke and Martha thought of him. The last thing he wanted was to air his transgressions, not that Luke hadn't guessed a few of them already.

"I would like to hear about that plumb line sometime," he said, reaching across the leather seat and taking the note with the promised information from Luke's hand. "Thank you, sir. Thank you for everything."

The doorbell rang at nine o'clock the following morning. Taite and Victoria had just climbed the attic stairs to finish going through the last few boxes. Taite, thinking an early real-estate agent had stopped by, hurried back down the stairs to the front door. A feather duster stuck out of her hip pocket, and a bandanna graced her head. She stopped at the entry mirror and patted the mussed dreadlocks poking from beneath it.

She was starting to turn the brass doorknob when she thought better of it and peered through the peephole. She gasped. It was Sam.

Just the look of him tore at her insides. She leaned against the door, her forehead touching the wood, unable to face him, unable to turn him away, her hand still resting on the knob.

The doorbell rang again. Trembling, she finally turned the handle and swung the door open.

"Taite?" His voice was soft and husky. Standing there, his clothes crumpled and wrinkled, he looked as though he'd been up all night. He was holding a bunch of bright yellow tiger lilies, her favorite, wrapped in green tissue paper. "These are for you." Awkwardly he thrust them toward her.

The huskiness lingered in his tone, and the sound of it brought back the pain in her heart. "Oh, Sam," she said, her voice little more than a broken whisper. She took the flowers from him, biting back her tears, then stepped back and gestured for him to come in.

"Who is it, dear?" Victoria called from upstairs.

"Sam," she called back, her voice rough with emotion. "Sam's come home."

"I know I've caught you off guard," he said, following her into the kitchen. "I was worried that if I called from the airport, you wouldn't let me through the door."

Taite didn't turn to look at him; she didn't know how she could without melting inside. Instead, she busied herself at the counter, looking for a vase in the nearly empty cabinet under the sink. "I told you I didn't want you to come," she finally managed.

"We need to talk face to face."

She filled the vase with water and dropped in the bouquet, then turned and crossed the room to set it in the center of the table.

"Please, Taite," he said, "look at me." He moved across the few feet between them to stand closer.

She raised her eyes to meet his and saw that he had been crying. Sam never cried. His gaze caught and held hers, seeming to probe her soul. He touched her cheek with the backs of his fingers, tenderly, lovingly. When he opened his arms to draw her close, she stepped into them with a small cry.

His head bent over her protectively, and his cheek rested on top of her head. "We're in this together," he said. "I should have come to you immediately. Please forgive me."

She swallowed hard and shook her head. "You weren't ready. Neither was I." Pulling back slightly, she looked up at him. Something was different in his expression. She knew because of the vulnerability and pain she saw there. She knew because it was the same with her. She frowned and reached up to touch his forehead. "What is it?"

He took her hand, and they walked together through the sunroom to the back door and out into the garden. A small iron bench, dusty from neglect, was nearly hidden in the corner beneath an olive tree. They had sat in the same place long ago. Sam took out his handkerchief and dusted off the seat.

"How are you feeling?"

"I'm past the worst of it. The first three months were terrible."

"You're past your first trimester?"

His question tightened the knot of fear inside her. "Why do you ask?" What if he'd come here to try to convince her to have the abortion? Before she saw him again, it had been easier to deny her love, to think only of the child growing inside her. But now, seeing Sam, knowing that she loved him from the depths of her being, how could she tell him to leave?

How could she repeat the words she'd said to him on the phone? *I don't need you.* As she looked at him, memorizing the slant of his jaw, his luminous intelligent eyes, the sweep of hair across his brow, sudden tears blinded her.

He took her hand and held it tightly between his. "I'm not sure what I'm feeling exactly, or why. It makes no rational sense."

She understood and squeezed his hand. "Go on," she said.

"Just before I left Boston, I received some news about our chances of having a healthy child."

A simple birdsong from across the garden suddenly pierced her heart with its sweetness. She didn't dare speak for fear she hadn't heard him correctly.

"A doctor I respect, who knows about what's happened, came across some research that indicates that what happened to you might not have hurt the fetus." He drew a deep breath. "He thinks the chances of the baby being healthy might be better than we've been told. He recommends that we see a specialist, have some tests run." He gave her a close look. "Will you be okay with that?"

She studied him, afraid to believe. It was good not to be alone with this. "Can you go with me?"

"The thing about long flights," he said leaning back, "is that they give a person a nice long time to think matters through without distraction." He was looking at her now, his eyes filled with love. "I know that no matter what happens, Taite, I want to marry you." He smiled at her in that way he had, and her heart leapt. "If you'll have me."

"We have a lot to talk over, Sam. Your school, your chance for this research fellowship in Sweden." She was so in love with him she couldn't think straight. "And the fact that I'm pregnant... I never wanted you to marry me because you felt you had to."

He kissed her hand, not answering her question. "First things first. I would like to marry as soon as possible. You'll come back to Boston with me. And providing your doctor gives us an okay, you'll go to Stockholm with me." His eyes glistened when he mentioned Sweden. "We can make it work, Taite—for you, for our baby, for me." There was a pleading note in his voice.

She studied him and pulled back her hand, thinking about what he'd said. "We need to slow down a bit," she said. "First of all, I-I can't go to Boston with you. Or to Sweden, for that matter."

He looked worried. "Why not?"

"It's Naini." She told him about the disease with the strange name, dementia with Lewy bodies, adding that symptoms were already progressing, the dreams and hallucinations, the memory problems, and extreme fatigue.

"DLB," he mused softly. His worry showed on his tired face. "Dementia will follow, also Parkinson's-like symptoms. The next phase is terrible."

"I've committed myself to care for her, Sam. The house"—she nodded toward the big Victorian—"is on the market. The real-estate agent tells us it's priced well and should sell quickly."

"Oh, Taite, I'm sorry. I had no idea you were facing all this, too."

He jammed his hands into his pockets and seemed to slump forward with the weight of it.

Taite laid her hand on his shoulder. "My grandfather, years ago, left me an old fisherman's cabin on Pelican Island. I'm taking Naini there. For a while she'll be well enough to help me take care of the baby. I plan to get a job... I have some ideas that have grabbed my heart like nothing ever has before." She gave him a gentle smile and amended her statement. "Well, like nothing related to work or career."

"Taite," Sam said with a frown, "you've got your life planned. And there's no room for me. What about us? The baby?"

"Until a few minutes ago, I didn't think you'd left room for me...or our child." She extended her hand, and Sam took it. Her voice was gentler when she continued. "These are huge steps for us to take. And as soon as you mentioned going to Stockholm, it was clear that you plan for your life to continue the same as always, but..." She fought to find the words. "But somehow I don't think you're ready." At the sudden thought of using embryos for research, she touched her stomach and fought the urge to be sick.

Sam looked at her intently, his eyes searching her face. "You're turning me down?"

"We've both got a lot of emotional issues. I haven't faced all my ghosts yet. You've known about this for less time than I have. I don't think you've dealt with yours either."

"I'm willing to marry you right now. Today."

"Willing?" she said, her heart sinking. "We're back to my question about marrying me because it's the right thing to do. I think you just answered it."

"Oh, Taite..." The words came out as a cry. He stood and tried to draw her into his arms. "I love you, Taite. You're right about the issues.

I've got a lot to work through. But I want to do the right thing. Isn't this it? Isn't this what's right and honorable?"

She nodded, her eyes filling, but she pulled back from his embrace. "Honorable, yes—and I thank you for being willing. But right?" She started to cry. "I don't think so."

He pulled out the piece of paper that she presumed had the name of the specialist written on it. She braced herself, waiting for Sam to place it in her hands and then leave her standing alone in the garden.

18

From the attic window, Victoria watched Sam and Taite as they talked in the garden. She couldn't hear them, but she could read plenty into their body language. Of course they were deeply stirred, and though they were animated and troubled at times, their love for each other was evident. They reminded her of the other young lovers who strolled in the same garden at twilight. She rubbed clear a larger spot on the dusty window to see if they might be there now, perhaps with their sheep, but Sam and Taite were alone.

Taran and Gwynedd are a vision, a product of your illness, she told herself. *They are not real...maybe they never were.* What was real? What wasn't? Dark fears swept over her. How long would it be until she completely lost her grip on reality? Her attention again settled on Taite and Sam, and she breathed a prayer of hope that her memory would stay intact long enough to know their child. To tell the family stories.

Finally she could bear the thoughts no longer. She turned from the window and went back to sorting through pictures in old photo albums. But it was frustrating. Because of the fatigue that had begun to plague her, names and places sometimes faded from her memory, only to reappear later as if her mind were as clear as ever.

She gave up trying to concentrate on the albums and walked over to the pull-down attic stairs. She remembered how she once sprang up and down them with the ease of a rabbit. Not these days. It took total concentration, placing one foot in back of the other to descend safely. She rested at the landing, then, hand on the rail, continued down the wide staircase to the ground floor. She had just given herself a silent cheer for making it safely when the back door opened, and Taite and Sam burst in.

Sam came to her immediately, his expression full of concern, compassion. "Taite just told me about your diagnosis." He took her arm and helped her into the sunroom. Taite followed.

She knew he wanted to talk about her disease, but after they were seated, she purposely turned the conversation to Pelican Island. Once they launched into a discussion of her illness, the next step would be his research—specifically stem cell research. Until only weeks ago she'd been adamant about how she felt about the ethics of it; now she wasn't as clear. Her fears sometimes clouded her thinking. It might be easier to skirt the topic altogether.

Victoria watched Sam as they spoke about the move to the island. His expression told her what she already suspected: he wanted to be part of Taite's life but hadn't figured out quite how. She wanted the two to marry; she wanted Sam to accept Taite and his child with open arms of love and grace. Only divine intervention could bring about the heart changes needed for their union to be healthy. She prayed that God, in his timing, would bring these changes into being. *His timing.* Not hers. And knowing what lay ahead in her life, accepting the limitations that would surely come, almost broke her heart. She wanted to see healing in them both before it was too late.

So selfish on her part, she thought, watching them together, their quick repartee, the sparkling glances they exchanged. She ached for them to come together, united by the God who loved them more than they loved each other, the One who cared more about their child than any of them could comprehend.

Victoria knew enough about them to conclude that each was trying to work through emotions that ran much deeper than dealing with the coming child. At the core were issues of the heart, a place in each of them where only God's touch could bring healing.

"Great strides have been made in the treatment of DLB," Sam was saying. "Exciting research." Taite looked strangely uncomfortable.

"DLB" was easier to say than "dementia with Lewy bodies." Anything was easier than the word *dementia*. "Tell me about it," she said.

He sat forward, his expression rapt, and told of the research techniques being developed in Europe, the almost miraculous results. Victoria had done enough reading to know that he was leaving out some key elements as well as the reasons such research was illegal in the U.S. She wondered if it was out of respect for Taite's condition. Or maybe it was to shield them both from graphic indelicacy. Perhaps it was to hide something about the research that bothered him.

"It's been only within the last few years that embryonic stem cells were found to have the remarkable ability to grow into nearly every component of the body," he said, his eyes bright with enthusiasm. "This means that with research we can learn to guide them to become new brain tissue for DLB patients, new pancreas cells for diabetics, nerve cells for spinal injury victims…" He paused, shaking his head in wonder. "Can you imagine the miraculous healing for those and other diseases that we'll someday see? What if this were available now…for you…for others who have DLB?"

Victoria didn't answer right away. She glanced at Taite, sitting there so beautiful in the first round sweetness of motherhood. Already it plagued her that her mind, her memory, might be gone by the time the baby was born. Her heart caught again at the unbearable truth of what lay ahead.

What if she could be made whole again? Would the cost seem as dear? Was her life not worth saving?

Taite suddenly laid a hand on her abdomen. She tilted her head with a look of wonder. "Oh my," she said, grinning. "Oh my!"

Sam looked alarmed.

"The baby," she said. "I think...I can't be sure...but I think I just felt our baby move." She grabbed Sam's hand and placed it on her stomach. "There...," she breathed. "A flutter, almost like butterfly wings. Did you feel it?" Their gazes locked, and they stared at each other with a look of love so deep that Victoria's eyes filled.

The baby's first tiny kick was celebrated with laughter and kisses all around. When the excitement had settled, Victoria drew in a breath. "You asked me a question earlier," she said, "which I think is leading me to consider stem cell transplant. Before I can answer, I have a question for you. How is it done, this research?"

"On laboratory animals here in the States," he said.

"And in Europe...do they use human beings?"

"Human embryos," he said, his voice dropping. He let his gaze drift away from her for a moment. "It might help you to know," he said, again meeting her gaze, "that the embryos used for research are those that would be discarded anyway. Fertility patients usually produce more embryos than they need while trying to conceive. The extras are frozen until they attempt another pregnancy or decide the cells are no longer needed and have them destroyed."

Taite's demeanor changed, and she looked pale. "Discarded lives." Her voice was sad. "Your words are making me feel even guiltier over what I almost did. What I planned was worse. There wasn't even the redemptive value of helping another human being." She stood, still ashen, and left the room.

Sam made a move to follow, but Victoria held up a hand. "She may need to be alone for a few minutes. And I think there are some things that you need to know." He sat back, still looking worried, and Victoria went on. "She's had a difficult time with her choices. She was determined to have an abortion—and not tell you—until the ordeal at the clinic. It changed everything—but brought a lot of guilt in its wake."

"I can understand that," he said.

"Our God is a God of mercy and grace. We all make errors in judgment; we take wrong turns even when we know the right ones. As humans, we can't undo the damage we've caused by those mistakes or the harm we've done to others or to ourselves. Only God can do that." He was watching her intently, his expression more skeptical than sad. She was undeterred. "Neither can we live with ourselves—if we have a conscience at all—after we understand the consequences of our actions."

Sam's mouth was set in a stubborn line, and he worked his jaw, probably in annoyance. "We've gone from a discussion on stem cell research to God's condemnation," he said evenly. "You're telling me that my interest in scientific research is one of those 'wrong turns' that God must forgive?" A cynical chuckle escaped his lips. "That is, if one even believes in a personal God."

"Oh goodness no," she said quickly. "These are hard questions—all of them. And I can't pretend to know the answers. I spoke to that issue from my heart, from my own experience. I was talking about Taite and her feelings of guilt. Her pregnancy before marriage, her plan to have an abortion without telling you, and most of all, the harm to the baby that may have been caused by her actions."

"I don't know what all this has to do with me." The cynicism was gone, and she could see her words had shaken him.

Victoria nodded. "Your forgiveness might help her understand that forgiveness and grace are gifts from those who love her."

"Grace?" He looked puzzled.

She smiled, remembering the many times God had extended it in her life. "Yes, grace," she said. "That distance between where our efforts end and where God stretches out his arms to meet us. We can't bridge the distance; we can't earn his love; we can't earn his forgiveness, his blessings. But in his mercy, he reaches out to draw us into his love. It's his compassion for us that bridges the gap."

Sam met her gaze. Understanding such things might be possible for him, because beneath the mask of his self-confidence she sensed his own silent cry for forgiveness.

Just then Taite entered the room again, carrying a tray of cookies and tea. Sam jumped up and reached for the tray. "It's about time I started helping out around here," he said. He set the tray down on the side table and poured tea for Victoria and Taite. Then, with a smile he said, "Point me in the right direction, and tell me what to pack."

Throughout the weekend, Taite saw a different side of Sam. He wouldn't let her lift anything heavier than a feather duster. He brought her glasses of milk and made sure she rested with her feet up every few hours. She found herself grinning at him as he fussed. She rode with him in Victoria's 1977 Oldsmobile to gather more boxes and sat with her grandmother in the parlor as he gave tours of the house when real-estate agents dropped by.

By Sunday evening they had accomplished more than Taite had thought possible. Every stick of furniture was tagged and priced for the moving sale, already advertised for the following weekend. Dozens of boxes and bags had been dropped by the Salvation Army thrift shop. And she sat back with her feet up while Sam called for estimates from moving companies to take to the island the few necessities Victoria and Taite wanted to keep—beds, dressers, a table and chairs, and a rocker.

"You haven't said when you fly back to Boston," she said over Hawaiian-style pizza that night. The three were sitting at the kitchen table, bone tired but pleased with their progress.

"I called this morning and changed it to next weekend." He took a bite, raised a brow, and gave her a lopsided smile as he chewed.

Taite tilted her head, surprised, pleased, and worried. Thoughtfully, she took a bite of pizza and savored the mix of fresh pineapple and grilled ham. "You can't miss school, can you? You said this week was crucial because of midterms, papers, and such." She dabbed at her mouth with her napkin.

"I couldn't be sure when we'll get you in for testing. We'll call first thing tomorrow morning and find out." He paused and looked from Taite to Victoria, then back again. "Plus, as I see it, you're packed and ready to go. Though the house hasn't sold, there's really no reason why you can't go to Pelican Island now"—he grinned—"this week while I'm here to help you settle in."

Taite started to protest, but when she met her grandmother's piercing gaze, she thought better of it. They did need help. Naini was in no condition to lift and put things away. She had done what she could to the cabin before she left, but now that her grandmother was coming to live with her, it would need a more thorough cleaning.

Sam was watching her as he reached for another slice of pizza. "Thank you," she said. She watched him, full of contentment and love, conscious of the ache before tears she had felt too many times to count since Sam's arrival.

That night after they tossed their paper plates and put the pizza box in the trash, Victoria excused herself. Taite helped her up the stairs to her bedroom, grabbed a thick sweater, and then went out to the porch where Sam waited in the swing. He looked up, smiled, and patted the seat beside him.

When she sat down, he put his arm around her shoulders, and they gently rocked without speaking. The night air was chilly, but the fog hadn't rolled in yet. The old-fashioned gaslights that lined the street glowed under a spangle of stars. The breeze carried the sounds of distant waves pounding the sand and blending with the low hum of fishing boats putting out to sea.

"I'm not very good at this," Sam said.

She let out a small laugh. "You're good at everything, Samuel Wellington. You always have been."

His tone was somber. "I thought so until recently." Taite leaned her head against his shoulder and waited for him to go on. "I'm lousy at asking for forgiveness," he said.

"But you didn't do anything wrong." She leaned back to gaze into his face, her heart aching with love for this man. "Sam, I'm the one in need of forgiveness. But my need is so great, I can't even ask. After everything I did..." She couldn't finish. She looked away from him, overcome with her burden of guilt and fear.

Gently Sam pulled her close. "Oh, Taite," he cried softly into her hair, his shoulders quaking with silent tears. "Oh, Taite..."

Victoria walked to her bedroom window, pulled back the curtains, and looked out at the night sky. Below where she stood, underneath the porch roof, Taite and Sam sat in the porch swing. Long ago—on the same day he finished building it—she and Daniel sat in that same swing, speaking of their dreams, their hope for a home filled to the brim with children and love and laughter. Time seemed to stretch out ahead of them until it touched eternity.

She sat down on the window seat. Oh yes, time did stretch into eternity. She thought of Daniel and smiled. But neither of them had thought their time together on earth would pass so quickly.

When Isabel arrived, and along with her delivery the news that Victoria could bear no more babies, all the love they had saved for their houseful was rolled into one child, their daughter.

Once they were three, a perfect family, Daniel, Isabel, and Victoria. Now Daniel was in heaven, and Isabel seemed not to care one way or the other about Victoria and home. And soon the house would be sold.

She stood and moved back to the bed, unbuttoned her robe with stiff fingers, and sat down. Taite and Sam would face heartaches and challenges even greater than the ones they were trying to figure out now. Life was made up of such dilemmas.

The story of Taran and Gwynedd came back to her, and as she pulled back her covers and slid underneath, she tried to remember the rest of the story. She needed to tell Taite, that much she knew. It was something important, something that, though tragic, would help Taite understand the story of family, the story of grace.

Elusive images floated into her mind and then just as quickly disappeared as she tried to capture them. A strange fear knotted her insides. Trembling, she reached for the lamp on her bedside table and flipped off the switch.

At the very instant the light died, she saw a young shepherdess. Frantically she switched on the light again. There, sitting on the love seat, was Gwynedd, holding a lamb in her arms. Her garments seemed to be made of homespun wool in shades of brown, tattered and worn, from the bodice to the toes of her cloth shoes. She stood gracefully, smiling at Victoria as if she knew her. Inclining her head toward the window as if she were about to step through, she beckoned for Victoria to follow.

Victoria folded back her blankets and swung her feet from the bed. The girl, now standing on the window seat, beckoned again.

Victoria took one step toward the window, then froze. *What am I doing?* Frightened, she turned off the light and crawled back into bed, her heart pounding. *Has it already begun?* For a moment her fear was so great she couldn't catch her breath. Fighting the darkness, fighting to breathe again, she willed the image of the Point Solana lighthouse to fill her mind. She whispered the verse from Ecclesiastes: "Truly the light is sweet."

"Oh, my Father," she whispered, "there is never a sweeter light than that which shines after the darkness. Let me never forget your light, no matter how great the darkness."

For Taite, being near Sam that week and knowing he was there to help bear her burdens, both emotional and physical, and to listen to her fears, to hold her, made her feel she wasn't so alone in all that lay ahead.

Monday an offer was made on the house and all its contents, Tuesday the negotiations continued, and Wednesday morning Victoria signed the papers accepting the final offer. On Thursday morning, Sam drove Taite into the city to see the specialist, only to find out that the soonest amniocentesis could be performed was a few weeks into her second trimester. The doctor ordered an ultrasound and encouraged them to hold on to hope until amnio and alpha-fetoprotein tests could be performed. He checked Taite's blood and weight, recommended a high-calcium, high-iron diet, and made an appointment to see her the following month.

On Friday, J&J Movers pulled up in front of the house and loaded Victoria's few pieces of furniture: a dozen boxes of books, bedding and linens, and clothes; the old Underwood typewriter; a steamer trunk filled with keepsakes and photo albums containing pictures of Daniel and Victoria's wedding, Isabel as a baby, and nearly every milestone in Taite's life from infancy through her teens.

From the sidewalk near the J&J truck, Taite watched the movers wheel the dressers and stacks of boxes to the mechanized lift at the rear, and she worried about her grandmother's reaction to seeing her life's belongings reduced so rapidly, so severely.

But Victoria stood on the front porch, apparently at peace. "Amazing how at the end of your life," she said as Taite walked up the porch steps, "just about everything you need fits into such a small space. Yet it's somehow comforting."

"I thought it might disturb you to leave, Naini." Taite leaned against the porch railing, facing her grandmother.

Victoria looked as regal as ever, her hair swept up from her face, her clothing tailored and simple. Taite was reminded again of her resemblance to Katharine Hepburn. "I've always admired tortoises," Victoria said, smiling. "They carry everything they need on their backs. The older I get, the greater need I see for lightening the burden of things. Possessions." She took Taite's hand, and they walked together to the swing and sat down. Sam walked out the door carrying two dresser drawers. Trailing behind was one of the J&J movers, a gray-ponytailed, tattooed hulk of a man, carrying a stack of three drawers.

"I've never said so, but I always admired the way you fit most everything into your backpack," her grandmother said.

Taite laughed. "You're calling me a turtle?"

Victoria laughed with her. "You've always had your own style. Your mother tried so hard when you were a girl to dress you in the latest fashions. She couldn't afford to buy the brand names that your schoolmates had, but she worked hard to sew them for you."

Taite remembered the battles she'd had with her mother over the clothes. "They were too fussy," she said. "But until just now I didn't realize what it must have cost her to work all day, go to evening classes, then come home at night and sew. I remember hearing the sewing machine humming long after I'd gone to bed."

"Then you refused to wear them."

"It became a battle of wills. The harder she tried to fit me into her mold, the harder I resisted."

"You both were too stubborn." A shadow of regret passed over Victoria's face. "And not just the two of you, all of us were—and still are."

Taite's jaw clenched as she thought about Isabel. Too much pain, too many disappointments, too much rejection. Sam's signal that the truck was loaded came none too soon. Thankful for the distraction, she helped her grandmother to her feet.

Sam helped Victoria into the backseat of the Oldsmobile, then opened the door on the passenger side for Taite. He seemed to notice her mood, gave her a wink, and stooped to brush her cheek with a kiss. Minutes later, the truck pulled away from the curb, and Sam guided the big boat of a car into the street to follow along. As they drove away, Taite turned to have one last look at 99 Sea Horse Lane.

Victoria faced straight ahead and didn't look back even once.

Late afternoon, after the movers had unloaded and driven back into town to catch the last ferry to the mainland, Sam and Taite worked to make the cabin comfortable by nightfall, especially Victoria's bedroom on the main floor. Out came the broom and vacuum cleaner, the dustcloths and scrub rags. Sam made a trip into town for plumbing supplies and tools, then returned to set about getting the ancient bathroom into working order, and he put together both beds complete with headboards. Taite shook out the bed linens and quilts, spread the circles of colorful rag rugs on the floors, and stood back pleased at the result.

Near dusk, Sam and Taite flopped onto the overstuffed couch near the fireplace, exhausted. "One more thing left to do before we stop for the night—and right after I get a fire going," Sam said. He stood to set kindling in the fireplace, wadded some newspaper, and struck a match.

"And what exactly was that one last thing?" She grinned at him as her stomach growled.

"Dinner." He plopped down on the sofa beside her.

"Oh, I was hoping that's what it was."

"How about if I go into town for a pizza?"

"As long as it's got lots of pineapple, ham, and onions." She sighed, rubbing her stomach with a laugh. "I could eat a whole one all by myself."

Sam chuckled, his tone affectionate. "Don't tell me the cravings have begun."

"Hawaiian pizza is better than ice cream and pickles, wouldn't you say?" Then she sat forward and frowned. "Where's Naini?"

"She said she was going to sit on the porch for some fresh air." He reached the door in three long strides, Taite at his heels. "She's not here," he said, looking out into the rapidly falling dusk.

Apprehension shot through her. In her alarm, she pushed past Sam to step outside. It was growing darker now, and the wind off the ocean had kicked up, salty and biting cold. She hurried down the dirt path to a clearing, turning in a slow circle. "Naini…," she called. "Naini?" She walked a few steps and called again, louder.

Only the moan of the wind answered. She turned to Sam. "She's gone." Her heart twisted at the worry in his face, barely visible in the darkness.

"Where would she go?"

"I don't know. I should have paid closer attention to where she was while we were working," she whispered hoarsely. "If anything happens…"

"I'll grab a flashlight." He ran to the cabin.

"Hurry!" she called after him, thinking about the slippery cliffs, the sheer drops to the ocean below, the wild, pounding surf. She began to shake as the fearful images built in her mind. She pictured Point Solana and bit her lip. She knew exactly where her grandmother's heart had drawn her.

"I think I know where she is," she called to Sam.

"Where?" He slammed the front door behind him in his hurry.

"The lighthouse," she said. "The most dangerous place on the island."

19

Victoria sat on a low, flat rock near the twisted trunk of a Monterey cedar. She didn't remember walking to the point; she knew only that she was happy to be here. The wind was wild and invigorating, stinging her face and making her feel alive again. Young again. It lifted her hair, tearing strands loose from the tortoiseshell clips that normally secured it. Unexpected tears filled her eyes as the sensations carried her back in time to when she and Daniel first came to the island. How often she had come to this place, sometimes after a spat with Daniel, other times to simply sit in quiet reflection. Usually she'd come here to quiet herself before the Lord, to listen to his voice in the wind, in the thundering surf, and in her heart.

She fixed her gaze on the lighthouse at the end of the rocky point. "Father, here I am again. I thought I had given you everything in my heart all those years ago. I didn't know there would be so much more I needed to release.

"I didn't know about the fear of aging, the fear of losing my memories… I didn't know about the heartaches that would someday be mine. Father, how I miss Isabel! I love her even now, even at this great distance that divides us.

"I want to see her again…while I still recognize her face, while I still know her name. I want to see her take Taite into her arms.

"But the time is short. Already I feel my mind slipping." Waves crashed against the rocky point in a majestic rhythm, a sound so full of strength and beauty that for a moment she couldn't breathe. "I know you're with me, Father, and I'm trying not to be afraid.

"But I plead with you for the gift of time. It passes so quickly, and it seems no one recognizes that but me right now." She dropped her face into her hands.

Taite spotted her first, though in the growing darkness her silhouette was faint. The wind was almost howling now, and she shuddered with both cold and fear. Her grandmother was dangerously close to the cliffs. In daylight, they were treacherous enough; at night they were deadly.

"I see her," Sam called, a few steps behind Taite.

They trotted along the path until they reached the knotted cedar where she was sitting perfectly still, her head in her hands. Puffing with exertion, Taite sat down on the rock beside her grandmother and laid an arm across her shoulders, squeezing her close. "Naini…"

Victoria looked up in surprise. "Honey, you look worried." Then she laughed. "You don't need to be. I came here to gather strength for my journey." She patted Taite's arm and looked astonished that Taite hadn't known.

"You're freezing. You should have worn a jacket."

"I didn't even think of it, child." She looked puzzled. "The truth is, I don't remember how I got here. I just came."

As Taite helped her stand, she exchanged a glance with Sam. Slowly the three headed back up the path to the cottage. As soon as Victoria and Taite were settled inside, Sam left to pick up dinner.

Taite tended to the fire, starting the kindling again, then adding larger pieces of wood. She sat down near Victoria. "Naini, you had us worried."

"I had some thinking to do." Her eyes were bright from the adventure, her cheeks flushed from the wind. She reached back to tuck her hair into its clip, laughing as she fastened it in place. She'd never looked more normal. "It did me a world of good to find the lighthouse—even if it was dark."

"Promise me that you'll not head off on another adventure without telling me."

Victoria gave Taite a quizzical look. "It's not that I won't intend to." She drew in a deep breath as if wondering how much more to say. "You know, dear, that this is part of what we have to face. That's why I've explained to you that staying here is only temporary."

Taite didn't protest aloud but was even more determined to see her plan through. She hadn't done many things in her life that she was proud of. This might be the first thing, this caring for Naini. And she didn't intend to let go of the chance. "If you feel the urge to wander, if you're having trouble remembering things, just tell me," she said lamely. "Please."

Victoria laughed out loud. "Taite, sweetheart, it doesn't work that way." Then she quieted. "I wish it did." She stood and moved closer to the fire, holding out her hands to warm them. "Some memories are tucked so deep in my heart that I can't imagine they'll ever disappear. Others linger somewhere on the edges of my mind. I fear they'll fly away before it's too late. That's what I was thinking about, praying about, at the lighthouse. I want to see Isabel."

"I don't think it's a good idea," Taite said quickly. It would be better if her own memories weren't so vivid. "We've talked about why." She paused and stoked the fire vigorously. "I'm just not ready."

"It's not about you," her grandmother said softly. "It's true that Isabel might not be ready for reconciliation, but I must at least try to see her. I want to write to her, tell her what has happened, where we are, and ask her to come home."

Taite turned and poked at the fire again. Sparks flew upward with the chimney draft, crackling. When she spoke, her voice was softer. "She abandoned me, emotionally and physically. I think my father's accident had something to do with it, Anna's death, too, though at this point I wonder if I'll ever find out why she couldn't love me."

"She loved you then, and she does now. She's had tragedies to bear more difficult than you know. But all that's in the past, and time now is too short to worry about all that," Victoria said, surprising Taite. Always before she had agreed with her about Isabel.

Frowning, Taite sat down in the chair by the fire. "I can't just forget it, Naini. You know that."

"Grudges can become like open sores, unable to heal. You've got to let go." Her voice dropped. "Just like I've had to."

"I can't."

"If not for yourself, can you do it for me?"

"Please, Naini, you're asking me to do the impossible."

Victoria didn't let her off the hook. "True heroes," she said quietly, "are those who, knowing the impossible, do it anyway." She paused. "Just like you've already shown me about yourself."

"Me, a hero?" She laughed, tossing her dreads. "Boy, that's a new one."

"I'm talking about what's in here." Her grandmother thumped her chest. "I'm talking about decisions of the heart. What you're doing right now—keeping your baby, taking care of me. You're a hero, Taite."

"Why do I think you're about to add a *but* to that?"

Victoria smiled. "But there's more."

Taite tapped the stud above her lip. "Forgiveness? Can't do it."

"To be forgiven, we must first forgive."

To be forgiven? Taite was immediately indignant. "I didn't do any-thing to Mother," she protested. "She's the one who abandoned me. I'm the child, for goodness' sake. She's the one who needs to ask for forgiveness."

"Have you ever thought about how God is already at work, prepar-ing hearts as if they are dry, hard ground in need of weeding, plowing, and watering before the planting?" She looked wistful as she stared into the fire. Then she turned back to Taite. "We're not alone. No matter how difficult the task, he's beside us."

Taite hesitated, torn by conflicting emotions. She had enough to deal with, didn't she? The baby, Sam, her grandmother's care? How could she possibly be asked to do more? No matter what Naini thought, she was no hero.

The sound of a car pulling off the main road interrupted them. Soon the Oldsmobile's telltale rumble and crunching tires on the rocky drive told them Sam had returned. The car door slammed a moment later, and he burst into the house holding two pizza boxes and shiver-ing from the frigid night air.

"Two pizzas?" Taite stood to meet him.

He waggled a brow and set the boxes on the table. "You're eating for two now, remember? I figured I'd better get a whole one for you. Victoria and I will split the second one." He shot a conspiratorial glance at Naini, and they both laughed.

They dove into the pizza, talking of life on the island, the coming winter, and what to expect from the Pacific storms that would hit the coast beginning in December. "That reminds me," Sam said, "I ordered two cords of wood while I was at the pizza parlor. Saw an ad on the bulletin board and called the guy while I waited for the pizza to bake."

He sat back, his arms crossed. "It'll be delivered tomorrow afternoon. They said they'd stack it for you."

"It sounds like you won't be here," she said, wanting desperately for him to disagree.

He nodded slowly as if knowing how she felt. "I've gotta go back, babe."

She drew in a deep breath and closed her eyes. These extra days with Sam at her side had made her almost forget he wouldn't be there forever, that he belonged in a different world, a world she didn't think she could ever be a part of. After a moment, she looked up at him, wanting to hold in her heart the memory of his face, the line of his jaw, the warmth in his eyes. "I figured it wouldn't be too long."

"We'll talk after I do the dishes," he said, standing.

Victoria laughed. "Why is it you always volunteer when 'doing the dishes' means throwing out the paper plates?"

The sight of Sam patiently escorting Naini as she shuffled toward the fireplace made Taite's eyes smart. So tender and caring. "You two stay here and visit," Taite said, getting up to gather the paper plates from the table. "The time is short till Sam leaves."

"But I'll be back," he said, sitting down on the sofa across from Victoria. "Though just how soon depends on your granddaughter." He paused, searching Taite's face from across the room. "I think a fall wedding would be lovely."

She saw the heartrending tenderness of his gaze, but her feelings about marriage hadn't changed since the day he arrived. The obstacles remained.

A few minutes later Taite worked the hand pump at the sink, tears flowing as she waited for the water to run clear. Between the squeaks of the pump, she heard Sam walking toward the kitchen, and a moment later he wrapped his arms around her waist. "We've gotta talk, honey."

"Nothing's changed," she said.

"My being here with you this week hasn't meant anything?" He gently turned her and lifted her chin with his finger. "I'd hoped my 'love in action' would make a difference."

"Love in action?" She smiled, knowing it was true. "I've seen a new tenderness in you…" When she glanced up at him, her gaze was clouded with tears.

He took her hands from the sink full of mugs and glasses and forks and dried them with a towel. With a determined smile, he steered her to the front door where their jackets hung on a coatrack. "We're going on a walk," he announced to Victoria, "while I try to talk some sense into your granddaughter's stubborn head."

Victoria looked up from the book she was reading and laughed. "Good luck," she called after them. "I've been trying to do that for years."

They walked beneath the starry sky for several minutes without speaking. In the distance the lighthouse loomed dark, but they turned away from it toward a path that led through a small wood. When they emerged on the other side, they came to a rocky clearing on the east of the island.

Taite gasped when she saw where Sam had brought her. The shoreline lights of Carmel and Monterey Bay lined the coast, sparkling like a string of jewels. A small wooden bench had been placed, probably by her grandfather decades ago, facing the mainland near an outcropping of boulders.

She was incredulous. "How did you find this?"

"I came across it this afternoon while gathering firewood." He grinned. "Pretty spectacular, isn't it?" He gestured to the bench. "Madam?"

Taite sat down, and Sam settled next to her. She took a deep breath and began. "We can't get married, Sam. Not yet."

He hunched forward, elbows on his knees, hands dangling, and stared across the water as the night sounds carried on the wind: the lapping water below, an owl hooting softly, the rustling of a small animal in the underbrush. Finally he turned to her. "Something must be hurting you deeper inside than you've already said."

"I'm still becoming…," she began, then halted, unable to finish the thought in her own mind, let alone form the words. After a moment she started again. "Change is happening too rapidly, like a wild ride at an amusement park. I need to stop, to breathe. I can't take such an important step without, well…being certain it's the right one. All my life I've reacted instead of acted. I need time to make sure this is right."

"Are you still worried that I'm marrying you just because it's the right thing to do?"

She stared up at the night sky, misery sweeping over her. "I don't doubt your love." Turning to him, she reached for his hand. "We've talked about marriage for a long time. But before this news"—she patted her stomach—"you weren't sure enough to put a ring on my finger. Our last conversation before you left for Boston made that clear."

"Don't punish me for that, Taite. I had no way—"

She touched his lips to shush him. "I'm not blaming you, Sam. I did for a long time, but not now. I just know that if you—if we—weren't ready then, you're not ready now. You need to finish med school, take advantage of these research projects, do what you must to figure things out in your own life before taking on the burden of a wife and a child you weren't expecting."

"You make it sound like you're back to releasing me from any commitment." He sounded desperately sad.

"Maybe I am." She swallowed hard, knowing she was about to break down and cry.

"What will you do?"

"Figure out my life."

He took her hand in his and kissed her fingertips. "Oh, Taite," he whispered, his voice hoarse, "I don't know how I can go on without you." They sat in silence for a while, and then he added, his voice still low, "Is it still the guilt that plagues you?"

She swallowed hard and nodded. "Is it the same with you?"

"I think about how we let our emotions carry us away without thought of the consequences. And now, this life you carry will pay for our actions."

"Acting irresponsibly without thinking about the consequences," she said, "the hallmark of my behavior. Then reacting to those consequences and having to mop up my own mess." Tears filled her eyes, but she didn't brush them away. "That's what has to change in me, Sam. I guess I just need to grow up." She pulled his hand close and laid her cheek against it. "The scary thing is, I don't think I know how."

"Promise me this isn't good-bye," he said, gathering her into his arms. "Promise me."

"I just need time," she said, melting against the warmth of his chest.

He pulled back after a moment and, tilting her chin upward, bent to touch his lips to hers. His kisses were feather soft at first, then he covered her mouth with his lips. "I love you, Taite Abbot," he murmured, his lips brushing against hers as he spoke.

She wrapped her arms around his neck and gazed up into his eyes. "Nothing will ever change my love for you, Sam. Nothing." Her words came out in a choking whisper. Burying her face in his neck, she breathed a kiss and tasted the salt of her tears on his skin.

Then with a small cry, he crushed her to his chest so tightly she wished he would never let go.

Sam and Taite left the cabin before dawn the next morning. As his ferry pulled slowly into the bay, Sam watched her walk out to the end of the dock, her dreadlocks bouncing in the wind, her long skirt billowing and snapping like a parasail. She was still waving and blowing him kisses when the ferry glided around a bend in the shoreline and she disappeared. Anguish lodged in his heart.

"That little gal sure looks like she'll miss you," said a voice near Sam.

He turned to the older man standing near him at the starboard rail. He grinned. "Not half as much as I'll miss her."

They talked companionably about the weather, the island, and time and distance to the mainland. They had almost reached the wharf when he took Sam's hand and introduced himself. "Doc Firestone," he said with a nod. "Pleasure to meet you."

"Name's Sam Wellington." He laughed. "Hoping someday to have 'Doc' precede my name."

The man brightened. "You're in med school?"

Sam nodded. "At USC, though I'm doing part of a year-long fellowship in Boston right now. Flying back this afternoon."

Doc Firestone leaned one arm against the rail. "What specialty are you going into?"

"Not sure," he said. "Research has always intrigued me."

"I thought so myself once upon a time," Doc said with a chuckle.

"Didn't take me long to figure out that the endless hours in a lab setting just weren't my cup of tea." He laughed. "I mean not my beaker of H_2O." He laughed again. "Sorry."

Sam couldn't help grinning. He liked the man already. "You practice here on the island?"

"I'm the only game in town."

"I hope you're not planning to retire soon."

Doc raised a brow and laughed. "You want me to wait until you're ready to take over?"

Sam held up a hand, palm out. "No, no! Not my meaning at all. Plus I'm fairly certain that a small-town practice isn't, ah…" He couldn't bring himself to say it.

Chuckling, Doc slapped him on the back. "Isn't your beaker of H_2O." Then he sobered. "You'd be surprised how rewarding this little practice is. You might stop by sometime. I'll show you around."

"I'd like that." He paused. "What I started to say earlier is that my girlfriend and her grandmother have just moved to the island. I'm glad to know you're close by. "

"We'll take good care of them," he said. "I'll let Gracie know to watch for them. What are their names?"

"Victoria Kingswell and Taite Abbott."

Sam wondered if he'd imagined it or if he'd seen a flicker of recognition in Doc Firestone's eyes. He started to ask, but the doctor was approached by two friends from the island, and he moved off with them after a friendly wave to Sam.

As the ferry bumped across the choppy waves, he relived the velvet softness of Taite's lips. He closed his eyes against the pain of missing her; the slicing wind dried the tears that squeezed from the corners of his eyes.

That night, while a Pacific storm wailed, Taite sat with Victoria by the fire. She had been worried about the roof leaking, but even after all these years, her grandfather's workmanship held up well. The stout, solid cabin didn't creak or groan; only the windows rattled from time to time in the stronger gusts.

"Mercy," Victoria said, raising a brow at a particularly strong blast from the wind. Then she laughed, glancing up at the twin oil lamps on the mantel. "At least we don't have to worry about the power going out."

Taite laughed with her. For days she had been meaning to tell Naini her plan. She took a deep breath. No time like the present. "There's something that's taken hold of my heart," she said, "and won't let go."

Her grandmother laid aside her book and leaned back in her chair.

"Storytelling," Taite said, glancing at the old Underwood sitting next to the Welsh letter box. "My dream has to do with storytelling."

"The family stories? That's quite a gift...of time, of commitment." Victoria didn't look as pleased as Taite expected.

She rushed on. "It's high time someone in the family did it. That's one of the reasons I wanted to bring you here, be with you before..." She couldn't finish.

"Before my memory fades?" Victoria's expression said she didn't want, or need, sympathy.

"You taught me not to beat around the bush. So, well, here it is: I want to write down the stories you tell."

Her grandmother still looked puzzled. "Why not use a tape recorder?"

Taite quirked a brow. "You know me; that would be too easy." Then she sobered and leaned back, trying to read her grandmother's expression. "There's something inside me just itching to write the stories. Not record them the way a stenographer would. But tell them from the heart—the way you do." She smiled. "With all the flourishes and emotion that you put into them."

Victoria stilled and grew even more serious. "Did you know that that's how we all do it? How each generation retells the stories? They become uniquely ours in the telling." She paused. "It isn't easy. In some ways it's a burden."

"I didn't think it would be easy," Taite said quietly. "You never told me that each generation gives the stories a different spin." She didn't hide her disappointment. First she discovered her grandmother's illness had some role in the stories, now this. "You never told me," she repeated.

"I didn't, did I?" A half smile now played at the corner of her mouth. She looked enormously pleased. Her eyes sparkled as if she were savoring a secret. "Have I ever told you the old Welsh saying about riches?"

"No."

Victoria grinned. "I have a sudden hankering for popcorn and storytelling. While I fix the popcorn, I'll tell you about the riches of the Welsh. The riches of your heritage."

Taite followed her into the small kitchen. She reached for two bowls as Victoria pulled out an iron skillet and placed it on the stove. She measured oil and popcorn and dumped them into the pan, put the lid on, and turned up the damper.

The kitchen, lit by a single oil lamp, was cozy and warm, with a fire crackling in the old-fashioned iron stove and the popcorn just beginning to sputter. Soon it gathered force and rose to a lid-pinging, fragrant clatter. Taite melted a small pan of butter, and picking up a potholder, she moved the skillet to the warmer at the back of the stove.

Taite scooped the popcorn into the bowls as they stood at the counter. "You were about to tell me about the riches of the Welsh."

"Ah yes," Victoria said, daintily digging into the popcorn bowl. "Listen to this…and keep it in your heart always."

"I'm listening."

With a merry look, she quoted:

> To be born Welsh is to be born wealthy.
> Not with a silver spoon in your mouth,
> But with a song in your heart,
> And poetry in your soul.

Taite reached for a handful of popcorn and took a crunchy, buttery bite. Outside the rain poured down, beating on the roof, sheeting off the windows. Naini bustled back and forth, setting a tray with the popcorn bowls, napkins, and soft drinks. Then holding the tray, she took a few steps toward the door. She glanced back to see if Taite was following. Her face reflected the glowing embers in the kitchen stove…and the simple joy of the moment. She had never looked so beautiful.

"I'll remember," Taite whispered.

20

For weeks Gwynedd followed the North Star during clear nights, sometimes finding it easier to keep moving in the cold and sleep in forested clearings in the daytime. From time to time she discovered villages the marauders had not touched and was brought in by friendly families, given food and a warm bed and worn but clean and mended clothes. When she reached the edge of Ridley Wood, a farmer gave her a goat when he learned of her mission, then farther down the road, a widow, hearing of Gwynedd's plight, presented her with a donkey. The shaggy brute was old but gentle of spirit and carried her without complaint.

Rumors of Gunnolf's merciless advance toward Caer were whispered in nearly every village, and by cook fires in thatched-roof dwellings, Gwynedd told and retold the tale of the attack at Han-mere, until she could spin the tale in her sleep. She found deep satisfaction in storytelling, something she'd always left to Taran. By the time she reached Farndon at the River Dee, news of her arrival had preceded her. It was the first time—and many would follow—that villagers left their homes and came to the road at the village gates to greet her, eager to hear of the Han-mere battle and to see for themselves this brave young woman on her mission from God.

She tried to dispel rumors of her bravery, finding them embarrassingly untrue, but the legend of her courage seemed to race like wildfire, fueled by people's desperate need to believe their God had not forgotten them in their struggles. In the village of Trevalyn, the villagers were astounded to find she was alone; they had heard she had gathered a small army to lead against Gunnolf to rescue her own true love.

When the hours of sunlight grew longer each day, and she had traveled through two full moons, her sickness began. At first it was the smell of cow dung and peat fires that triggered the emptying of her stomach. Then, at first light, no matter if she was sleeping in a hayloft or upon a feather tick, she heaved the contents of her stomach, even when there was nothing to heave.

At first she thought she had obtained traveler's sickness from bad water or perhaps, worst of all evils, Saint Anthony's fire, though the bread she had been given had not contained rye seed, the usual cause of death from the malady.

On the morning the sickness left her, she noticed a nesting sparrow and smiled, at once certain of the cause of her discomfort. She set forth on that day's journey with new hope in her heart and firm resolve in her step. Once she reached Caer and was quit of her mission, she intended to go after Gunnolf's army, even if it took a lifetime.

When she reached Cynwyd-Cilcain, the villagers met her, this time with terror written on their faces. Two swift riders from Trevalyn had told them of her approach a fortnight ago, and they knew of her mission. They had also heard the tales told by an old woman who was said to be a witch.

The toothless old woman, stooped and carrying a walking stick, touched Gwynedd's garment in a way that made her halt in midstep. "What is it, old woman?" she asked gently.

"It came to me in a dream," she said in a quavering voice, "a pretty young woman with child would walk this way, and that I was to warn her."

Gwynedd swallowed hard. She had told no one of the babe she carried, and her tunic hid the small bulge in her stomach. How could this old woman know such a thing about her? "And what else did the dream tell you?" She tried to sound calm, but a chill slithered up her spine.

"Do not go directly to Caer, but go a different way—to the sea itself."

"Your eyes have never seen the sea, old woman," a grizzled man shouted from the back of the crowd. "How can the way be known by the likes of you?"

"I saw a sailing ship in my dream," she said, glaring at the man. "Where could it be but on the sea?" She turned to Gwynedd again. "'Tis as true as I tell you. As real as I am standing here, this sailing ship and its cargo of human lives." Her lined face seemed to take on the sorrow of the world. "They suffer, dearie," she whispered, close to her ear. "They wait for you."

Gwynedd shook her head. "'Tis Caer that awaits me. For 'tis my mission, clear told and true. I cannot change my course now. I cannot delay." She touched the old woman's hand. "But I kindly thank you for caring enough to speak up, old woman. I prithee, remember me in your prayers." She turned to leave, leading her donkey by a tether, the goat following along behind.

She had gone only a few steps when the old woman called out, "'Twas a shepherd who told me true, m'lady. He said to tell you he is with you to this day."

Gwynedd stopped, thinking she had not heard the old woman aright. Around them the villagers' voices fell silent, sensing a change in the old woman's credibility. "Who told you?" she whispered, drawing closer and looking into the woman's eyes.

"A shepherd," she said and described him.

Warm tears came to Gwynedd's eyes as the old woman described the same shepherd Gwynedd had seen near the ruins of Han-mere Abbey. "And he is with me still?"

The old woman nodded. "And you must know this," she said, moving close enough for Gwynedd to see the flame of love for God in her eyes. "I am no witch. I am a woman of God. I would go to a priory to spend the rest of my days if my legs had the strength to carry me there. Instead, I have given myself to God in prayer, here in this village, in my home." She gestured to the villagers, who hung back looking fearful and worried. "When our Lord answers and people are healed, or when storms miss our village or Gunnolf's army skirts us, they blame it on witchcraft, no matter how I tell them otherwise." She touched Gwynedd's cheek tenderly and gave her a toothless smile. "Go to the sea. Take the road to Pen-y-ffordd," she said. "I will pray for you and the wee one in your womb. Godspeed, m'lady. Godspeed."

Gwynedd nodded and was on her way, this time taking the road that led northwest to the sea. But as she rode the donkey and led the goat on a tether, a dark forest rose before them, appearing sinister even from a distance. She grew fearful of the old woman's words. What if she was wrong? What if she was a witch, using trickery to lead her astray? She reached the edge of the deep wood just before dark. No villages lay close enough to ease her heart of fear; no welcoming fires burned in cheery thatched homes.

She found a clump of early green grasses for the animals, then looked for firewood at the forest's edge. The branches that had dropped to the ground were too large to burn, so she walked deeper into the tangle of trees, looking for twigs and dried branches of the right size.

Dusk and thick branches shaped like grotesque arms and hands caused her heart to knot in fear. She glanced back toward the patch of grass where the donkey and goat grazed peacefully, gathered up her courage again, then moved farther into the forest. She had taken only a few steps when she heard what sounded like a groan. At first she thought it was a wild animal and turned to flee.

Then it came again, and she halted. The sound was human. She moved closer, almost tiptoeing on the bed of decaying leaves. Again the moan carried from the deep wood. This time she hurried toward the place, just beyond the fat and gnarled trunk of a giant tree.

"*Os gwelwch yn dda...*" The words were clear this time, and she breathed a sigh of relief that they were spoken in her own language. For a moment she worried her Lord might have required her to be a good Samaritan to one of Gunnolf's men.

Touching the trunk of the gnarled tree, she squinted into the dusky shadows at its foot. All she could make out was a bundle of cloth, seeming empty of human life. "Who's there?" she asked in a shaky voice, every tale of haunted woods coming back to her.

" 'Tis but a weary traveler," came the tired voice. "I fear I've twisted my foot, and I am unable to travel any longer. I lay down here to die, urging my fellow travelers to carry on without me. Great danger they faced, and I could not have them tarry."

The voice sounded familiar. Puzzled, she moved closer. "Cadwallen?" She was afraid to hope. "Brother Cadwallen of Han-mere?"

He blinked, peering up at her through the darkness. " 'Tis I indeed." Then his lined face broke into a weak smile. "Is it Gwynedd herself?"

"Herself." She knelt beside him, cradled his shoulders with her arm, and helped him lean back against the trunk. She sat on a squat stump beside him, frowning at his sad condition. "Tell me what has happened and what are your needs."

"Gladly, dear one. But first, there is a spring just beyond the stand. Could you help this old man stumble to the place for a drink? I have crawled to the pool three times, and methinks I have not the strength to do it again."

"Better than trying your strength once more," she said, "I will retrieve my earthenware cup and bring the drink to you."

He nodded and, sagging against the tree, closed his eyes. Gwynedd returned to her pack of goods, retrieved the cup and some provisions, and ran back into the forest. Then she found the spring of clear water and brought Brother Cadwallen his drink. "An answer to prayer, m'lady," he said, his voice thick with emotion.

" 'Tis God who brought me this way," she said, and told him about the old woman's dream. "If not for her, I would be nearing the road to Caer Abbey by now."

He nodded slowly. "My companions, a handful of villagers of Han-mere, are not two days' journey from here. They, too, are traveling to the sea to rescue their children, wives, husbands, or parents who've been taken by Gunnolf and his army."

"We will find them," she said. Then she paused. "Why did they leave you? Surely not because of your foot."

"They did not desire it, but I insisted. They had no horses, and one lame among them served only to slow the party down." He gave her a gentle smile. "And you must leave as well, dear child."

"Several villages back a widow presented me with a donkey for my mission." She gave him an affectionate nod. "Methinks finding you was part of my mission. We will bind your foot so you are fit to travel, find a walking stick, and then mount you atop Eirin Mair."

His smiled widened. "Eirin Mair? Gooseberry?"

She laughed. It had been so long since her heart had been merry she'd almost forgotten the sound. "And my goat's name is Mêl."

Cadwallen leaned back and laughed with her. "Allow me to guess. You named her 'honey' for her sweet disposition? She does not kick when you milk her?"

"She does not kick at all, and her milk is sweet as honey," she said. She unbundled her food, provided by the villagers in Cynwyd-Cilcain. She drew out a hunk of dark bread, broke it in two, and gave Cadwallen half. "I have already milked Mêl today, but on the morrow we shall have fresh, sweet milk." Next she pulled out some cheese and again broke it to share. "God has provided," she said.

"Still your heart sorrows," he said, seeing through to her soul.

"Aye."

"For your Taran, for your family?" He tore off a chunk of bread, chewing while she answered.

"Taran and I remained after you left us. We waited until we thought it safe to leave the cave, then slipped out to find devastation beyond our worst night terrors." She went on to explain the events that followed and told him how she had retrieved his ring and why. She pulled it from beneath her tunic and, after holding it in her palm a moment, handed it to him.

He held it, examining it with a slight smile. " 'Tis your wedding ring, Gwynedd of Han-mere. Did you not know?" He gave it back to her.

"I had not dared to hope," she said, feeling a sting of tears in her eyes, as she retied the cloth that held the ring. "My heart is full of gratitude for your care, then and now." When the ring hung safely around her neck again, she bundled her supplies and stood. "We should get back to the animals. If they wander off, we will be afoot once more." She could see them through the clearing, still calm in the falling dusk.

Cadwallen leaned against her, and slowly they moved to the edge of the wood. She settled the monk near the animals, then headed back into the forest for firewood. She had just reached for the last of those branches she needed when the sound of pounding hoofs caused her to drop the armful of dried branches and hurry back to Cadwallen.

He had struggled to stand and now, leaning against a small tree, pointed down the road toward Cynwyd-Cilcain. A man on horseback was riding like the wind, his tunic flapping behind him. When he spotted Gwynedd's small band, he waved frantically and turned his horse toward them.

"Caer has fallen," he called to them when he halted, his horse dancing sideways nervously, "and Gunnolf is headed this way. Take cover!" And he was off to warn the next village.

Brother Cadwallen met Gwynedd's gaze. She could not stop herself from trembling. He reached for her hands. "Do not be afraid," he said quietly. "God has been with us each step. He is with us still."

" 'Tis more for my loved ones I fear than for myself."

He nodded slowly, "And for the life you carry inside."

She dropped her face to her hands then, and she wept. "Aye," she whispered, "for that most of all. More precious than my life—or beloved Taran's—for it is part of us. Perfect, because my babe is fashioned by God, like no other…a gift of love from him to us." She looked up at him tearfully. "Is it heresy to believe my wee babe is a miracle of life within me?"

Brother Cadwallen put his hand on her shoulder. "Not heresy at all. Scriptures tell us that your child is 'fearfully and wonderfully made,' " he said, first in Latin and then in Welsh. "And covered by the very hand of God within your womb. Rest in this knowledge, dear Gwynedd: you, your child, and Taran, too, no matter where he is, remain in God's keeping. None of you is hidden from him."

21

Isabel twisted her hands, breathless in her nervousness, as the gallery doors opened and the first of the London patrons entered. Her midnight blue Armani gown was exquisite, her dark hair perfectly waved and artistically bobbed, her sapphire earrings sparkling. The tender music of the madrigal singers' medieval chants carried through the gallery from where they performed in the champagne reception room. The lighting set off her Sacred Doorways paintings in a way that caused an almost spiritual hush as people approached them.

Everything was perfect. So why did her old insecurities pick today to rush into her heart, making her want to run from the gallery and hop on the first plane to San Francisco?

Taking a deep breath, she moved in among the crowd, looking more confident than she felt. She shook hands with lords and ladies, commoners, and other artists. Three newspaper reporters arrived, and she spent a few minutes with each, answering questions about her artwork and inspiration. A reporter and camera crew from the BBC came in midway through the evening, and she spent a half hour answering still more questions and smiling into the camera until her cheeks ached.

Weeks earlier the rumors had begun about the Queen asking for a private showing, though no official request ever came. But almost at closing, a limousine pulled up to the outer entrance, and a few minutes later, with great fanfare, the Queen's son Edward and his wife, Sophie, the Earl and Countess of Wessex, appeared in the lobby.

Isabel curtsied as the countess approached, Edward following a few steps behind. She was taken immediately by the genuineness of them both but especially by Sophie's friendly manner and knowledgeable questions about the Sacred Doorways. After they'd spoken a few minutes, Edward excused himself to view the paintings. Sophie asked about the painting *Mary*, which had been featured in the London papers, and they walked together to where it hung in an alcove by itself.

The expression on Sophie's face as she beheld Mary seemed to capture the same emotion that Isabel had felt when she had painted it: a mother's longing, love, and heartache. She stood so still and for so long, obviously moved by the painting, that Isabel slipped away to give her a few minutes of solitude. Not long after, their limousine pulled to the door, and the earl and countess passed through the gallery crowd, said their good-byes, and were gone.

After the rave reviews by critics had died down, the transactions completed for three five-figure sales, and arrangements made for another showing in six months at the same gallery, Isabel quietly made inquiries as to the protocol for making a gift to members of the royal family. The day before Isabel left for Hanmer, Wales, *Mary* was sent by special courier to the countess.

Isabel was still basking in the wonder of the Sacred Doorways exhibit as her dark BMW headed northwest to Wales. The driver had picked her up just after dawn, and now, after passing through Oxford, Cheltenham, and Worcester, they were nearly to Whitchurch where they would turn west toward Hanmer.

As the fields and hedgerows passed, she settled into the luxurious leather seats and let her gaze sweep across the landscape, empty of man-made structures. Always in the back of her mind when she traveled to Wales was the question of how the topography might have changed since the ancient days. She squinted into the fading light, imagining the people who had trodden the broad meadows and virgin forests. Her forebears probably walked along this same route on a path now buried beneath centuries of soil, plant decay, and crumbled dwellings of thatch and mud.

Their bones lay here too, hidden in the rich earth of their homeland. Perhaps in church graveyards, perhaps in grassy fields such as this where they fell in battle.

She looked out across the autumn grasslands of sepia and pale gold, beyond the ribbon of road that stretched to the horizon, and felt a beckoning. As if drawn to a place she should know.

This was her third trip to Hanmer, and she was surprised that each time she returned, the sense of homecoming grew stronger.

She was still basking in the strangeness of it all when the driver's voice broke into her reverie. "We're nearly there," he called over his shoulder. "The village road is just beyond the next roundabout."

The sign said six kilometers to Hanmer, and the driver slowed and swung the car left onto an even narrower road. Ten minutes later he pulled into the parking area for the Hanmer Arms, the country inn where she had reservations. He parked, then got out and rounded the back of the vehicle to open her door.

Isabel stepped outside and stretched. Darkness was settling in, the air was brisk, and a light drizzle fell, but it didn't matter. She turned a full circle and breathed in the scents of wood smoke and damp hay and the robust fragrance of something roasting inside the inn.

The driver removed her bags from the trunk, or boot, as it was called in the U.K., gave her a nod, and followed her to the entrance. The innkeeper, Albert, spotted her through the glass and, with a wide smile, opened both sets of double doors for her to enter. She hurried through and, after his words of welcome, shook his hand; the driver followed, wheeling her bags behind him.

Karen, the innkeeper's wife, was standing behind the desk and greeted her warmly. "It's good to see you again, Isabel." Her Welsh accent was musical.

"You have no idea how good it is to be out of the London craziness."

"Ah, but I think I just might," Karen said with a grin. "I lived in the heart of the city while at university. I used to complain to my mother how backward Hanmer is, but I was never so grateful as the day I returned home—as a bride with a man content to leave the big city for life in the country." She tapped a few keys on the computer. "We've held your favorite room for you, Isabel. Room seven—on the end, upper level."

"Perfect. And my friend Adam will be joining me in two days."

"You requested room six for him?"

"Yes."

Karen consulted the computer, then looked up with a smile of relief. "Charlie took the reservation. He's new. I'm glad to see all is in order." She retrieved a key attached to a small square of wood from the row of cubbyholes behind the desk and handed it to Isabel. "The dining room is closed, but we're still serving in the pub."

Isabel glanced across the now-closed buffet into the pub. In the U.K., pubs were gathering places for families, more like cafés in the States. When eating alone, she preferred the bright, friendly atmosphere of the Hanmer Arms pub, the chatty Welsh servers, and the unfailing friendliness of the families at tables near her as they commented on the inclement weather, upcoming country fairs, or church services, or asked about her accent.

Turning back to Karen, she grinned. "Actually, I think I would have chosen the pub anyway."

Karen chuckled. "Only the locals know the same chef prepares for both rooms."

"And as I recall, it's gourmet."

"Indeed. Our chef trained in the south of France."

Albert wheeled her luggage along the outside corridor to her room, a cozy Welsh country-style space, the kind that brought a sigh of contentment the moment she stepped inside. A small stone fireplace graced one corner. It was flanked by two worn tapestry chairs, each with two pillows depicting scenes of cattle and sheep, a shepherd and shepherdess standing watch nearby. Someone had laid wood for a fire, and before Albert left, he lit the kindling and pulled the screen closed.

An hour later she entered the pub for dinner. Lively chatter, mingled with laughter and the music of children's voices with their lovely Welsh accents, filled the place. She chose a booth near the street entrance, and after a moment Karen spotted her and left the front desk to join her.

"There's someone here very interested in your heritage," she said, sliding into the booth. "I told him you'd be checking in tonight. He said he might stop by for a visit." She grinned. "Just wanted to give you a bit of advance warning."

Isabel was pleased that Karen remembered the connection to Hanmer; she had mentioned the Americanized version of her family name, Hamner, on her last visit.

"It's our new vicar," Karen said, a sparkle in her eye. "Like me, he was born and raised here. He then left for a few years, only to return as the vicar at Saint Chad's."

"Is he a Hanmer?"

"No. But he's done some research recently on two of the original families, the Hanmers and the Kenyons. The descendants are instrumental in the upkeep of the church. They still own the town."

"This place, too?" Isabel asked, raising a brow.

Karen chuckled. "And everything around it. Each of the town's one hundred twenty-six houses, our country store, and the petrol station. Those of us leasing from Sir John Hanmer line up once a month outside the inn's doors to pay rent."

Isabel was surprised. "I'd heard they still owned the town, the mere, and all the land around it, but it never occurred to me that they might still be operating it like the feudal system."

"I suppose it does seem a bit archaic to outsiders," Karen agreed.

"Both names are in my family tree—the forebears of Nicolas Hanmer who came to America in the 1600s. We've traced our ancestry to the youngest of his four sons."

"That's why we welcome you with open arms," Karen said with a grin. "You're our long-lost American cousin." She stood. "I'll give your order to the chef, if you like. Tonight I recommend the wild mushroom and bacon fricassee in a phyllo basket for an appetizer and the chicken breast stuffed with Camembert and apple, drizzled with walnut sauce, but make sure you save room for one of our homemade desserts. The tiramisu with amaretti is superb."

"I don't even need to see the menu. It sounds delicious, but if I'm going to save room for dessert, I'd better forgo the appetizer."

Karen left for the kitchen. A moment later the street door opened, and with a cold blast of wind a young man stepped in and closed his umbrella. He greeted the servers by name, and as he was unbuttoning his trench coat, Karen returned from the kitchen.

Her smile broadened as she approached him. They spoke for a moment, then she led him to Isabel's table. "Isabel," she said, "this is the vicar of Saint Chad's—Father James Warner." She glanced toward him and added, "James, this is Isabel Abbott from the States."

Isabel stood to shake his hand. "Father Warner…" He had a wiry, athletic look.

He motioned for her to sit down. "I don't want to disturb your meal," he said. "And please call me James. All my parishioners do."

Karen laughed. "When anyone calls him 'father,' he looks around to see who we're talking to."

"Please join me," Isabel said. "Have you eaten?"

He sat down. "My wife is home fixing supper, and I daren't be late. But I was wondering if you might like to stop by for tea tomorrow. That is, if you're not busy."

"I would love nothing more."

"You see, I've come across a letter that might interest you. It has a direct connection to your family in the New World, a legend that ties us all together. Saint Chad's was founded nearly a thousand years ago. Though we've lost many of the records in fires from time to time, many remain intact. But this letter…" He shrugged. "I won't get into it now. I'll explain tomorrow."

"My mother used to tell me stories from those times. I didn't pay much attention, but lately…" Her voice dropped off as she thought about the peace she felt here, the people with whom she felt a growing kinship. "Lately I've wondered why I didn't listen more closely." She leaned back. "I'm always skeptical of histories put together by people who research their family tree in a way that fulfills their wishes, embellishing as they go."

"That's always the danger. It is strange, though. We have people arriving here from Australia and New Zealand and, of course, the States. Some do find their roots; others just spend a delightful holiday in Hanmer and throw in the towel, as you Americans say."

A tall, teenage girl, her hair twisted into a loose knot, her lean figure sporting a turtleneck knit top and dark jeans, approached the table, balancing a large plate on her forearm and a breadbasket in her hand. James stood and nodded first to the girl, calling her by name, then to Isabel.

"Around three tomorrow, then?" he said to Isabel.

"I'll look forward to meeting your wife and hearing about the family tree."

He paused. "I think you'll be surprised," he said. Then he turned and moved to the entrance, drew on his trench coat, and picked up his umbrella from the rack. With another quick wave, he slipped out the door.

The next morning Isabel donned her jeans and a heavy sweater, a hooded down parka, and hiking boots. She stopped by the dining room for a quick breakfast of poached eggs and toast, then headed outside for a walk around the mere, taking a mug of coffee with her.

The day was overcast and windy, and though the rain had stopped during the night, the ground was soggy. She kept to the winding one-lane road that led through the village. Lining both sides of the road were homes of red brick with peaked roofs. Here and there were scattered thatched cottages with half-timbered sides of wood and plaster. In the distance stretched the gray mere ringed by leafless trees. A swan glided across one end of the lake, causing Isabel to wonder briefly why it hadn't yet followed its kin to the Canary Islands or some other wintering ground. Stubborn, she supposed, and for some reason, she thought of Taite.

She imagined her daughter standing there with her, looking out across the gray waters to the stretch of empty fields beyond. She wondered what it might be like in spring, when the daffodils painted the landscape gold, or in summer, when the earth awoke with vibrant life—dragonflies, starlings, chaffinches, and robins. She would have loved to invite Taite to join her someday, but in her heart she feared the answer would be a haughty, "Are you kidding me, Mother?" Sadness descended on her, and she turned away from the scene. How could love cause so much pain?

On a small rise to her left stood the square tower of Saint Chad's, rebuilt in the sixteenth century after fire had destroyed it a second time. When she had visited Hanmer on previous trips, she had been unable to stay through Sunday, and on weekdays the ornate gate leading into the churchyard had been locked. But that was before the new vicar arrived. James Warner might have a different policy.

She headed up the winding road to Saint Chad's and tried the gate. With a click it swung open, and she stepped inside. A brisk breeze had kicked up, and in the east the sky looked lighter as if the sun were trying to break through. Surrounding the church were ancient grave markers; the more recent ones, less than a hundred years old, stood tall and straight among older ones in various stages of decay—some leaning, some crumbled, others little more than rubble.

Fascinated, Isabel wandered among the more recent, kneeling to read the carved names, surprised at the number of Hanmers and Kenyons. She rounded the church to the back, where the obviously ancient markers lay. Celtic crosses—some crooked, others curiously upright even though centuries old—were interspersed among the crypts and monoliths. Three blackface sheep grazed in a patch of grass around one of the oldest-looking graves, and a scatter of chickens scratched the bare soil near a half-dozen others.

Isabel headed across the uneven damp ground to the marker where the sheep were grazing and tried to make out the name on it. The last name was almost certainly Hanmer, but the first was too worn to read easily. She could make out "GWY... WYF OF..." The rest was illegible.

It made no sense to her, and she turned away. With so many centuries of Hanmers, there were surely dozens, maybe hundreds, of such markers. Though the first letters of the name reminded her of the stories her mother once told, they didn't bring to mind a name.

She turned away with a sudden shiver as the wind whistled through the graveyard. She jumped in fright as a rabbit bounded from behind a stone pillar. She giggled nervously and pronounced it the Hanmer hare.

Slowly she circled the church, stopping to study the markers, then moving on. When she reached the entrance, she climbed the stone steps, again with the eerie feeling that she was being drawn into this place. The tall wooden double doors were unlocked. Somehow she wasn't surprised. Without hesitating, she pulled back on the iron handle, and the door opened with a groan.

She halted in awe just beyond the doorway. The sanctuary was utterly silent and glowing with a pale kaleidoscope of color from the stained-glass windows. The stone floor seemed to swallow all sound, even her footfalls, as she crossed the back of the sanctuary. She stood for a moment at the center aisle, taking in the wooden beams, the family chapels that lined the room, each set apart with ornate ironwork. Turning, she looked up at the sign on the rear chapel. The name "Kenyon," in bronze, marked the family's private chapel, the largest in the sanctuary.

To the right of the altar, a smaller chapel caught her attention, and she headed down the aisle to have a closer look. Just as she suspected, it was the Hanmer family chapel. A long altar stood inside, an open Bible at the center of its linen-covered surface, a single unlit candle at each end.

Curious, Isabel stepped inside. A window depicting Christ praying in Gethsemane cast crimson, royal blue, emerald, and golden hues across the Bible. After a few minutes, she started back through the ironwork doorway leading to the main sanctuary.

But as she turned toward the raised pulpit, a plaque at the outside entrance to the chapel caught her eye. Written in old English script, the words were difficult to follow at first.

Isabel caught her breath as she reread the words, slowly taking them into her heart.

HANMER FAMILY BLESSING

Almighty God, our heavenly Father,
fill these your beloved children with faith,
virtue, knowledge, temperance, patience, and godliness.
Knit together in constant affection your son Taran of Han-mere
and your daughter Gwynedd of Han-mere
from this day forward.
For their children, their children's children,
and for all who will follow through the ages:
turn the hearts of parents to children,
and the hearts of children to parents.
So enkindle fervent charity among them all,
that they may evermore be filled with love one to another
as members of your family through
your Son, Jesus Christ our Lord.
In the year of our Lord, eleven hundred and thirty-two

Could it be that this blessing belonged to her family? Astonished by the idea, she stumbled back into the main sanctuary and sank into the nearest pew. The prayer, a blessing from someone unknown, had been meant for this family, her family, in 1132 and down through the ages.

She couldn't take in the wonder of it. *Turn the hearts of parents to children...the hearts of children to parents...* Her mother's image came into her mind, followed quickly by Taite's. Her wonder gave way to the realization that her relationship with them could not be anything other than what it was right now. The pain ran deep, too deep perhaps for both her and Taite. And then there was Victoria, in the middle, a role that she could use to bring about healing. Yet she chose to keep things as they were: status quo as always.

Sitting in the hush of Saint Chad's, Isabel tried to rid her heart of bitterness. She had asked forgiveness more times than she could count. She had emptied her heart before the Lord, begging him to heal them all. Yet had she been willing to drop career and London life and return home, to literally go the extra mile? It was easier to pray than to act. Such honesty shamed her.

She lifted her gaze to the altar, to the place where on Sunday the sacraments would be served, the body and blood of Christ, given for her, a life once dead, now gloriously alive. His life. Hers.

In him all things were possible; she knew that in her head. She only wished she could believe it in her heart.

The vicar's wife, Terri, met Isabel at the door of the vicarage and, with a warm smile, welcomed her into the cozy country home. It was located in the shadow of Saint Chad's and the school just opposite the church property where James served as headmaster. While they waited for him to return from the school, Terri showed Isabel her studio where she dyed and spun yarn. The wool came from her prized herd of Australian Corriedale sheep, raised on their small acreage just outside town. Many of her sweaters, hangings, and throws were on display, and Isabel could see why her work had won awards at country fairs throughout Wales and England.

James came through the door just as school let out, the shouts and laughter of children drifting behind him from across the grounds. When he saw Isabel, he smiled and extended his hand. "I'm so glad you could join us," he said and motioned for her to join them around the kitchen table.

Isabel was touched by the informality and felt more like family than a guest. Terri put on the kettle and pulled out the canister of tea. "Hope you don't mind that it's not English," she said, pulling out a variety of herbal tea bags. Isabel didn't mind; in fact, it was a refreshing change.

"Leftovers from living outside my home country," James said, sitting down beside her at the table. "We've got into organic gardening, baking our own breads, keeping away from red meat and caffeine. A bit odd, I suppose, since we live in sheep and cattle country."

"Not to mention turning our backs on the Earl Grey tradition," Terri said with a chuckle as she sat down opposite Isabel. "We provoke some raised eyebrows from time to time, but"—she laughed again, exchanging a glance with her husband—"for the most part people seem to accept us for who we are."

James talked about their return to Wales after years away, the progress of the school since he had taken charge, and the new spirit of warmth at Saint Chad's. "We're working on the interior rooms," he said as Terri poured their tea. She carried the mismatched mugs to the table on a tray with a pot of honey, then returned to the counter for a plateful of zucchini and carrot breads. A small crock of sweet butter was placed beside it with three delightfully misshapen antique silver spoons.

James slathered butter onto a slice of bread. "We've redone some of the chapels, and oh my, did they need it!" He took a bite before continuing, "And now we're starting on the small room just off the vicar's office. We have records there dating back nearly a thousand years. Most are copies. Let me correct that. I would say all are copies of the records kept at the cathedral in Chester—a city called Caer in medieval times." He took another bite and looked thoughtful as he chewed.

"This is delicious," Isabel said to Terri.

She laughed and gave James a loving look. "Thanks to my husband, the bread maker in the family."

"Terri finds the recipes on the Internet, prints them out, shops for the ingredients. Then I get the pleasure of putting them together." The love between them was obvious.

"But back to my housecleaning at the church," he said. "After you were here last time, Karen mentioned your ties to Hanmer. Your mother's family is from Wales, yes?"

"Yes. Centuries ago."

He nodded. "I remembered that one of your forebears was a neighbor to Thomas Jefferson in Albemarle County, Virginia."

Again she agreed. She didn't know much about her family history, but she had somehow tucked away that fact and had mentioned it to the innkeepers. "True."

"That's what caught my attention as I was going through the records. It makes your branch of the family stand out from the others, so I thought you might be interested in what we've discovered."

She leaned forward in interest. "Having to do with Thomas Jefferson?"

"He's mentioned only in passing. It's about a letter from your American ancestor Nicolas Hanmer written to his second cousin, Jenkin Hanmer, here in Wales. A very interesting letter. Nicolas mentions almost in passing that he and Thomas Jefferson were both vestrymen at Saint Anne's parish in Williamsburg, and he refers to a meeting they had both attended the night he penned the letter." He paused. "But the more interesting fact is that he refers to a letter he received from Jenkin Hanmer that tells some little-known details of the legend of Gwynedd and Taran of Han-mere."

"Those names I do remember," Isabel said. "My mother is the keeper of the family stories. She must have mentioned them."

"The young couple was instrumental in saving some irreplaceable ancient manuscripts. We know they existed and were the first to adopt the surname Han-mere, which later became Hanmer."

"Which then became Hamner in the New World," Isabel added. "The name was changed, we think, by a clerical error in one of the early census records."

"Apparently, from what we can deduce," James said, "Nicolas was the grandson of Humphrey, the first Hanmer to sail to the new country. Humphrey's birth records are here at Saint Chad's, and his death is recorded in Virginia."

"You mentioned the legend… Is there some mystery to it?"

"Yes, there is." He sat back as Terri poured steaming water into their cups and passed around the basket of tea bags. "The abbey that once stood on this very ground was destroyed by an invading force from the north. The Vikings had conducted their predatory raids centuries before, and this group was led by the legendary Gunnolf, a descendent of Eryk, an early Viking warrior. Vengeance might have been his motive. We don't know. Maybe he wanted to bring back the glory of the earlier years. I suppose much like the neo-Nazis today imitating what they see as the power and glory of Hitler.

"They arrived by sea and set upon the abbey, killing the monks who worked here and the men who tried to defend this little village. Those they didn't kill, they took captive as slaves, including the women and children. A few escaped, unknown to the young Taran and Gwynedd who were hiding in a cave not far from here. Eventually, even Taran was caught in Gunnolf's snare."

The story was familiar, but sitting on the ground where the abbey actually existed made it come to life.

"From what we know, some were willing to give their lives so that others might be free," he said. "Even the young bride Gwynedd faced death to save her beloved Taran."

"So the end of the legend is known, then?"

"There was a fire at Saint Chad's in the early sixteen hundreds. The interior was destroyed, all but a small section. The loss was devastating. Many of the early birth and death records had been transferred to the cathedral archives in Chester, so not all was lost."

"But the end of the story…"

"That's where you come in. No one knows what happened to Gwynedd after she sacrificed everything to free the others."

"But the family line…"

He nodded slowly. "There was a child—she and Taran had been given the rite of marriage by a monk at the abbey. But no one knows how that child survived or if Gwynedd lived to raise the child or even to see Taran again."

"And you think my branch of the family might have the answer?"

He laughed. "It's a long shot, I know. But perhaps in the National

Archives or at the University of Virginia where Jefferson's papers are kept, maybe at Saint Anne's in Williamsburg, there might be a collection of Nicolas Hanmer—or Hamner—letters. We think that the collection might include the letter from Jenkin to Nicolas—and will give us the missing details of the story."

Terri laughed. "What he's trying to do is to get you to do some sleuthing for him on the other side of the pond." She patted her husband's arm. "He's something of an amateur historian, and he's got a vested interest in this too."

"Let me guess," Isabel said. "You're a Hanmer too?"

He raised a brow. "I'm a descendant of Jenkin Hanmer," he said with a chuckle. "So, cousin, I'm hoping to enlist your help."

"I spend most of my time in London or on the Algarve coast," she said tentatively. "So I can't promise how soon I might be traveling back to the States. It's been a number of years since I was last there."

"You don't have family in the States then?" Terri said sympathetically.

Isabel sipped her tea as silence fell between them. "I do, but we're estranged." Outside, voices rose into the evening air as people passed by the vicarage on the main road. A child laughed, and the sound was followed by the loving murmur of a woman's voice.

"I'm so sorry," Terri said.

"Is the situation something we can help you with?" James asked gently.

Isabel drew in a deep breath. "Just pray," she said, "that the family blessing from centuries past might still be true for us today."

"For their children, their children's children," he said, as if in prayer, "and for all who will follow through the ages: turn the hearts of parents to children…"

"Yes," Isabel whispered, her eyes filling.

"And the hearts of children to parents."

Outside, some schoolchildren had begun playing a game of cricket just beyond the vicarage, and their squeals and laughter filled the air. Through the kitchen window, in the dim light of dusk, she could see a lone little girl sitting off to one side. Dark-haired and slight, even bundled up in sweaters and woolen scarf, she reminded Isabel of Taite.

She looked back to Terri and James. "Maybe it's time for me to think about going home."

22

After she left the vicarage, Isabel walked along the mere before supper, praying for the courage to face Taite and Victoria. She looked out across the waters rippling in the moonlight. A low mist came off the lake and drifted among the barren trees, obscuring the village, and then lifted again, showing the glow of lights in the cottage windows on either side of Main Street.

Her thoughts returned to Taite, their estrangement, and the story of the past that she rarely considered; it was too painful. But if healing could come, and it must, she had to face those difficult years and her own culpability in what had happened between them.

First there was Anna. She stopped by an old-fashioned street lamp and swallowed hard. The child had been so easy to love: sweet-tempered, bright, curious, affectionate. When Taite came along, completely Anna's opposite, she quickly let it be known that she was her own person: prickly, stubborn, prone to temper tantrums. Everything Isabel saw in herself and didn't like, she also saw in Taite.

Brady adored both his daughters, but there seemed to be something in Taite that tugged at his heart and made him laugh. Even when he no longer spoke to Isabel, he showered Taite with affection. After Anna's illness and death, she and Brady should have sought help, but they chose to plow through the process on their own, keeping up appearances on the outside, dying inside a little more each day. Now, thinking back on it, she realized that if they had talked to a grief counselor or if they had been surrounded by the love of a church community, perhaps Brady would have kept on trying.

By the time he died they were hardly speaking to each other. He'd begun spending more after-hours time at his office, sometimes working into the early morning hours, and attending weekend conferences. What Isabel didn't know was that to dull his pain he'd started drinking and gambling and had taken up the fast life that went with it. One winter night his car slid off the road into the rain-swollen Sacramento River. She found out later he'd seen their accountant that afternoon, and they were penniless. He'd gambled away everything, including their house.

Taite seemed to change once her daddy died. She became calmer, which was a relief to Isabel, who had too much to cope with—the loss of her home, Brady's debts to pay, and her fears that she didn't have the resources to take care of herself and Taite. She hadn't finished college when she and Brady married, and she'd never worked outside the home. If her mother hadn't stepped in to help with Taite, she never would have made it through those years of working two part-time jobs and completing her degree. She saw Taite slipping further away from her emotionally, but she thought that once the hard work was done, they could start over.

After graduating with honors in art history, she landed her first real job at the upscale Kensington-Peters gallery in San Francisco. She threw a party to celebrate, for getting through, but mostly for Taite as a thank-you for putting up with her Mom with a Mission, or MWM, which was what Isabel had jokingly called herself those years.

She expected Taite to be proud, to celebrate with her. Mostly, she wanted Taite to know how much she loved and appreciated her. By then Taite, who was in her early teens, already seemed to be drifting. But Isabel didn't worry; now she could be a full-time mom, at least in the evenings and on weekends.

She also had the mistaken belief that she had set an example for Taite of persistence, hard work, and dedication. She didn't realize until it was too late that her daughter held Isabel up as a measure of her own failure.

She planned the party to celebrate their new life, and she wanted it to be memorable. She rented a small room off the main restaurant at the top of the Mark Hopkins and sent invitations to Taite's friends with instructions to keep it a secret; she invited Adam and only a few of her friends—for after all, this was to be Taite's night. She kept her list small, inviting one of the executives from the paper, a friend of Adam's, the gallery manager, his wife, and Victoria, who asked to bring along some of her close friends. There were about fifty altogether. It would cost a fortune for the sit-down dinner and live band, a little young and wild for older tastes, but she knew Taite and her friends would adore dancing to their music. Such an expense was far beyond her means, but figuring the outcome would be worth it, she borrowed the money from the bank. She enlisted Victoria's help and asked her to take Taite shopping, supposedly on a lark, to buy special party dresses for them both.

When Taite came in after her day of shopping, her cheeks were the color of roses. She went on and on to Isabel about Naini's generosity, her no-expense-spared attitude about buying their dresses. Her eyes were bright with wonder, but there was also something new in her attitude toward her mother. Isabel should have seen the warning sign— Taite's pointed look as she talked of the sacrifices her grandmother had made through the years.

"You're lucky I turned out as well as I did," Taite said with a toss of her hair. "Being abandoned the way I was."

The night of the party Isabel had arranged for a limousine to pick up Taite and Victoria and to bring them to the Mark Hopkins.

Dressed in sweeping deep-garnet silk and jeweled sling heels, she stood by Adam's side at the entrance to the restaurant, waiting for the elevator to open and her daughter to appear. Behind her, in the Crystal Room, Taite's friends had already gathered.

Things had been strained between them for too long; this occasion, Isabel just knew, would change everything. Taite would see how much she was loved, and their closeness would blossom at last.

The elevator opened. Standing inside, her grandmother at her side, Taite looked confused, agitated. As soon as she helped her grandmother from the elevator, she headed stiffly toward Isabel without so much as a nod to Adam.

"What's going on here?" she demanded with a frown. Her voice echoed in the large room. At the corner of her vision, Isabel saw the *Register* executive cast a quizzical glance toward Adam. Standing a few feet away, Isabel's new boss from the gallery looked embarrassed as she watched the interchange.

Taking a deep breath, Isabel put her arm around Taite's shoulders and led her a few yards down the exterior hall. "Taite," she said quietly, "this party is for you."

"Yeah, right," she said, scowling at the Kensington-Peters woman. "You're just trying to impress your new boss." She laughed, shaking her head. "Pathetic."

"Taite, I'm ashamed of your behavior tonight."

She shrugged. "Like you should care."

Isabel felt the tears begin as a sting in her throat, but she willed herself not to cry. Taite was a still a young teen, and her behavior showed it. Troubled and unsure what might come next, Isabel forced her voice to remain calm, light. "Okay, step through the door and check out the guest list. If you still think this is all about me, I'll eat my handbag." She tried to laugh, but it came out dry and falsetto.

"It's always about you, Mom. Ask Naini. Ask anyone. Always has been. Always will be," Taite muttered, but she turned around and stomped, stiff-shouldered, into the Crystal Room.

Isabel followed, feeling sick. Adam fell into step with her. "What's wrong?" he mouthed as they headed into the dining room.

"I-I think Taite may be a bit overwhelmed," she said, not wanting to get into it. He didn't ask any more questions. She just wanted the evening to be over.

She stood back and watched her daughter walk haughtily across the empty dance floor to a cluster of her friends. She looked anything but happy. In the background the band played, but no one seemed inclined to dance. Suddenly she wondered if the music was all wrong. What did kids listen to these days, anyway? The restaurant manager had recommended the group, telling her they were popular among teens. But maybe he didn't know what he was talking about.

Isabel drew her shoulders straight, willing herself to make the best of a bad beginning. She marched toward the band, signaled the leader to drop the volume, and then she took the mike. For days she had planned what she would say to Taite in front of the group. But now she paused, unsure of her thoughts and words.

"Friends," she finally began, "tonight's party is in celebration of my daughter. It isn't her birthday—or Christmas or any other holiday— but it's a gift from the heart to say, 'Thank you, honey, for all you've done to help me through these hard years. I couldn't have done it without you.'"

There was a smattering of applause, and now even Taite's friends looked uncomfortable. Taite looked as if she'd just swallowed a thundercloud. Awkwardly the band started up again. At a round table in the back of the room, Victoria sat with her friends, all of them shouting to be heard over the music. One held her hands over her ears, a couple others shrugged and gave up talking, and Victoria shook her head as if in dismay over what Isabel had wrought.

Adam walked over to stand beside Isabel. "Are you okay?"

"Other than having thrown away several thousand dollars and wishing the ground would swallow me up, I'm fine."

"Teenagers," he said.

"True."

"The head server was by a few minutes ago and asked when you want dinner served."

"The sooner the better."

"I'll tell him."

Adam left Isabel's side at the same time Taite started toward her. Relief settled over her like a warm cloak. Taite would apologize and reach out and hug her the way she used to when she was a little girl. She smiled to encourage her daughter.

But Taite didn't meet her eyes. Instead, face straight forward, chin almost jutting, she marched past her to the doorway. Isabel followed her into the hall and caught up before she reached the ladies' room.

"Taite," she said, "what's wrong?"

"You just don't get it, do you?" Her daughter's eyes were brimming with tears, her face twisted in anguish. "You ruin everything. You always ruin everything." Her tears spilled, trailing down her cheeks.

"Honey," Isabel said softly and reached out to gather Taite into her embrace.

Taite's arms flew up, palms straight out. She pushed Isabel backward, not hard enough to make her stumble, but hard enough to make her heart ache with pain. One explosive single-syllable word from Taite completed the assault.

Isabel almost doubled over, her pain was so intense. Her first thought was that she couldn't survive the night; her second was that she had to. She wanted to get on the elevator and go home. But the guests she'd invited, the guests who knew this whole night was for her beloved daughter, waited inside.

So she pasted on a smile, patted her hair, and swept back into the room. Strangely, her daughter did the same. Soon the dinner was served, the nonalcoholic champagne flowed, the laughter began, and so did the dancing. Not once did Taite speak to Isabel or she to her daughter the rest of the evening.

The next morning before Taite left for Naini's, Isabel said, "What was last night all about?"

To her credit, Taite looked pale and sad. She spoke in a low voice that almost sounded ashamed. "I've got a news flash, *Mother*," she said. "It's not always about you." And without another word, she was gone.

Things were never the same between them after that night. Isabel played it over and over again in her head, knowing that her daughter's offensive behavior had more to do with her early life than with a single party. It had to do with Isabel herself, her failure to provide the emotional stability her daughter needed, her failure to love her enough. It hadn't been about Isabel ever, but Taite would never understand what it had been about.

Now, as she walked back toward the Hanmer Arms, she brushed away her tears. She hadn't realized she still cried when thinking about that night. She did know one thing. If she had it to do over again, she would give up her art, give up her world and everything in it, if she could only have Taite's love again.

Adam and Isabel sat in the dining room at the inn, lingering over a breakfast of yeast rolls, homemade berry jam, and Devonshire cream as they watched a light drizzle fall on the paved lot outside.

"Thanksgiving in Wales," he declared with a grin. "What's on the menu tonight?"

She laughed. "Karen said they'll serve us turkey and dressing if we'd like, but the chef does a much better job with duck. He prepares it with honey and cinnamon and serves it on a bed of wild rice and spiced berries."

He grinned. "I'm hungry already."

Their talk shifted to his trip to Lisbon and what he had accomplished during his three days there. She told him about visiting with the vicar and his wife, nosing around in church records, strolling along the mere, and finding the blessing that was meant for future generations of Hanmers.

"I'm thinking about going home soon," she said. "I just want to make sure God's timing is in this. When I've tried to approach Taite in the past, all my hopes and dreams for reconciliation have blown up in my face. I don't want it to happen for either of us again."

"It's been my experience," Adam said gently, "that when God keeps me from acting, it's usually because he hasn't completed a work he's doing in my life—or in the lives of those he wants to touch through me. Taite—and you—have needed extra time for him to work in your lives separately."

"There have been those dark days," she confessed, "when I've thought he'd turned his back on me. That the alienation was a direct result of my not being the full-time mother she deserved when she was little." Her voice dropped. "Punishment, I suppose, for my failure to love Taite as she needed to be loved."

Adam didn't look surprised. He knew her well. "You've thought that God was punishing you through Taite's actions?"

"I did for a long time. It's been a long journey for me to get beyond self-condemnation, and even so, I've hardly begun to understand God's mercy and forgiveness." She took a sip of strong, cream-laced tea. "I thought my failure at the one job more important than any other surely meant God's displeasure with me. After all, how could I hold my head up in his presence with all the muck and mire I carried in my heart?"

"He is the lifter of my head," Adam said, paraphrasing the psalm.

"Oh my, yes." She nodded and poured them each another cup of tea. "I can't earn his acceptance; I can't come close. It's finally sinking in that he loves and accepts me just as I am." She paused. "Oh, the feelings of guilt are still there; they'll probably always be." She smiled at him over the rim of her cup. "But I've also found a sense of grace that covers my false steps, stumbles, and wrong choices."

"They're part of being human," Adam said.

For weeks Taite spent every spare minute at the typewriter playing with words and images, drawing her scenes from the rich tales her grandmother had told. At the town's small library, she checked out armloads of books on writing and on the ancient history of England and Wales. She pored through them, hungry for knowledge and itching to actually begin her novel. She had been an honors student in school, but never had the quest for learning grabbed her mind the way it did now. Often in the middle of the night, she lit a lamp and sat down in front of the typewriter, which she had moved to a small table beside her bed. The *thunk* of keys and the soft *ding* of the carriage return seemed to speak to her in some secret heart language.

She became a regular at the Ink 'n Quill. The proprietor, Marihelen Westrick, took an interest in Taite, offering her a discount on lined pads, pencils, erasers, paper, and typewriter ribbons. When she found out that Taite was writing a novel, she insisted on making a gift of a white board and markers so she could keep track of scenes and characters and time passage. Marihelen also recommended a small writers group on the island led by Linda Sue Udell, the well-known mystery author.

A whole new world opened up to Taite, and she couldn't get enough of it. On her first visit, she was too intimidated to read the few pages she'd written the week before. But by her third visit, Linda encouraged her to read. She got through one page, her voice quaking with nervousness. The group applauded, and she flushed with pleasure.

After that, she couldn't wait for her weekly meeting. She set the goal of writing ten pages a week and to her delight found that some weeks she wrote fifteen. Then there were those weeks she struggled to get through three.

She began studying characterization and realized she didn't know what she was doing. The same thing happened with dialogue. Discouraged, she started rewriting and editing, wadding up pages, throwing them on the floor, and starting over again. She wrote chapter 1 twelve times, and still, she knew it didn't work.

"Writing is rewriting," Linda told the class. "It's part of learning your craft. Part of becoming."

The other writers in the class became her friends: Tillie, who wrote historical romance; Pearl, who wrote contemporary suspense; Noah, who was writing his life story for his grandchildren; Claire, who wrote and illustrated children's books; and Earl, a retired attorney working on a legal thriller. Once in a while Marihelen stopped by to join the class and read her poetry, the kind that brought both laughter and tears.

And her new friend Susan, the pastor's wife, joined the group a few weeks after Taite did. She began work on *Murder in the Box Hedge Maze,* the first book in a series of horticulture mysteries. Susan and Taite spent many wintry afternoons sipping tea in Susan's shop, Wild Thymes, talking about writing, and discussing novels they had bought secondhand at Books 'n Such, three doors down.

Victoria had her good days and bad, but the island air and her short walks near the cabin seemed to brighten her spirits. There hadn't been a repeat of the episode when she had wandered off, and Taite breathed a little easier when she left Victoria alone.

One night two months after the move to Pelican Island, Taite and her grandmother sat near the fire, Victoria reading, Taite jotting down thoughts on a yellow pad. Taite grinned, sighing as a tiny baby arm or foot bumped across her stomach. She rested her hand on the place and giggled, only to sense what felt like a somersault as the baby skittered to the opposite side.

Victoria looked up and raised a brow. "The butterflies are coming more often now?"

"More like a little kid doing jumping jacks." She grinned and patted her stomach.

A month ago she'd called Sam from a pay phone in town to let him know she didn't want the amnio tests. It had been the jumping jacks that clinched it. How could she possibly think of ending her baby's life after she'd felt him tumble and turn and skip and jump? How could he not be healthy? Sam reluctantly agreed but urged her to have an ultrasound, which she did. She watched the monitor with awe as the fuzzy image showed her baby sucking his thumb and blinking. But there were no somersaults and backflips that day, and gender couldn't be determined. Not that Taite minded. She was certain she carried a boy.

In the same conversation, he told her that he had been accepted into the Stockholm program and was struggling with his decision to go, worried about the timing and wanting to be with her. She cried all that night in her bed, visualizing, in graphic detail and terror, the research he was about to conduct. When she thought of their child and the horrible mistake she had almost made, she wept even harder.

The next morning she drove into town and called him just as he was leaving his room for class. He listened in silence as she voiced her objections to the overseas research, explaining why she thought it was wrong because it was illegal here, trying to appeal to the logical side of his brain. For a moment she thought he might decide to turn down the grant. "It's for our future," he said finally, sounding terribly sad. "It's a prestigious grant, awarded to top students."

She wanted to tell him about her fears, her nightmares about the babies, the graphic reality of what he was going to do that brought on heartache so acute it became physical pain. But she couldn't bring herself to say the words.

For several days they didn't talk, and she wondered if he was avoiding her or if something inside him was dying. How could he consider dissecting a human embryo and not kill a part of his soul?

Naini's voice brought her back to the present. "I'd like to go into town with you tomorrow."

It would be good for Victoria to get out. She smiled at her grandmother. "I'd love to take you by the Ink 'n Quill to meet Marihelen. I've told her so much about you."

Her grandmother nodded. "Let's save that for another time. Tomorrow I would like to meet Doc Firestone."

Taite frowned, her heart skipping a beat. "Have the symptoms gotten worse?" She had seen Doc twice for prenatal checkups and had told him about her grandmother's condition. He'd said he would be glad to see her for symptoms not related to DLB but that Taite should take her to the mainland to her neurologist for regular visits.

"I just want to meet him, get acquainted. After all, he is our hometown doctor now."

Victoria looked paler than usual the next morning and fell asleep twice on the ride to the clinic. After they parked, Taite left her grandmother in the car while she spoke to Grace about getting Victoria in without an appointment.

Grace looked up as Taite approached the counter. "You're absolutely glowing, Taite," she said with a smile. "How are you feeling?"

"Never better." She patted her stomach, now round with life, and grinned. "Though my profile seems to change every day."

"I didn't know you had an appointment scheduled."

"It's my grandmother. She wants to meet Doc Firestone." She sobered. "There may be another reason, though she's trying her best to assure me otherwise. I'm worried. She hasn't looked well lately."

"He'll be in a little before nine." Grace glanced at the clock, then looked back to Taite. "Why don't you bring Victoria inside where she's more comfortable? We'll work her in before the other patients arrive." She glanced at Taite's round stomach and smiled. "How about if I help you with Victoria?"

They walked to the door, and Grace opened it to let Taite step through. "I think I told you that I attend Chapel by the Sea. Your grandparents are well loved here. The old-timers are eager to see your grandmother after all these years. But they understand her ill health, so they haven't been pushy."

They crossed the parking lot to the car. Before Taite opened the passenger door, Grace touched her arm. "We would love to have you join us at church some Sunday," she said, "you and your grandmother.

Please come. It's an informal service, full of love and joy and singing."

"Thanks, but no thanks," she said with a half smile. Susan had invited her too, but her condition ruled it out. Church was for saints, not sinners. Naini would fit in; Taite wouldn't. That was that. "Maybe some Sunday I'll surprise you," she said to Grace, "but not now."

Victoria smiled at Doc as he sat down on a wheeled stool across from her. He picked up a blank chart and began writing as he asked questions about her health.

"I can have my neurologist send my file," she suggested when he was finished.

"As I told your granddaughter, I'd prefer that your neurologist continue to follow you closely. But I can handle anything else that needs more immediate attention."

She considered his words for a moment, wondering how much she should say about her new symptoms. She didn't think they were related to DLB, but she couldn't be sure. "I'm experiencing some shortness of breath," she said. "It's become worse over the last few weeks."

The lines on his face deepened. He stood and stepped toward her, hooking on his stethoscope. He thumped her chest and back, asking her to breathe in and out slowly. Then he took her pulse, returned to his chair, and made some notes.

"Is there anything else?" he said, frowning as if he knew.

"A feeling of pressure when I'm lying flat," she said. "Like there's a boulder on top of my chest, a butterfly inside it."

He nodded and again scribbled something on her chart. "I think you'd better make the trip to your specialist immediately. Will you promise me you'll do it soon?"

She looked at him evenly, lifting her chin. "I'd rather not. Isn't there something you can prescribe here?"

"I don't have the facilities for your care. If I order tests, you'll have to go to the mainland to have them done. Your specialist knows your background and can recommend the best care."

She tucked a loose strand of hair into her chignon. "You don't understand, Dr. Firestone. DLB leads to dementia; I've done a lot of study on the disease, and the last stages are…"

She let her voice trail off. He nodded, understanding in his eyes.

Clearing her throat, she began again. "The visions are increasing, coming nearly every evening at dusk. I try not to say much to Taite, because she gets frightened for me. The dreams are bad, so vivid I think I'm part of the nightmare landscape."

He made notes on her chart, then looked up again.

"It's my fading memory that causes me the most distress. Sometimes I forget where I am and why I'm there." She leaned forward. "For right now, I just want to be comfortable; I want to live every day to the fullest. But as for prolonging my life, no thank you."

He sat back, concern clouding his eyes. "Maybe you should have those charts sent," he said quietly. "Your memory loss," he said gently, "does it seem to be increasing?"

"I cover it up as best I can for my granddaughter's sake. And about this other—the breathing problems that I'm assuming are heart related?—I'd rather she not know…"

He wrote out a prescription and handed it to her. "This will make you more comfortable." He stood and offered his hand.

"Thank you," she said. "And remember—no one is to know."

"With one exception," he said. "I would like to talk with your neurologist. Grace will have the release form ready to sign on your way out."

"And no heroics when it comes to the end. I would like that in writing too."

He patted her hand and smiled. "That will mean more paperwork, but it's fairly simple. I've got a living will in my own file. It's especially wise in your case."

Victoria warmed to the kindness in his eyes. "Thank you."

In London, Isabel spent two weeks wrapping up the details of the exhibit. She met with the curator to go over details for the next Sacred Doorways showing, met with her accountant to analyze her projected profit and expense margin, and declined an invitation to take tea with Sophie, the Countess of Wessex, at Buckingham Palace, which was to take place the same day as her flight to San Francisco.

She had scheduled the trip carefully: she would arrive the week before Christmas and spend the holidays with Victoria and Taite if they were willing, with Adam if they weren't.

It was early afternoon when she checked her luggage at Heathrow, and two hours later the plane was banking into its polar route. And eleven hours later, after several airline meals and snacks, the jet circled San Francisco to line up for landing. Isabel stared out at the Bay, the Golden Gate Bridge, and the brilliant sky with its scattering of clouds. She made her plans to rent a car and drive directly to Crescent Bay and the house she grew up in, the big Victorian that had always symbolized home.

She didn't know where her daughter was now; last she had heard, Taite was renting a guesthouse in San Francisco and working as an aide for the elderly. But no matter where Taite was, Isabel had no doubt that her mother would be in Crescent Bay. She thought about calling first but decided to surprise her by simply knocking on the door.

She settled into a new calm as the plane touched down smoothly on the runway. An hour and a half later, after dealing with customs, retrieving her luggage, and finding the rental car agency, she was driving south. But when she pulled up in front of 99 Sea Horse Lane, she stared at her mother's home in surprise. It was nearly dark, but she could make out its new coat of paint, yellow with white trim and dark green shutters, and the landscaping that looked professionally done.

The gate to the side yard had been removed, and just beyond where it used to stand was a children's swing set. And three young children, bundled in sweaters and jeans, were swinging and laughing and calling out to each other.

The porch light came on suddenly, and a young woman Isabel assumed was their mother came through the front door, glanced at Isabel's car, and then called the children inside for dinner.

Isabel got out and walked up to the woman just as she was turning to follow her children into the house. "I-I'm looking for Victoria Kingswell…"

The woman brushed her strawberry blond hair from her face. "Oh yes, the former owner."

"I'm sorry, did you say former owner?"

"Yes, we bought the place from her three months ago."

Isabel looked up at the lovely home, almost too weary to speak. She'd endured the long flight and a kick of adrenaline during her drive from the airport, but now the disappointment of her mother's move and the fear she might not find her caught up with her. Her knees threatened to buckle.

"Are you okay?" the young woman asked. A little red-haired boy clung to her leg, watching Isabel with big eyes.

"Yes," Isabel finally said, "I'm just surprised. I didn't know she planned to move. Do you know where she lives now?"

She shook her head. "I'm sorry. She never said."

Isabel turned to leave, but the young woman said. "You might check at the real estate office. I'm sure I've still got one of their cards if you'd like to take it."

"Yes, please." She waited while the woman headed into the house, the boy trailing along behind, sucking his thumb.

She returned after a few minutes, holding the child on her hip, and handed a business card to Isabel. "This is the agent who handled the sale. He may not know either, but it's a start." She glanced at her watch. "You'll probably have to wait and call first thing in the morning."

"Yes, thank you," Isabel said. "I'll do that." She opened her car to slide behind the wheel.

"Oh, one more thing," the woman called to her and then hurried to the passenger door as Isabel lowered the window. Still holding the little boy, she bent to peer inside at Isabel. "I did hear that when the seller moved out, she was with her granddaughter. It seems she was in poor health."

Apprehension shot through her. "Victoria or Taite?"

"I didn't know the granddaughter's name. But it was the older woman, Victoria." She hesitated. "It sounds like you know them well."

"They're my mother and my daughter," Isabel said.

A girl with curly pigtails called, "Mommmmeee," from the front door.

"Thank you for your help," Isabel said as the woman straightened to walk back into the house.

She turned and nodded, her little boy now resting his head just beneath her chin, his arm wrapped around her neck. Isabel watched until the young mother entered the house and turned off the porch light, all the while thinking about the tender, sweet smells of toddlers when they are still small enough to cuddle against their mothers' necks, their puppy-dog scents after playing in the sun, their powdery sweetness after a bath.

She could hardly breathe for the pain in her heart.

23

On the mantel, next to the place of honor where Taite had placed the antique letter box, her new cell phone played a Mozart aria. Her heart skipped a beat as she crossed the room and picked up the phone, a birthday gift from Sam a week earlier. They spoke every morning at dawn, sometimes again in the late afternoon. Mostly she left the Stockholm research question alone now that the time was approaching for his departure; she figured it would come up again, causing the same sadness on her part, the same stiff response on his.

"Hey, sweetie," Sam said. "I'm on my way to class but wanted to check in." He was breathing hard, as if he was sprinting across campus. "How are you feeling?"

"Great," she said, smiling. "I'm certain our little guy has already started playing basketball. Knows how to jump and dribble. Maybe a slam dunk."

Sam laughed. "Maybe our little guy is really a little girl, and she's skipping rope."

"Or maybe *she* is jumping and practicing her dribbling. A future WNBA star."

"We can't have her interested in sports only," he said. "I want her to be studious, too," he said. "Are you reading to her every night?"

Taite settled deep into the easy chair, a pillow supporting her back, one arm draped across her large, round stomach. "I picked up some books of poetry at the library right after you mentioned it the first time. Robert Louis Stevenson for one, and a funny collection called *Where the Sidewalk Ends.* And I'm sure the baby's listening to Naini's stories." She hesitated, glad her grandmother had gone outside to sit on the porch so she could speak freely.

"You still there?"

"Yeah. I was just thinking about her storytelling. In some ways her stories are more dramatic than ever." She paused, musing aloud about the worries that plagued her. "But the visions are also more vivid. She doesn't always tell me when the ancient ones come to her, but I see it in her eyes, the wonder on her face. Sometimes she tells me what they're doing. Mostly it's Gwynedd who comes."

"I've done a lot of study on DLB since I was there. She's exhibiting the classic symptoms of stage two."

"I know stage three's the worst, and I keep holding my breath, hoping she's not close."

Sam's tone was soothing. "It sometimes takes years to reach the worst of it…"

"Dementia." Her voice broke as she spoke the word.

"You okay?"

"I was just thinking how frightening dementia must be in the early stages. When you know your memory is fading and there's nothing you can do about it."

"Does she seem scared?"

"Now and then I see the fear in her eyes, just a flicker, before it disappears. Last week she told me that Gwynedd sometimes beckons to her, wants her to follow. She looked so scared when she told me how much she wants to go. It's as if she knows she's hallucinating, but it shorts out in her brain somehow. She said it seems perfectly logical to go with Gwynedd." The baby bumped across her stomach, and she followed the skittering with her fingertips. "She said that quite often Gwynedd is as real to her as I am." She started to cry.

"Oh, honey…"

"I-I'm okay, really. I just think how frightening this must be for Naini."

"And for you."

She fought to keep her tears under control. "Yeah, me, too," she finally managed.

"Maybe it's time to think about Happy Acres. You could visit her every day."

"Not yet," she said. "I know it will come eventually, but she's still as normal as blueberry pie most of the time. We can wait."

They fell silent for a moment, both evidently thinking about Victoria. Then they both started to speak at the same time.

"When are you—," Taite began.

"What music are—" They laughed together. "You first," Sam said.

But Taite wanted to put off her question. "No, you go," she said.

"I was going to ask about music. The same study I told you about earlier suggests that unborn babies respond to different kinds of music, different beats, that sort of thing."

Taite was touched at his interest in their baby. "I found a second-hand radio in town. It's battery operated. Gets one radio station, classical from San Francisco."

"Classical?" He sounded amused.

"Our baby seems to especially like Beethoven," she said. "He almost danced across my stomach to something called the *Emperor* concerto." She had never heard it until a month ago, and now, when she did catch it, her spirits soared. She had called the station three times to request it.

"I'm at my building, Taite," Sam said. When he spoke again, his voice sounded thick with emotion. "What you're doing…," he said and then stopped to clear his throat. "All you're doing…for our baby, for your grandmother…" His voice dropped. "Talk about a class act…"

Quick tears came to her eyes. "Thank you," she whispered. A heartbeat passed, and she almost asked him to come home. But she couldn't bring herself to say the words.

Sam cleared his throat again. "Well, I've got to get inside. It's snowing out here for one thing. Class begins in ten minutes for another."

"Thanks for calling, Sam."

"Oh," he said before she could say good-bye, "you were going to ask me something a minute ago. What was it?"

She swallowed hard. "I-I was going to ask about Stockholm," she said. "Do you have your ticket yet?"

He didn't answer right away. "Yeah," he finally said. "I'm leaving a few days before Christmas." She heard a door slam in the background.

"Just before Christmas?"

"The fellowship begins the day after. I'll need a couple days to sleep off jet lag, get my bearings."

Silence hung between them again.

"Oh," Taite finally said, willing herself not to cry.

"Well, class is about to begin, Taite," he said. "Gotta go. I'll call you later."

With a click he was gone. Taite flipped the top to end the connection and laid the phone back on the mantel. A lonely restlessness settled over her.

Victoria came inside for a sweater, complaining of the chilly morning. She halted a few steps from the door and frowned. "Is something wrong, honey?"

"Sam flies to Stockholm right before Christmas." Taite sank into a chair, elbow on the padded armrest, and let her forehead drop into her hand.

Her grandmother settled into a chair beside her. "Maybe it's time you told him that the two of you must work things out."

She looked up in surprise. "I thought you agreed with me that my life needs direction first." She managed a smile, even quirked an eyebrow. "You're the one who said, 'One dysfunctional person plus one dysfunctional person equals two dysfunctional people, not one healthy, whole person.' Well, add an innocent baby to the equation, and you'll someday have three dysfunctional people."

With a chuckle, her grandmother settled back. "Sometimes I should keep my mouth shut," she said, her eyes bright. "And when I made that pronouncement, it was before I saw what you could accomplish if you set your mind to it."

"You mean my job?"

"I mean everything about you these days."

Taite's cheeks warmed at the compliment. Her grandmother wasn't one to give them lavishly. "It's not a real job...a career, I mean. But it will be enough to take care of the baby and us." She grinned. "As long as we don't order pizza too often."

She had landed a dream job at Happy Acres. It didn't pay much, probably never would, but she and the baby would be covered with full medical benefits, a godsend since she knew firsthand the horrors of healthcare without insurance. For years to come, she would be paying a little each month toward her hospital visit. Grace was chairman of the board and had been delighted when Taite made a proposal to help the residents write their family stories. She worked with small groups once a week and collected their stories as they wrote or tape-recorded them. When Grace found out Taite planned to type each one on her manual typewriter, she set up a small office, complete with an old computer, in a room once used for storage.

For the first time in her life, Taite felt she was doing something she believed in. Most people just wanted someone to listen to the stories of their life, what defined them and gave them dignity. Maybe that's all she had wanted through all these years. Someone to listen.

She would give that gift to others. She would be their listener, their recorder. Their voice long after they ceased to speak.

"It is a real job," her grandmother was saying, "and I couldn't be prouder of you."

"If I'd finished my degree..."

Victoria held up a hand. "It's never too late, but what you're doing now you can do without a degree."

"Someday maybe I'll take some online courses. But I would never go back to full time. I know what happened to me when my mother went back to school. I wouldn't do that to my kid. She was a normal stay-at-home mom; then bingo, all at once she was gone."

"Did you ever stop to think how, or why, your mother needed to return to school?"

"Anna died. Then Daddy. I know there were money problems, and maybe she needed something to do. You know, get her mind off things. Off herself."

Her grandmother was persistent, obviously unwilling to let the subject rest. "Do you remember your father being home with you and your mother?"

She hesitated as images came back to her: a big handsome man pushing her in the swing, tossing her in the air, and laughing with her squeals. "Glimpses, I guess," she admitted. "But I don't really remember him at home. It was usually just my mom and me…after Anna died."

"He was gone a lot, Taite. A lot."

"I remember Mother saying later that he was busy at his office." She shrugged, wondering why they were getting into this now.

"He chose to be away."

She leaned sideways to stretch. "What are you saying?"

"Your father led a double life before he died. Your mother didn't find out until much, much later. The signs were there, but naively, she didn't pick up on them."

"What?" Taite sprang upright, stunned. Her breath caught, and for a moment she couldn't speak.

"The whole story is your mother's to tell. But you need to know there are two sides. You blame her for abandoning you, but there were issues she had to deal with after your father died, serious issues."

Victoria narrowed her eyes, obviously upset by the memory. "For one thing he left her deeply in debt. And when she returned to school, it was so she could bring in more than minimum wage. One of her jobs was as a salesclerk in a discount shoe store. She was on her feet for entire days. On weekends, she worked as a hostess at a dinner house. You can imagine her fatigue."

Victoria's gaze slid toward the window, and for a moment she stared out as if lost in her memories. "When she decided to get back to work on her degree, she chose something that had been a passion all her life"—she paused, then turned back—"something to help her get through all the sorrow she'd endured."

"Painting," Taite said, feeling strangely ashamed but also understanding.

"She knew it would be hard on you, but she also knew she was placing you in loving, capable hands." Victoria brushed a stray lock of hair from her forehead. She was pale with fatigue. "Mine."

"Naini, if this is too difficult for you to talk about, we can wait until later…until some other time."

"No, it needs to be now. Honey, think about what she gave up." Her eyes pierced Taite's. "I drew you into my heart like I was a mother robin sitting in an empty nest. I took you in, often excluding your mother—though not really meaning to. It just happened. A jealousy rose between us, unspoken. It was like the elephant in the room that everyone pretends isn't there."

"But what about Anna? Mother always seemed to love her most, and when she died, something in my mother's heart died with her."

"She did have a terrible time getting over Anna's illness and death. She went a little crazy with grief." Victoria leaned back and closed her eyes for a moment, and when she didn't speak, Taite thought she'd drifted off. "There's more, honey," she said after a moment, "but I can't remember what it was I needed to tell you."

It didn't matter. Taite knew enough without hearing more of her grandmother's analysis. She stood, her chin trembling. "I was a little kid. It isn't fair that she would dwell on her own needs and ignore mine." She walked to the window and looked out at the slant of the morning sun striking Point Solana. "I was so young. I needed her. I needed her love." She wanted to shout, *And I still do.* But instead she turned back to her grandmother. "What about later? Surely enough time had passed by the time she left for Europe for her to have gotten over the worst of her grief." Her voice dropped. "She abandoned me."

"If you remember, the first time she left, you weren't even in your teens. She wanted to take you, but I encouraged you to stay with me. Now I realize you should have had those months together." She paused. "When she decided to move to London, you were older."

"Maybe. But I was still young enough to need her." She paused, remembering. "It wasn't long after that horrid party." She sighed. "I do admit to being a brat that night. No wonder she left."

"You'll have to ask her yourself about that." Victoria studied Taite for a moment. "About that party," she said. "You never would tell us why you were so upset."

"She was trying to make up for too much in one night. Like, 'Okay, Taite, here I am, your mom again. Forget about all the times I wasn't there for you. Forget about all the times I loved Anna more than you.'" She winced. "And I was embarrassed. It wasn't the kind of party my friends were used to—at the Mark Hopkins, for heaven's sake. In those years, the cool things were clubs, funky places with loud music and laser lights. Plus, they knew how I felt about my mom. I worried about what they'd think if we were lovey-dovey toward each other."

Suddenly ashamed again, she dropped her gaze from her grandmother's piercing eyes. She thought about what was really important right now: her baby's health, her grandmother's quality of life, Sam…and even her broken relationship with her mother. Her hands rested on her stomach as she reflected on how her thinking had changed.

"Your mother has come back," her grandmother said suddenly.

Taite didn't think she'd heard her correctly. "Pardon me?"

"While you were in town yesterday, Rory Miller stopped by. Isabel had called him, thinking that if we were here, someone from church might know. He's one of the old-timers, knew your grandfather." She paused. "Isabel remembered his name and took a chance that he might still live on the island."

Taite felt a moment of sorrow, thinking about Isabel's shock at finding her mother had moved. "She must have gone to the house first." Then the old bitterness and anger rushed back.

Victoria nodded. "Apparently. Then she started out to find us."

"That's why you wanted to talk about this now."

"Yes." She smiled gently. "It had to be now."

"Did she tell Rory Miller when she was planning to come? Or if?" How many times when she was a child did she wait for her mother to come home, only to cry herself to sleep because Isabel had been detained at school or work? "I don't know if I'm ready to see her." Her voice dropped when she saw her grandmother's disappointment. "I may never be, but for your sake, Naini, I'm glad she's back in the States. The two of you must put things back together."

Late that afternoon as her grandmother rested on the sofa, Taite zipped her parka over her swollen stomach and pulled on her hiking boots. A wind had kicked up off the frigid waters of the Pacific, so she wound a long woolen scarf around her head and neck. She tucked a small writing pad in one zip-up pocket and a couple of pencils in the other.

"Certainly not the height of fashion," she thought wryly, looking down at her attire. She was nearly eight months pregnant and had let her dreads grow out to a loose thicket of curls. So far she wasn't very good at the upkeep, but even in its messy state, it went with her new, strangely tender and prickly writer's heart.

The day was clear, and once outside, she headed toward the lighthouse. She had cautioned her grandmother about the damp and dangerous cliffs but figured that even pregnant she was as surefooted as a mountain goat.

Besides, Taite needed time alone. As much as she loved Victoria, solitude was a precious commodity these days. Swinging her arms in rhythm with her stride, she breathed in the scent of decaying leaves and loamy earth, saltwater spray and wet granite rocks drying in the weak sunlight. Waves surged with a soothing beat, with the occasional high crest crashing louder than the others. Gulls circled and called overhead, and a few low-flying brown pelicans studied her curiously as they swooped and soared, then dove gracefully into the surf for food.

As she walked, she thought about Sam. She stopped in the shade of a cypress tree. She wanted to call and ask him to come home to her, to their baby. To let him know that her heart cried for him, that she ached for him, that she wanted to spend the rest of her life with him.

But something stopped her from extending the invitation. It was fear, deep in the pit of her stomach. She was afraid of his rejection, perhaps not now, but months or years from now when he started resenting her for her part in the unexpected pregnancy and marriage before he finished med school. Rejection? She'd known too much of it in her life. She thought she might die if that happened. So calling him, inviting him home now was out of the question.

She found a flat boulder and settled onto it, facing the sun. Her thoughts turned to Isabel's arrival. She thought about calling Adam Gilchrist in San Francisco, knowing her mother would probably be in contact with him. She could then invite her to the island, give her some warning about Victoria's health.

She leaned back and closed her eyes. Her anger toward her mother had almost become an old friend. Could she give it up even long enough to press the numbers on her cell phone?

One little phone call. An invitation to talk. A step onto the bridge of reconciliation. She couldn't bring herself to do it.

In the ocean beyond the lighthouse, a sea otter floated on its back in the dark, gleaming seaweed, cracking open oysters with a small stone. Closer in, a stilt-legged sandpiper pecked in the sand.

Had she been so busy blaming her mother for all that was wrong in her own life that she hadn't seen the truth in front of her face? Had her bitterness and blame altered the course she had taken? Had she admitted her many failures only to justify the blame that always followed? How often had she thought, *I would have done better, been successful, if only I hadn't been abandoned...if only I'd had a proper upbringing?*

Tears crept from the corners of her eyes. She closed her eyes, feeling utterly miserable. Filled with anguish. She stood to get her bearings, to banish the darkness from her soul, the ache from her heart.

But neither would flee. Gingerly she walked along the edge of the rocky overhang, looking for crabs and starfish among the rocks below, searching for anything to distract her. She spotted a tide pool near the bottom of the cliff and, careful to keep her balance, climbed down to the sandy soil below. Squatting, she ran her hand through the shallow waters, watching for life. But there was none—at least, none that she could see. The pool held only a scattering of seaglass on a sandy bed, a strand of seaweed, a jagged piece of granite.

She sat down on an outcropping of stone near the tide pool and looked up at the lighthouse. If Isabel appeared this minute, how could she face her? She would rather wade into the sea and swim to China than look into her mother's eyes and see reflected back every angry word, every bitter jab, every mean-spirited thing Taite had ever done.

The baby kicked just then, and she rested her hand on her stomach. Life grew inside her. Her baby! With relief, she turned her thoughts to images of him scooting his tiny foot or sucking his thumb. Just then the sun reflected off the lighthouse glass and gleamed brilliantly for a moment before sliding away as the earth continued its slow turn.

Taite smiled, thinking of the verse her grandmother loved from Ecclesiastes: *Truly the light is sweet.* And most often she was quick to add, "There is never a sweeter light than that which shines after the darkness."

Taite stood and stretched awkwardly, glancing out at the ocean.

The tide was coming in, and it was time to get back before her grandmother began to worry. She took one step, stopped to regain her balance, and then tried another. The wet sand slid beneath her boots, and the cliff was steeper than it had seemed when she had climbed down. For the first time she felt alarmed about her own safety. Climbing down the cliff had been foolish. No one would hear her calls if she needed help. On the other hand, the rising tide gave her no choice but to work her way up the embankment.

She mustered her courage. All she had to do was put one foot carefully in front of the other, then do it again, over and over. She took a hesitant step, then another, and soon had settled into a steady rhythm, watching her path rather than the ocean below. She had almost reached the top when she found a patch of winter-dead fairy lanterns to give her the final boost she needed.

The little shrub came out by its roots. She tumbled backward like a rag doll, half rolling, half flying helplessly down the sandy slope. With a sharp crack, her head hit the outcrop of granite by the tide pool. Pain flashed through her. She lay utterly still, afraid to move.

24

Taite groaned as gentle, strong arms lifted her off the rocks. She leaned against a broad chest, feeling secure, and caught the smell of damp wool mixed with the salty scent of the ocean on his rough jacket. The man must be a fisherman. In her wooziness and pain, she thought she remembered seeing a rowboat bobbing in the surf, but she couldn't be sure.

Slowly they climbed. She felt the steady rhythm of his footfalls and heard the crunch of gravel beneath his feet as they moved to higher ground. It didn't seem long until he stooped to lay her down. She was shivering now, and he laid his palm on her forehead just as she remembered her father had done when she was a little girl. She heard him unzip his coat, and a moment later he smoothed it around her shoulders and neck.

"Your arms…," he said. "Can you move them?"

"No," she whispered. "I tried earlier."

"Try again," he said.

"They ache."

"That's a good sign. They're not numb."

She moved her fingers, making a loose fist, then slowly lifted her right arm. Next she tried her left. "I feel like I've been run over by a truck."

"Now your legs," he said. "Can you move them?"

She moistened her lips and scooted her legs slightly. He lifted one foot a few inches, then the other, and placed them again on the ground. "You've got some scrapes and bruises, and you may have a concussion. But no broken bones. Help will be here soon."

If he was a fisherman, he apparently had radioed to another boat farther offshore, perhaps the Coast Guard.

"Would you like some water?"

She nodded. He carefully tipped a trickle of water into her mouth, being careful of her neck. The pain was still intense, but curiosity got the best of her. She opened her eyes and stared up at him. His image was blurred, and he was backlit by the bright sun, but she could see kindness in his expression, strength in his jaw line and in the build of his shoulders in silhouette. "Thank you," she breathed and closed her eyes again. She worried that if help was on the way, he would leave her. "Don't go," she said, clutching her stomach with the sudden realization that her baby was as still as death.

"You don't need to be afraid."

"You don't understand. I'm pregnant. I can't feel my baby move…" She began to weep and lifted her hand to her face. "I don't know why I'm telling you this. But now, this fall, and my baby not moving…it's just that I'm so afraid." Her voice broke off. "It's my fault…the abortion, now the fall."

"You couldn't have stopped yourself from falling. It was an accident."

"My baby…if anything's wrong…" She started to cry again. "I wasn't careful. I'm never careful. I-I should have realized what the cost would be."

The touch of his hand comforted her, and she drew in a shaky breath. "I'm sorry," she whispered. "I shouldn't be telling you all this. It's my business, my pain, my ugliness. I can't even tell Sam about the darkness in my heart. I can't even tell Sam why I'm so afraid he won't love me."

"You can tell me," he said. "I understand." Something about his voice told her he did.

"If I hadn't tried to have the abortion, I wouldn't have hurt my baby. I didn't know I loved him until then, until I almost lost him. I saw the bloody discharge and thought I'd killed him." She was sobbing now, her face wet with tears. "My arms ached with love…ached with emptiness…and then I woke up…only to find what I'd done to him. I may as well have killed him. He might be born"—she groped for the words—"unhealthy, unwhole, handicapped."

"Would you love him any less?"

Her heart swelled, and a sob burst from her. "I think I would love him more."

"I think you would too," he said. "Tell me what else burdens you so."

"I've hurt others. Sam. I deceived him. He wants to do the honorable thing and marry me, but I keep pushing him away."

"Why?"

Sam's image filled her mind, and she whispered, "I love him."

"That's why you can't marry Sam—because you love him?"

She nodded and squinted up at him again. She could see him no better than the first time, but the same gentleness and strength seemed to radiate from him. She wasn't afraid to tell him anything; it struck her that nothing she said would change what he thought of her.

"I want him to fulfill his dreams."

"Yet you don't agree with his dreams."

She didn't ask him how he knew. "Not all of them. He wants to—" She couldn't bring herself to describe the research. "It makes me sick each time I think about it."

"Have you told him?"

Ashamed, she shook her head. "Not in so many words. I guess I expected him to know. After all, I'm carrying our child. Just the thought of anything, of something…" She wept again, thinking about the abortion she'd once wanted.

"Have you told him?" he asked again. "Have you told him all that is in your heart?"

The silence that fell between them seemed heavy with both love and sorrow. "Not as plainly as I might have," she whispered. "I was afraid."

"That he might turn from you and choose what grieves you?"

"Yes. That's what made me afraid. Other things too."

"You think that because others have chosen to leave you, your life means little—whether to Sam or your mother."

"You know about her?"

But he didn't dwell on Isabel, just as he hadn't with Sam. He took her hand. "There are angels in heaven," he said, "who rejoice over you, Taite Abbott, did you know?" He seemed to be smiling at her, though she felt it rather than saw it. "Don't you know your worth, child? God rejoices over you with singing," he said, quoting a verse she had heard a long time ago. "He will quiet you with his love…if you will let him."

Tears welled in her eyes.

"You saved the life of your child, refusing to give in when others advised you differently. You have given yourself to your grandmother in her need. All of heaven has watched as you turned from pleasing yourself, wallowing in despair, to looking for ways to help others."

"There's still so much dark ugliness inside me. I'm scared that I've brought Naini here to the island selfishly, because I didn't want to be alone, because I wanted to hear her stories. In the end, she'll need more help than I can give her. I don't want her to suffer."

He didn't speak, causing Taite to look inward, to weigh the consequences. Above them the seagulls cried, the pelicans soared, and the lighthouse had turned a crimson gold in the setting sun. "There are so many times I've been selfish—and still am," she said. "My mother. I don't want to see her."

"Difficult things are made more difficult when you try to do them on your own. God never gives you an assignment expecting to send you out alone to accomplish the task. He goes with you, to help, to guide, to comfort."

"But I've always been on my own," she said, tilting her chin. "I've always had to do things for myself." She heard both pride and complaint in her voice. Her protest felt hollow, and she was ashamed.

"The One who loves you," he said, "wants your heart, not your sacrifice."

"I'm not good enough to come to him." Thinking of the darkness in her soul, she pulled her hand away, shaking her head. "How can anyone love me after all I've done?"

"Do you think you have to be perfect to come to God? Do you think that by striving to change, by trying to be perfect, you'll then be deserving of love?" He reached for her hand again, clasping it between his two. She felt scars and turned his palms in wonder, touched them with her fingertips, then just as quickly decided it was her imagination. They must be calluses.

But when he spoke again, his voice seemed to hold all the sounds around her: the wind in the pines, the trill of birdsong, the thunder of the ocean. "You don't have to change to come to him," he said. "He loves you…just as you are."

It didn't seem possible, and as much as she wanted to believe it, her fears crowded in. "I'm scared," she said, letting her gaze drift from his face to her stomach. "My baby…" She pulled her hand from his and felt herself sinking back into the semidarkness of unconsciousness. "My baby," she sobbed. "He still hasn't moved." Forcing herself to look up again, she squinted into the deepening twilight. But the fisherman was gone.

She was lying in the dark near the lighthouse when she heard voices approaching. Isabel was the first to reach her and with a small cry dropped to her knees beside Taite.

"Taite," she kept whispering over and over. "Taite, honey. Wake up."

When Taite opened her eyes, she looked beyond her mother to search for the fisherman. But there was no one.

"Did you see him?" she said, reaching for Isabel's hands. "There was a man, a fisherman. He carried me up from the rocks. The tide was coming in…" She fell back on the sand, her head throbbing. "He checked to see if I had broken bones. He said I might have a concussion."

"I didn't see anyone," Isabel said and exchanged a worried glance with Naini. "Maybe he went for help."

"He said help was coming."

"Don't talk, honey," her mother said softly, checking her limbs much as the fisherman did. "You fell?"

Taite glanced toward the overhang several yards away. "I-I was over there, climbing from the rocks below. I slipped…I think. It's hard to remember." She tried to lift her head, but the pain was still too intense. "The next thing I knew I was being carried up the cliff by the fisherman. He covered me with his coat." She looked down. She was wearing her parka. There was no coat.

"I don't think we should move her," Isabel said to Victoria. "Is there a doctor—a paramedic—in town who would come out here?"

"Doc Firestone at the clinic on Bay Shore." Naini sat down on some flat rocks. "You go. I'll stay with Taite."

Standing, Isabel glanced at Victoria, her face lined with worry. She touched Taite's cheek affectionately. "She's going to need blankets. I'll bring some over before I go into town." Her words were comforting. Taite reached for her mother's hand, but Isabel had already turned and was gone.

Naini leaned forward and shone the flashlight on the soil near Taite. "I notice there are footprints around you," she said. "There, in the sand." She smiled. "They do look like fisherman's sandals, I would say."

Taite closed her eyes, remembering him. "I'm certain someone was here."

"There was another time," Naini said softly, "long ago, when a similar tale was told."

Gwynedd and Brother Cadwallen kept themselves hidden from Gunnolf and his army by weaving in and out of the dense forest, keeping their animals nearby for safekeeping. The gooseberry-colored donkey named Eirin Mair was the only means of transport for lame Cadwallen, and Mêl, the honey-sweet goat, provided milk, their only food once they'd finished the bread and meat the villagers at Cynwyd-Cilcain had given her.

Each night they waited for a glimpse of the Han-mere prisoners, Brother Cadwallen softly sang evening vespers, translating from Latin Psalm 121: "I will lift up mine eyes unto the hills, from whence cometh my help. My help cometh from the LORD, which made heaven and earth. He will not suffer thy foot to be moved: he that keepeth thee close to his heart will not slumber.... The LORD is thy keeper: the

LORD is thy shade upon thy right hand. The sun shall not smite thee by day, nor the moon by night."

Gwynedd quickly learned the words in Welsh and sang it with Cadwallen, their voices mere whispers. Then Cadwallen prayed, speaking to God with an intimacy that Gwynedd had never known. She found herself becoming bolder in her prayers, going to her Lord as a beloved child, speaking to him in the silence of her heart in the deep night.

And when the sky was clear, she stared up at the North Star and thought of Taran, wondering if he lived. She could not keep in one place much longer. They needed food, the animals needed new grass for grazing, and because there was no sign of the Han-mere prisoners, she felt the urge to move on to the sea.

The old woman's dream haunted her. Prisoners on a ship—could they be held there? But Brother Cadwallen prayed and cautioned her not to act boldly. Not yet.

Midsummer night, long after the sun had sunk into the shadowy earth, Gwynedd felt the first stirrings of life, wee ripples and bubbles that brought her a secret smile. The following morn, when she looked across the field where the enemy camped, she noticed for the first time that a fine carpet of bell heather and red clover had spring to life.

Horsemen in the encampment rode out daily, swords gleaming in the sun, and returned with shouts of triumph, swords bloodied and often with captives in tow. Gwynedd kept watch at the edge of the wood for signs of Taran, Mary, and the others.

"Do not despair, child," Brother Cadwallen said one morning. "We will know when it is time."

"But 'tis what to do that troubles me."

"We will know."

"'Tis hard to trust," she said, knowing that's what Cadwallen meant. She was learning that he did nothing without first feeling God's nudging. "I want to march into that encampment this minute and demand to see my husband. Surely these brutes if they knew my condition would allow a wife to see—"

Cadwallen held up a hand, looking alarmed. "Do not attempt such a reckless act," he said. "You called them brutes, truly their rightful name. I fear what they might do..."

She crossed to the other side of their small clearing and, standing beneath the branches of an ancient tree, looked back at him. "We cannot stay here forever," she said, trying not to wring her hands. "We need food. We must go. I have a plan, one that was successful for Taran and me. I will wait until they slumber, then I will slip into the encampment and forage for food."

Brother Cadwallen looked stricken. "That is too dangerous," he said quietly. "I will pray through this night for guidance."

And he did but the next morning, he had no answer. He prayed through a second night, and still God did not let his will be known. The lines beneath his eyes creased deeper with his exhaustion. The third night Gwynedd knew he was determined to stay the night on his knees in prayer, but he collapsed and drifted off, snoring lightly after only an hour.

The next morning she said, "We will go toward the sea. The old woman urged me to head northwest; mayhap her dream is the only sign we need."

Brother Cadwallen's voice was solemn. "There is still the problem of getting word to the Bishop of Caer. If something happens to us, no one will know of the cave and the sacred Gospels."

"'Tis that which is most important," she agreed, meeting his gaze. "Mayhap that is why we have been reluctant to move our little band on to the sea. Can it be there is a certain order to our mission?"

"I have concluded the same," he said.

"We are within a day's walking journey of Caer," she said. He nodded, and she went on. "I can move fast on foot. If you remain here with the animals, I will skirt the encampment, staying hidden in the trees, until I spot Caer from yonder hill. If it appears to be in smoke and ruins, I will return here, and we'll devise another plan. If the bell tower stands, I will make my way to the abbey."

He looked down at his swollen foot. "It strikes against my nature to put you on this path."

She touched his arm. "Promise me this, that you will stay hidden in the trees. No moving around while I am gone. Keep Gooseberry and Honey near you."

He smiled. "Godspeed, and be quick with you."

She would take nothing with her save the ring that hung at her neck beneath her shift. She knelt before Cadwallen, and he asked God's blessing upon her. Then he made the sign of the cross upon her forehead with his thumb.

She stood and met his eyes briefly. They seemed to shine with a deep peace, as if he had settled something important with God. He smiled, touching her cheek briefly. "God be with you," he said, "with your wee one, and with those who will follow through the generations."

She smiled. "The family blessing," she said softly, affection for the godly man welling up inside her heart. On impulse, she stood on her toes and kissed his cheek. He looked surprised but pleased. Without another word, she sprinted from their covert into the deep forest.

The morning shadows were still long as she picked her way through the tangle of trees, always keeping just out of sight of the encampment. She drew close enough to smell their cook fires and hear the guttural sounds of their voices but tiptoed as if upon goose eggs to avoid being heard.

The sun had risen higher when she arrived at the most dangerous part of her journey. To gain the road to Caer, she would have to cross a clearing. She stood at the edge, gauged her distance, and prepared to run like the wind to the trees at the far side.

Standing behind a tree, she looked to Gunnolf's camp, back to the trees, then to the hiding place where Cadwallen was surely watching. He was more cautious than she and likely would advise against the foolish run across the meadow.

She touched the ring and drew in a deep breath. How else would she get to the abbey? This might be her only chance. Before she could change her mind, she raced from behind the tree and into the open.

At precisely the same moment, as if planned, a shout in Welsh came from behind the encampment—where Cadwallen had been hiding. "*Bore da!* Good morning! *Ydi hi'n ffordd dda?* Is this a good road?" He shouted, limping toward the encampment and pointing to the road leading back to Cynwyd-Cilcain.

Several of the brutes shouted back in surprise and charged toward him, waving swords. They gathered round, jeering and poking at him with their weapons.

"*Bore da!*" he shouted merrily, smiling and nodding at them all.

The encampment was in an uproar, all running toward the crazy monk. Gwynedd stood rooted to the spot in full view, though no one was looking, tears streaming down her face. Cadwallen had saved her life. She watched as his face was bloodied, his garment rent. Still he shouted in Welsh, asking God to forgive his enemies and save the sacred places in his country.

Sobbing, Gwynedd ran across the clearing. When she was again hidden in the trees, she looked back. The warriors, still jeering and hollering, carried Cadwallen's limp and bloodied body back into their camp. Eirin Mair, tethered around the neck, was being yanked along by a young red-haired soldier. Behind him, Mêl squealed in terror as she was carried, lifted high in triumph, over a big-shouldered brute's head.

Gwynedd fell to her knees and emptied her stomach, then wept until the sun was high in its heavens and she had no strength left in her bones.

Cadwallen had given his life for her. She couldn't comprehend such love, such passion to see his mission accomplished. What if she failed after all he had done? He'd done it to see that she passed safely beyond the army and reached Caer Abbey. She held her stomach, feeling sick again, and doubled over, her forehead touching the bare, damp earth.

Her losses had been too many to bear. She was too worn in spirit and body, too tired of fighting to go on. She closed her eyes, willing herself to die on the spot. The Enemy was too strong.

Then she felt herself being lifted and carried like a lamb in a shepherd's arms. She rested her cheek against the warm cloth of his garment. Though she never once opened her eyes, she knew it was the same shepherd who carried her, the one she had seen near Han-mere Abbey. She wasn't certain how long she was carried, or how far, or if she had been dreaming.

She only knew that when she woke, refreshed, she was near Caer Abbey and far from where she had fallen asleep. And the first thing she felt was her child moving inside her, and she knew she must live.

Cadwallen's words seemed to float like music from a shepherd's harp through her mind: "He that keepeth thee close to his heart will not slumber.... He that keepeth thee close to his heart will not slumber..."

Standing, gathering her courage, she looked toward Caer and faced what she needed to do.

Doc Firestone bent over Taite. He checked her heart and lungs with his stethoscope, then gently probed her limbs. Taite was feeling better and grinned. "That's the third time today," she said. "The fisherman, my mother, and now you. It should be time to pronounce me fit as a fiddle."

He removed the stethoscope and rocked back on his heels. "You're a fortunate young woman. Your mother described the fall. Do you remember climbing to the top?"

"There was a fisherman—" She noticed the glance exchanged between her mother and Doc and said nothing more. Clearly Isabel had told him she was hallucinating. Old resentments crept into her heart.

He checked her abdomen, the lines on his face deepening. She kept her eyes on his, searching for a sign of hope, as he moved the stethoscope over her stomach, stopping every inch or so to listen carefully. "I hear a heartbeat," he said, "but it's faint. I fear there's been some trauma to the baby."

Taite met Isabel's gaze. Her mother's expression was unreadable; Taite was sure her own was defiant. Nothing mattered right now but her baby, not what her mother thought, not the condemnation that might be in Isabel's heart.

"We need to get you to the clinic," he said, now probing Taite's neck and the base of her skull. "Do you feel like standing? I'll be here to support you."

"Yes," she said shakily. "Earlier I didn't think I could move my legs. But now…" She wiggled her foot, then flexed her knee. Doc supported her shoulders and neck as she struggled to sit up. The pain hit full force again, bringing with it a wave of nausea. She brought her hand to her mouth and closed her eyes, forcing herself to breathe deeply. Behind her, she heard the worried voices of her mother and grandmother. "I'm all right," she whispered. "Just give me a minute."

A moment later he wrapped his arm around her waist and she leaned against him, her mother on the other side, as they moved slowly to his waiting SUV. He raised the rear door and gently helped Taite into the back of the vehicle. After struggling with her painfully stiff limbs, she gratefully lay down on a rubberized pad. It appeared to have been used for emergency transport before. Doc pulled a dark green army blanket from a stack of blankets and covered her, then closed the rear door and climbed into the driver's seat. With a spray of gravel, they drove down the bumpy road toward town. Taite heard a second car behind them, which she assumed was her mother's rental.

That night Grace took Victoria home, and Isabel stayed at the clinic. Taite was too weary, worried, and headachy to wonder how they decided who would stay and who would not. As soon as Doc had treated her wounds and run a sonogram, she gratefully settled into the one room at the clinic with a bed. Her mother took the chair beside her.

Taite kept silent, not so much because of all she'd been through, but because she didn't know what to say. Her head told her one thing, her heart another. Old resentments still lay buried deep inside, and for healing to begin, they needed to surface.

She wondered what her mother was thinking, if she was dismayed after all this time to find her daughter in such a state: pregnant and unwed. She was probably thinking about Anna and how different things would be if she had lived. Perfect Anna. Instead, she had come home to Taite. Unlovely, unlovable Taite.

Tears crept from the corners of her eyes. She sensed her mother's gaze and looked up. "Mama," she said. It struck her how much hope was in that single word. And vulnerability.

At once it was as if Isabel had removed a mask. Her face earlier had seemed a poised, passive blank. Now Taite saw tender concern.

Isabel moved her chair closer. "Do you feel like talking?"

"A little, maybe."

"Tell me about your life, Taite. It's been so long…I don't know anything about you, about what's happened to you since I left." Her hand fluttered nervously.

"You mean about how I dropped out of college, wasting your hard-earned money? Or maybe you mean about the baby?" She tried to bite back the bitterness and self-condemnation, but it was impossible. "Or my lack of a husband and father for my child?" She was ready to go on, then she remembered the fisherman. "I'm sorry," she said, her voice a whisper. She turned her head away from Isabel's probing gaze. "I know you must be ashamed of me. My attitude isn't making it any easier."

When Isabel didn't answer, Taite figured she was right. She felt weighed down with weariness, with the bitterness that had always seemed to rule her life. "Mama," she said, not daring to look Isabel in the face, "I-I need to ask you something." Tears started to slide from the corners of her eyes again.

"I'm here, honey." Her words reminded Taite of the same words she'd spoken at bedtime years before. The memory made her tears flow harder. Had dwelling on the bad memories blocked out the good?

"I-I don't th-think I can say it…," she said, knowing she had to.

"May I go first then?" came the answer. "Maybe what I need to tell you will make it easier for you."

She turned to look into Isabel's face, so familiar, yet instead of the harsh critical look she expected, she saw something new. Oh, she was still very different from Taite and her dreadlocks, hiking boots, and oversized sweaters. Isabel's hair lay in a dark, sleek bob, and today she wore a broomstick velvet skirt and billowy top with a necklace of natural stones on a silver and leather chain. She had always been pretty, tiny like Taite, but perfectly made up and willing to wear heels, usually on fancy boots. An artist from tip to toe, in bearing, in style.

Now something new emerged, an expression Taite had always longed to see. For a moment she just blinked, afraid she'd misread the affection.

"I need to ask your forgiveness, Taite."

Taite was stunned. "M-my forgiveness?"

"When I left for Europe the first time, I wasn't happy—to say the least—when you chose to stay here with Mother instead of going with me. I wish I'd either insisted that you come with me, no matter what you or your grandmother said, or that I'd stayed here to be with you during those years when you were still growing up."

"It was me. I told you what I wanted."

Isabel held up a hand, shaking her head slowly. "You were too young to make such a decision. I abnegated my responsibility. You'd been through so much: Anna's death, your father's, losing your mom to work and school." She paused. "There hasn't been a day since then that I haven't grieved over the choice I made."

"I didn't know," Taite said. She turned toward her mother, wincing as she moved her head. "Why didn't you come home?"

"When you didn't answer my letters, I thought you didn't want to see me."

Taite settled into her pillow. "I didn't."

"And the timing wasn't right, until now." Her voice dropped. "I needed to be here. Today."

Taite turned her head, feeling shy about what she must say next. "I know all this happened years ago, but I've been so bitter. The way I acted…" She swallowed hard. "I've been angry—full of blame—and I still am sometimes. I can't help it. But I'm sorry."

Isabel stood, walked over to the bed, and sat on the edge by Taite's knees. "That's okay. I'm still angry too sometimes, honey. Mostly about the circumstances that brought us all to this bitterness, blame, and separation."

"Daddy?"

Isabel nodded. "You asked me once about what happened on the day he died. I thought I was protecting you by not telling you the truth. I see that I only caused a deeper rift between us." She smiled gently. "Are you ready...or shall we wait until you're feeling better?"

"I want to hear it now." She closed her eyes and pictured the fisherman carrying her in his arms, and Isabel told her about the day her daddy died, about his gambling debts and his heartache over Anna's death and his wife's growing emotional distance.

"Regrets are insidious," her mother said. "There are so many things I'd like to change about the past if I could. I look back now, and I see clearly what led to his death."

She closed her eyes, afraid to hear the words spoken. "Suicide?" The word was barely audible.

For several heartbeats her mother didn't answer. Finally she said, "He didn't leave a note. But his world had come crashing in around him. We both were emotional wrecks... He just couldn't cope any longer." Her voice broke. She dropped her head and dug in her handbag for tissues. For a moment Taite heard only the soft sound of her weeping.

She reached for her mother's hand. Isabel looked at her with tear-filled eyes. "Mama, can we start over? Try to fix things between us?"

"That's why I came back."

"I'm pretty awful at relationships."

"So am I."

"I have a temper, though I'm trying to learn to control it. I look pretty strange most of the time."

Isabel blinked at her with proud, watery eyes. "I think you're beautiful."

Taite couldn't stop smiling. "Really?"

"Really."

Taite fell asleep with Isabel holding her hand. Just before two o'clock in the morning, she awoke with a strange tightening of her abdomen. The stinging lasted for only a few seconds, then disappeared.

Turning to one side, she groaned in pain. Her whole body ached, her head worst of all. She glanced across the nearly dark room to where her mother sat sleeping in the chair and felt comforted that she was near. With a sigh, she settled deeper into her pillow and closed her eyes.

She was drifting off again when the second pang spread across her stomach. This time it felt like a searing iron. She felt a gush of liquid and wept, knowing that her labor had begun. And that it was too early.

"Mama," she cried.

25

T he snow was falling so fast that Sam couldn't see farther than a few feet ahead. He raced into the building where the orientation meeting for Stockholm was scheduled, stopping just beyond the double doorway to stamp the snow from his boots. He hurried down the hall and opened the classroom door just as Dr. Jed Barnes, one of the top stem cell researchers from Johns Hopkins, was opening the session. He sat down at the U-shaped table with a half-dozen other students.

Dr. Barnes wrote a few notes on the whiteboard near a small lectern, then turned. "Before we get to what you'll be doing at the institute, I want to quickly review where we are in the debate here in the States.

"As you know, the human embryonic stem cell lines isolated to date have all been grown on beds of mouse 'feeder' cells—the only method allowed us since August 9, 2001. These mouse cells secrete a substance that prevents the human stem cells from differentiating into more mature types—such as nerve or muscle cells—which could create appalling errors in our research.

"Infectious agents such as viruses within the mouse feeder cells can migrate into the human cells. If these infected human cells were transplanted into a patient, they might cause disease, which could eventually be transmitted to the general public.

"At Johns Hopkins we found that human bone-marrow cells can also act as feeder cells for human embryonic stem cells without causing contamination and can still prevent those embryonic stem cells from morphing into more mature cell types.

"In Sweden, we are not restricted from using human bone-marrow cells as a feeder medium, which greatly reduces the risk to humans involved in the studies. You will be working with bone marrow as feeder cells for embryonic stem cells." He smiled at the group seated in front of him. "Legally.

"We not only question our government's decision to eliminate stem cell research, we need to fight for changes right now to allow for the creation of new, uncontaminated stem cell lines such as those currently being produced in other countries. We need them, ladies and gentlemen, and as soon as possible. Our institute in Stockholm is dedicated to continuing the global fight for legalization of stem cell research. You, we hope, will return as warriors dedicated to our cause.

"We're not sending you there for research training only; we're also hoping to ignite a fire of passion for saving lives through this exciting new frontier of research.

"I don't need to remind you that we are likely to find new therapies for diabetes, various cancers, spinal-cord injuries, Alzheimer's, and many other illnesses and disabilities as a result of the advances achieved by human embryonic stem cell research.

"I commend you men and women who have been accepted into our program." He went on to describe in detail the layout of the Stockholm research facilities and the duties expected of each participant.

Sam knew from his own research that the embryonic cells used were mostly taken from embryos produced in laboratories around the world to help infertile couples. The embryos that weren't implanted or discarded were frozen and stored. He'd heard that frozen embryos numbered over one million. So why did he give this a second thought?

Perhaps he was still trying to convince himself that the small clump of fewer than a hundred cells, the so-called inner cell mass, hadn't yet developed into a human being. A baby.

In the Stockholm program he wouldn't be experimenting on real human embryos. Not really. These were just cells, a blob in the blasto-cyst stage. Clinically, they were called ES cells—embryonic stem cells—expected to have the ability to grow into nearly any type of cells in the body. Clinically, it was easier to accept. Morally, spiritually, humanly, he was having trouble.

He couldn't get around the fact that a human life was sacrificed so the research could happen. Did it matter that millions of these cells would be destroyed anyway? Did it matter than he would be working with hundreds while he was in Stockholm? What about cells purchased through the abortion trade? Could that come in the future? Was it hap-pening now, illegally, here or abroad? The thought sickened him.

The professor had moved on to their specific assignments and rotations in Stockholm. But Sam was listening halfheartedly, thinking now of Taite and their baby, longing to see her, to hold her in his arms.

When the meeting was dismissed, he filed out with the others but strode for the door without stopping to talk. A thick snow was falling, and he took shelter beneath the building's extended roof. The campus was decorated for Christmas, and though classes were out for the break, people of all ages, bundled and wrapped with woolen scarves, walked in clusters along the snowy pathway to the chapel for the annual Christmas program. His gaze followed them toward the small church, and he couldn't help smiling.

It was a welcome scene, especially in contrast to the unpleasant graphics that had stabbed his conscience in the meeting. Pale gold shone through the chapel windows, and a single row of twinkling white lights outlined the bell tower and steep, icicled roof. Christmas tree–shaped pines on either side of the path leading to the front door wore spangles of the same lights.

"Currier and Ives," he thought with a grin and wished Taite could be here with him. He could just see the widening of her eyes as she took in the winter wonderland; he could almost hear the music of her laughter as she pulled his hand, trying to lead him into the chapel. Knowing Taite, at the last minute she would more than likely fling a snowball at him. He would of course give chase, then gather her into a hug as she threw her arms around his neck. Closing his eyes, he could almost smell the faint scent of wildflowers.

But Taite wasn't here, and he was leaving in three days for Europe.

The choir inside the chapel began to sing. Drawn to the music, Sam hunched his shoulders against the snow as he walked to the entrance. He crossed the narthex and was greeted warmly by a portly gentleman who handed him a program. "Do I need a ticket?"

The usher smiled. "No sir. But there are very few seats left. You might find one toward the back."

Sam slipped through another set of doors, just as he had once before. This time the sanctuary was dark except for candles lining the aisles. The choir stood to one side of the altar, and in the center a soft spotlight shone on a living nativity scene: Mary, Joseph, and the infant Jesus. A real baby lay in the manger, his little hands waving in the air. The baby started to fuss, and Mary lifted him from the bed of hay to her shoulder, bent over him, and rested her cheek on his head. Her tender touch caused Sam's heart to ache with longing for his own child.

The harpsichordist began playing a simple melody, which Sam recognized as "What Child Is This?" A hush filled the sanctuary as a soloist lifted her voice in the loving lullaby,

> What Child is this who, laid to rest,
> on Mary's lap, is sleeping?
> Whom angels greet with anthems sweet,
> while shepherds watch are keeping?
> This, this is Christ the King,
> whom shepherds guard and angels sing;
> haste, haste, to bring him laud,
> the Babe, the son of Mary.

The woman dressed as Mary smiled at the infant in her arms, stroked his silky, fuzzy head with her fingers, and kissed his cheek.

Sam's throat stung as he considered the profound, fragile beauty of an infant's life. God had sent his most precious gift to the world in the form of a child, a human infant. Even this infant had begun as a group of cells, those same few inner mass cells in the blastocyst stage. Could anything be a greater, dearer treasure? The image of his own baby filled his mind...followed quickly by the throwaway embryos he would be using for research.

"What child is this...what child is this..." filled his mind. He felt ill, and as soon as the soloist had finished, he bolted from his seat. He hurried through the doors without speaking to the usher, ran to the far side of the light-spangled Christmas tree, and bent double, expecting to lose his dinner. "What child is this...what child is this..." He gulped in the frigid air, forcing himself to breathe deeply until his stomach calmed.

He covered his face with his hands. "O God, what am I doing?"

Luke and Martha Stephens were sitting two rows behind Sam. They had watched him enter the sanctuary, his expression tight with anxiety, and they had exchanged a worried glance as he seated himself. When Sam stood suddenly, looking ill, and raced to the narthex, Luke picked up his overcoat, wool tam, and scarf and followed.

The snowfall had almost stopped, and he could see Sam near a small, decorated tree. He was kneeling, his face in his hands, just beyond the icy walkway.

He stepped close and placed his hand on Sam's shoulder. "How are you doing, my friend?"

"Must've been something I ate." Sam stood, looking shaken.

"We were sitting a couple rows behind you. I worried when you got up and left so quickly." He looked across the wintry landscape. "You want to walk a bit? Maybe it'll help clear your head."

"It's cold out here."

"I could use a bit of fresh air myself." They sauntered along the center of the green, almost automatically turning toward the brightly lit hospital in the distance. "You want to talk about it?" Their boots crunched in the packed snow on the sidewalk.

"A few weeks ago you mentioned a plumb line," Sam said, to Luke's surprise. Ever since Sam had returned from his trip to California weeks before, he had seemed to avoid Luke and Martha. He'd turned down two invitations to dinner. When Martha gently suggested they give him space and wait for God's timing, Luke had agreed. They had prayed for him daily, for his career choices, for Taite and their baby, for God to manifest his power and grace in their lives.

"Ah yes, my plumb line," Luke said. "I did mention it, didn't I?"

"Choices," Sam said, frowning. "It all comes down to choices. For years my course was clear. I thought my life's work was settled. It all seemed so easy." He shot Luke a puzzled glance. "I've thought about that plumb line you mentioned, how it gives you moral guidance, and I'm wondering how you discovered it."

"If you're speaking of a moral compass, I think you're finding it already," Luke said.

"Something tells me you're about to add a *but*," Sam said. They skirted a fallen branch, stepping off the walkway into the pristine blanket of snow and back again.

Luke chuckled, his breath coming out in white puffs as they both stomped the snow from their boots. *"But,"* he said, "if you're speaking of spiritual matters—how they relate to my plumb line—that's something different. A moral man can be a godless man. A moral man—a good man—may well have no inkling that he was created by a God who loves him and wants a personal relationship with him."

He stopped near a gaslight on a squat brick column and met Sam's gaze. "A man who longs after God, whose heart listens for his Savior's voice, is a spiritual man. This man doesn't have to be perfect or know all the answers. He may have made mistakes, terrible mistakes, but when he comes to Christ, he is made new. Forgiven, washed clean, because of the Cross."

"Does that include causing a child to suffer?" Sam's voice was hoarse with emotion.

"You're worried that your child will be born less than whole?"

He nodded mutely. "Tonight when I saw the babe in the manger and later in his mother's arms, I thought about our baby." He choked up and looked away from Luke. "My culpability in the harm I've caused this child.

"One night months ago I went into the chapel, and some words of condemnation came to me that I can't get out of my mind." He paused, then said, his voice heavy with sadness, "Better a millstone be hung around the neck of the one who brings harm to one of these little ones... Better he be drowned in the depths of the sea." He stared at Luke. "I'm not even a believer, yet this verse has stuck in my heart as if God himself etched it there."

"Do you know the verse just preceding that one?"

Sam shook his head slowly. "No."

"Whoever receives one little child like this in My name receives Me."

For a moment Sam remained utterly silent. "Say that again," he said, and Luke did.

"You have opened your heart to your child already. You went to California to make a momentous decision. And you did—quite the opposite of what you thought when you left Boston. But from that moment you determined the destiny of this child." He laid his hand on Sam's shoulder and said again, "Whoever receives one little child like this in My name receives Me." Sam's eyes filled, and Luke continued, "He was talking about you, Sam. And Taite. He was talking about receiving this little one into your hearts, into your arms."

Sam's cell phone rang, and he hesitated for a moment, apparently unwilling to let it go. He flipped open the cover on the fourth ring.

For a moment he listened with a worried expression. "What happened?" he said after a moment. "Oh no!" he breathed. "How is she? The baby...how's the baby?" He listened intently for another few moments, then said, "I'm on my way. I'll be there on the first plane I can catch." He fell silent as the person on the other end of the connection said something more. His face reflected his grief. "Tell Taite I love her," he said into the phone. "Tell her I'm on my way." He flipped the phone closed and looked at Luke.

"Taite?" Luke said.

Sam nodded. "She fell, and now she's gone into labor." He shook his head. "She's not even eight months along."

"Babies can make it at seven, Sam. It's a struggle, but they can make it."

"So many strikes against him…" He paused, seeming lost in anxious thought. "They're going to transport Taite to the hospital on the mainland. By helicopter. The neonatal ICU is on standby." He shook his head slowly. "I just hope they make it in time."

"God has his hand on this little life, Sam. I've seen it already." They turned to walk back to the chapel.

"Thank you for reminding me," Sam said with a grateful look. "And thank you for all you've said tonight. It's helped me beyond what you can know."

"It looks like your decision about Stockholm has been made for you."

"I made it tonight in the chapel. Sometime between when that baby's tiny hand waved in the air and when the soloist seemed to sing directly to me 'What Child Is This?' I knew I couldn't go through with it."

They reached the chapel and stopped at the entrance. "You grab what you need from your dorm, and I'll let Martha know I'm taking you to the airport. She can catch a ride home with friends."

"Are you sure you want to drive in this storm? I can grab a shuttle."

"Wouldn't hear of it. Besides, the plows are out by now." He gave the young man a reassuring pat on the shoulder, knowing he probably didn't want to be alone as he waited for a standby flight. Sam flashed him a grateful look and trotted off toward his dorm.

Luke watched him set off into the snowy night. "Thank you, Lord," he whispered, "for the miracle of your Son's birth—and for the light it's brought into Sam's heart. Now I bring his baby before you. O Father, already this little one has had a struggle to live. I ask that you cradle him in your arms. However this turns out, hold him fast in your love. He is yours…" He smiled. "Or she…"

Victoria sat with Isabel in the waiting room of the clinic. Doc had called the mainland for a helicopter. But the island was fogged in, and after making two attempts to find the tiny airstrip outside town, the pilot had flown back to the airport to wait for clearing.

Footsteps sounded from down the hall, and a moment later Doc rounded the corner into the waiting room. "She's resting," he said gravely. "The amniotic sac broke last night, which prompted the onset of labor. I've given her a sedative to slow down the process, in the hopes that we can safely transport her. The baby will be about seven weeks premature and will need neonatal intensive care. They've got a top-notch NICU there. Taite and the baby will get the best care possible."

Victoria glanced at her daughter, acknowledging the grief in her expression. She felt the same sorrow. "And what if Taite can't wait that long?"

He sat down wearily across from them. "I've got a ventilator that can be adapted to a preemie, also IVs, but it all depends on the baby's size and any other complications." Concern etched his face, and he reached for her hand. "We'll do the best we can for them both."

His expression softened. "Have you heard of kangaroo care?" Isabel and Victoria frowned at each other, puzzled, shaking their heads as he continued. "When a premature baby is born, the best care comes from skin-to-skin contact with the mother. The infant is placed beneath the mother's clothes, cuddled and warmed. The mother's heartbeat, her voice, her movements, are familiar. Studies show that the tiniest under-weight babies with kangaroo care improve faster than those in NICU incubators."

"We may not have a choice," Isabel said, looking skeptical.

"I won't minimize the dangers," Doc said. "With a baby at seven weeks shy of term, with the lack of oxygen to the fetus during the first trimester—" His words broke off, and he took a deep breath. "Without an NICU and its specialized doctors and nurses, this will be challenging." He stood. "Let Taite rest for now. You two do the same. I'll come get you if there's any change."

He left the room, and Victoria leaned her head back against the nondescript sofa and closed her eyes. But instead of resting, she could focus only on Taite, the baby, and the fact that her daughter sat near her and they needed to talk. But she was weary, so weary. Her heart thudded too rapidly, fluttering every few beats like two battling moths. She didn't think she could find the strength to speak of all that was between them.

"Mother?" Isabel said, breaking into her thoughts.

She opened her eyes.

"Last night Taite told me all that you've been going through."

"The DLB?"

"Yes." Her expression was full of compassion. But there was no pity. She was glad of that.

Isabel questioned her about the disease, more concerned with how Victoria was handling the emotional impact on her life than the coming mental and physical deterioration. "I'm here now, Mother. And I'll stay as long as you need me."

Victoria leaned back and closed her eyes again, ashamed that she had worried about losing Taite's affections now that Isabel was home.

She woke with a start when Doc Firestone tapped her on the shoulder. "Victoria?"

"Where's Isabel?"

"She's sitting with Taite. Your granddaughter's awake now and is asking for you."

Victoria stood shakily and took his arm. As they passed the reception area, she glanced out the window behind the desk. A deep gray fog blanketed the ground.

She met Doc's gaze. He nodded slowly as if to tell her it was going to be a long, long night.

26

Victoria stood in the doorway, feeling strangely left out. Isabel sat on the edge of the bed, speaking in low tones with Taite. The bond between them was tentative and fragile, but newborn hope shone in their faces. Her heart was filled with love for them both, but she'd been Taite's only family with Isabel on the other side of the world. Now that Isabel had come home to her daughter, it was time to step into the background.

Even swollen and pregnant, Taite looked too small for the hospital bed. Her dreads, as she called them, hung in messy ringlets around her head. Victoria wondered what Isabel thought about her daughter's tattoos and multitude of earrings. At least she'd recently removed the jeweled stud above her lip, saying she didn't want to scratch the baby when she kissed him.

When Taite saw her grandmother, she smiled and reached out to her. "Naini, I was getting worried."

Victoria laughed as she took Taite's hand. "We're supposed to be worrying about you, child, not the other way around." She touched her forehead and tucked a stray lock of hair away behind her ear. She sat down heavily in the chair nearest her granddaughter. "I talked to Sam earlier. He's coming on the first flight he can catch out of Boston."

Taite's face lit up like the dawn. "He's coming?"

"From his tone, I'd say he couldn't wait to get here." Victoria leaned back, hooking her cane over the chair arm.

Taite nodded. "I hope he arrives in time. The doctor thinks we can put off labor for a few hours. Maybe long enough for clear skies to return."

"He told you about transporting you to Monterey Community?"

"They have a unit there especially designed to treat preemies." Her eyes were bright with hope. "He said if we're lucky, the baby will be over three pounds. That'll give him a fighting chance. Can you imagine a child that small?" She winced and leaned back, closing her eyes.

"Taite…," Isabel said, frowning.

Taite swallowed hard. "I think it's beginning again. Maybe. No, wait. I'm not sure."

But Isabel had already bolted for the door. "I'll get Doc."

Victoria prayed softly for her granddaughter, then looked up to meet her gaze. "Naini, I want to hear the end of the story."

"Not now, surely," she said. "There's too much going on."

Taite chuckled. "Actually, there's not much going on." She patted her stomach. "At least not yet."

A moment later Doc was next to her bed with Isabel standing anxiously behind him. He lifted Taite's wrist and took her pulse. Then, bending over her, he listened to the fetal heartbeat with his stethoscope. He looked up at the clock, then made notes on her chart. "How are you feeling, Taite?"

She nodded and bit her lip again. "Maybe it was a false alarm. I-I thought maybe it was starting. It was a stinging sensation, a tightening, just like before."

"If it starts again, I want to know the first instant. Just holler, okay?"

He left the room, and Taite looked at her grandmother a bit mischievously. "You're on, Naini, if you're up to it."

Isabel looked puzzled. "On for what?"

"Telling me the rest of Taran and Gwynedd's story."

Isabel frowned as she pulled up a chair beside Victoria's. "Taran and Gwynedd?"

Taite laughed. "They lived in the twelfth century—do you know them?"

"I feel a bit like I do. I've just come from Wales—Hanmer—where I heard stories about them…legends, really."

Taite looked ready to clap her hands in delight and again met her grandmother's gaze as if wanting her to share her joy. She turned back to Isabel. "You were there? In Hanmer itself?"

"The very place. Apparently there's a mystery about what happened to the couple in the end. The vicar gave me a copy of a letter and asked me to search for another." She waved her hand. "But that can certainly wait." She looked to Victoria. "It's been a long time since I've heard your stories. I would love to hear one again."

Victoria had prayed for the day when her daughter and granddaughter would be reunited. Her mind was slipping, and she knew it well. But her prayer had been that she would live to see—and still recognize—her beloved Isabel and Taite in the same room, loving each other, just as mothers and daughters should.

How often she had complained that no one would listen to her stories. And now, in the shadowy world of DLB, here they were, longing for her to tell them. Both had changed, it seemed, toward each other, even toward the stories of the past.

She leaned back and regarded her precious granddaughter who'd once wanted to be rid of the life she carried. She was still the quirky, lovely, lively Taite, but in these most difficult hours, a new peace seemed to fill her spirit, as if she knew she was loved beyond all measure.

Victoria thought of the fisherman and smiled at Taite, knowing.

The gifts present in this room were the most precious of her life, Victoria decided. No matter what happened tomorrow, today was to be treasured.

"The story?" Taite asked, raising a brow. She patted the side of the bed by her left knee and scooted over slightly. "Come sit beside me, Naini. I want to savor every word."

Gwynedd headed into Caer Abbey as the pealing bells called the monks to nones. She passed through the gate with a knot of villagers on their way to market. Donkeys and oxen plodded among them, and geese fluttered and squawked alongside. She was surprised to find life going on as if the bishop himself, his monks, and the villagers were unaware that Gunnolf's army was grouped, ready to attack, just beyond the gates.

She moved past the market stalls into the heart of the village. Doves in a cage fluttered and squawked as she hurried by; vendors called out, hawking their wares. Surprisingly, the closer she got to the abbey, the greater her sense of foreboding, as if a strange pall hung over the city. She slipped into a doorway, off the cobbled street, and stared up at the bell tower, following its shadow to where it fell across the manicured abbey grounds and encircling walls. The area nearby was quiet, eerily quiet, making her want to back away and flee.

A monk walked past, his head bent in prayer. She stepped from her hiding place and fell into step with him. "Tell me," she said, "is it possible to see the bishop?"

He halted and stared at her in surprise. "Perhaps if you were King Stephen," he said, raising an amused brow.

"As you can see, I am not," she said, lifting her chin a bit defiantly. "But I have important information for his ears only. I have just come from Han-mere at great peril, and it is of utmost importance that I see him immediately."

" 'Tis impossible, miss." The monk bowed his fringed head and continued on his way to the abbey.

She followed, undeterred, trotting along in an attempt to match his purposeful gait. "Where would I find the bishop," she said, "should I convince someone to allow me to see him?"

The bells tolled a second time, and the monk increased his speed, the hem of his gray robe snapping as he walked. "You have recently come from Han-mere?"

"Aye," she panted, trying to keep up with him.

"I knew a monk from there many years ago. Cadwallen was his name. A gentle soul whose heart was tuned to God's own."

She touched his arm, and he stopped. "Brother Cadwallen was my friend and with me until this morn." Briefly she told him what had happened.

"And why have you come at such great risk? Why would Cadwallen give his life?"

"Because of the sacred texts," she said, "the illuminated Gospels, hidden away from Gunnolf. I must tell the bishop where they may be found."

The monk's expression darkened, confusing her.

"I have proof," she said, "of my mission and of him who sent me." She pulled on the cloth that held the ring, further alarming her companion.

"I entreat you," he whispered, "to hide the ring away. It is not safe here." He glanced nervously toward the abbey gate and the gardens beyond. "You must hide yourself until after nones. I will come for you." He looked beyond a group of monks approaching briskly from a cluster of outbuildings. "You will be safe in the gardens—near the far wall behind the well."

Her earlier sense of peril returned at the fear in his eyes, and she nodded. "Aye."

"Do not speak to anyone." He turned to leave, then looked back. "Especially do not speak to the bishop."

She hid in the shadows of the church wall, listening to the monks' chanted prayers through the open windows. Behind her, village women hurried in and out of a doorway leading to what she supposed was the abbey laundry, their lively chatter mixing with the chants. After a time, she paced, then sat again, twisting her hands in worry. When the monk returned, she breathed a sigh of relief and stood to meet him.

"I neglected to tell you my name," he said, drawing her further into the shadows. " 'Tis Brother John. And yours, brave woman?"

"Gwynedd of Han-mere, kind brother." She gave him a small bow. "I have a plan," she said, thinking how often she had said those very words to Taran. "I can give you the bishop's ring—because of your friendship with Cadwallen I trust you—and you can tell him about the Gospels. I will explain where they are hidden, how the fathers here can find the caves. For you see, I cannot spend more time at this place. I have another mission. I must find my husband and the captives with him."

Brother John sighed. "Bishop Jerome cannot be trusted, dear Gwynedd of Han-mere. You told me yourself that the ring was given you by Cadwallen. You must keep it in memory of your friend and wear it proudly someday." He looked around again to make certain they were not overheard. Only the laundresses were visible, hanging monks' robes, gowns, and scapulars on twine strung between two trees.

Brother John pulled her back, hidden from even the abbey laundry. "Gunnolf was here."

Her eyes widened as she tried to comprehend.

The monk touched his lips to signal she should not speak. "There is an exchange happening this hour. I do not know what the bishop has promised to Gunnolf—likely riches, perhaps of a sacred nature—in exchange for the safety of Caer Abbey." His expression turned dark. "'Twas overheard by one of the brothers that the bishop's personal wealth is pledged, as well as our abbey and outbuildings."

"That is no concession," she said, her heart sinking. "They will make your people slaves—those they do not kill—just as they did in Han-mere. You might have standing buildings, but they will be empty of life."

Brother John nodded sadly. "'Tis as you say." He paused, looking up at the tower, now turning golden in the late afternoon slant of the sun. "I think our weak bishop wanted only to save his own skin. Rather than fight what he thought was a lost battle, he made the decision to side with the invaders."

"Gunnolf will kill him anyway," she said.

"Or crown him king to keep the villagers from rebelling."

She nodded in agreement. "I must tell you about the sacred treasures." He stepped closer, and she whispered the details of the tunnel and the cave deep inside. When she was certain he understood, she gave him a nod. "My mission here is done, then."

He touched her arm, and she could see in his eyes the same flame of sacred passion that was in Cadwallen's. "You have been brave, dear warrior, showing more courage for God and your people than anyone else I have known. You have brought your news here. I will tell others I can trust, so if any of us is killed, the knowledge will live on. Even one man of God"—he nodded—"or woman of God can keep the flame alive with an obedient heart. Some of us will someday return to Han-mere to rebuild. Because of what you have done, the work of Cadwallen and the others will live on." He smiled. "I believe he knew this when he gave his life so that you might live…and reach Caer."

She took in his words, feeling strangely warmed by them. "And mayhap a handful of others can join you to rebuild," she said, staring at the monks' robes hanging by the laundry.

"Where will you go now?" Brother John asked.

"Sometimes God provides a vision of a journey's next step in the least likely places," she said with a small smile and hope in her heart. "I have another task to complete. I will bid you farewell and be on my way."

Brother John bent and kissed her hand. "Godspeed, m'lady, as you go out."

"May our Lord bless and keep you," she whispered and turned toward the laundry. When the women bent again to their work, she slipped closer to the drying garments. After another furtive look around, she sidled next to a gray hooded robe, snatched it from the line, and tucked it under one arm. Her heart thumping wildly, she hurried from Caer Abbey to the winding cobbled streets, passed the market vendors, and reached the city gate without being noticed or detained.

As the sun hung near the horizon, in a small tangle of saplings beyond the abbey walls, she donned the gray robe and adjusted the hood to cover her hair. She brought the bishop's ring from where it was hidden, discarded the worn cloth, and slipped the circle of gold with its embossed lily cross onto her finger.

It would be a sign to Gunnolf that she had come in the name of the bishop of Caer. She only hoped her disguise would get her into the encampment to find the prisoners, her family and loved ones from Han-mere, now enslaved.

As she made her way through the gray mist of eventide, she thought of Brother John's words about Cadwallen: "He gave his life so that you might live." Could she do any less for her people, for Taran? They carried in their souls the memory of Han-mere Abbey, what it once stood for as a place of God. They had worked together creating the lambskin vellum and inks. They had listened to the songs of praise and supplication, a sweet fragrance rising heavenward above the mere.

"This remnant of those who escaped must return," she thought, "for they know what was there and what must be rebuilt." The falling dusk dimmed the sky, and she paused at the forest edge, looking out at the enemy encampment, the tall tents surrounded by standing torches. She heard sounds of a raucous celebration. As usual, the camp seemed beset by disorganization. She planned how she would step up to the guards, disguised as the bishop's emissary, but she did not want to think about what they would do to her when they discovered her deception.

A rustling in the cat's cradle a half furlong away caught her attention. She turned, worried that a wild boar might be nosing about.

But instead, a hind stood like a statue, watching Gwynedd, her dark eyes luminous and knowing. The doe was young, delicate, and perfectly formed, so comely she made Gwynedd's heart ache. She stood firm, perhaps because a fawn lay curled nearby in a warm bower.

Rebirth followed death. Light followed darkness. The oil of joy followed mourning. It was God's way.

Lightly touching her stomach, Gwynedd whispered a prayer for her baby, remembering the blessing of Brother Cadwallen for her children and her children's children. "May it be so, dear Lord," she breathed as she stepped into the clearing.

Then she raised her eyes to the North Star and thought of Taran's love.

27

Taite leaned against the pillows Doc had piled against the headboard to support her back. The next pang hit with full force, and she gasped aloud, squeezing her eyes closed. "Heavenly Father," she prayed silently, "help me…help me." The pain eased, and she tried to breathe again.

Her mother kept vigil on her left, Naini on her right. She looked up at them with a heart full of gratitude. "Thank you for being here," she said to her mother, who had tears in her eyes. Then she looked to Victoria and reached for her hand. "Naini? Thank you for…" She smiled, thinking of all the love and acceptance her grandmother had showered on her through the years. "For everything." This was totally unlike her, to be so sentimental; she hoped it didn't mean she was about to die.

Naini squeezed her fingers. "Just concentrate on your breathing, honey. Short little puffs, and look up at the painting when the next pang hits. Don't think of anything else but the light in the tower, the sunlight on the water."

She relaxed against her pillows again. Her mother gave her a piece of ice, and she slipped it into her mouth. "Thank you," she whispered. She turned to the window. It faced the small harbor, the wharf, and the few businesses lining the boardwalk along the shore. Nearest the clinic was the Ink 'n Quill, and though it was veiled in fog, she could just make out the outline of Christmas lights along its steep roof, chimney, and front windows. A week ago she and Susan, whose six-month-old baby girl was cozily tucked in a pram, had helped Marihelen decorate a small tree on the wide porch, and even on this cloudy night, its lights glowed through the mist, the star on top brightest of all.

Doc came through the door. "Susan just called and sends her love and prayers. Little Evangeline has a stuffy nose, and she can't take her outside. Otherwise she said she'd be here with you. Pastor Tom had to make a trip to the mainland, but she assures me they're both praying for you."

He scanned the monitor beside her bed, moved to the IV drip, checked the glucose level, and changed the bag. "How are we doing?" he asked when he'd finished.

Taite grinned at him. "I don't know how you're doing, but this isn't much fun for me."

"That's what I like," he said, "a mom-to-be with a sense of humor." He put on the stethoscope again to check the baby's heart rate. "You'll need it when he's a teenager. Or she."

Another birth pang began, gradually growing in intensity.

"The painting, honey," her grandmother reminded her.

Taite forced herself to look at the seascape, the crashing waves, the lighthouse in the distance. She concentrated on the brushstrokes, the pastel colors, the dark colors, the everything-in-between colors. The pain grew stronger, and she moaned, breathing fast and clutching her mother's hand. "Oh, Mama," she cried at its peak. Then slowly it ebbed again. "Whew," she breathed, exhausted.

Doc was looking at his watch. "Fifteen seconds," he pronounced.

"It seemed like an eternity." She paused, remembering what she'd read about childbirth. "They get longer, right?"

He nodded. "Right."

"Until one simply morphs into the next one."

Chuckling, he raised a brow. "Morphs?"

Until her baby was born. Closing her eyes, she anticipated the moment. This little one already had so many strikes against him, and now she wondered how he could make it. Quickly she pushed away her fears.

She sat up slightly. "Doc?"

He was heading out the door but turned when she called him.

"Tell me about what will happen if my baby's sick, really sick. What can I expect?"

He came back into the room, scooted his round wheeled stool toward her, and sat down. "You want the whole scoop?"

She nodded. "Everything. The good and the bad. Every detail."

He described what to expect, depending on the birth weight of the child—the care she and the child would receive when flown to the mainland, the emergency measures he and Grace could handle at the clinic in case transport was delayed.

Her heart plummeted as he spoke. "What are the baby's chances?" Her hand rested on her bulging stomach.

"We're hopeful," Doc said kindly, "that his chances will be good." He paused. "Again, it depends on birth weight. The bigger he is, the greater his chances. And of course much depends on any other complications that might come up." He patted her hand, and gave her an encouraging smile. "Did your mom and grandmother tell you about kangaroo care?"

"Kangaroo care?" She smiled at the image. Doc nodded and explained about the skin-to-skin contact with a preemie, and she lay back against her pillow, imagining her little one. She was at once both frightened and awed.

He turned to leave, then glanced back. "By the way, you keep refer-ring to your baby as a he." He winked. "Your *he* just might be a she."

She laughed. "I'm just certain I'm carrying a little boy. I keep pic-turing his Little League uniform, his little jeans and shirts, how he'll laugh when he plays with bugs and lizards." Still grinning, she added, "You were the first to mention it, you know…the first to put a human face on what I thought was…" *Disposable.* She couldn't bring herself to speak the word.

He nodded, and she could see he remembered. "Thank you for what you shared that day," she said. "It was the first time I began to think—" She caught her breath and rolled to her side as another pang overtook her body.

The pain hung over her, a white-hot cloud, pulsating, drawing her into its depths. "Oh dear," she moaned. "Oh dear…"

"The painting, child," Naini whispered in her ear. "Keep your eyes on the lighthouse. Concentrate… Remember…"

The fisherman. That's what Naini meant. Taite looked at the light-house, the sea, the sun's reflection. Riding on the crest of the pain, she remembered being carried to safety. Oh yes, she remembered.

And Gwynedd and the shepherd, how he held her through her darkest night… He was the same yesterday, today, and forever. He had been with new mothers since the beginning of time. Through his Spirit he was with her now. She didn't know how she knew; she just did.

Sam landed in San Francisco at dawn. As soon as the plane rolled to a stop at the gate, he flipped open his phone and called information for the number of Monterey Community NICU. A nurse answered on the first ring, but Sam's heart dropped when he found that Taite hadn't yet been admitted. The nurse told him that they'd been on standby all night, awaiting the helicopter's arrival from Pelican Island. She also said, sadly, the island airstrip was socked in under a heavy fog that had settled along the coast.

That also meant he couldn't get a flight into Monterey Peninsula airport. He rented a car and sped out of the airport parking area, heading south on Interstate 280. Only to come to a dead stop because of morning rush-hour traffic.

He again pressed the auto-dial number for information, this time asking to be connected to the Pelican Island clinic.

It was before office hours, and as he dialed, he prayed someone would be there to answer. Doc Firestone picked up after the first ring.

"This is Sam Wellington," he explained quickly. "Taite Abbott's fiancé. Is she still there? And how are things going?"

"Taite is a fighter. It's been a long, difficult night for her. She's dilated to seven centimeters, and it seems things have stalled for now. It's been over twenty-four hours since her water broke. It's too dangerous to wait much longer. Forty-eight hours is max."

"You're talking about a C-section?"

"No anesthesiologist. And I can perform that role only in an emergency. I'm afraid I'm pretty rusty." He paused. "How soon can you get here?"

Sam told him about the traffic.

"We probably won't see you until noon. If the weather clears and things are stable, I still want her transported to Community in Monterey. Worst case scenario is to transport her by ferry. The seas are rough. It would be dangerous. Besides..." He paused. "I hate to move her."

"Can you have someone call me if you do get her off the island?"

Doc agreed and took Sam's cell number. "You want to talk to Taite?"

"Are you sure she feels up to it?"

"She's tired, but from what she's told me, there's nothing she'd like better than to hear your voice and know you're close. I'll put you on hold. Can you wait?" He sighed after a moment. "Grace is usually here to operate this antiquated phone system. If I lose you, we'll call you back from Taite's room."

"I'll be waiting. Thanks."

After a moment Taite spoke. "Hi, papa-to-be." Her voice came through the phone a tired whisper. "Where are you?"

He told her, trying to sound as optimistic as possible. "How are you doing, honey?"

"Trying to remain hopeful," she said quietly. "But I need you, Sam." She fell silent. "If there are decisions to be made..." She fell silent and then continued. "We need to make them together."

"That's not why I want to be there," he said. "I want to see my little girl the minute she's born."

Taite chuckled. "You and Doc both call him a *her*." She fell silent for a moment. "Either one will make me happy. I just want our baby to be healthy. Tiny is okay, but healthy."

"That's what I want too."

"Hurry," she whispered.

"I'll be there as soon as I can." For a moment, neither of them seemed willing to break the connection. Then Sam added, "I'm praying for you, Taite. And for our baby."

"I've never known you to pray," she said.

"I'm not very good at it, but that's all I've done in the last twelve hours."

She didn't answer, but he thought he heard her weeping.

Taite fell against her pillow, smiling. Sam was coming! And he was praying. She touched her stomach and lifted her eyes to the painting, thinking of the fisherman in her dream. "Carry my little one to safety," she prayed. "Just as you did me, carry him in your arms of love."

The next searing pain struck harder than any before; Taite drew in a quick breath. This time it built, and she sank into a formless pool of pain where she thought she might drown. On and on it whirled around her, threatening to pull her under.

When the pain diminished, she barely had enough time to suck in a breath of air before it grew again, this time even more fiercely. She cried out and felt her mother's hand on hers.

"I'm here," she said, her voice both tender and strong. "And Naini is right here beside you."

Naini lovingly wiped her forehead with a cool, damp cloth. The next wave of pain hit, rising and falling, carrying her on its crest once more. Taite heard her voice crying out, almost unrecognizable as her own.

Unconsciousness threatened, but Doc pulled her back. "Stay with us, Taite. Don't leave us now."

She tried to moisten her lips, and at once her mother was beside her with more ice chips. "It's time?" she croaked after a moment.

"We're almost there, honey."

"No helicopter ride?" She started to laugh, but the sound was broken by a cry as pain exploded, so overpowering that she sank into it, lost.

Doc's voice, low and concerned, was the last thing she heard, and even then, it seemed at a huge distance. It sounded like he said, "We've got a problem here…"

Isabel stepped back as Doc called for Grace. "We're ready to go," he said. "I need you here." The lines on his face were more pronounced than before. "Stat."

Within a half minute, she was in the door, dressed in surgical scrubs. "The delivery room is ready. I'll help you scrub."

They were gone only seconds it seemed before they rushed back in to move Taite to a gurney. He glanced toward Isabel and Victoria, who stepped back to one side of the room. "You need to wait outside."

Isabel nodded and reached for her mother's arm to help her down the hall. When they were seated, Victoria surprised her by smiling. "I would imagine when you decided to come home for Christmas, you had no idea we would be spending it in a clinic on the island waiting for your grandchild to be born."

"Christmas…" Isabel sat back shaking her head. "So much has happened I completely forgot about it. What day is it anyway?"

Victoria chuckled. "You're asking the wrong person. Some days I can't even remember what I had for breakfast—or if I had breakfast."

Isabel ached for her mother. "Has it gotten that bad?"

"Some days are worse than others. Coming here to the island has helped. I feel more at peace somehow. I wasn't for it in the beginning. I thought Taite wanted to use caring for me as a crutch to hide from real life, from her responsibilities. Instead, she's blossomed into the woman she was intended to be. She seems to have started living from inside out instead of outside in."

"I'm not sure I follow."

"For years Taite has focused on her own pain—her preoccupation with having been abandoned—at least her perception over what happened between the two of you. In the last few months she's turned some kind of emotional corner, started caring more about others than herself. She began writing our family history, turning it into a novel. She developed a program for seniors at Happy Acres—helping them write their own family histories. They've met her and love her and can't wait to get started. She's made friends of all ages in town, from the stationer to the local mystery author. I think it was the child that made a difference in her life." She gave Isabel a smile. "Motherhood changes everything, doesn't it?"

"But she's having a child out of wedlock." She drew in a deep breath, thinking about the entanglements to come. Hurting on behalf of the child and Taite.

Victoria leaned forward. "Taite knows better than any of us the consequences of her actions. You have no idea how she's grieved." She paused, her gaze meeting Isabel's. "If you knew where Taite has come from, you'd see that God's hand was on her, on this baby, from the beginning." She settled back. "It's all about his grace, Isabel. Without it, where would any of us be?"

Isabel's eyes filled as Victoria described Taite's determination to end her pregnancy, her experience at the abortion clinic, the worry about what the lack of oxygen had done to the fetus, then how she fell in love with the child she was carrying.

They fell silent, each seeming almost shy in the other's presence. Isabel felt it, and she wondered if her mother did too. "This is quite a homecoming," she said.

"Three generations of women, all of us together again," Victoria smiled. "I prayed it would happen."

"Perhaps there will soon be four." Isabel grinned.

"Now, wouldn't that be a wonder?" Victoria looked happier than Isabel could ever remember seeing her. "And at Christmas."

When Taite awoke, the room seemed bathed in haze. At first she didn't know where she was. Then she heard the *beep-beep* of a heart monitor. Around her rose a maze of tubes, IVs, and contraptions she couldn't begin to understand.

As the fuzziness subsided, one sound took precedence over all the others. It sounded like a machine that was breathing. In. Out. In. Out. A steady rhythm of whooshing sounds as steady as a heartbeat. A ventilator. But there were no tubes in her nose or throat.

She lay still with her eyes closed, afraid to hope that the warm weight against her chest was something more than her imagination. Then she felt the slight movement of breathing. Not hers, but the breath of a child as if from little lungs taking in and then expelling air, a small chest rising and falling. It moved in rhythm with the ventilator.

She bit her lip as tears welled in her eyes. Her baby was alive. She kept perfectly still, savoring, almost tasting, this first moment of knowledge that her baby was alive.

"Taite?" whispered a voice by her ear. "It's me. Sam."

She turned her head and grinned at him. The light in his eyes melted her heart. He was dressed in hospital scrubs, even to the mask over his mouth.

"We have a baby," he whispered. "Did you know?"

"How much does he weigh?"

Sam laughed in a hushed tone. "She weighs four pounds, one ounce."

Taite gasped with surprise. "She?"

"She," he said proudly. "We have a daughter."

Closing her eyes, she took in the news, unable to stop smiling. "Four pounds. That's big."

Doc, also wearing a mask, was standing at the foot of the bed. "Big for a preemie, but we'll still need to get you and the baby to the NICU." He stepped closer to speak to them both. "Tests need to be run, of course. I've taken a preliminary blood sample from her foot—something that needs to be done within twenty-four hours of birth—and the NICU will do the rest. But she looks healthy, very healthy, for someone so tiny." His eyes smiled above the mask. "You made it through without anesthetic—something that gave her a healthy boost into our world."

Taite laid her hand on the warm bundle cuddled against her heart. "I thought I heard you say, 'We've got a problem' as I blacked out."

"The cord was wrapped around her neck." Doc stepped closer and put his hand on Taite's, where hers still rested over her daughter's tiny body. "But she cooperated fully. Turned just as needed, just in time." He laughed. "Enjoy the moment. Give her a dozen years or so. She won't always be so willing."

"May we see her?"

Doc turned to Sam and explained about kangaroo care. The baby was held fast in a triangle of soft white flannel that wrapped around Taite's back and tied at her waist. "We can't let this little one get cold. So just a quick peek for now." He gently opened the pouch and stepped back like a maestro who'd just conducted a masterpiece. Taite almost expected him to bow.

Taite peered in first. The baby's head was perfectly formed, without the slightest bit of fuzz for hair. Her shoulders seemed no bigger than a doll's. She was smaller than Taite had even imagined. She blinked back her tears at the sight of the ventilator tube and IV needle taped to the baby's pencil-thin arm. "My precious little one," she whispered, touching her cheek with her fingertips.

Sam bent over Taite's shoulder. "She's beautiful—" He choked up, and for a moment he seemed unable to speak. Then he stood and looked down at Taite, holding the whole world in his eyes.

Doc helped Taite retie the triangle of flannel. Sam stood off to one side as they worked to get the baby snug against her.

"When we get to Community," Sam asked when Doc was finished, "will they take her from us—put her with the other babies in an incubator?"

"They may for a few days. They'll do what they think is best." His voice was reassuring. "They're good. Best around, in my opinion."

"How long do you think we have before the helicopter gets here?" Sam had a slightly mischievous gleam in his eye.

"I just checked the weather forecast. I would say we'll have enough clearing in a couple of hours."

Sam grinned at Taite. "I have an idea—if you're feeling up to it." He bent down and whispered in her ear, then stood back and gave her an adoring look.

It didn't matter that she was too sore to move, from her fall, from bearing this wee miracle. Nothing mattered except the new life she was about to begin with Sam. "I am if you are," she said.

"Do you think we can get someone to marry us?" he asked Doc.

Doc grinned. "I know just the one." He glanced at Taite.

She nodded. "The pastor at Chapel by the Sea. His wife is a friend."

"I'll get Grace to call and see if he's back." He shook his head slowly. "This'll be a first." He winked at Sam. "You never know what excitement a medical practice in a little backwoods clinic might bring."

When they were alone again, Taite couldn't keep her eyes off Sam. "You came," she said.

Above the sterile mask, his eyes crinkled at the edges. "A thousand kangaroos couldn't have kept me away."

She sighed deeply and wrapped her arms around the baby sleeping at her breast. "What about your work...the research?"

"Do you know the old English song 'What Child Is This?' "

Taite nodded.

"About the same time you went into labor, I stepped into the campus chapel. The choir had just begun their Christmas program. I expected to hear the usual fare.

"But the soloist began singing, and our child's image came into my mind... It all came together: my uncertainty about the Stockholm research and the embryos I would handle, my questions about the sanctity of life. There was a child, a baby—a real one—in a manger..." He looked at a loss for words. Finally he said, "It was so obvious in the end." He walked over and placed his hand on hers. "Can you forgive me for what I put you through? For not being more responsible from the beginning?"

She gazed up at him, her heart so full of love that she almost could not bear it. "I need forgiveness too," she said. "I've made so many mista—" But before she could answer, Sam touched her lips with his—still behind the mask—smiled into her eyes, then kissed the tip of her nose.

"I've always said I needed proof of God's existence to believe," he said softly. He moved his hand and tenderly rested it on their daughter. "He answered my prayer…before I even knew I was praying. This child is my answer."

Taite couldn't speak, she was so overcome with love for this man.

"I'd like to begin afresh," he said. "The three of us, you, me, and…" His eyes brightened above the mask. "Have you given it any thought?"

"I've thought of little else," she said, grinning wide. She still curled one arm around the baby, and with the other she reached for Sam's hand. "I've been so immersed in Naini's tales that I almost feel I know my ancestors. I would like to honor them. Their story helped bring a sense of wholeness to my heart."

His expression told her he understood. "Taran and Gwynedd, isn't it?" She nodded, and he went on. "Are you thinking about Gwynedd? It seems a bit cumbersome."

She quirked a brow and grinned. "I've always been a little unconventional."

The smile in his eyes warmed her heart. "To say the least." Then he paused. "You're not thinking…"

"I am thinking," she said, reading his mind, "of Taran. Though I'm a bit worried my ancestors might spin beneath their headstones. Giving a little four-pound girl the name of a brawny Welshman." She thought of Taran, his shepherd's soul, his heart full of song, his love for Gwynedd. Somehow it felt right. Perhaps he would be pleased if he knew.

"It's a beautiful name," Sam said, crossing his arms and squinting as if trying it on for size. "It might have been a boy's name in the twelfth century, but who's to say it can't be a girl's today?"

"Taran Wellington," she said. "I like the sound of it." She looked down at the sleeping bundle in her arms. "Taran," she breathed, and reaching inside the blanket, she touched her daughter's shoulders, letting her fingers trail along the flannel on her arm to the back of her tiny fist. She was so beautiful that Taite could hardly bear it.

The helicopter landed on the wharf, and even through the clinic walls, Taite could hear the *whop-whop* of the whirling blades as they waited to take off again.

Around the bed stood her mother, Naini, Grace, and Doc—all in surgical masks and covered with sterile gowns. Pastor Tom and Susan, dressed in the same manner, turned to Sam and Taite. Everyone was smiling, but because of the masks, only their eyes showed. Taite would remember her wedding guests' attire forever.

"Dearly beloved," Pastor Tom began, "we are gathered together here in the sight of God, and in the face of this company, to join together this man, Samuel Wellington, and this woman, Taite Abbott, in holy matrimony, which is an honorable estate, instituted of God, signifying unto us the mystical union that is between Christ and his church: the holy estate which Christ adorned and beautified with his presence and first miracle in Cana of Galilee."

As he spoke, Taite felt her mother's gaze and turned toward her. Above her mask, Isabel smiled with her eyes and gave Taite a nod that seemed to overflow with pride and approval and love. Taite was in awe of the change in her own heart. Only God could bring about such healing, take away her pain, and, in its place, fill her to overflowing with peace. She smiled at her mother. *I love you, Mama,* she said with her heart.

Before the pastor arrived, Taite had written out a personal request to be added to the ceremony, and when the time was right, Sam took her hand, and Pastor Tom read the blessing: "Almighty God, our heavenly Father, fill these your beloved children with faith, virtue, knowledge, temperance, patience, and godliness. Knit together in constant affection your son Samuel Wellington and your daughter Taite Abbott from this day forward. For their children, especially Taran, their daughter, and their children's children, and for all who will follow through the ages: Turn the hearts of parents to children, and the hearts of children to parents. So enkindle fervent charity among them all, that they may evermore be filled with love one to another as members of your family through your Son, Jesus Christ our Lord."

The helicopter rose from the landing pad, and the island fell away. Sam sat next to Taite's stretcher, his arm around her shoulders, one hand resting lightly on the bundle over her heart. The aircraft banked as it turned toward Monterey. Slanted rays shone through pillows of clouds with shapes like medieval castles and rocking horses and skipping lambs. It seemed God had created a masterpiece of design in his heavens just for her. For this moment. Taran moved slightly against her skin. Sam felt it too and met Taite's gaze with an almost startled look of wonder.

God had created a masterpiece. Oh yes, he had!

EPILOGUE

Taran skipped ahead of Taite and Sam as they walked up the slight incline above the mere. Isabel ran after her, calling and laughing, until she finally scooped the child into her arms. Taite exchanged a glance with Sam. "It seems Naini Isabel has her hands full this trip."

Sam laughed. "She spoils her rotten, but isn't that what grandmothers are for?"

A twinge of sorrow twisted Taite's heart as she thought about her beloved Naini. "Yes, but there's something about a grandmother's love…" She couldn't finish and looked away as she drew in a shaky breath. Her grandmother had died in her sleep two years earlier, not long after Taran had learned to call her Naini, but the pain of her loss was still sharp. How many times had she reached for the phone to call Victoria and tell her something she knew she would enjoy?

Every time the church bells tolled at Chapel by the Sea, echoing throughout the island, it seemed Victoria was with them still. During the last year of her life, she became passionate about collecting funds to restore the beautiful bell and its tower. Even when she began forgetting names and places and everyday details, she remembered the bell.

It tolled for the first time the morning Victoria died. Taite had often wondered if she had been waiting for that moment.

Sam took her hand to help her climb a circular stone pathway leading to the caves where Taran and Gwynedd were said to have hidden during the assault on their village. No one was allowed inside these days, but a bronze plaque honoring the young couple had been placed on a stone wall near the entrance sometime in the last century.

Taite touched the raised lettering, still visible despite its weathering. Beneath Taran and Gwynedd's names was the Cadwallen family blessing, written in Welsh. She knew it only because the vicar at Saint Chad's had given her a printed copy in English.

"Family blessings," she mused.

Sam grinned, looking down at her very round stomach. "And we have them in abundance," he said, gathering her close. She laid her head on his shoulder, taking joy in his love. "Do you have any sense of having been here before?"

"No, I don't believe in that sort of thing, but I do have the sense that this is a holy place." They stood holding each other for a moment, then turned to walk down the grassy knoll that overlooked the blue gray waters of the mere. Around them daffodils bloomed in profusion, creating a carpet of golden sunlight. Taran squealed in delight as she ran through the yellow field toward her mother.

Taite stooped to catch her daughter in her arms, lifted her, and planted a kiss on her nose.

Isabel wasn't far behind. She tromped up the hill, breathless from chasing her granddaughter.

"Naini," Taran said, reaching her hand toward her grandmother. Opening Taran's fingers, Isabel kissed her chubby little palm, stooped to pick a bright daffodil, and tucked it atop Taran's ear. Taran turned to Sam and gave him a coy smile. "Am I pretty, Daddy?"

"Like a princess," he said, and she reached for him to take her in his arms.

"I wonder where Cadwallen stood when he arrived here," Taite said to her mother, "and decided this was the place to build the abbey."

"Do we know that actually happened?" Isabel said. "Your grandmother has been known to make a good story better. And that was before her illness."

Taite laughed. "I think I inherited it from her." Then she thought about the letter box and its contents. "We do have evidence now that the story—most of it, anyway—is much as she related it."

Taran was chattering about the swans on the lake, and Sam set her on the ground, took her hand, and trotted down the path leading to the mere to have a closer look.

Taite watched them go. "The letter ties the legend together. It was as if Gwynedd wanted us to know the end of the story, wanted us to know the story didn't end when she entered the encampment."

"Did you tell the end in the book?"

Taite laughed lightly. "I was tempted to leave it hanging, much the way we were left when Naini told us the end at the clinic."

"Speaking of the clinic, how does Sam like working with Doc?"

"He's never been happier. Doc has brought him in as a full partner and plans to sell him the practice when he retires." She paused, watching her husband lift Taran into his arms. "He's still fascinated with research and will apply for fellowships, taking leaves of absence as he needs to."

"Back to your book," Isabel said. Taite could hear her mother's pride each time she let the words *your book* skip over her tongue. "Tell me how it ends."

Taite grinned. "Every author knows better than to give away the ending."

"But I'm your mother."

They laughed together. "I'll give you a hint." She shook her head slowly. "She was one clever young woman. She tricked Gunnolf, giving him a dose of his own medicine. She moved among them as a representative of Bishop Jerome, ordering the release of the Han-mere prisoners in exchange for more of the bishop's great wealth. She escaped with the villagers before Gunnolf discovered she wasn't a monk. They were miles away by the time he found he'd been tricked."

"And Taran?" They shared a smile. Her mother knew the story as well as Taite did. They had pored over the letter side by side, delighting in their discovery.

"Suffice it to say that their first child had many siblings," she said. "They grew old together." Then her thoughts sobered. "Do you think Naini truly didn't know the contents of the letter box? That the monk's ring was inside? Or the letter?" She shook her head slowly. "To find such a treasure was astounding."

"I think it was talked about from generation to generation, but no one wanted to open the letter box and find out the stories might be little more than wishful thinking...or fairy tales. So it was passed from hand to hand with instructions not to open it."

Taite grinned. "I was the maverick. Took it to a dealer in antiquities and had it unlocked."

Her mother put her arm around Taite's waist. "That's one of the things I love about you, dear one—your individuality, the rebel in you." She paused. "Taite, I want you to know how proud I am of you. Not just because of the gracious doctor's wife and loving mom you've turned out to be, or because *Family Blessings* is about to be published, or that your writing program for the elderly is flourishing, but just because you're you." Her eyes filled as she beheld her daughter. "Because you're Taite. A beautiful woman of God who's like no other."

"Dreads, tattoos, and all?"

Her mother laughed. "Especially all that. Did I tell you I'm getting a tattoo?" She raised a playful brow.

Taite groaned. "You, too? When I got my first one, Naini said she wanted one. Took a lot of creative determination to talk her out of it."

"Good practice for you," Isabel said, still smiling. "You'll need it when Taran reaches her teens."

Taite gasped in horror. "You don't suppose she'll try such a…" She caught herself and laughed. "But you'll be there to help me keep her on the right path."

"Always," her mother said as they walked back to the car.

"Chester Abbey, here we come," Sam said. When they were all buckled in, she and Sam in the front, Isabel and Taran in the back, he backed the car away from the parking area near Saint Chad's.

"Caer Abbey in Welsh," Taite said, thinking of Gwynedd's brave journey nearly a millennium earlier. A doe gracefully leapt across the road in front of them. Two fawns skipped behind. Sam slowed the car so Taran could watch them.

The automobile moved slowly along the country roads, and Taite opened the letter box one last time. She picked up the velvet drawstring bag inside, loosened the tie, and turned the bag over in her hand.

The ring slid into her palm. "Caer Abbey is its rightful place," she said softly, "but to think of its history, where it's been." She turned it in her hand, admiring the worn Celtic-knot design, the unique rose hue of Welsh-mined gold, the resurrection cross.

"The stories it could tell," Sam said.

"It's obviously up to me to tell the stories on its behalf," she said with a half smile.

"Have you thought that you are the last in the family to touch this ring?"

"And the last storyteller," she said. She remembered Naini's saying, *To be born Welsh is to be born wealthy, not with a silver spoon in your mouth, but with music in your blood and poetry in your soul.* Being Welsh suited her soul just fine.

She placed the ring on her finger and held it up to the light, turning it in the sun. From the backseat, Taran reached for it. "Let me see it, Mommy!"

Isabel took it from Taite and carefully slipped it over Taran's thumb. Taite watched her daughter turn it this way and that, her eyes wide with wonder. "Once upon a time there was a princess," Taran said solemnly. "And this pretty princess had a ring…"

"Actually," Taite said to her mother and Sam, "maybe I'm not the last storyteller after all."

Acknowledgments

Heartfelt thanks to my early readers and advisors: my dear friends Fr. Tom Johnson of St. John's Episcopal Church, Indio, and Susan Johnson, marriage and family therapist; Dr. Dennis Hill of Salisbury, NC, neurologist and the most wonderful brother in the world; and above all, Tom, my husband, best friend, chef extraordinaire, and resident historian, who makes all this possible. Thank you all for your generous gifts of time and expertise during the birth of *The Last Storyteller.* Our lively conversations about the moral and ethical issues in this work were priceless—and encouraged me to mine deep to discover the hidden layers of my characters' motivations and conflicts. I hasten to add two important points: the views expressed by the characters in *The Last Storyteller* are not necessarily those of these dear readers; and if errors, technical or otherwise, are found in this work, it is entirely the author's doing. A special thanks to Paul Hawley—once again!—for your enthusiastic, sensitive, and astute editing skills.

I'm happily in debt to you all!

READER'S GUIDE

The following author conversation and suggested questions are for personal reflection or group discussion and are intended to help you find new and interesting layers of meaning in *The Last Storyteller*. We hope that these ideas will enrich your enjoyment of the book.

A Conversation with Diane Noble

Q: You have blended contemporary and historical story lines in *The Last Storyteller*. Why did you choose to tell these parallel stories? And why did you choose ancient Wales as the setting for the ancient story line?

A: First of all, stories seem to find me, not the other way around. In the summer of 2002, I visited the little village of Hanmer, Wales, while following up on the research of my ancestry. I had the California coastline setting firmly in mind for the contemporary story, but the historical story line didn't become clear until I visited Wales for the first time. My family lineage has been traced back a thousand years to this same village by the mere. I walked through the church graveyard and stood in awe before the altar at Saint Chad's, the church built by my forebears. I knew this was the setting for Taran and Gwynedd.

As I walked across the ancient stone floor in Saint Chad's and stepped into the family chapels of the Hanmers and Kenyons (both are in my family tree), I imagined the people whose soles had touched these same stones. Living, breathing, *real* people who had no idea that their progeny would scatter to the far corners of the earth, that a daughter from these unimagined world corners would someday return to stand in the same place.

A sense of life's sacredness struck me in that hushed sanctuary. If any of the women in my ancestral family had terminated a pregnancy, by accident or on purpose, the line might have died. What-if questions filled my heart: What if a young woman in today's world is pregnant, planning to abort the fetus? What if her grandmother, the keeper of ancient family tales, desperately wants the young woman to keep her baby? What if the family line has been blessed and the blessing includes everyone who is to follow? What if the grandmother tells the story, hoping her granddaughter will understand the connection? What if there's not much time because the storyteller is suffering from memory loss?

Thus, the seed of an idea was planted—for both the contemporary story and that of Taran and Gwynedd, the twelfth-century couple whose love for God and each other spurred them to courage beyond their imagination. Their fictional story sprang from my research into life in twelfth-century Wales and the English border region, particularly within the sacred communities of monasteries and abbeys such as those at Shrewsbury and Chester.

Q: Taite is one of your most multifaceted and complex characters, full of contradictions from page 1—fiercely stubborn but unsure of her next step, tremendously gifted but lacking confidence, achingly tender but easily rejecting love. What was the germ for Taite's character journey, and how did it grow?

A: Taite actually arrived in my heart full blown, telling me who she was and how she would approach almost any situation I might place her in. In the beginning I hadn't planned for her to have the major role in the story. I thought Victoria, Isabel, and Taite would have equal thirds. Taite quickly took over and would have insisted on more "onstage" time had I not reined her in now and again. Originally I had planned for Isabel to be more central to the story, but as Taite "dictated" into my ear, it became obvious that her mother needed to remain in the background. (See what I mean?!)

Q: In the world of *The Last Storyteller,* the mother-daughter relationship is an emotional minefield: at times ambivalent, at times tinged with rejection and anger, at times tender and thoughtful, but always incredibly complex. What is it about this relationship that caused you to give this theme such prominence within the story line?

A: I am the mother of two daughters. I am also a daughter. I've *lived* that emotional minefield: joys, sorrows, misunderstandings, heartaches, frustrations, forgiveness, grace—all of that and more. Yet the mother-daughter relationship can be one of the most rewarding of our lives. I am blessed with two beautiful adult daughters and a wonderful mother. I think they would agree with all the emotions I've listed and add a few more of their own! I hasten to add, though the story line and all characters in *The Last Storyteller* are completely fictional, I believe the emotional landscape is one all mothers and daughters may recognize as familiar.

Q: You touch on some political hot potatoes in *The Last Storyteller*—embryonic stem cell harvesting, which has been outlawed in the U.S.; human cloning, which was recently found to be successful in South Korea. Why did you choose to bring these issues into the story?

A: My brother is a neurologist who's keenly interested in stem cell research from a medical—and ethical—viewpoint. We've had many conversations in recent years about this research. He helped me tremendously with the issues, often playing devil's advocate on behalf of Sam's character.

These issues will become increasingly important to discuss as research progresses, people live longer, and the incidence of dementia and Parkinson's and other diseases takes an even greater toll on family caregivers and our healthcare system. There are no easy answers.

I chose to bring this debate to the forefront of *Storyteller* as a result of another of those what-if questions novelists ask themselves: What if the father of Taite's child sees the developing cells as a potential cure for disease rather than the life of his son or daughter? What would be the crucial turning point in his thinking? How would it affect his growth? Asking these questions helped me define Sam's character journey.

Q: We see Taite toward the end of the book, lying near a lighthouse in the deepening dusk. She has fallen and suffered a head injury and dreams that she is rescued by a fisherman who is a Christlike figure. Throughout the story, her grandmother has blended fact with fiction, in large part because of her illness. Was it your intent to cause the reader to wonder whether Taite's encounter also stems from her imagination or if it is "real" within the universe of the story? E. L. Doctorow has said the element of truth is never more crucial than in the arena of fiction. What does *truth* mean in *The Last Storyteller*?

A: A guiding principle in all my novels is to point the way to the living Christ. I often use allegory to portray some aspect of his care over those he loves. Sometimes I show his love, his wisdom, his truths through peripheral characters, such as Luke in *The Last Storyteller;* other times, in a more abstract way, such as through the fisherman who cared for Taite, piercing her heart with his compassion. In the Welsh story, Gwynedd sees a shepherd on a barren hillside and no longer feels afraid. Later, when she comes to the end of her physical resources, he lifts her into his arms and carries her to safety. Both are portraits of the living Christ, the One who says, "Never will I leave you; never will I forsake you" (Hebrews 13:5, NIV).

   The Scripture that came to me during both scenes is found in Deuteronomy 33:12: "Let the beloved of the LORD rest secure in him, for he shields [her] all day long, and the one the LORD loves rests between his shoulders" (NIV).

Q: Who do you think your readers are? What do they want from a novel?

A: Most of my readers are women, though I do get reader mail from men who have especially enjoyed *The Veil* and my California Chronicles series. I've heard from married couples who write to tell me they take turns reading aloud to each other from my books in the evenings. I hear from readers as old as ninety and others as young as twelve. Some of my novellas, especially the ones that have been adapted for the stage, have appealed to all ages as well, even to children as young as seven and eight. It is gratifying to appeal to such a wide range of readers.

   No matter the age, readers want a novel that makes them think and lets them feel and leads them to discover some vital truth, particularly one that relates to their own lives. Sometimes in the smallest story detail a reader finds the greatest delight, the most breathless moment, or a life-changing truth.

Q: How and when did you begin writing fiction? Did your parents and teachers play a role in your early dreams of writing?

A: I was already a nonfiction writer when I began writing fiction twenty years ago. I had always wanted to write a novel, never dreaming, even as I headed toward my goal, that I would actually write more than one, which was frightening enough. (*The Last Storyteller* is my thirteenth full-length novel.)

My parents were great readers, which influenced me in an indirect way. Books seemed to be everywhere—stacked on lamp tables or beside my parents' bed. My mother read to me when I was small—nursery rhymes and fairy tales mostly—until I could read to myself, which I did avidly through my growing-up years. My only brother was a master storyteller and entertained me with his plethora of zany characters set in a make-believe universe. Early on, storytelling became as natural as breathing.

One teacher stands out as hugely important in my early life. His name is Al Schiebelhut, my fifth- and sixth-grade teacher. I'll never forget how his delight came through in tone and animation as he read from *Tom Sawyer* or *Huckleberry Finn* every day after noon recess. (There were others as well, but the Twain books stand out.) I will always be indebted to the love of story that he beamed right into my little ten-year-old heart. *Thank you, Al!*

Q: What are you working on these days? Tell us about your new project.

A: I'm currently working on *The Butterfly Farm,* the first book in my new Harriet MacIver mystery series. Harriet, a travel writer in her early sixties, is a bit like everyone's favorite aunt: more than a little eccentric but no shrinking violet when gumption is required. In *The Butterfly Farm* she flies to Costa Rica to rate the accommodations on a small adventure ship. When the ship docks at an obscure village port, Harriet accompanies a group of passengers on an excursion to a butterfly farm and health spa. After a passenger is murdered and a young woman disappears, Harriet becomes entangled in a deadly web of political and medical intrigue—with direct ties to the U.S. government.

    The Butterfly Farm will be followed by *Those Sacred Bones,* which is set on a five-star Mediterranean cruise line.

Questions for Book Club Discussion or Personal Reflection

1. When the book opens, Taite is struggling with her decision to abort the baby. Why do you think this decision is difficult? How might the rejection she felt from her mother affect her thinking? How about her relationship with Sam? Why can't she tell him?

2. The story in *The Last Storyteller* is told from the perspective of three generations of women. Did you find yourself empathizing with one character more than the others? If so, which character and why?

3. Sam struggles throughout the story with the ethics and morality of embryonic stem cell research, especially after he discovers Taite is pregnant. The cluster of cells she carries suddenly becomes more than a scientific method for research purposes—or a "medicine" to be used for a cure. How do you feel about using stem cells to research and possibly stop diseases such as Alzheimer's and Parkinson's? If someone you loved suffered with a debilitating disease, how would you feel about this loved one receiving harvested embryonic stem cells as a cure?

4. Discuss Luke's role in the story. How does he influence Sam's ultimate decision about his career within the medical community? Take a few minutes to reflect on God's sovereignty. When have you seen God bring people into your life for a purpose? How did they reflect God's compassion and grace? How did they give you a greater understanding of a struggle you were going through?

5. Discuss the relationship between Victoria and Taite. How is each character important to the other? What part did Victoria play in

Taite's character growth? Who in your family profoundly influenced you during your own spiritual journey?

6. Mother-daughter relationships are complex. What did you think about Isabel's reasons for leaving her daughter in Victoria's care? Is Taite correct in assuming she was emotionally abandoned? Does Isabel deserve Taite's rejection? Why?

7. Do you believe Victoria's stories about Taran and Gwynedd are the result of a vivid imagination, elaborations of true stories handed down through the generations, or the product of her illness and approaching dementia? Why?

8. Allow yourself to play novelist for a moment and imagine Taite's and Sam's lives beyond the years of the novel. In what ways do you think the knowledge of the family blessing might influence how they rear their children?

9. In *The Last Storyteller*'s final scene, Taran slips Brother Cadwallen's ring on her finger, saying, "Once upon a time..." After Taran becomes an adult, which of the family stories do you think will be the most important to her and the one she might pass along to future generations? Why?

About the Author

Diane Noble is the award-winning author of nearly two dozen titles, including novels, novellas, devotionals, and nonfiction books for women. Her works, ranging from historical fiction to contemporary romantic suspense, have won numerous honors and received critical acclaim. She is currently at work on *The Butterfly Farm,* the first book in her new Harriet MacIver mystery series.

Diane and her husband live in California. For information about Diane's new releases, works in progress, research trips, and reader contests and to sign up for her newsletter, please visit her Web site at www .dianenoble.com or write to her at the following address:

Diane Noble
P.O. Box 10674
Palm Desert, CA 92255-0674

DISCOVER
the LIFE-SAVING POWER
of TWO FAMILIES' STORIES

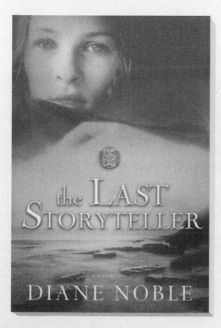

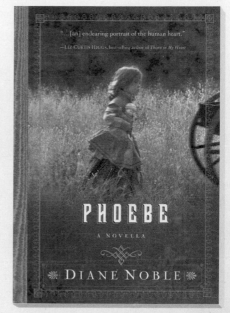

Rebellious Taite Abbot finds loving purpose through her dying grandmother's stories of the family's twelfth-century Welsh origins.

A series of heartwarming, interconnected stories follow the history of an antique doll—and tell a greater story of love and grace.

Available in bookstores everywhere.

WATERBROOK PRESS
www.waterbrookpress.com